Intentions

I Found My Heart in
San Francisco
Book Nine

Susan X Meagher

Susan X Meagher

INTENTIONS

I FOUND MY HEART IN SAN FRANCISCO: BOOK NINE

© 2009 BY SUSAN X MEAGHER

ISBN (10) 09799254-7-9
ISBN (13) 978-0-9799254-7-4

THIS TRADE PAPERBACK ORIGINAL IS PUBLISHED BY BRISK PRESS, NEW YORK, NY 10023

FIRST PRINTING: OCTOBER 2009

Acknowledgments

I hope she doesn't get tired of hearing it, because I never get tired of stating it. This book is for Carrie.

By Susan X Meagher

Novels

Arbor Vitae
All That Matters
Cherry Grove
Girl Meets Girl
The Lies That Bind
The Legacy

Serial Novels

I Found My Heart In San Francisco

Awakenings
Beginnings
Coalescence
Disclosures
Entwined
Fidelity
Getaway
Honesty
Intentions

Anthologies

Undercover Tales
Outsiders

To purchase these books go to
www.briskpress.com

Chapter One

The stately black BMW 735i sat in the circular drive for a long while, the occupant reluctant to leave the cozy confines of his leather-appointed cocoon. Something about the car—practically any car, for that matter—made him feel safer, and more in control, than nearly any home he had ever lived in.

His hands gripped and released the steering wheel, uncertain as to whether or not he would be welcomed, or even allowed, into his own home. *Accuracy is your business,* he upbraided himself, *let's be accurate. It's not your house. It's never been your house. It's Cat's house... bought with her money...decorated with her money...maintained with her money...all hers.*

He looked up at the imposing edifice, where he had spent the better part of the last twenty-two years. *The best years of my life,* he admitted. *And now, now I don't even know if I'll ever sleep another night in my bed.* Taking in a calming breath, he exited the car and walked up to the front door, his shoes crunching loudly on the stone drive. *Don't even think about using your key,* he reminded himself. *That would* not *be appreciated.*

Ringing the bell, he stood awkwardly at the entrance to the home, hoping that Catherine was inside. Afraid of being rebuffed, he hadn't called ahead to check. The door opened and he cocked his head, unfamiliar with the woman who stood in the doorway.

"Is Catherine at home?" he asked, not knowing what the accepted greeting was for an estranged husband trying to visit his wife.

"Who is calling?" the woman asked, a trifle formally.

"I'm uhm..." he paused, unsure of his correct title. He finally opted for, "I'm her husband," then noted the slight widening of the woman's eyes.

"Please, come in, Mr. Evans," she said immediately. "I'll see if she's home."

Well, it's obvious that she hasn't given the staff an order to shoot me on sight, but she also didn't tell them to welcome me with open arms.

He cooled his heels for several minutes, wandering around the living room, picking up photographs and staring at them as though they contained the images of strangers. He didn't recognize the seemingly happy family that gazed back at him from pictures spanning the years of his marriage. *Did these represent the truth?* he wondered, holding a photo of him, Catherine and Jamie, taken when their child was around three. *Or is this the truth?* He looked around the house that he was no longer welcome to explore, thinking that the previous happy times had probably been illusory.

"Hello, Jim," Catherine's soft voice called out as she crossed the room and stood far enough away to indicate there would be no physical contact. "Did I know that you were planning to visit?"

Ouch. "No, I uhm…I'm going to the airport to leave for Washington, and since I was in the neighborhood, I thought I'd stop and say goodbye."

"That's nice," she said, wearing the same face she had pasted on for the last twenty-two years to meet every one of his clients. "Well, goodbye."

She started towards the door, seemingly to lead him out, but he stood his ground and gave her a pleading look when she turned his way. "Have you talked with Jamie since yesterday afternoon?"

"Yes, as a matter of fact I have," she said, the pleasant half-smile still affixed to her face.

"Did she tell you that she and I are going to try to start over?"

"Yes, she did. I'm glad for that." Continuing to urge him towards the door, she said, "I don't see what that has to do with us, but I'm glad for it, nonetheless."

"But, Catherine," he said, trying not to lose any further ground, "our problems were mostly because of the problems with Jamie. Can't we start again, too?"

She cocked her head quizzically, asking, "Did you ever see that doctor I suggested? You really shouldn't rule out a physical cause for your delusions."

Turning on the heel of her handmade Italian shoes, she started to walk back in the direction she had come, traveling just a few feet before his pleading voice stopped her once again. "Catherine… Cat…please, don't throw me out. I came here to apologize… really."

Turning only her head, she gave him a pointed glance and said, "That wasn't your stated purpose."

Shoving his hands into his pockets, he let out a frustrated sigh. "For God's sake, Catherine, I'm nervous. Give me a chance, will you?"

She turned completely and gave him a weary look. "When is your plane?"

"Not until one," he said. It was currently 10:30, giving him a good hour and a half to kill.

"Would you like some coffee? Perhaps some juice?"

"Coffee would be great," he said, his relief evident at being offered some level of hospitality. "I've missed Marta's coffee."

"Marta's not here," she said over her shoulder. "She's out shopping. Helena will make it for us."

When she returned, he was sitting on one of the couches, feeling like it was all right to get comfortable. He gazed at her somberly and launched into his spiel. "I want to apologize to you, Catherine," he said, his eyes locked onto hers. "I not only treated Jamie horribly, I used information that I'd obtained about you to try to make her hate you as much as she did me." He looked down at his hands, feeling so adrift that he barely recognized them as his own. "I know that what I did is unforgivable, but I swear that I would do anything in the world to make it up to you."

"I don't think that's possible," she said. "Trust is a very fragile commodity. It can only be broken so many times before it becomes irreparable. I think we've passed that number this time."

He looked over at her, seeing so many familiar items scattered about the room—some they had purchased together, some of them gifts from him—and felt as though he were sitting in a stranger's home. His wife suddenly looked like a very different woman as well, all of the familiar warmth gone from her brown eyes. "Is there nothing left?" he asked, unable to look at her again. His head had dropped, and he gazed at his shoes as he awaited the pronouncement of his fate.

"Of course there is," she said, sending his heart soaring, but it fell back to earth when she qualified, "We'll always be connected through Jamie."

"I see," he acknowledged, feeling the tears coming and knowing that he would be unable to stop them. He stood and fumbled in the inner pocket of his suit, pulling out two sealed envelopes. "I know that Jamie and Ryan will be here this weekend for the volleyball tournament. I haven't had time to contact Ryan personally, but I'd appreciate it if you'd give these to her and Jamie."

He handed the envelopes to his wife, turning for the door, knowing that his composure would dissolve if he had to see the absence of any connection in her eyes once again.

"Good luck in Washington. I'd appreciate it if you'd do your best to support the arts in any way you can."

He blinked at her, amazed at the formal, businesslike tone. "I...I'll do my best," he said, not having any idea what else to say. His feet moved, and he got halfway across the living room before his eyes made the mistake of landing on one of their wedding pictures. It was a posed, formal portrait, taken at Catherine's parents' home, the site of their wedding. The innocent, happy expressions on their faces grabbed him and he stopped abruptly, reaching out with a shaking hand to grasp the picture. "Can I...can I have this?" he asked, unable to turn around.

She didn't respond immediately, instead, coming up along his side to look at his face. "Why do you want it?"

"I want to remember who I was," he said, the words nearly incomprehensible through his tears. "Who we were." He began to cry so hard that he had to lean against the piano for support.

Catherine's veneer of disinterest collapsed, and she went to him, gently running both of her hands down his back. "It's okay," she soothed, turning to scowl at Helena when she tried to enter with the coffee. "It will be all right."

"No, it won't," he gasped. "It'll never be all right again. I'll be lost without you, Cat. I swear I can't make it alone."

"Of course you can. It will hardly be different. We've barely been roommates for the last year."

"That's not what I want," he sobbed. "That's never been what I wanted. I was just trying to give you the space that *you* wanted."

She cocked her head thoughtfully and let his words sink in. "Maybe the way we've been hasn't been the way you've wanted it to be," she conceded, "but I refuse to be the woman that you come home to when you can't do any better." Some of the rage that she had kept carefully bottled up started to erupt, and she continued, her voice growing stronger and more forceful. "I've been giving you second chances again and again since Jamie was five years old. She's grown and gone now, and we don't have to keep up the façade any longer. She knows about you, and she knows about me, thanks to you," she added bitterly. "It's over."

Her rising anger seemed to quell his sorrow, and he was soon able to stem his tears. "Why can't we go on like we had been? We always had a nice time together when we went out. I was always proud to escort you to every function that you asked me to go to—isn't that worth something?"

She gazed at him for a long minute, finally shaking her head in disgust. "I don't want an escort, damn it! I want a husband. I want someone to love me, and care for me, and want to share my bed. I want to be desired again. I will have that again—or for the first time—if you were *never sincere* in your affections." She knew this last statement was unfair, but at the moment she honestly wasn't sure if he had ever loved her or if it had always been a marriage of convenience and opportunity.

He looked as though she had slapped him, actually staggering a bit as he stared at her with wide eyes. "How can you even *say* that? I loved you enough, and I loved our unborn baby enough, to get married a good five years before I wanted to. I discarded every bit of my youth to be the best damned father that I could be. I didn't do that just for Jamie, I did it for us. How can you look at me and say that I didn't love you? My God, Catherine, how can you say that?" He looked more wounded and more distraught than she had ever seen him, and she immediately regretted her harsh statement.

"I'm sorry. That was wrong of me. I know that you loved me as well as you could…it just didn't last long."

"That's not true. I loved you then and I love you now. Just because I slept with other women, didn't mean that I didn't love you. I know you have a hard time believing that, but it's true. The sex that I've had with other women is no reflection on you or the love I still have for you."

She turned on him, her eyes blazing with anger. "How can you say that? How can you have the nerve to say that cheating on me has nothing to do with me? How can you say that?" She was nearly panting, her rage spilling out in waves. "You've destroyed my self-confidence, Jim Evans. You've made me feel unattractive and old before my time. I've squandered my youth on you."

In all of their years together, they had never, ever, yelled at each other like this. Throughout all of their arguments, there had always been a level of civil restraint that had characterized their interactions, and neither of them had any idea how to deal with the maelstrom of feeling that was flying around the room.

Feeling like a small boy being scolded by his mother, he mumbled, "I…I didn't know that you felt like that."

"You didn't *know*?" She grabbed his lapels and gave him a good shake, her anger shocking him speechless. "You didn't know?" She continued to glare at him, fire sparking in her brown eyes, her hands still clutching his suit.

"No, no, I didn't know," he insisted, backing away from her to escape her reach. "I knew you were angry and disappointed at first, but you never really seemed to care that much."

"Didn't care." She said the words like they were foreign to her. "Didn't care," she said again, shaking her head in amazement. "I was a twenty-five-year-old woman with a five-year-old daughter who thought the sun rose over her daddy's shoulder. You and I didn't have the closeness or the intimacy that I had always dreamed of having, but I believed we were happy. I believed that you desired me." She faced him and stared intently into his eyes. Unconsciously he shrank back from her, the pain that he saw reflected in the brown depths too much for him to bear. "The first time I caught you, I honestly thought that I would have preferred to die than face that rejection." Her voice was quiet, but filled with fifteen years worth of unexpressed misery.

"I didn't know," he whispered, wishing he could turn back the clock and make it up to her—anything to take away the pain that filled her eyes. "You seemed more upset about the…other thing."

Her eyes flickered closed as she shook her head in amazement. "Forgive me for having a tough time deciding what was worse," she spat, her voice dripping with sarcasm. "Finding out that my husband was snorting cocaine, or realizing that he was getting high in another woman's bed." She advanced on him again, standing toe to toe. "I love you enough to spend all my energies helping you overcome your drug habit without anyone finding out. I honestly believed that the drugs led you to make choices that you wouldn't have otherwise made. You proved me wrong, Him, time and time again."

His eyes were tightly closed, and he looked like he wanted to put his hands over his ears to block out her words. "I know I did. I know that you don't believe me, but I honestly thought that you understood my...need. The other women didn't mean anything, Catherine. You're the only woman I've ever loved."

"Given the choice," she said dryly, "I might have preferred to be one of the women that you didn't love."

His shoulders slumped dramatically. "I suppose this means that you'll file for divorce."

She shook her head, saying, "Not yet. I'm not in the mood for a fight right now. And knowing you, that's exactly what I'll be in for."

His head started to shake, increasing in intensity until his hair was flying around his head. "No, no, no," he insisted. "I won't fight you. I would like my cars, but you can have the rest. I would never be able to enjoy Pebble Beach without you, and this place has too many memories to even think about living here alone."

"I'd love to have that statement in an affidavit," she said, her tone harsher than she wished.

The hurt that filled his green eyes was nearly palpable as he quietly said, "All right." He turned to leave, one hand still clutching the photograph.

Surprising herself, Catherine reached out and placed a restraining hand on his shoulder. "Wait, Jim. Please." He turned, regarding her with grief-stricken eyes, his head cocked in question, and she said, "Stay and have coffee with me. I hate to think of you sitting in the airport alone."

He nodded, surprised and somewhat heartened by her offer.

While Catherine went to fetch the coffee, he dried his eyes with his handkerchief, wondering where his legendary control had disappeared to.

She had obviously decided that a change in topics was called for, because when she returned, she focused on his move to Washington. "Where will you be living?"

Just the question caused tears to form again, and he silently cursed himself as he swiped at his eyes in frustration. "I'll be at the Hay-Adams for a while. It's easier than having my own place."

"That's a nice hotel," she said, finding the conversation more than a little strained. "Will you take anyone with you?"

"Yes. I'm bringing two associates from the firm. I doubt that I'll sponsor much, if any, legislation, but I'll still need to conduct a lot of research. I need people that I can trust, who don't have an agenda to foster."

"That's good. At least you'll know someone."

He gave her a look of incredulity, amazed that she would even think that associates of the firm could make up for the loss of his family. "I regret agreeing to do this," he said softly, staring at the carpet.

"Really? I would have thought that this would be quite beneficial for the firm."

"It is," he said somberly, his eyes boring into hers. "Sometimes the firm isn't the biggest consideration."

Since when? she wanted to say, but bit her tongue since they were trying to be civil.

He saw the look of doubt in her eyes and added, "I'm learning—for the first time—that my life can't be fulfilling if it's centered on work. It's just not enough."

She cocked her head again and gazed at him for a moment, trying to gauge his sincerity. "I'm sorry that you had to learn that lesson the hard way, but it's a valuable one."

"Yeah, as though it matters now."

"It will still be good to know. I know you're upset now, but you will go on. I hope you enter your future relationships with that perspective."

"I don't want future relationships, Catherine," he said earnestly. "I want us back."

"You can't have that. I'm sorry." She actually did look sorry, but she also looked completely determined, and he knew that he didn't have a chance.

"Does Jamie know?" he asked tentatively.

"Not in so many words. I don't tell her much about us. It's not good for any of us."

"You've always been the more mature one," he commented, drawing a knowing glance of agreement from his wife. "Will you tell your friends?"

"Again, no. I don't want to tell a soul until we decide what we're doing. I don't want to feed the rumor mill one minute earlier than I must."

He nodded, knowing that his wife hated being the subject of gossip. "I won't tell anyone either. I'll just tell my staff that you have too many commitments to join me in Washington."

"That's not that odd, anyway, dear," she said, unconsciously reverting to her usual term for him. "Many senators live alone in hotels and apartment buildings in Washington."

He laughed bitterly, admitting, "That's because most of them are about the caliber of husband that I am. If you really love your spouse, you go with them."

"That's probably true, but I'm sure you'll do fine there. You've never backed off from a challenge."

"I've never been so ill-prepared emotionally to face one, either," he said, his hair falling into his eyes as his head dropped again.

She fought the urge to push the errant strands back into order, and instead gave him a small smile. "You'll get through this. It will just take a while to adjust."

He sighed and stood, looking awkward as he loomed over her. "I've spent years trying to have my own life—apart from you and Jamie. It always made me feel safer to have something that was mine alone. Well, I've got it now." He turned and walked towards the door, pausing when his hand grasped the knob. "It stinks." Without turning back, he walked out the door, their wedding portrait nestled securely against his chest.

Ryan was going to Palo Alto with the volleyball team, so Jamie decided to go down early to spend the afternoon with her mother, and she arrived just after noon. For a change, she used her key to enter, feeling more comfortable at her family home than she had since she left for college three years previously.

She strolled around the first floor, poking her head into the kitchen and seeing a stranger standing near the sink. "Hello?" she said.

The woman turned quickly and blinked at her. "Miss Evans?" she asked warily, wondering how many more of the family members she would meet that day.

"Yes. Jamie, please," she said immediately, extending a hand.

The woman smiled and said, "Marta told me that you did not like to be too formal." She shook Jamie's hand and said, "I'm Helena. I've just been here a week."

"It's good to meet you, Helena," Jamie said, smiling pleasantly. "Is my mother at home?"

"Yes. I believe she is upstairs. Shall I tell her that you're here?"

"No. No, thanks. I can find her." She turned and headed upstairs, looking in the places her mother usually spent her days in. When she didn't find her in her office or the small, but well-stocked library, she decided to look in her bedroom. A light knock heralded her arrival, and she waited patiently as she heard her mother cross the room to open the door, which, Jamie realized as she heard the click, was surprisingly, locked.

"Yes?" Catherine asked, opening the door warily. "Oh, Jamie," she said, wrapping her arms around her daughter. "I'm so glad to see you."

Leaning back in the embrace, Jamie lifted a hand and brushed it across her mother's cheek. "You've been crying."

"Your father was here earlier."

"What did he do to you?" Jamie asked sharply, her eyes narrowing.

"Oh, honey, don't worry, he didn't do anything. It just made me sad to see him. As much of a sham as our marriage has been, it's still hard for me to face that it's over. We've managed to be friendly to each other through the years, for the most part," she sniffed, dabbing at her eyes with a tissue. "I lost my husband many years ago, but now I feel like I'm losing a friend. My oldest friend," she added sadly. "It's so much harder than I thought it would be."

Jamie tucked her arm around her mother's waist and guided her to a small love seat near a window. "How could it not be hard, Mom?" she asked as Catherine's head dropped to rest on her shoulder. "You've been married for twenty-two years."

"It's funny," she said, her thoughts drifting to her earlier conversation with Jim. "We yelled at each other at the top of our lungs today." She cocked her head slightly as she added, "Things might have been different if we could have done that at the very beginning." She pursed her lips as she reflected, "We've always been so careful with each other."

"Jack and I were that way for the most part. When he broke up with me, I think our entire conversation took less than five minutes. No argument, no yelling. He said it was over, and I accepted his decision." She shivered noticeably as she said, "Lord, what a mistake it would have been to marry him."

"You would have had a marriage like mine," Catherine said. "Now I'm hoping that one day I can have a relationship like yours."

Jamie smiled at her, giving her knee a tender squeeze. "That's exactly what I wish for you. I want you to have someone who loves you like you deserve to be loved. Someone who thinks you're the center of their universe."

"I'm so glad that you have that," Catherine said, sighing. "Nothing can make a mother happier than knowing her daughter has someone in her life who loves her so well."

"Then you should be downright giddy," Jamie chuckled, giving her mother another squeeze.

"Having you and Ryan care for me makes me giddy. I don't know how I'd get through this without you."

"We're with you permanently, Mom. We're a team."

Jamie's cell phone chirped as she and Catherine were leaving the room. "Hello," she said.

"Hey, James," Mia's perky voice said. "I need some advice."

"Sure. What is it?"

"I want to come down and see the girls play tonight, but I don't want to look like I'm chasing Jordan...even though I am."

"Ooh, that's kinda tough. What's up with her, anyway? Has she called you?"

"Nope. Not a word. It's weird, James, I know that we really hit it off the other night, and I sat around all day on Tuesday waiting for her to call. I really thought she'd ask me to come to the game to watch her."

"Is that why you weren't at the party after the game?"

"Yeah. I thought it would work better to act like I didn't think it was a big deal—but it clearly hasn't worked. I'm really frustrated, James. What does the lesbian rule book say about this situation? Can I call her?"

"Hmm...I haven't received my copy of the rules yet. Why don't you just come down to the game and sit with us? Maybe you can stay with your parents tonight, and since Stanford is so close..."

"Good idea. I'll come down and sit with you." She paused for a second and said, "Oh, it might be weird to see Conor, though. Jesus. I've gotta start dating outside of this incestuous little circle."

"You parted on good terms with Conor. It should be fine."

"I guess you're right. Damn, if I was anywhere near ready to settle down..."

"I know, but you're not. It's really better not to have the temptation."

"Yeah, I know you're right. At least Jordan's where I am in terms of being serious. Or even further behind," she added wryly.

"As I've told you, I don't know Jordan really well, but I'm pretty confident that she's not ready to settle down."

Mia laughed softly. "I'm not even sure she wants to date, much less settle down."

When they reached the kitchen Catherine said, "Should we have the O'Flahertys over for dinner tonight as well as tomorrow?"

"Sure, that'd be nice. I'm not really sure who's coming tonight, but I can give Martin a call."

She found him at work and he agreed that he and Maeve would

love to come, but that none of the other family members would be able to make it since they all had to work until at least five. The drive down to Palo Alto was almost always a tough one, but crawling through stop and go traffic after a long day at work was a sacrifice that Ryan didn't expect her brothers to make.

After having a bite of lunch, Jamie decided that she needed to take care of one little matter and now was the perfect time to do it. Marta had prepared their lunch, but as soon as the women were served she'd gone into her room to allow them to enjoy their meal alone. The servants' quarters were just off the kitchen, and when Marta wasn't in the kitchen proper she could usually be found in her spacious room. Jamie knocked and heard the softly accented voice reply, "Come in."

She opened the door and stuck her head in to find a smiling face looking at her questioningly. "Do you need something else, Querida?"

"No, no, I just wanted to talk to you for a minute. Do you have time?"

"Si, si," she replied as she motioned Jamie into the room. There were three bedrooms in this section of the house, each with its own bath, and Marta clearly had the best of the bunch. She predated Jamie's nanny Elizabeth by five months, so she had been able to have her pick of the rooms twenty-two years earlier, when she had joined the staff.

After immigrating to join her sister in Palo Alto, Marta had come to work for the Evanses as her first job in the States. Jamie had always wondered why she had never shown any interest in men or dating, but Marta seemed content with her life. Her only job was to cook meals for the family, and since Catherine ate out so often, Marta might only cook once or twice a week now that Jamie was gone. She'd had to cook for quite a few large parties, and seemed to thrive on running a busy kitchen, appearing to get a great deal of satisfaction from successfully handling a big affair. Her interests seemed to revolve around visits with her sister, and devotion to her church. She had belonged to a large Catholic parish in San Mateo for over twenty years and was very involved in many aspects of parish life.

"What is on your mind, little one?" Marta asked in her flawless

English.

"Let's speak Spanish," Jamie suggested. "I don't get a lot of practice."

Marta had worked with Jamie extensively when she was a child to perfect her grammar and accent. It had been hard for the child to keep her languages straight, since Italian was so close to Spanish, but Marta was an excellent teacher as befitted her many years teaching English as a second language at her church.

Seamlessly switching to her native tongue, Marta looked at Jamie carefully and asked, "What is it, little one?" applying her usual pet name for Jamie.

Clearing her throat nervously, Jamie began, feeling a little tentative. "I don't know if you know this, but I live with a woman named Ryan. Ryan O'Flaherty," she added, thinking that neither "Ryan" nor "O'Flaherty" sounded very good with a Spanish accent.

Marta nodded. "Yes…the woman you brought here for dinner this summer." An enigmatic look showed on her handsome face.

"Yes, that's Ryan. I'm sorry I didn't introduce you then, but that was a…that was a difficult night," she said, shivering at the memory.

"Do not be concerned. I took no offense."

Jamie smiled at the older woman and continued, clearing her throat nervously. "She's…she's my very good friend, and I want you to get to know her. She's going to come down later today and stay here this weekend. I wanted you to know…" she said, clearing her throat again.

"Yes?" Marta urged, gazing at her sympathetically. "What would you like me to know?"

"Well, I…ah…she's very important to me…and…ah…"

"I know that you love her," Marta said softly as she placed a hand on the younger woman's knee.

Jamie's head jerked up in surprise but saw only acceptance from her old friend. "Do you understand…how…how I love her?"

"Yes, I understand these things." She looked down for a moment and said, "It is not my way. I do not know what causes a person to love someone of their own sex. But it is the way for you, and I can see that. If it is your way, and you are loved by this woman, then it is what you must do." She paused for a moment and turned her face to gaze into Jamie's eyes. "You are well loved, are you not?"

Brushing a tear from her eye, she nodded mutely. "I am," she said haltingly. "Very well loved." She took a deep breath and asked, "But how did you know? You've never even spoken to her."

"You act like a woman who feels loved. It shows," she said, shrugging her shoulders.

Letting out a relieved sigh, Jamie reached over and grasped the strong, warm hand of her old friend. "Thank you for understanding, Marta. Somehow I knew you'd support me."

"I know love. There is no greater power on earth, and I'm very happy that you finally have it." She opened her arms and Jamie tumbled into the embrace, just as she had when she was young. "I am very glad that you did not marry Jack, even though I liked him very much. It was obvious that it was not right for your heart."

"Why am I spending so much money on a therapist?" Jamie said, laughing. "I could have figured this out just by talking to you."

"I know you and I love you, Querida, but I would never tell you who to love. You must follow your heart."

Jamie gave her a gentle squeeze as she stood. "Thanks for knowing me, and for supporting me."

"It's my pleasure. Oh, one more thing," she added. "If you are patient with your father, I believe he will come to see who you really are. It may take a while, but I have faith."

"How…?"

"The house is big, but it is not that big," she laughed as she stood and tousled Jamie's hair.

Mia came barreling into the gym at seven-fifteen, having taken nearly two hours to get to Palo Alto. She quickly found the O'Flaherty rooting section, the small group consisting only of Jamie, Martin, Maeve, Caitlin, and Catherine. As the curly-haired woman climbed up into the stands, she noticed that Cal was beating BYU two games to one. The score of the current game was 12-6 in favor of Cal, so it was obvious that the end was near.

As Mia sat down, Jamie introduced her to Martin and Maeve, and within seconds, Caitlin was flirting shyly with her.

Stanford's game began at the conclusion of the Cal/BYU match, but since there was a separate admission for each match, the Stanford crowd was still outdoors, lining up to see the beloved Cardinal. The gym was so quiet Jamie noticed that for the first time, she could clearly hear the setter calling out instructions to the team. With the score at 14-7 the setter passed the ball high in the air to Ryan. Jamie laughed aloud when she heard her cry, "Boomer," as Ryan glided into position to kill the ball decisively with a powerful spike. As usual, Ryan seemed to know exactly where Jamie was in the crowd, and she gave her a smirk as she caught her eye. "Oh, oh," Jamie said aloud. "I've got to be more careful when I use pet names around Jordan."

After congratulating the players from BYU, Ryan headed across the floor, a shyly grinning Jordan in tow. As Ryan was congratulated, Jordan shot Mia a smile and said, "I was hoping to see you again. This is a nice surprise."

You could have called me, you big dope, she thought, but said, "I decided to come down for the weekend, and since I'm so close, this seemed like it would be fun. You really play well," she said, even though Jordan had not touched the ball in her presence.

"Thanks," Jordan blushed. "Uhm…well, it was nice to see you again. I have to go change so I don't miss the bus."

Jamie had one ear on the interchange and she piped up, "Come to the house, Jordan. No sense in going back if you just have to come down again tomorrow."

"Really?" she asked, hesitantly. "Are you sure…?"

"Mom?" Jamie said, getting her mother's attention. "Would it be all right if Jordan stayed over with us?"

"Oh. I assumed she would," Catherine said. "Didn't I mention that? I told Marta to prepare enough for eight." Looking past Jamie, Catherine met Jordan's eyes and said, "I'm sorry for not inviting you personally. Will you come?"

"Sure," Jordan said, her shy smile a little brighter now.

"Uhm, Mom," Jamie said, "that's only six…seven if Mia comes by."

"I know," she said, rather proud of herself, "but if Jordan eats as much as Ryan…"

"No one eats as much as Ryan does, Mrs. Evans," Jordan insisted. "She's a freak of nature."

"It's Catherine, Jordan," she decreed, giving the tall blonde a warm smile.

"Me too?" Mia asked, her sunny face curling into a grin.

"Of course. You should have been calling me Catherine for years now."

"Cool."

Jordan gave Mia a tentative look and asked, "Will you come to Jamie's? I'd like it if you could."

"Uhm, sure. I didn't get a chance to tell my parents I was coming down, so they're not expecting me." *All you have to do is ask, Jordan, and you've got a very friendly bedmate for the weekend.*

Jamie and Mia were patiently waiting when Ryan and Jordan came strolling out just a few minutes after they entered the locker room, their sweats replacing their wet uniforms. A reporter for the student newspaper was in attendance, and he snagged the women for a few post-match comments as Jamie made faces at Ryan behind his back. "Real mature, cupcake," Ryan said, after the reporter left.

"Cupcake, huh?" Jordan teased.

"Feel free to tell the announcer at her next tournament, Jordan," Ryan instructed. "Paybacks."

Mia gave Jordan a lift, and they pulled up into the large circular drive just behind Jamie and Ryan. Jordan didn't say much at first, standing still as her clear blue eyes took in the entire place. Jamie walked ahead, and the tall blonde gave Ryan a dramatic open-mouthed stare as she took in the mansion. Ryan laughed and said, "Based on the look on your face, I would have given anything to see my father's when he took this monster in."

Jamie knocked on the door, deciding to announce their presence so as not to overwhelm the staff. When the door opened, she guided her companions inside. Doffing her jacket, she said, "Helena, these are my friends, Ryan, Jordan, and Mia."

Helena stuck her hand out to grasp Ryan's offering and shook the hands of all three young women. Accepting their coats, she bustled away, indicating, "The others are in the kitchen."

Jordan finally found her voice and said, "Uhm, your house is really...nice, Jamie."

Sliding her arm around Jordan's slim waist, Jamie said, "I know it's terribly ostentatious, but thank you anyway."

She led the women into the kitchen where Martin and Maeve were sitting rather stiffly. Ryan sensed her father's discomfort at being in this palatial setting, and she asked, "When will dinner be ready, Catherine?"

"About twenty minutes or so. We're just having soup and sandwiches. Is that enough for you girls?"

"Perfect. How warm is the pool?"

"I keep it at 82 degrees. Would you like to take a dip before dinner?"

"I would, and I bet Jordan would, and I bet Mia would, and I know Caitlin would," she said, giving Catherine a winning smile.

A few minutes later, Jamie had secured suits for the adult women and Caitlin had been stripped bare. As Ryan jumped into the deep end, Jamie stood back slightly and observed Mia checking Jordan out. The lanky blonde looked absolutely fabulous in the too-small suit that Jamie had provided for her, stretching the bright gold bikini to its limits. "Put your tongue back in your mouth," Jamie joked, elbowing her friend playfully.

"I'd rather put it into *her* mouth," Mia said, rolling her eyes dramatically. "She looks tasty."

"I don't normally have the need, or the desire to look at other women, but I've gotta agree with you on that one. Jordan could stop traffic."

"Whew." Mia fanned herself playfully. "She makes my wheels squeal." She took a running dive into the pool, ostensibly to cool off, as Jamie shook her head and joined her, trying to land close to give Ryan a big splash.

The girls were all playing so joyously that within minutes Martin and Maeve lost their shyness and were acting like their typical selves. Marta and Helena brought the food out to the pool house and opened the wide double French doors to the space. It was fairly warm out, about 70 degrees, but they lit the large gas heaters that surrounded the pool anyway, and the adults were able to relax comfortably while the younger women played.

Caitlin particularly wanted to be with Mia and Jordan, since they were the new members of the Caitlin Appreciation Society, and to Ryan's delight, Jordan seemed happy to carry the happy baby all around the pool, even though she claimed to have no experience with babies whatsoever. When Jordan placed Caitlin on her shoulders and swam around like a shark, Caitlin was in heaven. She looked like she was riding Shamu as the water rushed over her chubby little legs, and she giggled so hard tears rolled down her cheeks. Jordan got tired fairly quickly, since she had to be underwater to make the trick work, but she kept it up much longer than most people could have. "It's fun to make her laugh," she said, handing the baby back to Ryan.

Jamie hopped out and loaded up trays with soup and the little tea sandwiches that Marta had prepared, placing them on the deck of the pool so that no one had to get out. Jamie and Mia kept the baby entertained while Ryan and Jordan attacked the food—both women nearly starving since they hadn't eaten since lunch. The adults watched in amazement while the hungry athletes snarfed up every bit of food they could get their hands on. Martin got up twice to fill their plates again, and as Ryan finished he admonished her, "Siobhán, you stay out of the deep water. I don't want to have to jump in and rescue you if you start to drown."

Jordan caught her eye, and Ryan realized that her friend had never heard anyone call her by her first name. She swam up alongside her and threatened, "If the whole team starts calling me Siobhán, you are toast, blondie."

"Why, Siobhán, I mean Ryan, why would you assume that I would mention this?"

Ryan pushed her under and held her down for a moment casually asking her father, "You don't mind if Jordan drowns, do you?"

The young women went from pool to spa and back again at least twenty times. The baby stayed in the pool with one of them, since they agreed that the 104 degree water would be too much for her delicate system, but Caitlin didn't mind a bit. Four babysitters was just about right for her tastes, and she enjoyed the newer members of the gang so much that she hardly even begged for Ryan to hold her.

At around ten Martin decided that it was time to depart, since Caitlin was starting to tire. She cried a little when she was taken from the warm pool, but she was so thoroughly exhausted that her tantrum faded out quickly. Martin had her wrapped up in an enormous towel as he bent to kiss his daughter good night. "We'll see you tomorrow, sweetheart," he promised. "And we'll have a much bigger contingent to root you on."

"Now Martin, remind everyone that we'll have another simple dinner here tomorrow night," Catherine said.

"We can't keep imposing like this," he protested.

"Imposing?" she asked, blinking. "I thought I was part of the family."

He looked totally abashed as he quickly amended his statement. "I don't know who was speaking before. Of course we'll all be here," he said firmly leaning in to kiss her cheek.

⚜

The pool denizens dreaded getting out since the ambient temperature had dropped to around sixty, and the house looked uncomfortably far away. After Catherine had seen her other guests to the door, she came back out and offered, "Shall I warm the sauna for you, so you can dry off?"

At Ryan and Jordan's bright-eyed looks, she laughed, "I think that's a yes."

Several minutes later, the foursome made a mad dash for the generously sized sauna in the pool house. Ryan got there first and started to strip off her suit, but Jordan gave her a pleading look and shook her head discreetly. Ryan was a little puzzled, but didn't want to make her teammate uncomfortable, so she left her suit on and the others did the same. The hot sauna felt so unbelievably delicious on her chilled skin that a shiver of pleasure ran up her spine as she collapsed on the teak bench.

The sauna had been custom built, and the benches that covered all four walls did not stint on space, allowing even the tall women to stretch out completely. Jamie suggested, "Why don't I turn down the heat a little and bring some cushions in so we can stay longer?"

"You're a genius," Jordan sighed. "It must be my Scandinavian heritage, but I absolutely adore saunas. I could stay in here all night."

"Be right back," Jamie promised, as she lowered the temp to 105 and carried in an armful of cushions. Another trip to the table Marta had set up yielded a large plastic pitcher filled with fresh lemonade and glasses for everyone.

They all sat up to drink some of the tart beverage, and as the temperature dropped Jamie brought her cushion over to snuggle next to Ryan. "Not too hot to be close, is it?"

"Never. I love to be hot, to tell you the truth."

"Makes sense," Jamie whispered into her ear. "You always make me that way."

"Behave," Ryan whispered back, giving her partner a playful little slap.

"So, Mia," Jordan asked, "does your family live around here?"

"Yeah. Actually, you could walk to my house from here, if you didn't mind getting hassled by the Hillsborough police."

"Is it against the law to exercise?" Ryan asked lazily, thinking it odd, but not altogether unbelievable, that the town would prohibit such conduct.

"No, but there aren't any sidewalks or streetlights, and anyone walking around after dark is immediate cause for suspicion. My mother likes to take our dog out for a walk at night, just to make the police nervous."

"Mia's mom's a free spirit," Jamie informed the others.

"That's putting it kindly," Mia said. "She's a hell-raiser."

"Were you adopted?" Ryan asked dryly.

"Funny, Shevun, or whatever your real name is."

"It's Siobhán," Ryan said, pronouncing the name properly, with just a hint of her Irish accent coming to the fore, as it always did when she used a Gaelic name. "I think it's a lovely name—quite suited to me, as a matter of fact. It means 'gift from God'."

"You are that," Jamie beamed at her, getting temporarily lost in the deep blue eyes that blinked slowly at her.

Ryan didn't hear or care if their friends had any further comments about her name. She grasped Jamie's chin with two fingers and held her steady while she zeroed in for a tender, slow kiss. The world actually faded away for a few moments as her body focused only on the delightful sensations that suffused her senses: Jamie's soft warmth, the faint scent of her citrusy perfume, the incredible softness of her lips, and her warm, lemon-scented breath.

A jolt of desire shot through Ryan's groin as Jamie's tongue slid into her mouth, and she heard a small moan escape her lips as she welcomed her lover in. Months of experience with her fiery partner told Ryan that Jamie was feeling amorous, and she knew that they could rapidly cause a scene. Not wanting to embarrass themselves or their guests, she pulled back a little and rubbed a calming hand down Jamie's back. "Soon," she whispered into her partner's flushed ear, drawing a small groan of protest.

There was not a sound coming from Jordan or Mia, and Ryan pulled away to spare a quick glance. Jordan was lying down, her eyes closed, seemingly oblivious. Mia, however, was shooting Ryan a lethal glance, and she mouthed, "Stop that." Properly chastised, Ryan nodded, giving her a "can't help myself" shrug.

Mia sat up and gave Jordan an appraising look, then asked, "Hey, do you like flowers?"

"Flowers?" she asked slowly. "I guess. Why?"

"Jamie's mom has a really cool formal garden back behind the pool. Are you dry enough to go for a walk before I have to leave?"

Immediately getting to her feet, Jordan smiled and said, "I love flowers. Let's go."

Feeling frisky, and not caring if her friends knew it, Jamie asked, "Will you be coming back in?"

"Probably not," Mia said. "I think I'll put my clothes back on. Why?"

"I'd like some quiet time with Ryan, and I wanted to know how uhm…quiet we could get."

Ryan gave her a startled look, but she didn't protest.

Jordan smiled at the pair and said, "I'm going to get dressed, too. It's a little chilly out, even with a dry suit. You two can be as quiet as you want."

"Thanks, guys," Jamie said, puckering up for a kiss. Mia dutifully gave them each one, ruffling Jamie's hair as she did so.

"We'll close the outside doors," Mia said. "Let the games begin."

"See you two tomorrow," Jordan said. "If you go for a run, come and get me Boomer, okay?"

"Will do," Ryan sighed. "Looks doubtful at the moment, but I won't forget you."

"Will I be able to find my room?" Jordan asked right before she left.

"Yes, I'm sure your light will be on and the bed will be turned down. When you get to the top of the stairs, turn right and go to the first open door. Do you need pajamas?"

"Hardly," Jordan chuckled. "I'm a natural kinda girl."

Mia watched her walk out, looking like she wanted to see her au natural very, very soon.

As the pair left, Ryan snaked her arm around her partner and pulled her down for a warm hug. "You're getting quite bold with your wishes, my pet. What happened to the shy woman I knew just a few months ago?"

"I'm still shy about some things, but I feel really comfortable around Mia, and I know you feel comfortable around Jordan, so I decided to be myself."

"I like your self," Ryan cooed, nibbling on a slightly salty earlobe. "I've missed your self."

Jamie looked up at her, realizing with shock that they hadn't made love since Ryan returned from her trip to Oregon five days ago. "God, what with your illness, and all of the things that have been going on, we've really been missing out on our close time."

"I know. But that's how long-term relationships are. When you haven't been intimate in a while, it makes being together special."

Jamie rolled onto her side and studied her partner seriously. "When you were single you didn't have to put up with some of this stuff, did you?"

"If, by 'this stuff', you mean the emotional roller-coaster we've been on with your father, of course not."

"No family drama?"

"I didn't care enough about anyone to get involved with their families. Ally was the closest I felt to any person that I slept with, and I don't have any idea what her parents do for a living. It's just not the same."

"But do you ever miss that? Do you ever miss just being able to find someone and have a good time, without worrying about them emotionally?" She looked very tentative as she asked the question.

Ryan trailed her fingers down Jamie's face, chasing a single drop of perspiration that trickled down her cheek. "What's up? That question doesn't sound like it's coming from your most secure place."

Jamie looked up at her and asked earnestly, "Just tell me. Do you ever miss that? Do you ever wish you could meet someone hot and take her to bed?"

"Jamie, the last woman I bedded like that was before Tracy. That's been almost a year. I was tired of the game before I even had a thought that I could be with you."

"It's been that long?"

"Yep. I didn't stop whoring around just because I knew that you wanted me to. I stopped because it wasn't pleasurable for me any more."

"I don't like it when you talk about it as whoring around. I don't like to hear that word applied to you."

"That's what it feels like to me now," Ryan said. "It didn't feel like it then, because I thought that's what sex felt like. But now that I've known what making love is, the way I used to act seems like a very poor, very cheap imitation of the real thing." She wrapped her arms tightly around her partner and murmured, "It hurts me to think that you could even question this. I tell you all of the time how much our intimacy means to me. Why have you forgotten that?"

Jamie sighed and nestled her head against Ryan's shoulder. "I haven't forgotten. I...I'm just a little confused tonight."

"Why tonight? What has you confused?"

"I guess it's from this afternoon with my mom. We spent a lot of time talking, and she told me some things that I didn't know before. I guess what upset me the most was when she told me that the first time Daddy slept with someone else, she was completely devastated. She had no idea. She thought they were deeply in love. She thought he was happy and satisfied with her." Peering up at Ryan with a frightened, worried look, Jamie said, "It scares me that she didn't have any idea. I guess I was under the impression that they had just drifted apart—not that he went out and found someone while they were seemingly happy."

Ryan nodded. "Okay, I can see that would make you feel very sorry for your mom, but I don't get why it makes you worry about me." The blue eyes were wary, and Jamie could see a glint of hurt in them.

"I'm sorry. I told you, I'm just confused." Jamie let her hand drop onto Ryan's stomach and rubbed her gently. "I can't understand how you could do that to someone that you loved." She shook her head. "It's more understandable to me if there are major problems in the marriage, you know? But just screwing someone else because you can shocks me to the core."

"I agree that it's a terrible betrayal," Ryan said slowly. "I also don't understand why you doubt me because of it."

"I don't doubt you." Jamie paused for a few moments, then sighed heavily and said, "There are just a lot of similarities between our situation and my parents'. They got married when they were around our ages, Daddy had been with a lot of women, and he hadn't really been in the market for marriage." She looked up at Ryan and said tentatively, "Neither were you. You've told me many times that you weren't interested in settling down until you were through with grad school. I just worry that you'll feel trapped—like he did."

Ryan sat up, consciously separating herself from Jamie. She looked like she was about to speak several times before finally taking a breath and doing so. "I'm doing my best not to take offense at what you're saying, but it's really a struggle." Her hands were tensed into fists, and she looked like she was poised for a fight. "I don't mean to be cruel, but it insults me to be compared to your father. He and I might have a similar history, but I'm not overly controlling, I'm not manipulative, I'd never hurt an innocent person just to get my way, I'd never try to ruin someone's reputation just because they were in my way, and I'd never hurt my spouse just to make myself appear better by comparison. I'm *not* like he is, and I can, and I will, keep my promises to you." She stood to leave, but Jamie grabbed her firmly by the seat of her swimsuit and refused to let go.

"Please don't leave, please."

"I don't want to say anything that I'll regret," Ryan ground out through her clenched teeth.

"I'd rather have you say something rude than leave me right now. Really." There was a look of abject begging in her eyes that seemed to break Ryan's resolve.

"All right. I'll try to be polite." She sat down across from Jamie, feeling too hurt to be close.

"I shouldn't have said anything. I need to work those fears out on my own. Telling you everything probably isn't a good idea." She looked sad and a little lost as she said this.

"Oh, shit, I…I got carried away," Ryan said. "I shouldn't get so upset when you're just trying to work something out for yourself. I have to show you a little more patience." Ryan's head dropped, and Jamie crossed the room to sit next to her.

"Is it okay if I sit here?"

"Yeah, sure. Sorry I got angry. It just hurts me when you say things like that, and I react by getting angry."

"That's understandable. I wouldn't like it if you'd said the same thing to me." She sighed heavily and added, "I think there's still a part of me that feels morally superior because I've been sexual with so few people." She leaned back against the wall and said, "It's not a part of myself that I'm proud of."

"Understandable."

"No, it's not. It's a part of myself that I want to change. It doesn't come out very often, but it's destructive for us when it does. I mean, I know that it's coming up now because of my father, but that's no excuse. Really, it isn't."

Ryan finally smiled, sliding an arm around her as she did so. "Let's call a truce. I know that I'll always be faithful to you. You can have your doubts, but do me a favor and try not to tell me about them unless you really have to, okay?"

"Okay," Jamie said quietly, resting her head on Ryan's shoulder. "I don't have doubts about you, really I don't. I'm just confused when I try to figure out how someone I'd always looked up to could have been so duplicitous. If I could have been so thoroughly fooled, I wonder about my ability to judge people and their behavior."

"That makes perfect sense. I'm sure my foundations would be shaken if I found out that Da had cheated on my mother. I'll try to keep that in perspective, Jamers."

"I think things like this will come up for a while. I'll just do my best to talk to Anna about it rather than hurting your feelings."

"Deal," Ryan said, leaning over for a kiss to seal the bargain.

"Ready for bed? You must be beat after your match tonight. You really played up a storm."

Ryan stretched—sticking her arms straight out to ease some of the stiffness that had settled in her shoulders. "I am tired, but I need a little connection tonight," she said, drawing her finger down her partner's thigh in a simple pattern. As she spoke, she expanded the territory that she covered, moving a little higher, into more sensitive spaces.

"What kind of connection were you thinking of, sweetheart?" Jamie cocked her head playfully and began to trail her finger down the tasty-looking cleavage that was so conveniently located.

"Well, we're almost naked...we're already a little sweaty...we're alone, and no one will disturb us...I think this would be a perfect place to connect, don't you?"

"Ooh...you want the intimate kinda connection," Jamie said, playfully acting obtuse.

"That's my favorite kind. I'm just afraid that we'll have a stroke if we stay in here. It's cooled down, but it's still pretty hot."

"Oh, there are plenty of places we could go in here if you want to stay. Let's go use that fabulous shower to cool down. Then I can heat you up anywhere you wish."

They spent a long, leisurely time in the shower, letting the warm water wash away some of the lingering tension that their little squabble had created.

"Ooh...perfect," Jamie smiled when they re-entered the sauna. It was warm, but dry, reminding her of sub-Saharan Africa on a nice spring day. Turning to Ryan, she cocked her head and asked, "Will you be comfortable here?"

Ryan arranged the cushions on the long, wide teak bench, nodding thoughtfully to herself. "Looks great." She spread a slightly damp towel over the cushions and lay down on her side, moving against the wall to allow her partner plenty of room to join her. As she patted the cushion invitingly, Jamie lay down next to her, moving up until their faces were level.

"I'm really sorry for being so rude earlier," Jamie said. "You don't give me any reason to doubt you. I'm just struggling."

"I understand," Ryan soothed as she tenderly brushed the damp hair off her forehead. "You've had your moorings rocked. It'll take you a while before you trust yourself again."

Jamie nodded, her smile growing as she took in Ryan's comment. "You really understand," she sighed. "It's not you that I doubt…it's myself, and my judgment."

"I do understand. I just have to remind myself that this is an internal struggle for you and doesn't reflect what you feel about me. That's hard sometimes," she said. Her big blue eyes blinked shyly as she said, "My feelings get hurt."

Wrapping her arms around her partner, Jamie kissed her gently and said, "I know, sweetheart. I hate to hurt you, but I know that I do sometimes." She gazed at her somberly and promised, "I never mean to hurt you. I swear."

"Oh, I know that. Neither of us wants to hurt the other, but we've hurt each other before, and we'll hurt each other again. It's unavoidable. What matters is that we try to learn from it."

"I've learned that I love you very, very much," Jamie said, her eyes beginning to tear at the emotion she felt flowing from her heart. "You're my life."

Moving closer, Ryan smiled gently and tenderly kissed every hint of a tear from the misty green eyes that she loved so much. "Sometimes it's almost too much, isn't it," she asked rhetorically. "It feels like your heart might just burst."

Jamie nodded, a smile showing through the tears that continued to fall. "It is too much sometimes. But it's a good too much."

"Yeah. That's the perfect way to put it." As Ryan spoke, her head dipped just enough to allow her to kiss her partner, trying to reveal the depths of her love through the gentleness of her touch. One kiss became many as the passion that so often lurked just under the surface of Ryan's personality started to flare.

Soon she was fully astride her partner, her body moving sensually against Jamie's as the kisses covered her face and neck. Jamie felt like she was standing naked in the simmering desert heat, with cool, fat drops of life-giving rain touching her parched skin.

Lifting her head to breathe, Ryan met Jamie's unfocused gaze. "I've been putting this off for as long as I can," she whispered, her own eyes filled with wanton desire. "I don't know why, but I'm completely fixated on your breasts today." She shifted her body just enough to allow her tongue to reach the flesh. Her head hovered just over the normally pale skin, now pink from the heat and the lingering effects of the warm shower.

"Tell me," Jamie urged, loving to hear Ryan put words to her yearnings.

Ryan smiled, and said, "It started when you got out of the shower this morning. I don't know why, but I had a very hard time stopping myself from taking your bra off as soon as you put it on." Her shoulders shrugged slightly. "I don't know what the reason was…I just needed to have my mouth on one of those little beauties."

"They're always interested in visitors," Jamie chuckled. "You should have dropped in."

"No time." Ryan shook her head roughly. "I didn't want to nibble and run. I just had a feeling that I'd get carried away."

"That's one of your best traits."

"I'm glad I waited. Now I can take my time and love them like they deserve to be loved." She placed her soft tongue at the bottom of her partner's breast and slowly licked up the warm, pink skin, passing gently over the stiffening nipple and continuing in an unbroken path until she reached the very top. Unable to resist, she nipped at the skin just above the breast, making a light mark with her teeth.

"They like that," Jamie sighed, a shiver running down her body.

"When we were in here with Jordan and Mia, you had a nice bead of sweat that started just under your ear," Ryan related. "I watched it slide down your neck and pass through the hollow between your collar bones. It started to pick up speed when it got here," she indicated, her finger recreating the journey. "Then it stopped for just a second, just a heartbeat, really, before it slid right between your breasts." She looked up at Jamie with longing in her big blue eyes and said, "I wanted to be that lucky, lucky little drop of moisture. It was all I could do to behave myself. I wanted to tear that sexy suit off you and nuzzle my head between your breasts until you cried for mercy."

Jamie reached down and placed her hands on the outside of the pink flesh and gently compressed it. Her eyes were blinking slowly, her desire for her partner pounding in her veins. "Jordan and Mia are gone," she whispered. "Make your dreams come true."

The soft pink tongue peeked out of Ryan's mouth, then moved sensually along her moist lips, readying them for the feast. Her head dropped as her hands covered her partner's, helping her to squeeze the sensitive flesh firmly, both women moaning in tandem as Ryan's lips captured a painfully erect nipple.

She used her mouth and her tongue and her teeth to stimulate the tender breasts in every possible way, loving them more thoroughly and with more enthusiasm than Jamie could ever remember. The sensations pulsing through Ryan's body were nearly as powerful as what Jamie experienced. Every few minutes, the dark head would have to lift so that Ryan could concentrate on her breathing just to avoid feeling lightheaded.

Jamie's hands were laced through her hair, clutching her to her breasts with reckless abandon. Her arousal was nearly painful by this point, and as much as she was enjoying the overwhelming sensations, she longed to touch her partner in the same way. Finally unable to suppress the urge, she forced Ryan onto her back and began to love her, making Ryan moan and twitch under her assault.

Their bodies were tingling, chests heaving with effort and arousal, both so sensitive that they drunkenly wavered along the line between pleasure and pain.

Shifting her hips, Ryan maneuvered one of Jamie's strong thighs between her own and began to glide against her, the delicious sensation building so quickly that she barely had time to bend her head to pull a rock-hard nipple into her mouth. She sucked firmly as her climax hit her hard, flashing through her body with a frighteningly fierce intensity.

Jamie held her tight, soothing her by running a hand down her back for a few moments. She knew that Ryan needed some time to rest, but her own need was so fierce, so demanding, that she made an offer, "I'll give you a million bucks if you'll lend me your tongue for a few minutes." Ryan's low chuckle caused her to clarify. "I'm good for it. Really. I just need that tongue immediately."

"You've got it," Ryan growled, her body coming to life as she easily tossed Jamie onto her back. She was already sliding down as the blue eyes locked on Jamie's to assure her, "No charge."

Ryan got right down to business, focusing on loving the writhing woman into a much-needed climax. Her preference was to tease her partner until she was nearly beside herself, but she knew she could always go for another, more leisurely tour a little later in the evening. *I love having a multi-orgasmic partner. Everyone gets what they want.*

After just a few minutes of Ryan's skillful ministrations, Jamie cried out loudly, her exhausted body barely able to summon the strength for respiration.

It took a substantial bit of time, but Jamie could finally speak again. Ryan rolled off of her, and she stared up at the teak ceiling, murmuring, "I love women." Ryan's chuckle make her laugh as well, and she clarified, "I love you above all women, but I love women."

She said this so emphatically that Ryan laughed once again, turning her head to gaze at Jamie, sharing a smile. "You've just begun to plumb the depths of your new affiliation. There's much, much more to come."

🐎

It was after midnight when Jamie and Ryan ran laughing across the lawn and reached the kitchen. The were both thirsty from being in the sauna for so long, even though the heat had been turned down to the lowest setting. Ryan was amazed at the assortment of beverages that the massive refrigerator held, and she had to think for a bit to decide. After chugging a twenty ounce bottle of cranberry juice, they started to make their way up to bed, holding hands as they walked towards the stairs. They stopped abruptly when a soft voice asked, "Going up to bed, girls?"

"Oh. I didn't know you were still up, Mom," Jamie said, startled. "We were just uhm…sitting in the sauna and…"

"It's all right, dear," Catherine assured her. "I'm very pleased that you're enjoying yourselves. But there was no way I was going to bed with you two still in the sauna. I was going to give you another ten minutes, and then I was going to send Helena out to check on you."

"That would have been…interesting," Jamie laughed, imagining the eyeful Helena would have received just a few minutes earlier.

"Better her than me," Catherine agreed, laughing.

"Hmm…Jordan's not in her room yet," Jamie said as they climbed the stairs.

"She wasn't out back. She's probably walking Mia to her car," Ryan said sleepily as she shuffled into Jamie's room. "Boy, I'm tired. Whew."

"Sleep in tomorrow. You've got a big day, and you need your rest."

"I will if I can. It's just such a habit for me…"

"I'll cuddle you extra tight," Jamie promised. "Then you'll be so warm and content that you won't have any desire to leave me."

"That sounds like the best cure for early rising that I've ever heard," Ryan agreed, placing a kiss on her partner's nose.

Chapter Two

When Jamie woke at eight o'clock, there was a note lying on Ryan's pillow.

> Your hugs felt great, but I'm wide awake. I'm going to drag Jordan out of bed and take her with me for a run. Stay in bed as long as you like—If you're still sleeping when I get back I might join you for a snuggle. I love you—R

Oh-oh, Ryan thought when she left their room and saw that Jordan's light was still on. Poking her head in, she saw that the room had not been slept in, and she began to wonder if her friend had left with Mia.

Just to make sure they hadn't been locked out or something, Ryan decided to swing by the pool. To her surprise, she was greeted by the sight of the twosome cuddling on a chaise, kissing so intently that they didn't even hear her approach.

She sat down on a facing chaise and regarded the pair, waiting until one of Jordan's blue eyes rotated in her direction. Jordan slowly disentangled herself from Mia's mouth and waved at Ryan. "It's nice out here," she said dully, looking like she'd been hit between the eyes with something heavy.

The pair had covered themselves with several of the large bath sheets that were stored in the pool house, and Ryan wondered aloud why they hadn't gone inside the spacious building to warm up.

Mia shrugged amiably, repeating, "It's nice out here."

"So I hear," Ryan said, smiling. "Well, I'll leave you to it. Marta will be in the kitchen soon, so if you don't want to put on a show, you might want to adjourn to Jordan's room."

"There's two rooms on the second floor of the pool house if we wanted to do that," Mia said absently. "We like to be outside."

"We were just saying good-bye," Jordan said. "I know Mia wants to spend the weekend with her family. Good thing you didn't tell them you were coming," she said as she gazed fondly at the curly-haired woman. "They'd be sending out the hounds by now."

"They're used to my schedule," she said easily. "But I should let you go running if you need to. I don't want to interfere with your training."

"How does keeping her up all night fit in with that?" Ryan asked, a little miffed at Jordan for pulling another all-nighter on the eve of a game.

"That's not Mia's fault," Jordan said, immediately coming to her defense. "She can't help it if she's an absolutely fascinating conversationalist." She was grinning shyly at the curly-haired woman, and Ryan had to force herself not to roll her eyes.

"Yeah, you looked like you were heavily involved in… conversation."

Jordan tossed off the towels, hopping to her feet in one graceful move. "Can I go with you, sport? I'd like to get my blood moving, have a little breakfast, then hit the sack for the rest of the day."

"Sounds like a perfect training regimen for game day," Ryan smirked. "Sure…I'll wait for you. Do you have any shorts in your gym bag?"

"Yeah. I've got a spare pair. Be right back," she said, addressing only Mia, who gave her a beaming grin in return.

As Jordan jogged off, Mia gave Ryan a long hug. "I'm so glad that you decided to play volleyball."

"Jordan's pretty special, isn't she?"

"Yeah," Mia said patting Ryan on her nylon-clad butt. "So are you, for that matter. Is everybody on your team extra-special?"

"Come to the game tonight and find out. You could actually come to this one on time and see some of the action." Ryan, of course, had noticed exactly how late in the previous night's game Mia had arrived, even though Jordan had not.

"Eh…not unless Jordan invites me. I don't want to chase her. I don't think she'd like that."

"I'm not really sure. You're the first person I've seen her with, so I don't know her likes and dislikes."

"Hmm…that doesn't make any sense. How could she not have women leaping into her arms when she walks down the street?"

"Got me."

"At least I don't have to fight anybody off."

Jordan ran back to the pair, hopping in place to warm up her long legs. "Ready, Boomer?"

"I've been ready for fifteen minutes. Let's go before the Hillsborough police sic the dogs on us."

Jordan smiled at Mia and gave her an incredibly gentle kiss, barely allowing their lips to brush against each other. "See ya. I had a great time last night."

"Bye," Mia said softly, lacing her fingers with Jordan's and giving her hand a squeeze.

Well, I guess she's not coming to the game tonight, Ryan thought, giving Mia a puzzled shrug as Jordan turned and started to jog down the springy grass that led to the street.

⚜

They had already broken a sweat by the time they started chatting with each other. "Nice neighborhood," Jordan smirked as they passed some of the most expensive real estate in the entire Bay Area.

"Yeah. I don't think there's a very high percentage of food-stamp recipients around here."

"Is Mia this well off?"

"I don't really know. This social stratum is so far above mine that it's impossible for me to judge. I've never been to her house, either. I know that her dad and Jamie's dad met at Stanford, and that they went to law school together, but other than that…"

"She's pretty cool, isn't she?" Jordan asked, getting a dreamy look on her face.

"Yeah, I like Mia a lot. She's been a great friend for Jamie, too. When Jamie was going through some tough times last year, Mia was the only one who was always supportive of her. For that alone, she's way up there on my list."

"She's so soft and cuddly." Jordan smiled, looking just a little embarrassed. "It's kinda weird to snuggle with someone so much smaller, you know?"

Ryan shot her a look and asked, "Have you generally been with women as big as you are? Where in the heck do you find them? Amazons 'R Us?"

Jordan just shrugged, ignoring the question.

Something about her attitude changed, though, and Ryan decided to follow up. "What kind of women do you normally go for?"

"I don't know," she said, staring straight ahead.

"Jordan…"

The lanky blonde gave Ryan an embarrassed look and said, "I don't *go for* any kinda woman. Women go for me."

"Huh? What do you mean by that?"

"I've…never approached a woman. I've been approached a couple of times, but even that's been a while."

Ryan saw the chagrined look on her friend's face and said, "Does it bother you to talk about this?"

"Yeah, but I should. I'm confused."

"What's up? I thought you were gayish."

"Yeah, emphasis on the 'ish'."

"Oh, I got the impression that you'd been with more women than men." Ryan was trying to tread carefully, but she was confused about the whole situation.

"Nope. Same number, as a matter of fact. Two each."

Ryan nearly tripped when she heard this news. "You've only been with four people?" It wasn't that the number was so shocking. It was that Jordan had given Ryan such strong vibes—and had indicated that she was a player just like Ryan had been.

"Yeah." She was blushing fiercely now, and she mumbled, "Kinda sad, huh?"

"No. There's nothing sad about being picky. I just had the impression that you uhm…got around."

"That's what gets around," Jordan admitted, an embarrassed grimace on her face. "The impression."

Ryan shook her head, trying to reconcile this information with the full-court press Jordan had put on her. "So, what about the women you *have* been with?"

"What about 'em?"

"Were you in relationships, or was it more casual than that?"

Jordan laughed, a bitter note in the sound. "Oh, they were a lot more casual than that." They ran on in silence for so long that Ryan was sure Jordan had decided not to continue, but she finally started to speak again. "The first one was at a volleyball camp when I was a junior in high school. She talked me into going for a walk one night, and before I knew it, we were rolling around on a tennis court. After a good deal of convincing I went up to her room with her, but I freaked and wouldn't even talk to her after that. Creeped me out," she said with a shiver.

"So you didn't really do anything."

"No, I ran out before we could. We kissed a lot, though." She gave Ryan a look. "It was enough."

"What was your other experience?" Ryan asked, almost afraid to know.

"It was the next Christmas—a holiday all-star tournament for some of the club teams from the L.A. area. One of the college players who was working at the camp invited me to her room. We had a nice chat about the school she went to—I thought she was trying to recruit me," she said, a mortified look on her face. "She was."

"God, Jordan, did she force you…"

"No, no, nothing like that. We kissed for a long time, but when she put her hand under my shirt I pulled away from her and ran. I think I ran around the UCLA campus half the night. My legs were so sore the next day I could barely jump an inch."

"So you've never really…been with a woman?" Ryan said, still unable to process the information.

"I've never been naked with one, no." She looked pathetically sad when she added, "I sure have wanted to, though." She shook her head a little, trying to remove the sweat that dripped into her eyes. "I dream about women."

Ryan was completely charmed by the guileless way that her friend said this. It sounded romantic—almost quaint, and once again she realized that it didn't fit with her image of who Jordan was. "Not to state the obvious, but I don't think you'd have too much trouble getting lucky if you wanted to. What's up with that?"

She shrugged, loosening her shoulders as she did so. "I don't know; it's seemed too dangerous, you know?"

"Nope. Not a clue."

"Volleyball comes first. I don't have time for all of the turmoil."

"Hey, I love volleyball too," Ryan reminded her. "And I think I'm pretty focused. Being loved makes life easier. Really."

"Eh, maybe it does. But you can't tell me that coming out is easy. I don't want to be in the closet if I fall for somebody. That's not me. I don't know if it's cool to be gay if you're on the Olympic team, and I'm not gonna hurt my chances by having anybody know about me. I've got the rest of my life ahead of me—there's no rush."

"Okay. That makes sense—intellectually, that is. But why were you flirting your ass off with me? You were giving off some unequivocal vibes, pal."

She blushed furiously, and stared straight ahead, unable to make eye contact with her friend. "I don't know." She was obviously mortified to be called on her conduct.

"That's okay," Ryan said. "Forget about it."

"No," Jordan said firmly. "This is important. It's been getting too strong to resist." She shook her head, long blonde hair sliding across her shoulders. "It's started to interfere with my concentration." She looked at her friend and said, "I can't afford to have my concentration ruined. This year is critical. It's probably the most important year in my life."

"Okay, so you've started feeling like what…like you wanted to go farther than you had before?"

"Yeah. I think I convinced myself that if I could just let a little steam off I could get back to business. I…I heard you were…"

"Easy," Ryan supplied.

"Well, yeah." She grinned, looking more like the person Ryan had come to know. "I thought you'd be a good place to start because you understand about focus and stuff. It was pretty obvious that you weren't into commitment—at least, that's what I'd heard."

"Oh," Ryan said, the light going on. "You thought I'd be safe—just a little playing around—no big deal."

"Yeah," she said, nodding. "I thought I could learn the ropes, too."

"I've taught a few women the ropes," Ryan admitted cockily, "But I wouldn't have done that with you. Teammates are dangerous."

"I don't know any of this stuff," Jordan said, looking thoroughly confused. "I just know I didn't want anything permanent, but sometimes it just hurts 'cause I want it so bad." She finally turned and gazed at Ryan with pained eyes. "Do you know what I mean?"

"I think so. I mean, I know what it's like to have desire. It's pretty hard to say no to it for long."

"I know," she moaned, wiping her face with the back of her hand. "It was so hard to lie on that chaise with Mia and not…touch her." She blinked at Ryan for a second and added, "I think she wanted me to."

Oh, Lord, knowing Mia, she wanted to do a lot more than just touch. "I've gotta tell you, you might not have any experience, but you sure don't act like a woman who hasn't done this before. Does Mia know?"

"Huh-uh," she said, shaking her head quickly "It's easy for me to act like I'm teasing or playing around, but I'm scared shitless to really do anything."

"What do you want to happen with Mia? Do you want to have sex with her?"

"God, yes. I've been dreaming about her every night since we met. I go to sleep thinking about how her lips felt, and I wake up wishing that I was holding her."

"How did you get up the nerve to kiss her for the first time?" Ryan asked. "Wasn't that a really big step for you?"

"Well, it woulda been if I'd done anything," she said with a grimace. "We had the best time that night, just talking. There was a part of me that felt so attracted to her—I really wished that I had the guts to kiss her. When she wanted to get something to drink, I sat down on a chair in your kitchen. She brought over a big glass of juice and asked if I wanted some. I said, 'Sure,' and she brought the glass up to my lips. She was leaning over to make sure that she didn't spill." Jordan gave Ryan a puzzled look and said, "I still don't know why I didn't take the damned glass out of her hand."

"I have an idea, but go on," Ryan said, smiling at her innocence.

"So she's leaning over me, and when she takes the glass away, there was a little juice on the side of my mouth. She gave me this look." Jordan shivered all over as she recalled the scene, "then she leaned over a little more and said, 'You dripped.' I looked up at her with what had to be the stupidest look in the history of the world, and she leaned over and kissed it off me." Jordan blinked, still obviously puzzled by the encounter. "Next thing I know, she's sitting on my lap, and we're kissing like I've never kissed anyone before. My God. If you hadn't come down right then, I don't know what would have happened."

"Again, I've got an idea…"

"I'm scared," Jordan said softly. "I really don't know what to do, and I don't want this to be a big deal." She gave Ryan a stern look. "Are you absolutely sure that she's not a lesbian?"

"No, I'm not sure of that for anyone—except myself, of course," she joked. "I know Mia's had a long-time boyfriend, and I know she really likes guys. I'd never seen her with a girl before, so this is all new for me. I think you need to ask her."

"Oh, that'll go over well. Uhm…Mia, I'd really like to have sex with you 'cause I think I'm gay, but I don't know what in the hell I'm doing, and I think you do. Being near you makes me ache, but I wanna make sure that you're not gay, 'cause I don't want you to fall in love with me or anything, 'cause I like volleyball more than you." She gave Ryan a droll look and said, "Smooth enough line?"

"I could make a few suggestions to spruce it up a little if you want."

"Go."

Ryan gave her a little snort of a laugh and said, "You remind me of my brother Brendan sometimes. He speaks in shorthand, too." Jordan gave her a smirk and she continued, "You could tell Mia the whole truth. Tell her that you're trying to figure your sexuality out, but that you aren't in the market for a relationship. She might be willing to help you get to the answers."

"Maybe," she said, nodding. "I just don't want to blow it with her. Whether or not I sleep with her, I really like her. She makes me feel like a different person. Do you know what I mean?"

Ryan shot her a smile and said, "Jamie makes me feel like I'm the best person that I can be. She makes me feel powerful…like I could do anything as long as she's with me."

Jordan laughed and said, "It's just the opposite for me. Mia makes me feel soft and gentle. I've never had so much desire for someone— and then wanted to touch them so softly. I always thought I'd feel passionate and kinda frantic, but it's not like that at all. I just want to hold her and stroke her body with my hands and my…" She shook her head roughly, censoring herself, obviously feeling that she had been too revealing. "I feel like I'm going nuts."

"Did you ever feel this way about guys? Were you ever in love?"

"No. Not even a little," she said dismissively, shaking her head the whole time.

"Did you have boyfriends? Or did you just sleep with guys you knew casually?"

"Uhm…" she gulped noticeably. "I'm pretty sure I didn't say I slept with either of the guys I dated seriously. We did a lot," she said, "but we didn't actually do everything. I went out with a guy from the soccer team last year, and we almost did but…" She grimaced. "I chickened out so many times he finally couldn't take it any more."

Oh boy. Mia's got her work cut out for her.

❧

Ryan was in the shower when it hit her. *Jordan wasn't flirting with me because she thought I'd play with her. She didn't even start flirting until she knew that I was with Jamie—that we were living together. She thought I was safe to flirt with because she knew I wouldn't reciprocate. Come to think of it, those guys she was flirting with at the bar that night were with other women.* She shook her head as the picture became clearer. *She's obviously scared out of her wits to be with anyone who's available…and Mia is certainly available at the moment. This could get interesting.*

❧

When Catherine came down at nine o'clock, all three young

women were relaxing at the kitchen table, sharing stories with Marta about life in Berkeley. The cook hopped up immediately when Catherine appeared, but Catherine placed a hand on her shoulder and urged her back into her seat. "I'll just have coffee, Marta. Relax for a change."

Marta rolled her eyes at Jamie and complained, "This is the first work I've done in two weeks. I don't get to cook anything but toast."

"Well, you'll be happy tonight," Catherine promised. "Ryan's family is coming for dinner."

"Wonderful. How many people?"

"I'm not sure yet," Ryan said, "but I'll call my father and ask for a head count. Probably fifteen or so."

"Oh, that is a good number. I'll start right now. I'm off to the market," she said as she grabbed her keys and headed for the door.

"You've made her happier than you'll ever know," Catherine said as she sat down and picked at remnants of the now cold breakfast.

Ryan stood and scooped the platters away from Catherine, stating, "I'm making you a decent meal, and then we're going to have your first weight training class."

"We are?" she gulped, looking up at the young woman with wide eyes.

"Yep. No arguments," she said menacingly as she leaned over and placed a gentle kiss on her cheek.

"Does she always get her way?" Catherine asked Jamie with a smirk.

"Ha." Ryan scoffed. "I don't think I've won an argument since August the twenty-fourth, the day I met your daughter."

After figuratively force-feeding Catherine some fresh fruit, low-fat yogurt, and a bagel, they all went up to put on workout clothes. Jamie lent Jordan some nylon shorts and a tank top and she had to laugh at her after she put them on. "We wear the same size, but we sure don't wear them the same way." She surveyed the way Jordan's long, lean frame stretched the clothes more vertically than when she wore them.

Ryan slipped on a black sleeveless unitard with short legs and a low neck that immediately had Jamie salivating. "I've never seen you wear this," she mused as she pulled at the skintight fabric.

"I think I've worn it when I've been with you, but I always wear a T-shirt over it so it just looks like shorts."

"Don't wear the T-shirt today. I want to see those muscles rippling."

"Your mom will be in the gym, too. Can you avoid trying to lure me into what we did the last time we worked out in private?"

"I promise I will not ravish you while Mother is there. But when I get you alone, all bets are off."

"I do have to play a match tonight. You don't want to drain all of the lifeblood from my poor body."

"When do you have to be there?"

"We don't have to practice since we played last night. So I don't have to be there until around 3:30."

"Excellent. I'll have time to drain you and fill you back up again," Jamie said with a gleam in her eye.

"I think I need a nap already."

After they were all dressed, Ryan asked Jamie, "Where *is* your weight room? I haven't seen it."

"It's on the second floor of the pool house, but it's not as extensive as the one in Pebble Beach. We put it in the pool house so you can just hop in the sauna or the spa after you work out."

Jordan interrupted to say, "I don't mean to offend you, but why on earth do you guys want to live in Noe Valley? I'd never move away from home if I had a setup this sweet."

"Ryan loves Noe Valley, I love Ryan, and that's the bottom line," Jamie said firmly, giving her lover a pat on the cheek.

When they reached the pool house, Jordan started to pepper Catherine with questions about the design. As they drifted away to discuss some detail, Ryan leaned back against the wall and asked, "Do you want to live in Noe only because I do?"

"Uhm, I guess so. I mean, I'd never been there before I met you, and I doubt that I would have ever gone there on my own. I was planning on living down here after I married Jack—so I guess the answer is yes, I want to live in Noe mainly because it's important to you."

Ryan blew out a breath and sighed heavily. "I guess I thought you liked the neighborhood," she said, a pout forming on her lips.

"I do, sweetheart. I've grown to love it. It feels like home to me now. But that's not what you asked me. I grew up here, and I would have been happy to live here for the rest of my life. It's comfortable and familiar, and I must admit that I like the weather better. But this is just a place to me. Noe is much more than that to you, and it's tremendously important to me to make sure you have the things that make you feel happy and secure. I can move to Noe Valley and be perfectly content, but you couldn't do the same down here. It's an obvious choice."

"But I should be able to be as flexible as you are," she murmured, still pouting.

"You're very flexible, sweetness, but this isn't an area that you need to compromise on. I want to live in Noe."

"But the weather really is nicer down here, and we could never have any real outside space. We'll never be able to have a pool or…"

"My parents have all of this stuff. It's a half-hour trip. No big deal. And since we're going to have to bring the kids down to see Granny all the time, I think it'll be nice to have a very different environment for them. Lord knows what will happen with my parents, but one of them will probably wind up living here. Hopefully we'll have a relationship with both of them by then."

Ryan gave her a quick look to confirm the talk might have made Jamie a little sad. Seeing the dimming of the normal sparkle in her eyes, she deftly changed the subject. "I don't think Granny will be the name of choice for your mother. You'll have to come up with something a lot more elegant."

"Good point. We'll have to work on it. Now are we settled on our living situation?"

"I suppose," she said. "You know, most people would agree with Jordan. It does look nuts to leave this life to live in my crummy little neighborhood."

Eyes blazing, Jamie said, "Don't you dare talk about our home like that. There is nothing crummy about Noe."

Ryan looked down at her shoes as she said with an embarrassed shrug, "I get kind of insecure when I'm down here. I guess I still think about your father telling me that you could never be happy with our lifestyle. And this all is so far from my experience that it boggles my mind a little."

"This is just stuff. Stuff can never replace family. Never."

"You're right. I'm sorry that I'm a little insecure." She was gazing intently at her shoes, embarrassed to be caught in such a vulnerable moment.

"I get insecure too. Quite often, if my memory serves me well. It's our job to help each other through it."

When Jordan and Catherine had finished their tour of the first floor of the pool house, they all trooped upstairs to hit the iron. Jamie's assessment of the space had been absolutely right on. It was not anywhere near as complete a gym as the gorgeous layout in Pebble Beach, but it had been very well designed to include equipment for working every muscle. In lieu of separate machines for most of the muscle groups, there was a large multi-function set up that contained weights and pulleys that could be configured to perform an almost endless variety of exercises. There was also a treadmill, an elliptical machine for cardiovascular training, and an exercise bike. Against the wall rested a graduated set of hand weights and a set of bar bells.

"Excellent setup, Catherine. You have everything that we could possibly need," Ryan said. Jordan wanted to work on her back and her abs, mostly to stay loose, so she walked over to the free weights to begin her program. Jamie was going to do her regular workout, but she wanted to watch Ryan start with her mother, so she pulled up a weight bench and sat down to observe. "Okay," Ryan began, "let's start with what you want to get out of a weight training program."

"I'm not sure," Catherine admitted. "I suppose I want to fight gravity and the clock."

Ryan nodded thoughtfully. "Weight training is one of the best ways to attack both of those. But let's talk about your overall fitness first. What do you currently do for exercise?"

"Not much," she conceded. "I walk on the treadmill a couple of times a week, but I'm not very consistent with it. It bores me to death, so I'm not very motivated."

"I don't blame you. I couldn't use a treadmill either. It's too much like a hamster on a wheel for me."

"Don't forget your tennis, Mom," Jamie piped up.

"Oh, I don't," Catherine allowed, "but to be honest, it's not a tremendous workout."

"Only 'cause you're so much better than your competition," Jamie said. Looking at Ryan she said, "Mom is one of those really accurate baseline players. She has great court savvy, and she gets to every ball that's hit anywhere near her. She's a lot better than her friends, and she barely breaks a sweat—even though her opponent is gasping for air."

"Oh, it's not that bad, honey," Catherine scoffed, even though she knew it was.

"Hmm…" Ryan said. "You really should get some aerobic exercise at least three days a week. You could play with a better caliber player at your club…"

"No, I'm not interested in that. I like to play for fun. A lot of the better players are too serious about the whole thing."

"How about walking in the neighborhood? It's so lovely down here that the walk could be enjoyable. And your pool is long enough to get a good workout if you could tolerate doing laps."

"No, I'm not a swimmer."

"How about a bike?" Jamie suggested. "It's much more interesting for me to ride than walk. I feel like I'm really getting somewhere on my bike."

"Hmm, I haven't ridden a bike since I was at Stanford. I enjoyed it then, but don't you think I'm a little old for that?"

"Not at all. Gosh, there were a couple of people in their 70s on the AIDS Ride with us."

"I might like that," she said with a twinkle in her eye. "It could remind me of my youth."

"That's why I do most of the things I do," Ryan said, grinning.

"Let's go get you a bike while the urge is still fresh," Jamie suggested.

"Really? So soon?"

"No time like the present," Ryan agreed.

"Okay," Catherine said, "as soon as we're through here, we'll go shopping."

"Works for me," Ryan said. "I'd like to start with a few exercises to get you started, but I don't want to overwhelm you. Over time we'll add to these to keep you interested, but first we need to build a base. So I'll show you exercises for your shoulders, chest, arms, back, legs, and abs."

"Okay, let's go."

Ryan led her through the most basic of exercises for each of her major muscle groups. Catherine was substantially weaker than Ryan would have guessed, but given that she did no work around the house and didn't stress herself at tennis, that wasn't too surprising. She could only manage ten or fifteen pounds on most of the exercises, but Ryan assured her that she'd progress quickly if she kept at it. Ryan urged her to do each exercise ten times but to do only one set at the beginning—as she got stronger she would increase the sets until she could do three, and then they would start to increase the weight on the machine.

Catherine seemed to like the process, and she agreed that she would work out three days a week and that she'd give Ryan weekly calls to report on her progress.

By the time they were finished Catherine's muscles were already beginning to stiffen up. Ryan wanted to suggest a massage, but since she wasn't sure how Jamie or Catherine would feel about it, she held her tongue.

"Oh, my, I'm going to feel this in the morning," Catherine said as she sat on a bench and watched Jamie work.

Without missing a beat, Jamie suggested, "Let Ryan give you a massage, Mom. You'll feel tons better."

Catherine looked at her a little hesitantly but Ryan assured her, "I'm happy to work on you if you feel comfortable."

"Yes, I think I do. I've never had a massage from someone I know, but I think I'd be fine."

"She's the best, Catherine," Jordan piped up.

"And you know my feelings on the matter," Jamie added.

"Okay, Ryan, work your magic," Catherine gamely replied.

As befitted the home that had everything, there was a massage room right off the main weight room. A professional table was set up, and Ryan noted that the room looked as if it were used frequently. "I have a massage here every week," Catherine offered, "but my masseuse doesn't come until Wednesday."

"That's good to know. Over time we can make Wednesday be your hard training day. I'll just step out while you get undressed," she said. "Call me when you're ready." She walked out of the room and dashed over to Jamie for a good luck kiss. "I'm more nervous than I was when I took my final exam in massage school. It's gonna be weird to see your mom naked."

"Just think of it as a preview of coming attractions," Jamie said as she gave her a playful pinch on the butt.

Jordan piped up, "I'd take that attraction right now—much less in twenty years. Your mom is a hottie, Jamie."

You'd better stick to a little safer game, Ryan thought to herself. *Jim Evans would shoot you dead if you touched his wife. Speaking of which—I'm going to touch his wife. Yikes.*

Ryan ran back just as Catherine called for her. Catherine was lying face down on the table with a pale blue sheet loosely wrapped around her body. Ryan felt her stomach clench as she entered the room. She was actually more nervous than she had ever been about giving a massage, and she wracked her brain to come up with some relaxation techniques for herself. "Would you like some music?" she offered, knowing that her voice betrayed her anxiety.

"That would be nice. There are a number of CDs in the cabinet there." Ryan opened the door and found a lot of new age instrumentals, but one disc caught her eye.

"Cool," she muttered to herself as she pulled out "The Irish Whistle."

"Pardon, dear?"

"Oh," Ryan said as she popped the disc in the very snazzy CD player, "I was just commenting on this CD. This was my first instrument."

As the strains of the Celtic harp wafted through the air Catherine turned and looked at her. "This one?"

"No, I play the whistle." Several bars later the ethereal tones of the whistle began. "That one right there."

"What a beautiful instrument. Do you play often?"

"No, as a matter of fact, I don't think I've touched it since I've been with Jamie. I used to express myself through my music, but I just don't have the need anymore. I should get in the habit again. I can't afford to get too rusty if I want to keep it up."

"Jamie would love to hear you play. I guarantee you'd have an appreciative audience."

"Good point," Ryan said, much more relaxed now that the calming whistle was trilling in the background. "I'll pull it out as soon as we get home." She approached the table and tried her best to get into her professional mode. "What type of massage are you used to?"

"The person I have now just does traditional Swedish massage, but I love Shiatsu also. Why don't you do whatever you're comfortable with."

I'd be comfortable making a run for it, Ryan thought as her stomach gripped again. She grabbed a bottle of lightly scented massage oil and warmed it in her hands for a few moments as she tried to decide where to start.

She delayed so long that Catherine finally turned onto her back and caught Ryan's wide-eyed gaze. "Are you as nervous as I am?"

"More," Ryan gulped, feeling better almost immediately just to have the issue out in the open.

"Do you want to just skip it, dear? I don't want to make you nervous."

"No, no, this is no big deal. I'm a professional—I just have to calm my mind for a minute."

"For what it's worth, even though I'm a little uncomfortable, I trust you completely." She gave her a warm, open smile, and Ryan felt the rest of her anxiety ease.

Returning the smile, Ryan said, "Let's start some place nice and safe." She stood on the left side of the table and took Catherine's arm in her hands and began to work the massage oil into her flesh. "Let me know how firm a touch you like."

"I'm tougher than I look. I like a lot of pressure."

Hmm, there's a family trait, she thought as she started to work on her mother-in-law's arms.

"I think I'd be more comfortable on my stomach," Catherine said, and Ryan helped her arrange the sheet after she had turned over. Getting back to business, she pulled both arms above Catherine's head as she dug into the muscles with her thumbs. "Perfect," Catherine hissed out in a pleasure-filled moan. "Just perfect."

Oh, God. Ryan cried inwardly as she realized that Jamie moaned just like her mother did. *I've got to get my mind on business.* She used every centering technique that she knew, but the only thing that worked was when she reminded herself that Catherine trusted her implicitly. *She knows I'm very sexual, she knows I sleep with her daughter, and she knows that her husband would kill both of us if he saw me massaging her. And yet, she trusts that she can be this vulnerable with me. I can't repay that trust by letting my mind wander all over the place. She's not my lover's naked mother. She's a woman who's putting her trust in my hands, and I have to respect that in the same spirit that it's offered.*

Once her little pep talk was finished she switched her mind off rather easily and concentrated like she always did. She was soon able to focus only on the tips of her fingers and the individual muscles that her fingers glided over.

Catherine was right on the money when she said she liked a firm touch. Ryan gave her everything she had, but the harder the pressure, the more she liked it. She knew that the aggressive massage would help Catherine's stiff muscles, so she was a little more forceful than normal, and before she knew it she was right back at the arms. *God, did I hit everything else? I completely lost track of where I was.* Just to make sure, she broke the silence by asking, "Any areas bothering you?"

It took a second for Catherine to realize that the voice was addressing her. "No, I don't have a care in the world," she murmured.

Ryan placed her hand on her back and leaned over to speak quietly. "Relax for a while. I'll leave the music on for you."

"'Kay," she muttered sleepily as Ryan gently closed the door.

Neither of her companions was in the weight room, so Ryan went down to the first floor to look for them. She put her hands on her hips and glared at the two naked blondes as they lounged in the sauna. "Am I the only one that has to work around here?"

"God, honey, you were gone for over an hour. What were you doing in there?"

"I had to concentrate really hard to ignore the fact that it was your mom, so I didn't pay any attention to time. The only reason I knew it had been a while was because my hands were starting to cramp. She likes it rough, too," she said with a waggling eyebrow at her lover.

"Me, too," Jordan reminded her as she held out the bottle of moisture lotion that she had carried into the sauna.

Ryan sighed heavily as she started to strip out of her clothes. "Do all of you only want me for my hands?" she sighed as she accepted the lotion and started to work on Jordan's lower back.

"That's only half of your allure," Jamie assured her. "Your mouth is equally important to me."

"Not to me," Jordan demurred, letting out a gasp as the powerful hands stroked her tired muscles. "I only need your hands."

As soon as Jordan's brief massage was finished, she wrapped herself up in a towel and announced, "I'm going to bed. Wake me up at the last possible minute, will you, sport?"

"Will do, sleeping beauty. Sleep well."

As Jordan left Jamie asked, "How late was Mia here last night?"

"She was still here this morning."

"Ooh, Mia finally had her way with Jordan, huh? Good for her."

"You're jumping to conclusions. They were lying on a chair by the pool, fully clothed, when I found them. I think they were talking most of the night."

"For someone who doesn't talk much, that Jordan sure is gabby when she's around Mia. What in the heck is up with her, anyway?"

"I don't know, to be honest. Jordan's a pretty complex person— she's not so easy to figure out."

"She'd better not hurt my Mia," Jamie said, her eyes narrowing. "It's obvious that Jordan is a love 'em and leave 'em kinda girl, and I'm afraid that Mia really likes her."

"Don't make too many assumptions about Jordan. As I say, she's more complex than she seems." *A lot more complex*, Ryan decided. *I think Mia would be in well over her head with Jordan.*

🐎

An hour later they padded into the house in their warm-ups, just making the turn for the stairs when Catherine's voice called out from the living room. "Jamie? Ryan? Can I have a word with you both?"

Catherine was also dressed in a nylon warm-up suit—probably one that she wore after playing tennis, Ryan considered. She looked young and relaxed and attractively casual in the simple cocoa brown outfit that emphasized her eyes, and Ryan considered once again what a fabulous catch the lovely woman was. *Jim Evans…you are a putz*, she thought, not for the first time.

"When your father was here yesterday, he left these envelopes for you both," Catherine said, handing both women matching buff-colored vellum envelopes.

Ryan and Jamie exchanged glances and Catherine said, "I think they're safe. Too many witnesses for him to put a biological weapon into yours, Ryan."

Ryan grinned at her with a look of embarrassment. "He continues to disappoint me," she said. "I'm a little wary of any communication from him."

"You're wise to feel that way. He has a tendency to disappoint." She gave Ryan a sad nod of understanding and waited for the younger women to take a seat.

"I'll go first," Ryan said, ripping open her envelope. A letter and a small plastic card fell out, and she gazed at the card for a long while, her mouth dropping further and further open. It was a credit-card sized piece of plastic with "S. Ryan O'Flaherty" stamped onto it. Below her name it said "Member since September 1999." The top of the card simply read "The Olympic Club."

Wordlessly, she handed it to Jamie and, opening the letter, read it aloud.

"Ryan,

"Please don't assume that I'm trying to buy your good will with this small gift. The harm that I've tried to cause you could never be ameliorated by so small a token. Instead, please accept this as a meager peace offering.

"I know that Jamie loves Olympic, and I think it would make her happy to play there in the future. Since you are a part of her future, it only seems fitting to include you in that scenario. The membership is yours to do with as you wish. If you don't want it, you can sell it back to the club—the choice is yours. I hold out the hope that one day we can play the course together and enjoy each other's company. I'm certain that I will like you once I get to know you, Ryan, and even though I don't hold out a lot of hope, I pray that the reverse is true, also.

"I am truly sorry for the trouble that I have caused you. I have no excuses—none are creditable. I can only try to make it up to you over time, if you will allow me the opportunity.

"Sincerely,

"Jim"

"Wow." Ryan leaned her head back against the sofa and took in a breath. "He's never predictable, is he?"

"No," Catherine smiled. "That's one of the things that makes him a good lawyer."

Jamie ripped her envelope open and found a matching card embossed with her own name. "Good news, honey. They're for the same club."

Ryan laughed, pleased that her lover was keeping her sense of humor. Jamie's letter was a little longer than Ryan's, and she read it in silence.

Dear Jamie,

I've done more terrible things in my life than I am willing to admit, even to myself, but the thing I'll always regret the most was willfully hurting you. I still don't understand what came over me, but I know that I have seriously harmed the most precious thing that I have— our relationship.

The happiest day of my life was the day after you were born, when your mother and I brought you home from the hospital. The hospital was filled with nurses and friends and family, and I didn't have the opportunity to spend a moment alone with you. But as soon as we got home, your mother went to bed to rest and I could get to know you a little bit. I came into your room and sat in the rocker holding you that first night, already so attached to you that I couldn't bear to put you in your cradle. I held you in my arms and cuddled you for most of the night, so filled with joy that I couldn't even think of sleeping. I spoke to you about my hopes and dreams for you, and I promised that I would always be there to take care of you.

I broke that promise, Jamie. I shattered it, all because of my need to control you and every other thing that means anything to me. I don't know how to stop behaving the way that I do, but I promise that I will try. I want you to know that no matter what happens, I will try to fulfill the promise I made to you on a cold, clear February night, twenty-one years ago.

Her father always used a fountain pen for personal letters, and she noticed that some of the letters were smeared, as if a few tears had escaped and fallen onto the paper. Wiping her own eyes with the back of her hand, she continued to read.

Forgive me for launching into lawyer mode, but I have a few matters to take care of, and not much time to do them before I leave for Washington.

I pulled a few strings and convinced the membership committee to waive the normal application process for you and Ryan to become junior members at the Club. Your mother's great-grandfather was one of the founding members of Olympic, and I think it's time you became a member in your own right.

Even though I arranged and paid for the memberships, they are in your names. You will be responsible for the monthly charges; I will not even be informed of them. I do this only so that you understand that I am trying to give up control over your spending practices, not to avoid the expense myself.

Towards that end, I agree to your request for a discretionary distribution from your trust. I've communicated my wishes, in writing, to Tuck, and he is prepared to follow your instructions whenever and however you wish to proceed.

It would probably be best for you to move your money to a money manager of your own choosing, honey. Having my firm handle your affairs is probably not a good idea for either of us. I'm sure your mother can suggest someone that she trusts if you need any advice.

I did some research and it appears that you should create a durable power of attorney to give Ryan the right to make decisions for you in case you are incapacitated for any reason. I know that she's the person you trust to make decisions for you now, and a power of attorney will enable her to do that.

Forgive me again if this sounds too businesslike, sweetheart. I'm trying to get all of my affairs straightened out before I leave for Washington, and I'll admit to feeling a little overwhelmed.

I'm very much looking forward to having a fresh start for our relationship. I hope that by taking care of some of these financial matters, we can put them aside and never have to revisit them.

As I've already told you, I'm feeling adrift with this change in my life. I would be forever grateful if you could come visit me, for even a weekend. I know I'll be busy, but I'll clear my calendar at a moment's notice to see you— government business be damned. (That was a joke, honey. Don't tell the President that I said that.)

I am more hopeful than I have been in months about the future of our relationship. I promise to do my best to be the father that you deserve.

Love always,
Daddy

She leaned against her seat back in nearly the identical pose that Ryan had struck earlier. "Wow, indeed," she murmured, unable to make another comment.

Laying in bed late that night, Jamie traced patterns on Ryan's belly as she asked, "Did you have as nice a day as I did?"

"Hmm, let's see. I had a nice run in a lovely neighborhood and a great breakfast, I had a good session training your mom, I gave two pretty awesome massages, I got a cool membership to one of the best golf clubs in the country, we got your mom hooked up with a really nice bike, my team won easily for a change, and then we had a truly stupendous dinner with nearly my whole family and I got to go swimming with Caitlin. I'd say that it'd be tough to beat this day, to tell you the truth. How about you?"

"Well, mine wasn't as athletically focused as yours was, but it was very nice. I'm still having a tough time getting my mind around my father's letter, but I feel really good about it."

"Feel free to share anything you want. But if you want to keep it private, that's okay, too."

"Thanks. The biggest thing we'll have to discuss is his decision to let me have my distribution." She snuggled up tight and said, "I think I want to let it stay on the back burner until we have a little more time. I just don't see that we are prepared to deal with the stress of all that money right now."

"Works for me," Ryan said, hoping to hold off on that for as long as possible.

Ryan yawned so widely that Jamie was afraid her jaw would crack. Giving her belly a playful rub she asked, "Tired?"

"I was tired before the game. Now I'm sleepwalking," she said through another massive yawn.

"Hey, what happened to your pledge to take one day off a week? I completely forgot you were going to do that."

"I guess I haven't been very successful, huh? The only days off I've had were when I was sick."

"Well, it's only 10:30 now. I want your sweet little butt to stay right in this bed until at least eight tomorrow morning."

"Eight o'clock? I don't think I can sleep that late."

"Who said anything about sleeping? If you're too tired to

perform your marital duties at night, you'll just have to take the early shift."

"I had no idea what I was getting into with you," Ryan murmured as she closed her eyes and snuggled up against Jamie's warm back. "But it's been a very welcome surprise."

Chapter Three

J amie was standing at the bottom of the stairs, her bag already over her shoulder. "Mom. We're leaving."

"Let me come kiss you both good-bye," Catherine called out, as she scampered down the stairs. "I don't know how you two can get ready so quickly in the morning."

"It's not hard when you're just slipping on a warm-up suit," Ryan smiled, indicating her Cal Volleyball outfit.

"You look marvelous in everything you put on, Ryan O'Flaherty, so don't even try to get away with that," Catherine scoffed, patting her daughter-in-law's cheek. "What time should I be there?"

"Well, Annie suggested two o'clock, so any time around then is fine," Ryan said. "Remember, Catherine, no presents."

"I understood your edict. That doesn't mean that I didn't try to circumvent it—but I understood it."

On the long drive home Jamie turned sideways in her seat and said, "We've been so busy I haven't had time to compare our stock portfolios for a while. How are you doing?"

"Just fine," Ryan smirked.

"That's all I get? You know exactly how I'm doing."

"That's because I'm the accountant," Ryan reminded her. "You didn't request full disclosure when we made the bet."

"Well, I'm requesting it now."

"It's gonna cost ya."

"Cost me? What do you mean, it's gonna cost me?"

"When you change the rules, you have to pay, sweetheart. Lord, you missed out on a lot, not having siblings."

"Fine," Jamie groused, turning her body to face forward. "What will it cost me?"

"We don't really have a specific bet," Ryan reminded her. "It was just who did a better job picking stocks. For full disclosure I think I want…I think I want you to buy me five shares of my favorite stock."

"You make it sound like you're a sure-fire winner," Jamie grumbled, narrowing her eyes a bit.

"Well, it pays to be confident. Besides, I am the sure-fire winner. Simple fact, ma'am."

"Okay, Alan Greenspan, tell me exactly how you're doing." Jamie's lips were pursed tightly and Ryan knew she was really getting to her…to her extreme pleasure.

"I'm up $110,000," Ryan said, both eyebrows popping a few times to emphasize her superiority.

Only Ryan's excellent hearing allowed her to pick up the mumbled "shit" that her partner spat out through her clenched teeth. *And she says* I'm *the competitive one.*

⁂

Caitlin's first birthday party was in full swing when Catherine arrived a little after two. "My goodness," she said, after kissing Jamie and Ryan, "Jamie warned me to come on time. Did everyone else just get here?"

"Nope. Most of my family likes to come an hour or so early, just in case. Just remember that you can't ever be too early for an O'Flaherty event."

The baby spied her good friend at the door and flew over to her, her body leaning forward, arms out at her sides, a slightly goofy look on her face. She had been walking unaided for just a few days, and she still hit the ground as often as she remained upright, but she was getting better day by day.

"Oh, my goodness." Catherine said, picking her up and cradling her in a gentle hug. "You weren't walking last night."

"She had the concept down yesterday, but she was in the pool all night and didn't really get the opportunity."

"Yeah, and one of us was carrying her the entire time we were at Stanford," Jamie added.

"Well, it's a fantastic accomplishment, Caitlin. You should be very proud of yourself." Catherine tickled the exposed tummy, causing the baby to shriek with laughter and wait for her to do it again.

Catherine made the rounds, smiling broadly as every member of the family greeted her like a long-long cousin, even though nearly every one of them had been at her home just the day before. By the time she finished her hellos she was parched and went into the kitchen for a glass of something cold to drink.

Maeve was in the kitchen and she greeted Catherine warmly, inviting her to sit for a spell while she finished the last preparations for the barbeque.

"So, what is the news on the wedding front?" Catherine asked.

"Well, not much there, I'm afraid. I think we've worked out an arrangement with Niall so that we could move into his little house sometime near the end of January."

"Oh my, that's quite a long wait. What's the problem?"

"He doesn't have all of his appliances in the kitchen yet, and he can't finish the bathroom until a certain tub enclosure comes in. Then it all has to pass inspection. He thinks it might be ready by early January, but I'm not counting on it."

Catherine gave her a sympathetic look, seeing the disappointment in her new friend's eyes. "That gives us time to start planning something nice," she said brightly.

"Oh, I don't know, Catherine," Maeve said, a worried frown on her face. "We'll have so many expenses. We'll have to buy a whole house full of furniture—Niall has absolutely nothing in the place, and we don't want our children to have to bear that expense if we take our things with us. I'm afraid we won't have much to spend on the wedding."

"What was your first wedding like?" Catherine asked. "Were you married here?"

"Oh, yes. It was a simple little affair. Just the two of us, and my husband's brother and sister-in-law standing up for us. We didn't have the money for a real church service, so we had the ceremony in a little chapel in the rectory. It was fine," she said, sparing a sad smile.

"Your family wasn't able to attend?"

"Oh, my, no. My sister Fionnuala was saving every little bit of money she could to be able to emigrate, my younger sister was still in secondary school, and our brother was younger still. My parents were not very happy with me getting married so soon anyway, and even if they had approved, they never could have spent that kind of money on a trip. No, it wasn't the kind of wedding that a girl dreams of, but one can't have everything in life."

"What do you think you and Martin will do?"

She laughed. "Well, we'll need the church this time—just for all of the relatives. I suppose we'll have tea and cake in the auditorium afterwards. It's not really important. All that matters is that I'll have my Marty."

Catherine rose from her seat and placed her hands on Maeve's shoulders, smiling a little when she realized that they were the same height. "It does matter, Maeve. Every woman should remember her wedding day fondly. Tea and cake is fine, but it's not enough for a special day. Let me help."

She said this with such determination that Maeve heard herself asking, "How?"

"Let me host a reception for you and Martin. I have a cook who longs to cater a big party, and enough china and silver to serve a small army. I would be forever grateful if you'd let me give you this gift."

"Oh, Catherine, that's too generous of you. We couldn't impose like that."

"Why do you and Martin keep saying that?" she responded with frustration. "Either I'm a member of this family, or I'm not. I see how the whole family pitches in to fix Niall's home, I see how you accept his home as your own, why refuse such a simple offering from me?"

Maeve pursed her lips and made a decision. "Why indeed?" she repeated, nodding her head. "I accept—with one proviso. You have to allow us to pay for the food."

Catherine narrowed her eyes and made a counter offer. "Only if I can pay for the liquor." *And the flowers,* she said to herself.

Maeve grimaced, knowing that she had been outflanked. Sighing heavily, she smiled and gave Catherine a warm hug. "It's a deal," she whispered. "Nothing too fancy, now. We're simple people."

"I promise to hide the caviar spoons and the paté forks," Catherine said, already planning the menu in her head.

"Now I just need to find a dress, make the arrangements with Father Pender, and tell my parents…in that order."

"Will this not be happy news?"

Maeve sighed and said, "They were never happy with Martin, to be honest. Even though we were poorer than church mice, Mam had great plans for Fionnuala. She was very talented musically, you know. Great promise. But she wanted to come to the States, and once she met Martin—well, you know how it is."

"Your sister didn't regret her choice, did she?"

"Oh, my, no. She was completely happy. She loved Martin and the children with every bit of her heart. She was very much like Siobhán that way. Her heart was as big as the North Sea. No, she was a very happy woman. It's Mam who never warmed up to Martin. Part of it was distance. She only met him twice—once, not long after they married, and the second time at my sister's funeral. Not the best time to make a good impression," she said. "Mam has always had the unreasonable notion that Fi would still be with us if she hadn't come to the States. She seems to think that we're surrounded by all sorts of carcinogens that they don't have in Ireland." She shook her head and rolled her eyes a little, amused as well as dismayed by her mother's beliefs.

"Will she be upset that you've chosen Martin, too?"

"Yes, she will. Distance wasn't the only problem," Maeve admitted. "The children spent a lot of time in Ireland, and Martin and my mother each have strongly held views on child-rearing. At one point they had a terrible row, and I'm quite certain that Mam has never forgiven him for it." Shaking her head again Maeve said, "I'll be fifty-seven years old this year, but I still hate to think of making my mother angry with me."

"Will you tell her by letter?"

"I have to. It would cost five hundred dollars for a ticket right now. We could buy a new sofa for that kind of money."

You can? Catherine mentally gaped, but politely held her tongue.

"It's September, right?"

"Right," Maeve said cautiously.

"I have enough miles for three first-class airline tickets to anywhere in Europe, but they expire at the end of the year. I'm certain that I won't use them, so will you use one of them to tell your mother and father in person?"

"Oh, Catherine," she cried, for the second time in the day. "Those are yours. You should use them. You could take the girls on a nice trip."

Catherine gave her a look and said, "I have a hard time getting both of them in one place for dinner. Jamie could get away around Christmas, but Ryan starts basketball as soon as volleyball is over. There is no way that she'll get any time off."

"What about your husband? Couldn't he…?" Maeve began, but stopped abruptly when she saw the look in Catherine's eyes. "Is something wrong?"

"We've separated. He left for Washington on Friday. I won't be joining him."

"Oh, I'm so sorry to hear that. We saw him on the television just the other night. He's such a nice looking man. He looks quite a bit like Jamie, doesn't he?"

"Yes, he does," she agreed, smiling sadly. "Nonetheless, we won't be traveling together in the near future. If you don't want these I'll give them to Stanford to use, but I would prefer that you take them."

"All right," she said, giving her another generous hug. "It would mean a lot to my mother, and I would love to see my father again. I truly miss him."

"Thank you for treating me like a member of the family. You've made my day."

The party raged on for the better part of the afternoon, so many people jammed into the small house that it seemed like the walls would bow. Jamie tried to catch her mother's eye several times, but for nearly forty-five minutes the woman was engaged in a rather serious-looking discussion with Tommy and Annie in a relatively private corner. Finally, at around six o'clock, Catherine came breezing over, saying, "I wish I could stay a little longer, but I'm exhausted. Being around you energetic people for a whole weekend has worn me out."

"Well, you still look marvelous, Catherine," Ryan said, taking a long look at her fashionable mother-in-law.

"We had a great time at the house, Mom. As soon as we have a spare weekend, we'll do it again."

"I know that will be a while, dear, but I'm happy with whatever time you can spare. I promise not to be one of those cloying mothers who tries to make you feel guilty for having your own life."

"Once again, I thank God for giving me the most wonderful woman in the world and her equally wonderful mother," Ryan said, giving both women one of her patented beaming grins.

"See you both soon," Catherine said as she kissed them both and bade a quick farewell to the others.

As she left, Jamie spared another glance back at Tommy and Annie, who were both sitting right where they had been when her mother was speaking to them. "Ryan, they don't look well."

"No, they certainly don't." She strode over to the couple and sat down, placing a hand on Annie's knee. "Are you two okay?"

"We're in shock," Annie said vacantly, a sheaf of papers in her hand.

Tommy nodded somberly. "In shock," he echoed.

Jamie came up and placed her hand on Ryan's back. "What's up?"

"They're in shock, near as I can tell," Ryan said, glancing up quickly at her partner. "I just can't figure out why."

Annie looked up at Jamie with a stunned, wide-eyed expression and said, "Your mom."

"What? What happened?" Jamie was getting a little anxious since the couple looked like they had seen several ghosts all at once.

"She gave us a present...for Caitlin."

"Darn it," Jamie said. "We told her no presents. What did she give her?"

"Four years at Stanford," Tommy said, as Annie extended the papers in Jamie's direction.

"What? She gave her a college degree?" Ryan was nearly speechless, but she had just enough air left to get out, "Holy Crap."

Jamie shook her head, knowing full well what her mother had done. "She's done this for a number of kids."

Ryan looked at her with such a blank expression that Jamie had to laugh. "It's okay, love. Breathe."

"What in the hell is this?"

"It's a program that some private schools have started. You pay for the child's education in today's dollars. There are all sorts of formulas based on the kid's age for how much you owe. The money earns interest—not a lot—but a decent amount. No matter how much tuition is at the time the kid is enrolled, his tuition and fees are covered. It's kinda like an insurance policy for the donor, and Stanford gets the money early…seventeen years early, in Caitlin's case."

"That's remarkable," Ryan gaped.

"Now, it's not guaranteed that she'll be admitted—she'll still have to qualify, but this guarantees her a free education if she wants to go there." Jamie smiled, pleased that her mother thought so highly of Caitlin and Tommy and Annie.

"Did you accept the gift?" Ryan asked, amazed that her proud, headstrong cousin would do so.

"Uhm…I think I did," Tommy said dully.

"He did, he really did," Annie vouched for him, looking equally stunned.

"She just talks you into stuff," Tommy said, looking like a truck had hit him.

Annie was coming around now that they were talking about it, and she said, "Catherine said that if we didn't want the gift in seventeen years, we could give it back. Since she'll earn interest on it, it's not really ours until Caitlin enrolls. Cait might not want to go there, and she might not have the grades or the scores to get in…"

"Not to worry," Ryan said, seeing some of her own talents already blossoming in her young cousin. "She'll be admitted anywhere she wants to go. So you're okay with this?" Ryan asked again.

"I guess so," Tommy said. "I mean, it's going to be impossible for us to save enough to send her to a private school. Catherine promised that if, for some reason, we don't feel comfortable when the time comes, we can just refuse it—no hard feelings. So it's almost not even real, ya know?"

"Your mom does this for other kids, too?"

"Yeah. She's awarded two scholarships a year to low-income kids who go to the school attached to my grandfather's church. She pays for tutors to help the kids get the grades to get admitted to Stanford, too." She shot Ryan a wide grin and said, "She's a pretty cool mom, isn't she?"

"The coolest," Ryan agreed, her sentiments echoed enthusiastically by her cousins.

The party was winding down, but the baby was becoming more and more frazzled as the guests began to leave. Annie approached Ryan and said, "Any chance you two would take her for a walk in her stroller to tire her out a little? We can get the place cleaned up so we can give her some attention by the time you get back."

"And the alternative is staying to clean up?" Ryan asked, smiling brightly. "Duh…I think I'd prefer the walk." She scooped Caitlin up and got her settled in her jogger, mostly ignoring the outraged squawks from the baby, who believed that her newfound ability to walk had rendered the stroller a thing of the past.

The threesome took off, deciding to go on a long walk down to Castro for some of Ryan's favorite ice cream.

They crested the hill and rolled down into Castro, the street fairly crowded on a warm Sunday evening. As they drew near the ice cream shop Ryan's face grew darker, her expression morphing from outrage to desolation. Finally, her nose was pressed up against the now-empty store window. "They can't close it." she cried, looking completely bereft.

Jamie rubbed a soothing hand on her back, confirming the obvious. "They already have, honey. We're gonna have to settle for something else."

Ryan turned to her with a pout affixed to her face. "This was one of our places. I thought we could come here for years and years, and tell our kids about how we came here when Mommy didn't know she was dating Mama."

Jamie's eyes fluttered closed at the adorable sentiment. She tossed her arms around Ryan's waist and hugged her tight, murmuring, "You are the sweetest woman on earth, Ryan O'Flaherty. You capture my heart anew nearly every day."

"Nearly?" Bright blue eyes peeked out of long bangs, making Jamie's heart skip a beat.

"Every day," she corrected. "You make me fall in love with you all over—every day."

"That's pretty nice, isn't it?" Ryan asked, returning the hug with fervor. "Falling in love feels so good—it's a shame to only do it once."

Caitlin didn't care for the unexpected stop, and she displayed her displeasure vocally. Jamie stooped to check her diaper, finding it in need of an immediate change. She volunteered to take her into the nearby GLBT bookstore to ask if she could change her on the floor, since there was no other horizontal surface in the immediate vicinity. Ryan stayed out on the street to keep her eye on the jogger, even though she thought it was safe to leave it. She leaned against the building and people-watched for a while, finally walking down the street just a few yards to look in the windows of the neighboring shops just as Jamie came out and began to put the baby back in her jogger.

Out of the corner of her eye Jamie saw a woman approach Ryan from behind. Ryan's arms were crossed over her chest, and the woman threw her arms around Ryan's crossed ones, lifted her off the ground, and began to spin her around in a very enthusiastic greeting. Jamie started to call out but she could tell from Ryan's body language that she knew the person who was tossing her around like a toy. *My God, how strong do you have to be to pick her up that easily? I know she's lost weight, but that is ridiculous.*

As Jamie struggled to get Caitlin settled, she intently watched the interplay between Ryan and the stranger. It seemed like the woman was intentionally showing off, still holding Ryan's body a good half a foot off the ground. The captive was giggling as her feet dangled off the ground, looking like she was well used to this game.

Jamie's eyes raked over the powerful woman who held her lover so effortlessly, starting at the soft-looking sandy brown hair that fell forward into her eyes. The cut was much like the one Brendan sported—a few inches long on the top, tapering to less than a quarter-inch on the sides and back.

Her face was attractive, though quite androgynous, with a strong jaw line, a broad forehead, and surprising gentle eyes that were nearly hidden when she smiled, which she was currently doing. She was tall…very tall…at least two inches taller than Ryan, and given that Jamie rarely met a woman who approached Ryan's height, she assumed that this woman must attract more attention than she wished for her notable size. She was muscular, too, in a way that was very different from Ryan. This woman looked like she had earned her muscles the hard way, through manual labor. She was far too bulky for Jamie's tastes, but she could understand the attraction that Ryan obviously held for her.

It was also very clear that this woman was not just a casual acquaintance. The sparks flashing between her and Ryan were almost visible, and only Jamie's iron-clad belief in her partner's fidelity prevented her from marching down the street, grabbing Ryan by the ear, and dragging her back home and away from this temptation.

When the woman finally set Ryan back on her feet, Jamie's eyes almost popped out as the tall stranger bent over and placed a very, very familiar kiss on Ryan's lips. The kiss continued much longer than Jamie was comfortable with, but in reality it was probably just a couple of seconds. Ryan pulled away before the other woman did, but the automatic gesture that followed was actually less preferable to Jamie's eyes than the kiss. As the stranger stood, Ryan laced her hands behind her friend's neck and leaned back in a gesture that looked well practiced and very familiar. There was something almost girlish about Ryan's body language, and Jamie marveled that she had never seen this softer, almost shy side of her lover. But the woman who gently held Ryan had obviously seen it, and seen it often.

Caitlin was secured by now and Jamie steered her quickly over to the twosome, unable to control her proprietary streak another moment. Approaching the woman, she stuck her hand out and said clearly, "Hi, I'm Jamie Evans, Ryan's lover," her emphasis on "lover."

The woman smiled widely and said with a slight Southern accent, "I'm very pleased to meet you," as she grasped her hand with both of her large ones. "I'm Ally Webster."

Jamie found herself a little tongue-tied at this revelation, but Ally rescued her when she added, "I have got to tell you that I think you've captured the most precious woman in the whole Bay Area. I really wish you both the best," she said with a beaming smile that Jamie could not help but return.

Just then Caitlin decided that the focus of attention had been elsewhere for too long. She cried to be picked up, and Ryan lifted her from the jogger immediately.

"Is this your little cousin?" Ally asked with delight. "Can I hold her?" Ryan immediately relinquished control, and the baby happily went to the large woman and snuggled up in her massive arms. "She's adorable." She grinned as she bounced the baby on her hip, but Caitlin wanted a better view, so Ally shifted her until she was nose to nose with the giggling baby. Caitlin grabbed each part of her face, to Ally's delight, but the baby was truly in heaven when she reached Ally's soft hair. After a moment of stroking it she leaned over and rubbed her little face on Ally's head. Looking up at Ryan's blush, Ally just raised an eyebrow to her friend's embarrassed nod. "I can certainly see the family resemblance," she said dryly, obviously sharing a private joke.

"Yeah, she's already showing evidence of the family charm," Jamie admitted.

"Well, she's got a long way to go to catch up with her talented cousin," Ally said as she patted Ryan's cheek fondly.

She's blushing like a schoolgirl, Jamie marveled. *I have honestly never seen this side of her. I've got to know more about this woman—as soon as possible.* Almost without thinking Jamie said, "I'd love to let you two catch up. Why don't you come over for dinner, Ally?"

It was hard to tell who was more surprised by the invitation, but Ally paused for a moment and looked at Ryan carefully. "Would *you* like that?"

Ryan paused for just a second, then made her decision. "Yes, very much," she nodded enthusiastically.

"Okay, when do you want me?" Ally asked Jamie.

"Are Sundays good?"

Susan X Meagher

"Yeah, Sundays are fine."

"Well, how about next Sunday? It's the only weekend date that Ryan has available for a few weeks."

"You're on," Ally said firmly. "Will my future girlfriend be there?" she teased as she pulled Caitlin up for a kiss on the cheek.

"No, her parents won't let her date for a while," Jamie said. "But you can bring a date if you want," she said, hoping that Ally had someone to replace Ryan.

"I might," she replied noncommittally. "Can I let you know?"

"Sure," Ryan said. "We usually have one or two joining us for dinner, so we always have extra."

"Great. Pager still 555-2345 Ryan?"

Jesus, she has her pager memorized. "Call her on her cell or at our house," Jamie said as she pulled out a slip of paper and wrote both numbers on it, hoping to remove the other number from Ally's memory bank.

"Will do," she promised as she leaned in for another kiss from Ryan. This one was shorter and much more chaste, to Jamie's satisfaction. Ally stuck her hand out and shook Jamie's once more. "I look forward to seeing you both," she said politely as she returned Caitlin to Ryan's grasp. "Bye-bye, Junebug," she said as she mussed Caitlin's hair.

As Ally strolled away, her determined gait almost mesmerizing to watch, Jamie switched her gaze from Ally to her lover, trying to imagine Ryan with this woman. She shook her head slowly as she muttered, "If I had to guess what she looked like, that would have been my last guess. I couldn't have been more surprised if she had a big penis."

Ryan leaned over and whispered, "She's got a whole box full of 'em."

🐎

There was no acceptable ice cream substitute in Castro, so they started the long climb home. "Are you okay with me asking Ally over?" Jamie asked.

Ryan had been thinking about that very issue, finding that she was less and less comfortable with the idea the longer she thought

70

about it. "Uhm, generally, I'd prefer that we discuss things like this beforehand. I don't think you'd like it if I decided I wanted to get to know Jack better and asked him over."

"Bu...but...he was my fiancé," Jamie gaped, grabbing onto Ryan's arm to stop her progress. "I had the distinct impression that you and Ally had a much more casual relationship than that."

Feeling intensely uncomfortable discussing her feelings for the other woman, Ryan consciously decided to back off. "We were much more casual than you and Jack were. I'm not saying that I don't want her to come—I'm just saying that, as a rule, I'd prefer to agree on things like this beforehand. Is that really asking for much?"

"No, it's not. I'm sorry, but my curiosity just took over. Why don't you call her and tell her that something came up? It's not worth doing if it makes you uncomfortable."

"No, it's fine," Ryan said, even though she wasn't at all sure that it was. "She was an important person in my life, and I do want to maintain the friendship, so now's as good a time as any."

They took a short detour on the way home, stopping in front of The Scoop Shop. Looking up at the sign, Jamie asked, "Ice cream? This close to home?"

"Yeah," Ryan agreed. "It's good. Probably my second favorite place. They mix up Oreos and M & Ms and other kinds of candy into the ice cream. I think you'll like it."

Grabbing her arm once again, Jamie looked up at her with an amused smile. "You mean to tell me that we could have been coming here for all of these months? This is three times closer to home than the other place."

"I know, but I like the other stuff about...oh, I'd say five percent more."

Jamie shook her head and took Caitlin out of her stroller, telling her, "One day when you grow up you'll be able to drive your boyfriend or girlfriend just a crazy as Ryan makes me. Won't that be fun? Yes!" she smiled as the baby enthusiastically agreed.

Jim Evans fought through the choked traffic around National

Airport late on Sunday night, cursing himself for not ordering a limo. He was early, much earlier than he usually was for appointments, but he had been nearly out of his mind with boredom and loneliness for the last three days and couldn't wait to leave his hotel. *Why did I come to Washington three days before I absolutely had to?* he grumbled to himself as he steered the car around the unfamiliar airport. *If I'd waited until today I could have come out with Kayla and had someone to keep me company.*

His thoughts focused on the young redhead, smiling to himself as he recalled her elation at being asked to accompany him to Washington. He didn't let himself believe that she was thrilled just to be in his company. Kayla was as determined and as ambitious as he had been at her age, and that was saying a lot. Being a junior legislative aide to a United States senator was a very prestigious opportunity for a young woman not two years out of law school, and he knew that Kayla would throw herself into the job with all of her usual passion. He gave himself credit for at least sleeping with a hard-working, bright young woman. *I probably would have offered the job to Kayla even if we weren't involved. Of course, we'll never know at this point.*

He found a short-term lot close to the proper terminal and quickly ran to the building, his anxiety palpable. *She'll think you're out of your mind if you act as excited to see her as you really are. Women don't like to be smothered. Especially young women. You think you would have learned that lesson from Jamie.*

The flight was on time, and he consciously forced himself not to crowd around the gate to greet her. He was sitting in a chair, acting as though he was reading "The Economist" when she approached. "Senator Evans," she said, her voice cordial and respectful.

He stood and almost kissed her, then remembered that he was now a public figure and might be recognized at any time. Mentally slapping himself, he raised his voice in case anyone was eavesdropping and said, "Kayla. Good to see you again."

"Always a pleasure, Senator. Ready to get to work?"

"I am. Shall we?" He shouldered her laptop, leaving her to organize her claim checks for her baggage. As soon as they had retrieved the three large bags, he asked a skycap to bring the bags to the curb and went to get the car. After the luggage was loaded in he pulled out into the heavy Sunday night traffic, the young woman sitting quietly until they were near the airport exit.

"Pull over," she said, her voice calm but determined.

He raised an eyebrow, but did as she asked, pulling into a no parking zone for what he assumed would be a quick stop. "What is it…" he began, but before he had completed his thought she had maneuvered herself against him, pinning him to the door. Her mouth crushed against his, her tongue slipping past his open lips as her body squirmed against him.

"I missed you," she murmured, her head lifting briefly before she dove back in.

Her touch felt so good, so incredibly good. His body ached with longing, needing to feel her skin against his. "I missed you, too," he sighed, squeezing her tightly. "Let's go to the hotel."

"I can't wait." She slid back into her seat after giving him a look so filled with desire that it nearly made him numb.

He shook his head roughly, trying to focus. "Remind me to order a limo next time, will you?" he asked wearily as they shared a smile. "I don't think I'm in any shape to drive right now."

※

On Monday evening, Ryan was sitting on the steps outside the gym buckling up her roller blades when Jordan sidled up. "Hey."

Looking up, Ryan nodded, then went back to her task. "What's up?"

"Not much. Got any dinner plans?" Jordan seemed a little tentative, which was unusual.

"Not really. You?"

Jordan blinked and pursed her lips. "Oh. I thought you'd be going home."

Now Ryan let out the laugh she'd been holding in. "Come on. We've always got room for one more hungry mouth. Let me call Jamie."

※

It took a little longer than normal to arrive home, since only one of the pair wore blades, but Jordan did a good job of running alongside, even after an enervating practice. When they arrived, Jordan plucked at her shirt and asked, "Can I borrow a T-shirt? Somehow mine got drenched on our leisurely walk."

"Sure. You know where they are by now, right?"

"Yep. Be right back."

Jordan took the stairs two at a time, managing to find herself in front of Mia's room even though it was further down the hall than Ryan's. Knocking lightly on the open door, she popped her head in as Mia looked up from the book she was reading. "Hi. Ryan invited me for dinner. Are you going to be eating with us?"

Mia graced her with one of her best smiles, hopped off the bed and walked to the door. "Yep. I was just going to go down. You look healthy today," she said, noting Jordan's ruddy cheeks. "Hey, you're dripping wet. Did Ryan make you run all the way over here? Don't let her push you around. She's going to make you catch a cold running around like this. Do you want a T-shirt? How about some sweats?"

"Do you have a shirt that's big enough?" she asked, even though she knew where an entire drawer full of extra-large shirts was just waiting for her.

"I think I can fix you up." Mia rummaged through her chest of drawers, finally pulling out one that she wore as a sleep shirt. "This one goes almost to my knees. It should work."

She handed it to the lanky woman, expecting her to put it on, but Jordan looked around and asked, "Bathroom?"

After pointing in the proper direction, Mia stared after her. *She's a tough one to figure out. I don't know anybody who's afraid to change shirts in front of me—especially an athlete. Don't they get dressed in front of each other?*

🐎

After dinner, Ryan went upstairs to study while Jamie staked out her usual position in the library. Jordan and Mia took off for a walk, so the house was quiet when the phone rang at about nine o'clock.

"Hello?" Ryan said absently, trying to figure out a chemistry problem that had been vexing her for twenty minutes.

"Ryan?" the deep, rather formal male voice asked.

"Yeah."

"It's Jim Evans."

Her heart rate picked up, as it always did when she heard his voice. "Hello. Would you like me to get Jamie for you?"

"Yes, in a minute, but first I wanted to congratulate you on how well you played this weekend."

"How well I…played," she said slowly, thinking that his private detective must still be on his payroll.

"Yes. I subscribe to the Cal Bears report, and I specified that I wanted information about women's volleyball and golf. I get a report after every game. Very good work against BYU. You should be proud of yourself."

"Thanks, Jim. Thanks a lot," she said, pulling the phone away from her mouth to take a better look at the device to make sure she wasn't hallucinating. "Shall I get Jamie now?"

"Yes, please. Thank you, Ryan," he said, his tone friendly and very casual.

As Ryan ran down the stairs she muttered to herself, "This guy has not presented the same face two times in a row. Will the real Jim Evans please stand up?"

When Jamie came up to bed, Ryan was undressed and waiting for her while working on her correspondence. She was wearing a grin that grew in intensity as she finished up the e-mail she was writing. "What's up?" Jamie asked, slipping into bed and trying to read the screen. "You look like the cat that ate the canary."

"I was just telling Aisling a funny story. I forgot to tell you this, but I think someone made a pass at me at the game on Friday night."

"What?" Jamie got on her knees and pressed her nose against Ryan's. "You tell your cousin before you tell me?"

"You're making me cross-eyed." Ryan put her arm around her partner and pulled her down so they were next to one another. "It was no big deal. I'm not really even sure that it was a pass." Her eyes twinkled merrily.

"What do you mean you're not sure? You've had enough passes thrown your way to know when someone's doing it."

"Well, it was hard to tell because they didn't speak and I couldn't see their eyes."

"What? What in the hell are you talking about? Was someone under the stands or something?"

"No. They were right next to me and kind of grabbed my butt every chance they got."

"Why do you say 'they'?"

"Well, I'm not sure what sex they are."

"Spill it or I'll tickle you until you cry," Jamie threatened as she began to do just that.

Through her laughter Ryan finally cried, "Okay, okay. The female Oski Bear kept putting her paw on my butt."

"Oh, Jesus, even the school mascots are hot for you?"

"Not the male, just the female," she said through her giggles. "Even a bear can tell that I'm a lesbian."

"You just wait until the next home game," Jamie threatened ominously. "She's *so* gonna wish she'd kept her paws to herself. It's hunting season, and I'm loaded for bear."

Getting up to brush her teeth Jamie commented, "Daddy pointed out something when I spoke to him that I think we should consider."

"What's that?"

"He thinks that I should take some money out of my trust. Kind of as an experiment."

"Huh?"

"Well, I think he has a good point. I'm worried about taking everything that I'm entitled to—mainly because it's so much money and I'm too busy to decide how to invest it. But as he pointed out, I'll never get comfortable until I do it. If you don't object, I might take out a portion of the distribution I'm entitled to and spread it between a couple of different money managers. That'll let me try a few people out to see what kind of relationship develops."

"I have no right to object…"

"Yes you do," Jamie said firmly. "It's our money."

"Okay." Ryan smiled sweetly. "I give you my explicit permission to do anything you wish with our money. How's that?"

"Sneaky, very sneaky. I'm going to call Mom and ask her for some recommendations." She grinned at Ryan and said, "Daddy didn't even try to make a suggestion on who I should use. Weird, huh?"

"I think we should have his DNA tested. He's clearly not the same guy."

Ryan walked down the hallway the next morning, absently packing her school supplies into her backpack. As she turned to descend the stairs she saw her roommate pinned in the corner of the loveseat, Jordan looming over her. The taller woman was kneeling on the cushion to improve her angle, with Mia's face captured between both of her hands. She was working on Mia's mouth with a determined intensity that looked like it was on the verge of getting out of hand. Mia, however, looked more than happy with this state of affairs. Her hands were laced through Jordan's silky hair, pulling the willing blonde to her body.

Great, just great. We need a back entrance to this place, since Mia seems to tend towards exhibitionism. She took another quick look, nodding her approval at her friend's technique. *You're doing great for a beginner, Jordan. Go get her, buddy.*

She had to walk right past them, since she wasn't going to give up her breakfast just to save them some embarrassment. As she passed by she ran her hand over both heads, giving each a pat just to let them know she was there. Jordan pulled away, yelping a little as Mia's tenacious grip nearly ripped the hair from her head. "Shit! Is it that late already?" She rolled away from Mia, putting her feet on the floor and scrubbing her hands over her face. Turning to Mia, her brow furrowed, she asked, "How did it get to be so late?"

"It's actually early," Ryan reminded her, "and if I'm not mistaken, you have an early class. You gonna skip?" she asked over her shoulder as she went into the kitchen to get something to eat.

"Shit, shit, shit." She got to her feet and shook like a wet dog, the sensations that had erupted from kissing Mia so passionately still pulsing through her body. Looking down at her rather limp-looking kissing partner, she said, "I have to make this class." She tugged at the hem of the tee she wore and quirked her mouth into a shy grin. "Need your shirt back?"

"Not until you wash it," Mia said, smiling. She got to her feet and wrapped Jordan in a gentle hug. "That way I can be sure you'll come back."

Ryan came back out into the living room, looked at Jordan and asked, "Shall I wait for you?"

"I'm ready," she said. "Can we stop and get me a gallon of coffee on the way?"

"Yeah." Ryan smiled. "I'll even buy if you'll shake a leg." She went out to the porch to put her blades on and give the pair a moment alone.

Jordan smiled down at Mia and fluffed her hair gently with her fingertips. "I've messed your hair up."

Mia reached up and returned the favor, smiling as she loosened a large tangle that her frantic clutching had created in the smooth blonde tresses. "You can't tell much with mine, but yours could use a good combing."

Ryan rapped sharply on the door, and Jordan leaned down for what was becoming her signature goodbye kiss. She once again touched Mia's chin with her fingertips, leaned over and gazed into her eyes until Mia felt her knees grow weak. Then, when she was about to grab Jordan and kiss her until her eyes crossed, Jordan allowed her eyes to flutter closed as she leaned in even closer, took in a deep breath and brushed her lips against Mia's with the barest hint of pressure. "Bye," she said softly, her lips so close that Mia could feel the moisture from her warm breath.

"Bye," Mia sighed in return, wishing that she could wrestle Jordan to the floor and ravish her without mercy.

Then she was gone, leaving Mia to collapse onto the loveseat and bang her fists against the cushion in frustration.

"Anyone I know?" Jamie asked from the top of the stairs.

"Ryan," she grumbled, giving the cushion another sharp blow. "She picks the worst damn times to show up."

"Huh? What are you talking about, and for that matter, what are you doing up?"

"I was really making progress with Jordan," she sighed, dropping her head to the cushion as she stared vacantly at the ceiling. "For the first time it felt like she was the aggressor. Know what I mean?"

"Yeah, I'm familiar with aggression," Jamie said, thinking that Ryan could teach a graduate level course in how to be dominant sexually.

"Well, we'd only been kissing a couple of minutes—as usual—when Ryan comes down and takes Jordan away. That's three times in a row. Why does she have to have Jordan with her all of the time? She's mine."

"I hate to spoil your fantasy, but Jordan couldn't pull Ryan away from me if she didn't want her to. Are you sure this is Ryan's fault?"

She gave the cushion another punch and admitted, "No. It's Jordan. I don't know what's wrong, James. I've never had to work this hard to even get a kiss. She seems to have no interest in going any further, and I've gotta tell you, that's not what I'm used to."

"I should think not." Jamie laughed. "You have a reputation to uphold."

"Funny," Mia said, not even a flicker of a smile crossing her face. "She's just so shy. I gave her a T-shirt last night, and she went into the bathroom to put it on."

"I hate to tell you this, but Jordan's not shy. Jesus, she's practically a nudist."

"You've seen her naked?"

"Oh, yeah." Waggling her eyebrows, she added, "It was worth a paid admission, to tell you the truth. She's got a body to die for."

"Great. Everybody but me gets to see her naked." Looking at Jamie curiously she reminded her, "She even wore a suit in the sauna the other night."

"Not the next day. We worked out, and she was stripping on her way down to the sauna. I swear she was stark naked by the time we got there. She seems really unconcerned with nudity."

"With you! What in the hell is going on here? Does she like me or not?"

"She acts like she likes you. Ryan said she invited herself for dinner, and it was obvious that it was just so she could see you."

"Then why doesn't she call me? She hasn't invited me to a game or for a cup of coffee or anything. Do you think she's ashamed to be seen with me?"

"You're adorable! Anybody would be proud to be seen with you. How can you even say that?"

Looking uncharacteristically embarrassed, Mia said, "This is really getting to me. My equilibrium is screwed up."

Jamie sat down next to her and patted her leg. "I wish I could help more, but if Ryan knows anything, she won't tell. I guess you'll just have to wait and see what happens."

"Great. Just great," Mia sulked, giving the defenseless furniture one more jab.

They had been trying to find an open date to spend an evening with Brendan and Maggie, and Ryan hurried home on Tuesday, thinking that they'd be rushed to have everything ready by the time her brother arrived.

To her surprise, Jamie nearly had dinner ready and Ryan gave a brief thought to how difficult it would be to have a social life if she lived alone, given the demands that volleyball put on her. She truly loved being able to entertain and build a family life, and she knew that she wouldn't be doing either if not for the dedicated efforts of her partner.

"I love being in love with you," she said in greeting when she wrapped her arms around her lover, who was stirring a delicious-smelling concoction on the stove.

"Well, that's a nice greeting," Jamie said, turning her head to kiss the only surface she could reach—the hollow between Ryan's collar bones. "What made you say it?"

"Oh, I don't know." Ryan stuck her finger in the pan and took a taste. "Mmm...delicious." She went over and sat down on a stool near the counter. "There's a difference between loving you and loving how it feels to love you. I was just thinking about the latter."

"I'm glad that both are true. Now run upstairs and put on some real clothes, and then set the table, will you?"

"Boy, I know I'm an adult when I have to put on real clothes for my brother," she mumbled as she left the kitchen.

The foursome was sitting around the dining table, waiting for their entrees to digest a bit before they could even think of dessert. Brendan was more voluble than Jamie had ever heard him, chattering away continuously—mostly boasting about some particularly cute trait that Maggie possessed. Ryan was a little more quiet than usual, mostly because her brother was filling up the room for a change. She'd been observing Maggie at every opportunity, and Jamie could tell that her partner approved of the woman. When Ryan was relaxed with someone, she wasn't usually interested in directing the conversation—she was content to participate only when she had something meaningful to say, exactly how she was this night.

"So Brendan says you're from a large Irish Catholic family also," Jamie commented. "Was it hard for you to leave them?"

"Yes," she said thoughtfully. "In a way it was devastating for me, but there must be a little independent streak in me from way back. I'd been groomed to attend Notre Dame from the time I was in diapers. My father and two of his brothers went there, as well as one of my older brothers and a sister. But when the time came, I shocked them all by choosing Georgetown." She laughed gently and related, "You would have thought I'd chosen Brigham Young. They couldn't get over it. But I wanted to make my own way. I didn't want to be just another Reardon trooping past the golden dome."

Ryan chuckled and commented, "You and Jamie have something in common. Her family laid the cornerstone at Stanford, but she's a big ol' Golden Bear."

Jamie patted her hand and said, "It's not quite that bad, but it's close. One of my ancestors was in the Pioneer Class, as they call it. The class of '01…1901, that is."

"Wow, that must have caused some raised eyebrows," Maggie said.

"A little more was raised than a few eyebrows," Jamie agreed, recalling her first real argument with her father. "My father was livid, but in reality, it's my mom who should have been upset. It's her family that carries the tradition. My Dad was the first in his family to attend."

"Hmm…why doesn't that surprise me?" Ryan said dryly, getting a playful scowl from her partner.

"Problems with the in-laws?" Maggie asked.

"On and off," Ryan said. "I think things will calm down over time. We've only been together officially since June. Jamie's dad's just going through a period of adjustment."

"Is he upset with you or…?"

Jamie piped up, "It's mostly the fact that Ryan's a woman, even though he won't admit that's the real issue. I didn't know that I was gay until we fell in love."

"Ooh, that must be an adjustment. One of my best friends from high school came out to me just this year. I'm sure it's easier to do when you're young."

"Ask Ryan," Brendan teased. "She was checking out the other little girl babies in the nursery at the hospital."

"Not true, Bren. I was in kindergarten before I even kissed a girl."

"You kissed a girl in kindergarten?" Jamie laughed. "You've never told me that."

"I've tried to forget her," Ryan said, looking like she was about to cry. "She went through the whole class…one by one. I was just a notch on her Cabbage Patch Kids pencil case."

Jamie reached over and grasped Ryan's hand, giving it a squeeze. "If she could see you now, she'd kick herself. She could have called dibs."

Mia had foraged dinner for herself, not returning home until Brendan and Maggie had already left. Ryan was on kitchen detail since Jamie had cooked, and Jamie was in the library preparing for a quiz she was having the next day.

"Hey," the curly-haired woman said as she flopped down on a kitchen chair. "How'd your dinner go?"

"It went well. I like my brother's new girlfriend. Did you get fed?"

"Yeah. I met some friends for a salad. Hey, can I ask you something?"

"Sure. What's up?"

"Do you think Jordan likes me?"

Ryan scratched her head for a moment, appearing to give the matter considerable thought. "Well, she doesn't French kiss me or Jamie, and I've never seen her slip the tongue to any of our teammates, so I'd say there's a good chance that she likes you."

"You know what I mean," Mia said, narrowing her eyes. "Do you think she likes me enough to date me?"

Ryan tossed her dishtowel over her shoulder and took a seat. "I can't tell you things she tells me in confidence. I'm friends with both of you, and I'd never tell her anything you told me, either. It's better this way." She put her hand on Mia's shoulder and gave her an empathetic smile. "Do you get that?"

"Yeah, I guess I do, but I'm really frustrated." She sat up a little straighter in her chair and said, "How about this? Would you tell me if she didn't like me? Like if she told you that she thought I was okay to fool around with, but not good enough to date?"

"I wouldn't hang around with her if she said things like that. Jordan's not a jerk." She sighed, trying to think of a way to give Mia some information without betraying Jordan's confidences. "Let me tell you this. This is my own observation, not something Jordan has told me. She seems to have a persona that doesn't really match who she really is. Do you know what I mean?"

"Mmm…kinda."

"She gives off the appearance of being very much in control and very aloof, right?"

"Right. But she's not really like that when you get to know her."

"Right. I know. I think she's like that in other areas of her life, too. She comes across as being apathetic over whether she sees you or not, but I doubt that's how she feels. I think she's just very, very cautious. Very much afraid of being hurt."

"Oh! So she's just going slow because she's shy and kinda afraid?"

"Something like that," Ryan agreed, knowing there was a lot more to Jordan than shyness.

"Cool. So I should just play it cool and let her do what she needs to do to feel comfortable?"

"I think that's all you can do. I know that if you put too much pressure on her, you'll scare her off."

"I don't want to do that. I really like her."

"Well, I like you both, and I hope it works out between you. You make a really cute couple, you know."

"Do we really?" Mia wrinkled up her nose.

"Yeah. It's kinda cool to see people who have almost no physical characteristics in common. Kinda like me and Jamie."

"Well, you're a pretty cute couple, too, so if we look like you two, I'm happy."

Chapter Four

When Catherine found Jamie in the stands at the Oregon game on Friday night, it didn't take long for the younger woman to lean in close and ask, "What's wrong? You look upset."

Catherine sighed and said, "I received a very troubling letter from your father today. I wasn't going to bring it up, but my attempt to look cool has obviously failed."

Jamie clasped her mother's hand and said, "Let's go out in the lobby, and you can tell me all about it, okay?"

"There's really not much to tell, dear. I made a flippant comment last week when he was at the house, and he obviously took it very much to heart." She reached into her purse and pulled out an official-looking set of papers atop a plain blue backing.

"He's filing for divorce!" Jamie said this much louder than she had wished, and she noticed a surprised look from Martin, who was sitting a few seats down the row.

"After a fashion," Catherine said. "It's my fault this time. I made an issue of it."

"Tell me what happened."

"When he was at home on Friday I made a comment about how much stress a divorce would be, and that I didn't want to pursue one—mainly because I knew he would make my life a living hell." She shook her head, angry with herself for being so snappish with him.

"Sounds reasonable to me. That's exactly what I'd think."

"He insisted that he wouldn't put me through that," Catherine said, "but I didn't believe him and said I'd love to have his assurances in an affidavit, where they meant something." She took the papers back and shook them as she concluded, "Here's his proof."

"So is he filing for divorce or not?"

"Not technically. He put the ball in my court. These are fully executed papers. All I have to do is sign and file them, and we're done."

"What did he ask for? Half of everything?"

"All he wants is his clothing, the gifts I've given him over the years, and the cars," Catherine said, shaking her head at the paucity of Jim's request. "He meant it. For once he told me the truth, and I doubted him. Now I feel like I've pushed him to do this when neither of us is ready."

Jamie took the papers from her mother and read the cover letter. "This doesn't sound like he's pushing you, Mom. He says that you can file if you wish, or wait and see how things progress. That sounds kinda hopeful."

"I suppose. It just looks so formal, so final."

"Don't do anything now, please. There's still a glimmer of hope that you can get back together. I can see it on your face, Mom. You're not finished with this marriage."

"No, I suppose I'm not. I felt a stirring of emotion for him on Friday that I haven't felt for years. Granted, much of it was anger, but it was still emotion."

"Don't give up yet. See what happens. You might pull this one out yet."

"Are we having dinner tonight?" Jordan asked brightly as they left volleyball practice on Sunday afternoon.

"Did you ever eat before you met me?" Ryan realized that her comment sounded a lot sharper than she had intended, and the flash of hurt she saw cross Jordan's face confirmed her worry. "Hey, I'm sorry. That didn't come out like I meant it."

"How'd you mean it?" Jordan's tone was wary.

"I meant that I'm really grouchy today. We've having a guest for dinner, and I think it's a very bad idea."

"Who's coming? You look pissed."

"We ran into an old lover of mine the other day, and Jamie asked her over for dinner. I'm feeling really weird about it, and I guess it's affecting my mood."

"What kind of lover?"

"Someone I knew really well, but we weren't really girlfriends."

"More physical than emotional?"

"Yeah. Very much so."

"How many times did you sleep with her?"

Ryan knit her eyebrows together and she was deep in concentration for a few moments.

"God, that many?"

"I would give a conservative guess of seventy-five times," Ryan admitted.

"Jesus, I bet my parents didn't have sex seventy-five times. Are you insane?"

"I didn't say I'd had sex with her seventy-five times. We had about seventy-five dates. Many of those dates lasted for three or four days. The actual number of times we had sex is beyond my ability to count."

She looked a little sick as she said this, and her mood was not improved when Jordan said, "Jeez, that's the last person you want to have at your house."

"I didn't invite her," she groused. "Jamie asked her without even asking me first. But once she asked her, I couldn't withdraw the invitation." She mused contemplatively, then said, "You know what really bothers me? It's that I know Jamie has an agenda. She always does with this kind of thing. I just have a feeling that I'm going to be under the microscope tonight."

"I can see why Jamie wants to investigate this a little bit. It surprises me that you slept with someone that much but didn't have an emotional attachment. That doesn't seem like you."

"I would have taken more, but it was never offered. Ally made it clear from the start that we would have sex only. I was just a kid, and she was such a good teacher that I forced myself not to fall in love with her. But I could have," she said wistfully.

"Is she like Jamie at all?"

Ryan choked out her first true laugh of the day. "They hardly seem like the same species."

Ryan was already home when Jamie came barreling up the drive. Ryan dashed out with a tension-filled expression to help her drag in the three bags of groceries. "Where have you been? We can't possibly get dinner ready in time."

"Hi," Jamie said slowly, blinking up at her partner. "I missed you too. Did you have a good day?"

Ryan ran her hands through her hair in one of her chronic nervous habits. "I'm sorry. I just expected you home a lot earlier. I didn't know if I should go to the store or what was going on, so I just stressed."

"Can I have a kiss hello?" she asked patiently.

"Of course you can," Ryan stooped to give her a kiss and added a hug. "I missed you," she said as the hug continued.

"Okay, you can let me go now. We've got dinner to prepare."

Earlier in the week Ryan had told Jamie that Ally was not a strict vegetarian, but that she leaned heavily in that direction. She also told her that Ally was very careful about her diet in general and didn't eat much fat or refined sugar.

When they reached the kitchen, Ryan pulled everything out of the bags, looking suspiciously at the contents. "What are we having?"

"Cannelloni with low-fat ricotta cheese, a vegetable salad with low-fat poppy seed dressing, and fruit and cheese for dessert."

"You remembered everything I told you," Ryan beamed with pleasure. "You are just the best partner in the world."

"Anything to keep you happy. Now you go get ready, and I'll start dinner."

"Uhm, I am ready," Ryan slowly said. "Do I look stupid or something?"

"No, of course not." She surveyed Ryan's big black Doc Martens, her skintight black sleeveless T-shirt, and her new custom-made black jeans. "You look too good for an ex, honey. You're supposed to tone down your magnificence when you're with people that can't have you any more."

"Oh, is that right?" she asked with a smirk. "Since I've never had a lover, I didn't know the rules. Should I wear my warm-ups?"

"No, those are too cute, too. Maybe one of my sports bras and your baggiest sweats."

"Your bra?"

"Yeah. It'll be skin tight so it can hold those beauties down," she said as she cupped one of the beauties in her hand.

"Do you really want me to change?" Ryan asked seriously as she looked into Jamie's eyes.

"No, I'll do my best to fend her off if she makes a grab for you."

Ryan gave Jamie a stern look. "We stopped seeing each other long before you and I were intimate. It's not like we were going at it hot and heavy until you came along. Ally decided to pursue a serious relationship with someone right about the same time I did. It was really mutual."

"I'm sorry if I'm acting jealous. I know that I have no cause to be that way."

"Absolutely no cause at all."

As it got closer to eight o'clock, Ryan got more and more tense. She had canvassed each stereo but had been unable to find what she was looking for. Mia came home as she rummaged through the CDs for the third time. "Mia, you're just the person I was looking for. Do you have any country CDs?"

"Yeah, I think I do. No—wait—oh darn, they're in my other trailer. Sorry." She smiled sweetly as she strolled past the scowling Ryan and into the kitchen.

"What's up with the odd musical selections that Ryan's looking for?" she asked after she had hugged Jamie.

"Oh, one of her old girlfriends is coming over for dinner, and she wants her to feel comfortable. Apparently she only likes country music."

"Ooh, old girlfriend, huh? Maybe I'll stick around and get introduced. I'm not too proud to take Ryan's rejects if I can't get anywhere with Jordan."

"I don't think this one would be your type."

"Not cute?"

Jamie thought about that question for a moment. "No, she's not the type that would ever be called cute. She's really big—taller and heavier than Ryan."

"Ooh, a beefy girl," Mia teased.

"No, not really. I'd bet that she has less body fat than Ryan does. She's just got an extra thirty pounds of rock-hard muscle on a very big frame. She also growing out what Ryan says was a crew cut."

"She sounds like one of those Bulgarian weightlifters."

"Not technically, but she is a body builder. She works as a personal trainer, but she spends most of her free time working out and training for competitions."

"Was Ryan with her long?"

"They were never 'together' per se," Jamie said. "They just slept together—a lot. Apparently, neither of them wanted a relationship, or they weren't that interested in each other at the time." Her mouth twitched into an impish grin as she added, "Whatever it was, I'm finding out tonight."

"I'm with you. I'm interested in seeing this specimen."

"Why don't you join us for dinner?"

Mia placed her hands upon her hips and glared at Jamie for a moment, "You're trying to hook her up with someone, aren't you, you little sneak."

Jamie tossed her hair as she said, "Why, Mia. That would be unseemly. Besides, you're interested in Jordan."

"Uh-huh. Like that would stop you."

⁂

"She'll be on time. Are you sure I can't help you move things along?"

"Ryan, we don't have to serve dinner the moment she walks in the door. Chill out. Everything is under control."

"Are you sure I look okay?" she asked with a hint of a whine in her voice. "You got me all worried when you told me to change."

"You've asked me five times now. May I remind you that you're not going to get to sleep with her this time? Goodness, you act like you're going on your first date." Ryan looked completely nonplussed, and Jamie immediately regretted shining a light on her insecurities. "Sweetheart, you look good enough to eat, and as soon as Ally leaves I plan on doing just that."

Ryan sighed and turned to walk back into the parlor to pace for a while, much to Mia's amusement. "Do I look okay?" Ryan asked worriedly as she checked her hair in the mirror—again.

"You look great," Mia said sincerely, deciding that since Ryan had asked her three times she must want a complete assessment. She crossed her arms over her chest and appraised her friend critically for a long moment. "I like how that shirt shows off the muscles in your arms. You have great triceps, you know," she said, her intent brown eyes critically surveying Ryan's body. "You have on a sports bra, don't you?" she asked, not waiting for confirmation. "I might choose something that gives your breasts a little more definition, but then you lose some of the softness that the sports bra gives you." Her eyes raked up and down the long form as she said, "Those jeans look really nice, too. They fit nice and snug on your ass, but they still look comfortable, not too tight in the crotch. I hate that," she said, making a face. "The Doc Martens are a nice touch…pretty butch, but nice." Grinning slyly, Mia added, "I'd do ya."

Ryan had been staring at her in shock through this entire soliloquy. Mia summarized by saying, "In my opinion, you look too good for an ex, and if I was Jamie I'd make you put on some heavy sweats."

Ryan's brain was still trying to accept the fact that Mia had been checking her out—thoroughly. One point stood out and she jumped on it. "She's not an ex. We just had sex."

"How often?" Mia asked conversationally. "Once, twice?"

"A few times a month for around six years," Ryan mumbled, as she ran her hands through her hair while gazing into the mirror once again.

"Oh, well then, I understand completely. Just sex partners."

Ryan was just about to explain once again when the bell rang. "Yipes," she said weakly as she moved towards the door. When she was almost there she looked over at Mia and whispered loudly, "You're not staying, are you?"

"Gee, thanks for the heartfelt invitation." She scowled. "Don't worry, I'm just staying for a peek."

Ryan rolled her eyes dramatically as she reached for the door. As she flung it open, Mia witnessed an astounding transformation. "Ally!" Ryan said, her face animated by a huge smile.

The very large, very well built woman stepped into the foyer and rumbled out, "Hey, sugar," as she wrapped her arms around her friend, lifting her slightly off the ground.

Mia was amazed to see that there was something shy and demure about Ryan's entire demeanor. She acted like a kitten being picked up by the scruff of the neck. And seeing a completely docile Ryan was quite a shock.

As the woman deposited her back on the ground, Ryan clasped her hands behind her friend's neck and leaned back to let Ally take a good look. "As usual, you're more beautiful every time I see you," the deep voice murmured. "Jamie is one lucky, lucky woman."

Ryan blushed so deeply that she looked like she'd been slapped. She leaned in and gave her friend a sweet kiss on the lips as Mia privately mused that it was lucky that Jamie wasn't there to see the emotion lurking just under the surface. *Sex partners my ass,* she thought derisively. *Ryan's totally into her.*

As they released each other, Ryan took her by the hand and led her into the parlor. "Mia, I want you to meet an old friend of mine. This is Ally Webster. Ally, Mia Christopher."

Mia hopped up from the sofa and extended her hand, "Good to meet you." She batted her eyes at the handsome stranger.

"The pleasure is all mine," she rumbled out in her soft southern accent.

"Mia is our roommate, " Ryan explained.

"Ah, will you be joining us for dinner?" Ally held onto Mia's hand just a little longer than necessary.

"Yes," Mia replied as Ryan concurrently said, "No, she's got a prior engagement."

Ryan shot her a glare but Mia shrugged it off as she said, "I can cancel that engagement. I'd much rather stay home tonight." She batted her eyes again and extended her hand to Ally. "Come sit down and tell me about yourself while Ryan gets you something to drink. What would you like?"

"Sparkling water?" Ally suggested.

"Coming right up," Ryan gritted out through clenched teeth. "Mia's staying for dinner." she hissed out as she passed Jamie on the way to the refrigerator.

"It's okay, I told her she could stay if she wanted to."

Ryan stopped dead in her tracks and glared at the back of her partner's head. "You did what?"

Jamie turned and started a bit at the look on Ryan's face. "I told her she could stay if she wanted to. Why, is that a big deal?"

"Do I have any say in anything around here? Or am I supposed to be put on display for the whole neighborhood?"

"Display?"

"Don't act like you don't have a hidden agenda," Ryan hissed out. "You always do." She stuck her head in the refrigerator and yanked out a sparkling water. As she passed by she muttered, "I'm just a pawn in your little game."

As she stalked out the door, Jamie stood rooted in place. She shook her head forcefully to clear it and muttered aloud, "I don't know who that is, but I'd like my Ryan back."

During the meal they spoke of common interests and current events in the Bay Area. Ally was unfailingly polite and expressed a quiet interest in almost all of the topics they covered, but she spoke very little of her own accord. Jamie tried to draw her out a bit by asking about her family. Ryan shot her a warning glance, having specifically told Jamie not to ask about them, but to her surprise, Ally easily began to speak about her history.

"So where are you from again, Ally?" Jamie asked.

"Chapel Hill, North Carolina," she said with a heavier accent than she usually displayed.

"Interesting," Jamie said. "I don't think I know anyone from the South. What was it like to grow up in a university town?"

"Well, my parents were both affiliated with the university so it was a little like a company town for me. Most of our social circle revolved around the school, so I suppose it just seemed like any other large employer in a small town."

Ryan had no idea that her parents were affiliated with the school;

in fact, she had even forgotten what town she was from. Jamie continued, "What did your parents do?"

"My father is a professor in the chemistry department and my mother is a lecturer in the English department."

Ryan's eyes bugged out at this revelation. She had always assumed that Ally was from a poor, uneducated family, and she had to admit that she'd been following a blatant stereotype. Since Ally was from the South, hadn't attended college, and had been molested by a family member, she had just assumed that she was poor white trash—but white trash didn't teach at the University of North Carolina.

"That's fascinating." Jamie said. "But you didn't go to college, did you?"

"Nope. I wanted to get as far away from academia as possible. I think I've done a pretty good job of it too. Hanging out in a gym all day is the antithesis of academia. I must say, though, that my mother's influence still shows up in my choice of reading material."

"Really? What do you read?" Jamie asked. Ryan couldn't wait to hear this since she had never seen a book anywhere in Ally's house.

"I'm a sucker for anything from the Victorian period," she said, looking a little embarrassed by her revelation. "I know I don't look like the type, but a good romantic heroine gets me every time."

"That's fascinating," Jamie said. "I'm an English lit major and the Victorian period is one of my favorites also."

They went off on a wide-ranging discussion of their favorite works while Ryan just stared at them, unable to contribute much since she had only read the bare minimum of fiction required to get through school. Instead, she sat back and tried to reconcile what she was learning with what she knew of Ally, and she found that nothing fit. She was just wondering where all of these books were stored, when Ally said that she didn't keep books in her house, since she thought they needed to be actively read. So a few years earlier she had begun to donate every book she bought to her local high school as soon as she was finished with it.

Ryan just shook her head as she took in each new detail about her friend. *Why haven't we talked like this? Did I just never bother, or didn't she want to share this stuff with me? Maybe she thinks I'm not well versed enough to have a serious discussion about the things that interest her. God knows I have no friggin' idea of what they're talking about.*

After their extended tour of English literature, Jamie brought the conversation back to something they could all participate in. "So, are you seeing anyone now, Ally?"

Subtle, Jamie, really subtle, Ryan thought.

"Yes, as a matter of fact, I started seeing someone just a couple of months ago. She's a student at San Francisco State. She's an English major too. I bet you'd like her."

"Why didn't you bring her?" Ryan asked.

Now it was Ally's turn to shrug shyly as she said, "I don't know if she's ready to meet my exes. Especially the ones that look like you," she said as she leveled her gaze at Ryan.

For the tenth time that night, Ryan blushed to the roots of her hair, and Mia actually expected to hear her say "aw, shucks" at any minute.

The ringing phone saved Ryan from having to reply, and she hopped up to answer it. "Mia, it's for you," she said as she walked back to the table. "Jordan."

When Mia returned, she announced that Jordan was coming over to take their usual after-dinner stroll. She dashed upstairs to put her running shoes on, then said her good-byes and went out to meet Jordan halfway.

After Mia took her leave, they went into the parlor to digest their meal prior to having dessert. Jamie sat on the end of the sofa and, since Ryan sat right next to her, she assumed she had been forgiven her earlier transgressions. Within moments Ryan's arm was around her, and she had her hand resting on the inside of Ryan's thigh, as usual.

"You two seem absolutely perfect together," Ally observed, smiling at them fondly. "You finish each other's sentences, and you seem to communicate without words a lot. It's really great to see you look so happy. You truly deserve the best."

Since Ryan's embarrassed grin didn't look like it was going away any time soon, Jamie jumped in. "You're the only person I know who knew Ryan when she was just coming out. Do you mind talking about what she was like when you first met her? I'm terribly curious about her youth."

Ryan started to protest, but Ally smiled and said, "Happy to. I have nothing but fond memories of Ryan."

"What was she like when you met?"

"Well, I'd have to say she was a lot different than she is now," Ally said thoughtfully. "She was very sweet—which hasn't changed—but she was so naïve that you could have convinced her the sky was green without half trying."

"I have a hard time picturing that," Jamie said.

"It's a little hard to explain. In some areas Ryan was very mature for her age, but she was clueless about dating and relationships and sex."

Ryan was again blushing furiously, and Ally gave her a concerned look. "Do you mind us talking about you, sweet pea?"

Jamie bristled just a bit at the endearment, but she reassured herself that it was probably a pet name that just seemed natural to them. Ryan shook her head lightly and said, "No, I don't mind. It's kind of interesting to see myself through your eyes."

Ally continued, "I don't know how many women you'd been with, but you were just like a big black Labrador puppy when I first met you. You were so enthusiastic and playful. You were willing to dive in and give everything you had, but I recognized that was going to get you hurt badly. So I tried to give you some advice on how to be a little more careful about giving your heart away. Up until now I've been worried that maybe you took me too literally. I was beginning to wonder if you'd ever find someone that you could love."

"You did me a bigger favor than you'll ever know," Ryan said. "I would have had my heart broken fifty times by now if you hadn't showed me how to determine if someone was right for me before I jumped in with both feet. And you taught me some lessons that Jamie here has benefited from also," she said as she pinched her lover on the side.

"I'll say," Jamie replied through her giggles. "And I owe you a debt of gratitude for teaching my sweetie about safer sex. She would have been on antibiotics all the time if you hadn't knocked some sense into her."

"My pleasure," Ally grinned. "This little one was too precious to waste." She laughed at her own joke and said, "Although I hadn't planned on conducting the safer sex lessons in person."

"What do you mean?" Ryan asked.

"Is it really okay if I talk about this? Most women would be uncomfortable hearing ex-lovers talk about their sex life."

"It's fine, really," Jamie assured her. "The only time we have trouble is when we don't talk about things."

"Okay, I can see that," she conceded. She furrowed her brow a bit as she began, "I've never told you this, but I think I should tell you why I was never interested in being exclusive with you."

Ryan sat up with a deeply interested look on her face. She cocked her head just a bit and gazed at Ally, urging her to continue. "I had a pretty tough childhood," she said as she addressed her. "I got involved with drugs and alcohol at a very early age. I'd say I was an alcoholic by fifteen. After I'd been in San Francisco for a while I met a woman who helped me get sober. It was really tough for me to stop, but I was managing pretty well. My sponsor worked very, very closely with me and I would say I'd been sober for about six months when I met Ryan. I've got to tell you, from the first day I laid eyes on her I was a goner."

Ryan looked up in surprise as she said, "You barely seemed to notice me. I didn't think you even knew my name when you took me to Good Vibrations."

"Oh, I knew your name all right. But as soon as I told my sponsor about you, she warned me to steer clear. It's usually dangerous to get into a relationship during your first year of sobriety, and she strongly urged me to avoid you. I didn't want to listen to her, but she told me something that has proven to be very true. She said that people with serious issues like I had should avoid people that they were very powerfully attracted to. She said that kind of visceral attraction generally led you to find people who appealed to your most wounded self. So I decided to follow her advice and ignore this gorgeous young thing."

"So that's why you acted like you didn't know I existed?" Ryan asked.

"Yep. But I heard you talking to one of the other trainers about going out with Shelly Sterns, and I knew you needed some advice. That woman had run through every lesbian in the city, and I knew you were headed for trouble if you started hanging out in her crowd. So I asked if you knew how to have safer sex and when you confessed your abject ignorance, I knew I had to instruct you."

"But why did you…?"

"Show you in person?" she asked with a wink.

"Yeah."

"Well, I am only human." She laughed, the sound ridiculously musical. "I decided to listen to my sponsor and not fall in love with you, but you were so willing, and beautiful and ripe; just like a luscious peach waiting to be picked." She shook her head a little as she shot Jamie an embarrassed glance and said, "Sorry, I got carried away."

"It's okay," she said easily. "It happens to me on a daily basis."

"Anyway," Ally continued, "I let my lust get the better of me, and I showed this innocent young thing how to have a very good time without putting herself at risk. Ooh, she was such a good student that I had to fight valiantly not to fall in love with her." She turned to Ryan and said earnestly, "That's why I couldn't see you very often, and why I didn't let you get to know me very well. I knew I was risking my sobriety every time we were together, but I just couldn't stop."

"I thought you just didn't want to see me that often," Ryan said softly.

"Far from it. It was only this past year that I came to terms with the fact that I had begun to use sex just like I'd used alcohol and drugs. That's why I decided to stop sleeping with you. I knew we shouldn't be together, but I also knew that I wouldn't look for another woman if I knew I could have you whenever I needed you, so I decided to go cold turkey."

"Was that hard for you?" Jamie asked sympathetically, wondering how one could voluntarily stop seeing someone as wonderful as her partner.

"It was nearly as hard as when I stopped drinking," she acknowledged. "But it really has been for the best for both of us. I can see how happy Ryan is with you. And I think I have a chance to build a relationship with Ellen. I think it's worked out for the best."

"It certainly has for me," Jamie said as she gave her partner a squeeze.

Ryan was still shaking her head as she commented, "I just never knew you felt like that about me. I wish I had known. It would have helped me figure some things out."

"That would not have been a good idea. I knew that you were interested in me, and I couldn't have stood my ground if you'd tried to convince me to get closer. I just couldn't risk it. You're not an addict, Ryan. You don't know how powerful the pull is."

"Do you really think I appealed to your most broken self?" Ryan asked, a confused and slightly hurt look on her face.

Ally looked profoundly embarrassed. Jamie took her cue from the look and said, "I'm going to get dessert ready." When Ryan started to stand, she pushed her down easily by just resting a hand on her shoulder. "You two stay and chat. I'll be back in a few."

Ally smiled at her departing form and said, "She's special."

"I know that," Ryan agreed. "I thank God every day for bringing her into my life."

Ally looked at her for a minute and said, "This is a little hard to explain. You weren't bad for me, in general. The real problem is that I'm trying hard to give up my need to control my partner in bed. I don't know if I could have done that with you," she said as she stared at the floor. "Our personalities fit together far too well."

Ryan pursed her lips and furrowed her brow, trying to understand Ally's statement. She came over to sit next to Ryan on the sofa, then lifted her hand and brushed her thumb down Ryan's pink cheek as she said, "I've told you that I was sexually abused by my brother." Ryan nodded slowly. "He was a few years older, and he overpowered me—not so much by force as by his presence and his personality. I found myself acting that out with you almost immediately. And there was a very big part of me that was afraid those urges would get worse over time. I've been fighting the need to physically dominate women, and I don't know if I could have fought it with you. There's something about you that just makes me want to own you," she said, bending down to place a very tender kiss on Ryan's lips. "You're just too tempting, my little peach."

Ryan rested her head on her friend's shoulder as she took in a deep breath. "I'm glad you told me. It hurt me that you didn't want to get closer. There was a part of me that thought you just didn't like me enough."

"Nothing could be further from the truth," she whispered, gathering her in her arms for a tender hug. "I love you, and I always will. But I want you to be with someone who can love you for yourself, without the echoes of the past invading constantly."

"I'm so glad you told me," Ryan sniffed as she tried to stifle her tears.

Ally grabbed a tissue and gently wiped the tears that threatened to escape from Ryan's red-rimmed eyes. "It's okay, sugar," she said as she patted her. "It's okay."

⁂

Jamie could hear nothing but low voices coming from the parlor, and she knew that if Ryan wanted her to come back she would appear in the kitchen, so she busied herself making a very attractive platter of cheese and fruit. She was in the middle of brewing espresso when she felt herself being enveloped in a warm hug. "Thank you," Ryan whispered as she leaned over her.

"For what?" Jamie turned in her lover's embrace.

"For inviting her, for asking her all of those questions, for being my lover, for putting up with me when I'm cranky, and for being the prettiest girl in the whole Bay Area."

"Most of those things are part of the job description, love. And I think you're a little biased about the prettiest girl thing."

"I am biased," Ryan admitted. "But I still think you're the most wonderful woman in the world."

⁂

It was quite late when Ally finally said goodbye. Jamie accepted a hug, but when Ally turned to Ryan Jamie suggested, "Honey, why don't you walk Ally out to her car?"

Ryan shot her a grateful look as she escorted her friend to the street. "She seems like a very understanding woman," Ally said, grasping Ryan's hand.

"She is that. And given my past, she has reason to be insanely jealous. But she seems more interested in my past than suspicious of it. Like tonight. I thought she wanted to know more about you, but I think she really wanted to know more about me."

"Well I think you did very well for yourself. I hope you bring each other a lot of happiness."

"We do," Ryan agreed. "We really do."

"I just find one thing kind of funny," Ally said as she folded her long frame into her small car. She looked up at Ryan with a grin and revealed, "I think it's cute that such a little woman can top you."

"Hey! I told you—I am not a bottom."

"Keep dreaming, sugar. But I will let you in on a little secret." Ryan leaned down into her open window. "The fact that you don't recognize it is what makes it so darned cute."

For the final time that night, Ryan blushed deeply as she shook her head and smiled down at her friend. "You keep in touch, big girl," she said fondly as she leaned in for a kiss.

"I will. Take care of your precious self." She gave Ryan one final broad smile and a short wave as she drove off down the dark street.

◆

When Ryan came back in the house, she stood behind her partner at the sink and wrapped her arms around her tightly. Jamie didn't speak, didn't ask her why she was nearly squeezing the breath out of her since she had a fairly good idea. Drying her hands quickly, she leaned her head back against her partner and stroked her bare arms for a few moments.

"Thanks," Ryan said, after a long time had passed.

Turning in her embrace, Jamie looked up at her and said, "You're welcome, sweetheart." She ran her hands through Ryan's hair, tossing it behind her shoulders and fluffing the bangs. "You had a pretty tough night, didn't you?"

With a ghost of a smile, Ryan nodded, pleased that Jamie seemed to understand that the discussion with Ally had taken a lot out of her. "How about you? Are you okay?"

"Yes, I'm great," Jamie said sincerely. "I learned a lot about Ally, and, more importantly, a lot about you."

"I learned a lot, too," Ryan agreed. "I guess I feel better, but I feel a little raw, you know?"

"Yes, I know. Why don't we go to bed now? We can finish cleaning up in the morning."

Ryan looked around suspiciously, her eyes wide as she said, "You don't think Da can see dirty dishes from Noe, do you? He'd rather we leave the front door open all night than leave the kitchen dirty."

"You look like you need some hugs," Jamie declared, taking her partner's hand. "Sometimes hugs are more important than anything else…even something as vital as a clean kitchen." She gripped the tip of Ryan's nose between her thumb and index finger and gave it a gentle tug. "That'll be our little secret. We'll never admit that we broke the cardinal rule of the O'Flaherty family."

When Jamie came out of the bath, Ryan was in the process of unlacing her boots. She kicked them off and stood to unbuckle her belt, with Jamie watching her out of the corner of her eye as she went to get a T-shirt for herself from the dresser. The jeans fell to the floor, and Ryan bent over to pick them up, showing off her butt to Jamie's appreciative eyes. The taller woman hooked her thumbs into her shorts to peel them off, but Jamie came up behind her and placed a hand on her arm. "Leave 'em," she said, meeting Ryan's surprised eyes.

The full, pink lips curled into a grin, blue eyes sparking interest as her voice dropped a little and she said, "All right."

Jamie pushed her back onto the bed and crawled up next to her, resting her head on Ryan's chest. Ryan still wore her sports bra and sleeveless black T-shirt, and Jamie decided to leave both garments on her for the time being. She pulled the shirt up just enough to be able to reach her hand inside the shorts and begin to rub gentle circles on Ryan's belly. "I don't think of you with other women much. I used to," she added with a chuckle, "but I don't anymore."

"Tell me about the used to part," Ryan asked, loving it when her partner talked about the beginnings of her sexual desire for her.

Jamie laughed softly, her fingers never ceasing their gentle stroking. "We had a few pretty intense discussions when I was with Jack. Especially when I got comfortable enough to tell you how bad things were with him sexually."

"Yeah..." Ryan said, urging her on.

"We had one when I was down at my parents'. I guess it was Thanksgiving...or maybe Christmas..."

"Thanksgiving," Ryan said emphatically. "We went for a bike ride and we stopped at a picnic table and started talking about sex." Her eyebrows popped a few times as she said, "It was fun."

Jamie sat up just enough to be able to face her, then asked, "Were you...uhm...did you think...did you...uhm...what do you mean, fun?"

"Not that kinda fun," Ryan smiled. "I didn't allow myself to consciously think of you in a sexual manner back then. But even though my mind didn't participate, I think my body was reacting to you." She smiled gently and said, "It was a long ride home."

"Ooh," Jamie smiled as her hand slipped out of the shorts and came to rest between Ryan's legs. She gave her a gentle pat and asked, "Got your motor running, huh?"

"Yep. I got home, stripped, and climbed into bed without even taking a shower." She gave her partner a rakish grin and added, "I had myself good that day."

Jamie smiled at her choice of words and echoed them. "I had myself, too. We'd been talking about oral sex, and I had this image that I could not banish from my brain. I saw you, on your back, with some unspecified woman between your legs, loving you with her mouth." She shivered violently as she recalled the image, still clear in her mind. "I could just feel what you were feeling as she licked and nibbled on you—thanks to your excellent powers of description, I might add," she said, patting Ryan's belly.

"I hadn't thought about the woman who introduced me to oral sex in the longest time," Ryan smiled. "But she had me again that afternoon." She chuckled low in her chest as she added, "She'd gotten even better over the years."

"I just bet she did. Anyway, back to my original point. I don't often think of you with someone else, but when Ally was talking about how you were when she was with you the first time, I started to get excited."

"Really?" Ryan smiled, rolling onto her side to see her partner more fully.

"Really. I had this image of you...all cute and innocent and naïve...lying in Ally's bed while she uhm...played with you." A very becoming blush stole across her cheeks, and Ryan had a need to find out what was behind it.

Ryan's voice grew low and took on a very sexy timbre. "What did you imagine her doing to me? Be specific," she added, nudging her partner with her hip.

"I don't think I can. I don't really know what you two did together, and I don't really know how it would be to use things on each other, so I just had this mmm...I don't know," she said, sighing heavily.

"Embarrassed to tell me?" Ryan's expression was welcoming and open, and Jamie found her head nodding up and down.

"I know I shouldn't be embarrassed," she said, her cheeks still pink. "I mean, I share everything with you..."

"Hey, don't feel like that." She wrapped her arms around her and gave her a comforting squeeze. "I was just trying to knock off a few minutes of foreplay, but I'm confident you can rev me up pretty quickly." Jamie still looked uncomfortable, and Ryan tried again. "It's perfectly normal to have some things you don't want to share. They're your fantasies."

"Thanks. I'm a lot more comfortable showing you that I'm excited than I am telling you how I got there." She let out a small, wry chuckle, and Ryan nodded her head in understanding.

"Makes sense. I'm that way sometimes, too."

"I can share one thing with you," Jamie said, her eyes beginning to sparkle again. "I got excited thinking about Ally being kinda dominant with you." She looked up at her partner with an embarrassed giggle. "You're normally pretty clear about what you need and what you want when we're together. I guess it was kinda hot to think about you being more...compliant."

"I'm not compliant with you?" Ryan asked as her fingers slipped under her partner's T-shirt and started playing with the soft skin they found there.

"Well, in a way you are, but in another way you're pretty forceful. It makes me hot to think of you being completely at someone's disposal...letting them totally control what happens." She cocked her head and asked, "Will you tell me what it was like between you two? How you touched each other? How she pleased you?"

It didn't take Ryan long to form her answer to the question. "No." She gave Jamie a warm smile, but her head was shaking decisively, emphasizing her refusal. "I don't think that's a good idea, love. I show you things we did together all the time, but the details of what we did together are between Ally and me."

"Embarrassed?" Jamie asked, returning Ryan's question.

"A little, yeah. But I want us to have a future relationship with Ally, and I don't want the things I tell you to get in the way." She hitched herself up against her propped up hand and said, "I used to go out with a certain woman fairly often, and one of her exes was a mutual friend of ours. The woman I was dating told me that her ex could only get off if she was lying on her stomach with her hands between her legs, masturbating. The woman I was going out with had to spank her—hard—at the same time." Ryan pursed her lips and narrowed her eyes slightly as she said, "I thought about that every time I saw this other woman. I wondered what had happened to her to narrow her sexual expression down to such a constricted form, and I wondered about the woman I was seeing, too. I knew she didn't like to spank this other woman, but she did it anyway, for a couple of years. It made me wonder if she was doing things for me that she didn't like. Do you know what I mean?"

"I do," Jamie nodded. "Sorry I asked. I don't mean to make you uncomfortable."

"You didn't. I just want you to understand why I don't want to talk about details. It's not quite like attorney/client privilege, but it's close." She chuckled. "You should be able to freely express yourself with a lover without worrying that the things you share will be revealed to others. It's kind of a sacred bond to be intimate with someone." She traced the gentle contours of her partner's face as she reflected, "Ally and I didn't just have sex. You were right about that. We were intimate with each other...very intimate at times, and I treasure those moments. She trusted me, just like I believe you trust me. I would never, ever, tell anyone the details of what we share, and I'm sure you feel the same way."

"I do," she agreed. "I guess what I was asking wasn't for details as much as for you to tell me if there are things you want that I'm not doing for you." She had her hand on Ryan's side, and she started to run her fingers up and down the smooth, well-defined muscles of her torso. "I want to please you in every way you've ever dreamed of."

"You do. I'm always very, very satisfied, and I can't think of a thing we're lacking. I never lie here and think 'if only she would…'"

"Sure?"

"Positive." Ryan wrapped her up in a hug, their faces just inches apart. "Absolutely positive. Now, all of this yakkin' has thoroughly cooled my engines. You've got your work cut out for you if you want to get busy." Her bouncing eyebrows indicated that her challenge was a playful one, but Jamie took up the gauntlet immediately.

Pushing Ryan onto her back, Jamie climbed aboard, always loving the feeling of lying completely atop her partner. A few playful kisses segued into many, each one growing a little hotter, a little wetter. In minutes Jamie was sucking gently on her lover's tongue, feeling her desire rise quickly as the agile visitor slid sensually into her mouth.

She needed more skin to work with, so Jamie rolled off and removed her shorts, then tugged the T-shirt over Ryan's head and eased the sports bra from her body. As she tried to toss it away, Ryan managed to hold onto it, and she methodically wrapped the fabric around her hands, gently binding them.

Jamie cocked her head slightly and locked eyes with her partner, seeing the shy, almost hesitant look in Ryan's dark blue orbs. It was clear that Ryan was making an offer, and she realized that the offer was to make herself vulnerable…compliant…obviously trying to satisfy Jamie's expressed fantasy. Jamie swallowed nervously, and then took a few deep breaths, reminding herself that this was just Ryan, and that she had nothing to worry about. They were just going to play a little, and if she didn't like it, she didn't have to continue.

Ryan blinked up at her and extended her hands in front of her body, asking, "Would you like to tie them?"

Shaking her head, Jamie looked at her speculatively and decided, "I don't think so. I think I'd rather see you struggle to control them yourself."

Oh, Lord. A born top.

Intentions

"I want you to keep your hands above your head," Jamie instructed. "You can hold onto the headboard, but I don't want you to touch me…or yourself."

"I won't."

"I think your eyes should be closed, too," Jamie decided, her brow slightly furrowed.

The blue orbs shuttered, Jamie looked around the room for something to tickle her partner with just to test her resolve. On the top of one of her bookcases was a dried flower arrangement that her mother had sent to her when she was out of town on some holiday or other, and she noticed that a few of the dried grasses would serve well as feather substitutes. She got up and walked over to the case, standing on her tiptoes to retrieve it. Two suitable specimens were found, and she came back to bed, intent on taking her partner to the limits of her self-control.

Rather than get onto the bed, Jamie stood next to it so her lover couldn't tell how she was leaning, or where she would strike next. She began to stroke Ryan's long body with the stalks, delighting as she saw the flesh begin to pebble wherever they traveled. A soft pink lip was drawn into Ryan's mouth, and Jamie could see her bite down firmly to keep from crying out. Ryan was essentially very ticklish, but she could suppress her urge to giggle when it was absolutely necessary. It appeared that she was struggling with her ability today, and Jamie was glad to see that this would not be easy for her lover to bear. She had no interest in actually hurting her or causing her pain, but she wanted to push her a little bit—just to watch her squirm.

Ryan was already squirming, and Jamie smiled as she directed her, "Put your feet together, and lift your legs straight up in the air."

Dark eyebrows lifted, but the eyes stayed closed as Ryan immediately complied. Jamie knew the position would be hard to maintain, but she wanted to tickle the backs of Ryan's thighs, easily her most sensitive spot. Ryan knew just what her intent was, and she renewed her grip on that lower lip, knowing she was going to need it.

The long, muscular legs rose straight up into the air, the muscles already twitching even though Jamie hadn't touched them yet.

Moving to the foot of the bed, Jamie could already detect the first faint signs of her partner's arousal, and she smiled in satisfaction. The stalks of grass swiped across Ryan's buttocks, causing her to jerk sharply and let out a strangled whimper. Quickly moving from the tip of her toes, to the backs of her knees, the arch of her foot, back to her buttocks, Jamie never let her prepare for the next touch. It was always a second faster or slower, and always fell onto a part of her body that she hadn't anticipated. By the time Jamie urged her to lower her feet, Ryan was shaking roughly, her hands grasping the underside of the headboard so fiercely that Jamie could see the tendons in her arms in raised relief.

She allowed her hands to roam all over Ryan's body—soothing and reassuring her that she would receive substantial pleasure in return for her compliance.

When Ryan's body was loose and relaxed, Jamie urged her onto her stomach, where the feather-torture continued. The sexy hips were twitching rhythmically, even though the touch was never predictable.

The soft moans that continued to flow were music to Jamie's ears and she cranked them up a notch when she took an ice cube from her glass and knelt between Ryan's spread legs. She popped the cube in her mouth, and started to kiss and lick her way down the ultra-sensitive body…letting the warmth of her lips and tongue contrast sharply with the cold, hard cube. Again, Ryan never knew if the touch would be hot or cold, soft or hard, wet or dry.

Once again, Jamie got up and stood next to the bed, trying to keep her partner's equilibrium off balance. She noticed that Ryan had shifted her legs far apart and was trying to get a little satisfaction from pressing her vulva hard against the mattress. Walking to the end of the bed, she placed the feet shoulder width apart, and instructed, "Keep them there." Ryan whimpered a little, but otherwise held her tongue. Next, Jamie took two pillows and placed them under her belly, effectively precluding her from obtaining any pressure against her most demanding need.

Now that Ryan was once again under her dominion, Jamie started at the sensitive instep of each delicate foot, and raked her short nails over the skin, watching in delight as Ryan's whole body convulsed, her struggle with control nearly at the breaking point.

The moan that issued from her throat was low and rough, more of a growl than a moan, and Jamie was determined to wrest a few more just like it from her before the night was over.

Her short, smooth nails carved fiery paths up and down Ryan's body, the skin growing heated under her touch. The force and intensity varied, sometimes gentle, almost a tickle, sometimes so intense that it left pink trails along the expanse of smooth skin.

Fishing out another ice cube, Jamie grasped her partner's legs and pulled forcefully until they were dangling off the side of the bed. She continued to urge Ryan towards her until the tips of her toes were touching the ground. Kneeling between her widespread legs, Jamie began to tease her trembling cheeks with the ice, alternating sharp quick bites with cold, wet, kisses.

Without the headboard to provide stability, Ryan's entire body was as taut as a bowstring, every muscle standing out as she struggled to not only stay still, but refrain from forcing Jamie's head right where she desperately needed it.

Jamie grasped her tightly around her thighs and forced her legs a little further apart, giving her clear access to her goal. Ryan sensed that she was finally going to get some satisfaction, and she let out a massive sigh of relief. Just as she did so, however, Jamie put the last bit of ice to good use, pressing the sliver into Ryan's overheated wetness, where it melted instantly.

"Oh, my God," Ryan moaned as Jamie's ice-cold tongue laved her indulgently, touching every aching spot, and wringing a deep, raspy growl from her. In seconds, her body flew into a shattering climax, her stressed legs giving out completely as she sank to her knees before tumbling to the floor, her partner holding on tight to cushion her.

Their entwined bodies lay in a sprawled heap, the sheet tangled between them—a casualty of Ryan's mad grasp for stability. It wasn't easy, but Jamie finally maneuvered onto her back and Ryan immediately sought the comfort of her embrace. The dark head lay pillowed against Jamie's chest, her breathing still ragged, her body still mostly limp.

"Like that?" Jamie chuckled, her partner just a few brain cells above plankton at the moment.

Ryan didn't speak…actually, she couldn't speak. Summoning every bit of strength she could amass, she raised one elegantly arched eyebrow and rotated one blue eye in her partner's direction—the sum total of her ability to comment.

When Ryan came home the following Monday, she had to shove the door open since the mail was wedged behind it. They had a large mail slot right in the door, and while it was convenient, sometimes it made opening the door difficult. Ryan wished their mail carrier would leave sizable items on the porch, but the young woman seemed to enjoy the challenge of forcing large items through the small slot.

Huh…United States Senate…well, la di da. She hefted the large envelope onto the desk.

When Jamie arrived home a few minutes later, her eyes lit on the package and she opened it with barely contained glee. "I *love* getting surprise packages," she said, her childlike enthusiasm showing brightly.

She shook out the contents, finding an attractive navy blue sweatshirt with the seal of the U.S. Senate on the breast, along with a similarly styled T-shirt. A few note pads, a fistful of pencils, and two lovely, engraved pen and pencil sets also littered the desk. She read the enclosed note aloud. "Dear Jamie and Ryan", her eyebrows popped up a few times as she read the salutation, and Ryan gave her a gentle smile of acknowledgement.

"I thought you two might enjoy a few mementos of my new job. I'm trying to turn over a new leaf now that I'm a public servant, so I'll have you know that I actually paid for these things. Your fellow taxpayers will not have to bear the expense of these gifts." Jamie looked up and said, "That was a joke."

"Got it." Ryan smiled. "Go on."

"I wasn't sure if Ryan liked to use her first name or not. I hope I guessed correctly. Love, Daddy."

Ryan picked up one of the writing sets and removed one of the pens. S. Ryan O'Flaherty was neatly engraved in gold on the dark blue pen. "Sweet," she said approvingly. "I love swag."

"Swag?" Jamie asked, tilting her head.

"Free stuff. You know, like stuff they give away to promote stuff."

"This is pretty nice swag," Jamie said, holding up the T-shirt. "Extra-large," she said, giving Ryan another pointed look.

"He can swag me all he wants. He can't buy my love, but he can make me happy about bringing the mail in."

The next morning Jamie used her break between classes to call her father and thank him for the gifts. "Hello," she said when a very official-sounding woman answered the phone. It was extremely odd to hear the woman refer to her father as Senator Evans, but she collected herself and said, "This is Jamie Evans, Senator Evans' daughter. Could I leave a message for him?"

"Oh, Ms. Evans, the senator has left explicit instructions that we are to find him when you call. Will you hold, please?"

"Uhm, sure. I can hold."

She waited almost five minutes, but his voice came on the line, sounding a little out of breath. "Hi, Jamie."

"Hi, Daddy. I was just calling to thank you for all of the nice gifts that you sent to us. It was really nice that you included Ryan. The extra-large fit her perfectly."

"That's good to hear, sweetie. I wear an extra-large, too, and even though she's not as large as I am, I know that people your age like your clothes to be a little roomy."

"Thanks for noticing. Also, thanks for telling your secretary to find you when I call. I appreciate that."

"I hope you're calling to say that you're able to spare a few days to come visit."

"Oh, I don't see how I can manage that during the fall season, Dad. My winter schedule will be much more open. Is it okay if we wait until then?"

"Sure, honey," he said, his voice betraying his disappointment.

An idea occurred to her and she suggested it before she had time to censor herself. "Could you manage a quick trip to Portland next week? I'm in a three-day tournament, and I'd love to have you there for at least one day if you could manage it."

Without even checking his calendar he said, "I'll figure out a way to be there. If not for the whole tournament, I'll come for the Monday match."

"Are you sure?"

"This means a lot to me. I'm sure."

"It's nice that golf means a lot to both of us, isn't it?"

"I wasn't referring to golf, honey. I was referring to the fact that you asked me to come."

"Oh…well…I want you to be there. Ryan can't come, and Mother isn't planning on coming either. We can have some time alone to just chat."

"Either I or my secretary will call you with my travel plans, honey. Thanks again for thinking of me."

"I think of you often, Daddy. I look forward to seeing you."

Chapter Five

Late Thursday night, or early Friday morning, depending on one's perspective, Mia glanced at her watch and suppressed a yawn when she saw that it was four a.m. As usual, she and Jordan had eaten dinner with Ryan and Jamie, then had taken a long walk around the neighborhood. For the past two hours they had been sitting in the living room, talking about everything that was important to either of them. Mia found herself opening up to Jordan about topics that she had never spoken about to another soul, and found her to be a fantastic listener. Jordan let her talk, sometimes lightly touching her knee for support or encouragement, but otherwise just listening, her blue eyes intent and focused.

For her part, Jordan seemed remarkably open, almost without barriers when it came to revealing her emotional self. After all of their lengthy chats Mia knew more about Jordan than she did about Jamie, with whom she'd been friends for seven years.

The only topic that didn't come up was Jordan's sexual history. Mia was fairly forthcoming about her own, but Jordan clammed up and changed the subject whenever Mia even hinted around about it.

It had been two weeks—not that long a time, but given the amount of time they had spent together, it seemed like eons to Mia. Every night the routine was the same. Talking until near dawn, then a yawned comment about the rising sun. Jordan would lean in for a good-bye kiss, and the floodgates would open, leaving them plastered against each other until Ryan or Jamie interrupted them, usually just a few minutes after they'd started.

As much as she enjoyed the time, Mia could tell that things were not going to go further unless she pushed them—so she decided to do so that very night. Basing her plan on their normal script, she decided to press the issue by suggesting that Jordan leave at four, rather than six, hoping that would give them two more hours to make a little progress.

She yawned pointedly, and Jordan took the hint. "You look tired. Maybe I should go."

"Yeah," she yawned again. "I think all of these late nights are catching up to me." Jordan leaned in for a kiss and Mia put as much of her sensual charm as she could muster into the embrace, causing Jordan to immediately return for more. As usual, the tender kisses turned passionate, but this time, both of their usual chaperones were snug in their bed, leaving no one to interrupt them.

Within minutes, Mia was throbbing from head to toe, her desire for the enigmatic woman nearly at the bursting point. Jordan was panting, appearing on the verge of losing control—just where Mia wanted her.

Trying to maneuver on the small loveseat was no easy task, but Mia finally twitched around until she was nearly on her back, then she pulled Jordan down on top of her. Now their bodies got into the game, with Jordan's lush, full breasts mashed against Mia's, whose heart began to beat so wildly that she felt faint. This was the most contact their bodies had yet experienced, and Mia could just feel some of the careful reserve leave the other woman's body.

Every part of her was beginning to cramp from the extremely awkward position, so Mia pushed Jordan up, then stood and extended her hand. Jordan looked up at her with stark confusion, but did as she was asked. Mia grasped her hand tightly and started to lead her towards the stairs, but Jordan's feet did not move. Her eyes trailed up the stairs, giving the impression of a condemned woman gazing at the path to the death chamber. Immediately realizing that she'd pushed too hard, Mia yanked the cushions from the loveseat and dropped to one, still holding on to Jordan's clammy hand.

"Come here," she said firmly, her eyes locked onto Jordan's frightened gaze. "Jordan," she soothed, as she would to a panicky kitten, "come sit by me."

Swallowing visibly, Jordan pursed her lips and allowed her body to fold itself onto the cushion, looking at Mia with eyes as wide as a terrified child's. "It's okay," Mia said, stroking her from her shoulder to her hand. "It's okay, I just wanted to get comfortable." She leaned close and rested her head on Jordan's chest, the rapidly beating heart thrumming against her ear. "Are you comfortable?" she asked, moving slowly so as not to frighten her any further.

"Uh-huh."

"Good. Can I have another good-night kiss?" Her voice was low and gentle, and she almost laughed when Jordan gave her a quick peck, obviously testing to see how far Mia would push her. Mia was still stroking her, trying to reassure her before moving forward. "That was nice. How about another?"

This time, when Jordan leaned down, Mia ran her tongue all over Jordan's lips, teasing, seeking entrance. Jordan was lost as soon as Mia's tongue entered her mouth, and within minutes they were completely horizontal, Jordan's long body covering Mia's as they sensually rubbed against each other. "Ooh, this is nice," Mia moaned, seeking Jordan's flushed ear and beginning to nibble on it.

As many times as they had kissed, Mia had focused exclusively on Jordan's mouth, leaving a world of unexplored territory that she was determined to claim. As she nibbled and sucked, Jordan began to shake, her entire body shivering as the delicious sensations washed over her. Mia kept right on her path, breathing softly into the pink ear, letting her tongue trail over every bit of skin, nipping and licking her way down past the ear and onto Jordan's elegant neck. "Mmm…you taste so good," Mia hummed, drawing an even stronger reaction from her prey.

Jordan was shaking so hard that Mia could hardly hold on, so she flipped her over, pinning the taller woman onto her back. Her mouth returned to Jordan's, kissing her with a fervent intensity that made their pulses pound so heavily they were nearly audible. As her tongue thrust, Mia's right hand slid up across Jordan's shoulder and grasped her breast, giving it a gentle but determined squeeze.

Jordan's hand immediately covered Mia's, and for a second it was unclear whether she would push the hand away or force it onto her breast more firmly. Her indecision was starkly evident on her face, which had abruptly pulled away from Mia's.

Mia felt her heart clench when she saw the raw panic. Even though a part of her knew that she could push Jordan past her fears, she didn't want it to be like that between them. Shifting her other hand up to Jordan's face, she brushed the disordered hair from her eyes and asked, "Does this make you uncomfortable?" she asked, her hand barely compressing the pliable flesh. "I'll stop if you want me to."

Jordan looked down, seemingly wanting to consult her breast to get its opinion. The look on her face was adorably indecisive, and Mia was finally hit with the reality of the situation. "Jordan?" she whispered, still stroking her to calm her, "have you ever made love with a woman before?"

She blanched. "N…n…no," she said, her head shaking rapidly. "No one. I've never made love to anyone."

She was blushing furiously, and Mia tried to hide her shock, saying, "That's all right. Really. Everyone has to start somewhere."

Jordan gave her a ghost of a smile, her body still shaking.

"Do you want to make love with me?" Mia asked, letting her hand twitch once again, smiling to herself when Jordan's eyes closed in pleasure.

"Ye…yes," the tall woman rasped when she had collected herself. "I want to. I really, really want to," she breathed, some of her suppressed desire showing in her darkening blue eyes. "But not tonight," she added immediately.

Mia laughed gently, bending to kiss her. "We'll make love when you're ready—and not one minute before." The sigh of relief was so enormous that Mia had to laugh again.

"You don't mind waiting for me to catch up?"

"Of course not. I love getting to know you. I love kissing you," she said, placing another sweet kiss on her lips. "It feels wonderful." She moved against her languidly, seductively.

"I love it too," Jordan gasped out, her eyes blinking slowly. She cleared her throat and swallowed before she mumbled, "I…I dream about it."

"Ooh, that's so sweet. Did you like it when I kissed your neck and ears?"

"Uh-huh. It felt…wonderful. Absolutely wonderful."

"How about this?" Mia asked, giving her breast another tender squeeze. "Do you like it when I touch you here?"

Jordan's entire body shivered as Mia's hand twitched upon her flesh. "Y...yeah. I like it...a lot."

"Where do you feel it?" she asked, her voice a deep, sexy purr. "Tell me."

Smacking her suddenly dry lips together, Jordan blinked slowly and revealed, "Everywhere. I feel it everywhere."

"Show me," Mia insisted, taking Jordan's shaking hand in hers. "Show me where you feel it."

With her eyes widening even more, Jordan complied, gently touching her own breast, then sliding her hand slowly down her body, her eyes locked onto Mia's glittering brown orbs. Her body shuddered as she tentatively slipped her hand between her legs and whispered, "Here. Here's where I feel it."

"That's just where you should feel it," Mia assured her. "How about now?" Her hand gave up possession of the left breast and applied the same kneading pressure to the right.

Jordan's head nodded furiously, the painfully aroused woman unable to keep her eyes open for another moment. "Yes," she gasped, her index finger rubbing along the seam of her jeans. "Right there."

Mia knew that she was pushing, and she knew that one more tiny shove and Jordan would be hers. But she didn't want the fragile woman to wake up in her bed and have even a glimmer of regret. She dipped her head and kissed her for a few more minutes, enjoying the soft warmth of Jordan's mouth, the sweet, shy innocence of the kisses they shared.

Pulling back she opened her eyes and gazed at Jordan for a moment, letting her make the next move.

The crystal blue eyes looked up at her with childlike innocence. "That's enough for tonight, okay? I'm about to pass out."

Smiling warmly, Mia removed her hand and bent her head to place a whisper-soft kiss right on the painfully hard nipple. "We'll wait until you're ready for more. You can trust me."

"I do trust you. I really do." She grasped Mia in a fierce hug and squeezed her until her ribs ached. "Thanks for putting up with me. I know I'm a handful."

Casting a pointed gaze at Jordan's full breast, Mia raised an eyebrow and said, "You're a delightful handful, and I can't wait to have my hands full of you again."

Blanching noticeably, Jordan rolled onto her side and squeaked out, "I've gotta go."

"But it's still dark out. Let me drive you."

"No, no, I've gotta go...now." Jordan grabbed her gym bag and ran out of the house at full speed.

Mia stared at the open door, rubbing at her face with her open hands. *My God, what have I gotten myself into?*

⚘

Ryan's internal motion detector alerted her to the presence of another person in the room seconds before she received a sharp slap on her ass. She flew into a sitting position, tearing away the sheet that covered her naked body, ready to leap to her feet to defend herself against her attacker. "What in the fuck...?" She blinked rapidly, focusing in on the obviously furious woman who was looming over her.

"You knew! You knew she was a virgin, and you didn't tell me. I swear I'll...I'll kick your ass, O'Flaherty. Get up and fight like a woman!"

Jamie's response to this invasion was, as usual, slow and muddled. "Ryan's not a virgin," she muttered. "I've seen to that myself."

Patting her gently, Ryan snugged the sheet up to her chin and whispered, "Go back to sleep, love." She kissed her cheek and slipped out of bed accompanied by her lover's unhappy grunt, grabbing the clothes she had worn the night before. She pointed at the door and Mia marched out, followed by Ryan, who hopped into her sweat pants as they walked towards Mia's room.

"I'd prefer not to fight you, but if you wake me up in the middle of the night by slapping my ass again, you're gonna get all you can handle."

"You just make me so damn mad," Mia growled. "You knew damn well that Jordan was a virgin, didn't you?"

"Yes, I did. She's very sensitive about it, and I would never tell someone her secrets. Just like I wouldn't tell yours. I don't care how mad you get, I'm not going to betray my friend."

"You're so fucking logical. I hate it."

Ryan was dressed now, and she sat down on the bed. "Tell me why it bothers you so much that she's a virgin."

"Because I really like her. I'm desperate to have sex with her, but I just know she's going to freak out and not want to. God, it's like trying to tame a wild mustang."

Ryan laughed, running a hand through her tangled hair. "That sounds like her. Look, it's true that Jordan's pretty complex, and she can drive you nuts, but I like her a lot. I don't want either of you to get hurt, so if this seems like too big of a problem to overcome, let her down gently—don't lead her on."

"Shit, I really like her. I don't want to stop." She sighed heavily and lay across the bed next to Ryan. "She's really sweet...and so fragile. It's like being with a kid in some ways, but in other ways she's really mature and sensitive. She's so good to talk to—better than anybody else I know."

"That doesn't sound so bad," Ryan said, running her fingers through Mia's hair to calm her down a little.

"No," she said as she rolled onto her side, "it's not bad. I just don't want to have this be a deal breaker."

"It doesn't have to be," Ryan said, the head rub relaxing her as much as it was Mia. "Take it slow and see how it goes. Talk about it before it gets to be too much of an issue."

"We did that tonight. She said she wants to have sex with me eventually, but she almost passed out when I touched her breast." She laughed wryly as she said, "I'm not used to a reaction quite that dramatic."

"Maybe you're really good," Ryan chuckled lazily.

"Well, yeah, I am, but still..." She snuggled closer, letting Ryan's soothing touch reach the back of her head.

"It'll be okay," Ryan said, already half-asleep. "Just be patient."

Where the heck is she? Jamie wondered lazily when she woke just an hour later. The bathroom was empty and Ryan's book bag was still lying next to her desk, so she obviously had not left for her trip to Los Angeles. A quick trip downstairs didn't shed any light on her whereabouts either, and she was about to give up when she saw Mia's door open. Poking her head inside she saw her partner lying crosswise on the bed, with Mia curled up against her side, her curly brown hair tumbling across Ryan's chest.

She shook her head, rolling her eyes as she walked over to wake the slumbering pair. *I've got to start getting up earlier. There's obviously a lot happening around here between midnight and six a.m.*

Ryan was more than a little groggy, but she tried her best to focus while she packed for the trip to Los Angeles. They had discussed travel arrangements several times, and each time Jamie tried and failed to find a way that she could accompany the team.

The issue was raised one final time as Ryan zipped up her gym bag. "I want to meet Bryant. It won't kill me to miss class."

"That's not what you said the last time we talked about this. You've had to miss so much for golf already, and you have to miss next week, too."

"I know," Jamie grumbled as she flopped down on the bed. "Does he ever come to San Francisco?"

"Mmm, he hasn't been back in a while. After Michael died he stayed in the city for about a year, but then he moved back to L.A. He said he just couldn't stand to watch his friends die one by one."

"Your Aunt Maeve talks about him so fondly," Jamie mused. "He sounds like a really special guy."

"He is. I want you to meet him at some point, because he's on my short list of sperm donors."

Now Jamie sat up and gave her full attention. "I didn't know that. I didn't know you even had a list."

"Oh, sure. I've been thinking about my list for years. Now that we're together it's kind of moot, but Bryant would be an excellent father."

"Moot? Why is your list moot?"

"Well, because we'll make our decisions together. Over time we'll come up with a list that appeals to both of us."

"That sounds right, but I really want to meet this guy. If he's good enough to be on your list, I can't imagine I won't like him. How do you think he'd feel about it?"

"Hard to say, but I don't think he wants to move back here. I've always thought that I wanted the donor to be involved with the baby, so his distance would be a problem."

"Do you still feel that you want the donor to be involved?"

"Mmm…I'm not sure. No matter how we do it, there are ramifications for the child. It's a very, very big decision."

"One that we have a lot of time to consider," Jamie reminded her. "I'm very disappointed that I won't be able to meet him though. You must really care for him."

"He's a very cool guy. Michael loved him very much, and he didn't give his heart away to just anyone." She smiled over at Jamie as she said wryly, "His body was another story."

"His diary told me all I needed to know. Don't remind me." She looked at Ryan with a puzzled, concerned look and asked, "What about AIDS? Is Bryant…okay?"

"Yeah, he says he is. He must have a hell of an immune system, or maybe they didn't have high-risk sex, but he's HIV-negative."

Jamie blinked and said, "I'm glad."

"Yeah, It would have killed Aunt Maeve to lose him, too." She shook her head to dispel the morose thought and said, "I know you want to come on the trip, but it's only two nights. We'll have Sunday afternoon together." Once she said it she realized that didn't sound like much time at all.

"Oh, shit! I forgot I had to leave for Portland on Sunday. Can't you come home on Saturday night?" She was nearly pleading, her whining tone rare enough to be cute.

"We never know how late our game will go, so it's a lot safer to make the reservation for the morning. Besides, it would be so late that it wouldn't be worth it."

"It's not worth it to sleep with me?" Jamie blinked her eyes beguilingly.

"It's worth anything to sleep with you. That's not how I meant it."

"How did you mean it?"

"Hey! Look at that big spider on the wall."

Jamie's head flew around to search for the dreaded arachnid. "Hey," she complained as she slowly turned back, "you're just messing with my mind, aren't you?"

"Me? Never." Ryan jumped onto the bed face first and squeezed her partner in a firm hug. "I love sleeping with you more than anything. I just don't want to put more pressure on myself this weekend. These are really big games for us, and I'm trying to relax as much as possible. If I have to worry about getting out of L.A. in time for the last plane, it'll just be one more thing on my mind."

"I'm sorry. I don't mean to add to your burden."

"You're never a burden. You make everything easier." She only had a few minutes, but every time she tried to get up, Jamie pulled her back down. She had her entire body wrapped around Ryan's back and seemed to be doing a pretty good job of holding her captive until Ryan said, "You've got to let me go. I can't be late."

"No," she pouted. "I'm keeping you."

"Actually it's the other way around." Ryan easily scooted to the end of the bed and stood up, with Jamie hanging off her back like a horizontal chimp.

"Put me down," she cried, tightening her hold to stop herself from falling to the ground.

"I thought you wanted to keep me." Ryan sat down and let her release her grip.

"Sometimes it's absolutely infuriating to have such a strong girlfriend. I can never win a fight."

"You win every one that doesn't involve brute strength," Ryan teased as she slapped her butt hard.

"Ooh, you are a brute." She rubbed her stinging seat. "But I kinda like it."

Ryan just rolled her eyes and hefted her bag onto her shoulder. She was dressed in her navy blue Cal warm-up suit and high-top basketball shoes and, from Jamie's perspective, looked good enough to eat. "I guess I'm driving myself?"

"I'm taking you, silly. Are we ready?"

"Well, one of us is stark naked."

"Yikes! Give me two minutes!"

Once the athletes were settled into the amazingly small coach-class seats on the airplane, Jordan leaned her chair back the full three inches and sighed heavily. "Well, I think I managed to scare Mia off last night." Her voice bore a weary, defeated tone.

"Odd. I wonder why she went out of her way this morning to tell me that she really likes you? She must be trying to mess with my mind." She narrowed her eyes in thought and tapped her chin.

Jordan gave her a wary glance and asked, "Did she really say that?"

"I wouldn't normally say anything, but I don't think Mia would mind. Yes, she said that she really likes you."

"What else?" Jordan asked, looking at Ryan with the beginnings of a bright smile.

"It wasn't a big deal. Just a comment."

Jordan shook her head, a grin poking out even though it looked like she was trying to stop it. "She must be a glutton for punishment. I don't think I'd have the patience to hang in there with me."

"Will you stop cutting yourself down? You act like you're a loser."

"I don't," she said defensively, a frown settling onto her face. "Well, not about most things. I just feel so out of my element about sex. It's like I missed my window of opportunity. You know what I mean?"

"I guess I do."

"Everybody else started having sex in high school, and they were all probably kinda weirded out about it, but they were in good company. You didn't stick out so much if you were inept, you know?"

Ryan chuckled deep in her throat. "I can't tell you how many times I got the dreaded tap on the shoulder. That 'don't bother—I'm never going to come, so you can stop now' tap." She shivered in memory as she added, "It's something everybody goes through."

"But I'm going through it at twenty-one. God, I acted like such a loser last night. Mia touched my breast, and I honestly almost passed out. If I was a guy, I would have come in my pants."

"I've done that," Ryan said playfully. "On MUNI."

Jordan slapped her on the leg and gave her a smile. "You don't have to try to make me feel better. I know the only way to get over my anxiety is to just jump in and do it. I'm just worried that Mia isn't the right one."

"Why? I'd think she'd be the perfect one. She has lots of experience, she's very playful and fun loving, she's amazingly easygoing, and she doesn't seem to be very clingy. Sounds perfect to me."

"I guess I worry because she's so gentle and understanding. I…I don't want to hurt her. Volleyball is my focus, and I have to stay on that path."

"Has she said that she wants a commitment from you?"

"No, no, of course not," Jordan said dismissively. "We haven't even really had a date. We just kiss."

"What's your agenda? I mean, you've done without for twenty-one years. Why start trying to get close to someone now?"

"It wasn't planned. I don't think I would have even gone to the bar that night with her if I'd known she was into women. I've gone out of my way to avoid the temptation—you know?"

"Yeah, I do know. That's not uncommon."

"I just feel like I'm on a train and I don't know how to get off. I really like Mia, and I really want to be close to her, but I'm as scared as I am turned on."

"Is it worth it to you? If you go further, I can guarantee that you'll feel even more out of control than you do now. I mean, it's possible that you'll fall in love with her."

Jordan dropped her head back against her seat, letting out a deep breath. "I don't feel like I have a choice. I let the genie out of the bottle this time. I don't think I can get it back in." Jordan stared at the ceiling for a few minutes and finally said, "I feel like I'm at the top of a steep hill, and that I've started to descend. I'm gathering speed, and I think I have to just let it roll."

Ryan patted her thigh, thinking, *I hope you don't crash, pal. Landings can be awfully rough.*

Jamie ran home after her morning classes finding Mia in her room watching cartoons and eating a big bowl of multi-colored cereal made for children. "Do you ever go to class?" Jamie asked.

"Yeah, when absolutely necessary. Why, what would you rather I do this afternoon?"

"How do you know I want you to do something?"

"You've just got the look. It's hard to describe, but you've got it now."

"How would you like to have a date with a hot woman tonight?" Jamie asked with a raised eyebrow.

"Hmm, let's see. How often do I turn down a hot date? Uhm…I'd say never." Her face grew pensive as she shook her head briskly and said, "Not this time, though. I uhm…I think I'll stick with Jordan and see how that plays out. Who am I turning down, anyway?"

Jamie smiled enigmatically and said, "Jordan."

"But she's in L.A. with tall, dark, and never home."

"I know. But if the hot dates won't come to us…"

"Cool! I'd love to go. But I'm almost overdrawn…"

"My treat. An all-expenses-paid weekend for the volleyball groupies."

"You have the best damned ideas, girlfriend."

Mia had a late afternoon class that she had to attend, so they couldn't leave until five. Breaking every speed law, they made it to the airport just in time for a seven o'clock flight. They carried their bags aboard and breathed a sigh of relief as the massive doors closed right behind them. "Ooh, first class," Mia purred, sliding into the roomy leather seat.

"Coach was sold out. Not that you're not worth first class treatment in any case."

They finally took off just as the game was scheduled to begin. "Are you sure I'm not going to scare poor Jordan to death?" Mia asked. "She hasn't even bought me a cup of coffee, and here I am trailing after her like a stalker."

"Nah, you're with me. It wouldn't be any fun to do this alone. Jordan will understand."

"She's quite the little mystery." Mia sighed. "I can't for the life of me figure out what's got her so freaked about sex. Do you think she was molested or something?"

"I have no idea. But speaking as someone who was also freaked out, I can assure you that you don't have to have been sexually traumatized to have issues."

"No, but it helps. She just acts so frightened, James. You didn't see the look in her eyes."

"Have you asked her?"

"No. She's really close-mouthed about her sexual experiences. That's part of the reason I think that something happened to her. I guess I have to ask."

"Yeah, you should know, especially if you're going to go forward with this. You don't want to do anything that freaks her out even worse."

Mia sighed and gave Jamie a small smile. "I feel protective of her. I want to make sure she doesn't get hurt. You know what I mean?"

"Sure. I feel that way about Ryan. It hurts me when she's hurt."

Mia chuckled softly. "I'm not that bad. I just feel protective of her. It's weird. I've never felt like that about anyone."

"Not anyone?"

"Uhn-uh. I was usually with guys who wanted to protect me. Not that I needed it."

"What about women? You've been with a few."

"Yeah, but except for Melissa in high school, they were all pretty experienced women who picked me up. There wasn't a whole lot of nurturing going on there, James. It was sex-centric," she said, chuckling.

"How does it feel to be in this role? Is it weird?"

The curly-haired woman gave Jamie a surprisingly shy smile and said, "I kinda love it."

"Really? Why?"

"I don't know. It just makes me feel tender and sweet towards her. It doesn't just feel like sex, James. It feels like…I don't know…like more than sex."

"More than sex can feel nice. I love having more than sex with Ryan." She had a dreamy, faraway look in her eyes, and Mia patted her softly on the leg.

"I'd love to have what you and Ryan have some day. You set a nice goal."

"The sex as sex part isn't bad either."

"From what I can hear from my room, you two are doing all right." she agreed, grinning impishly.

🐎

The flight was short, only fifty minutes, and they touched down right at 8:30. Jamie had called ahead to reserve a car, and they trotted over to the black-suited man who held aloft a cardboard sign that read 'Evans.' Jamie ran up to the driver and said, "We're the Evans party."

"UCLA?" he inquired, looking at his dispatch sheet.

"Yep. We need to get there on the double."

"Follow me," he said agreeably. Friday night traffic was slow, as usual, but the driver did his very best to get them there as quickly as possible. Luckily he knew where Pauley Pavilion was, and as he pulled up to the circular drive right behind the auditorium, Jamie hopped out to see if the game was still in progress. She ran up to the arena door and asked the attendant, "Volleyball match still going?"

"Yeah. It's the fifth game."

She ran back down the stairs and signaled Mia to hop out. After giving the driver a very generous tip, they grabbed their bags and ran back up the stairs to the gate. Since the match was almost over, the gentleman at the door allowed them to enter without tickets. Jamie flopped down on the bench as Mia said, "I'm going for nachos. Want anything?"

"Jeez, let me catch my breath." She looked up at the scoreboard and saw that the fifth game was knotted at ten, but her rumbling tummy got her attention and she handed her friend a twenty, saying, "Hold the jalapeños."

By the time Mia returned, Cal was up 14-13 and Jordan was set to serve. Mia had not yet attended an entire game, but she got so excited when she saw Jordan standing at the service line that she yelled out "Go Jordan!" at near ear-piercing volume. The entire team looked up into the stands, and both Ryan and Jordan's mouths dropped open when they saw their appreciative audience. Jamie, of course, was blushing to the roots of her hair, but she quickly got over her embarrassment when Jordan got down to business and aced her serve for the win.

Mia hopped up and screamed again and as the players congratulated each other, Ryan made eye contact one more time, her wink punctuated by a blown kiss that got Jamie an elbow in the ribs. "Ooh, she loves you."

"Eat your nachos," Jamie chided as she grinned and blew one right back.

The team was streaming out of the locker room much sooner than Jamie thought possible. When Ryan and Jordan came out it was obvious why. "You didn't take showers?"

"Unh-uh," Ryan said as she gave her lover a fond kiss. "We wanted to see our groupies."

Mia was standing next to Jamie, looking a little unsettled and unsure of herself as Jordan fussed nervously with her gym bag. She was finally set, and she gave Mia a wide smile, saying, "It was a great surprise to see you in the stands. I think it helped me concentrate."

Mia beamed up at her, maintaining a respectful distance. "Maybe I'll be your good-luck charm."

"Do you have a car?" Ryan asked.

"No." Jamie held up her carry-on as she added, "We took a limo, but I let him go. That was stupid, wasn't it?"

"No. We can take the bus with the team if you want to go to the hotel."

"I don't think this is the easiest place to get a cab, so I guess we'll have to."

They hopped on the bus and greeted all of the other players. No one knew Mia, but that didn't stop her from saying, "Good game," to everyone that looked in her direction.

The bus eventually turned onto the 405 freeway and Jamie looked up to ask, "Where are we going, anyway?"

"Down to USC. Our hotel is within walking distance of campus."

"But there's nothing to do down there," Jamie complained.

Ryan cocked her head and asked, "Why do you think they put

us there?"

"Ooh…good point. Coach is pretty smart, isn't he?"

When they pulled up to the hotel, the student manager hopped off and went to the front desk to sign them in. Jamie got in line behind her and asked the clerk for two rooms, trying to secure one for Mia if Jordan didn't want to sleep with her.

"Sorry, Ma'am, we're booked solid."

"You are?" she gaped, never having considered that possibility.

"Yes, Ma'am. There's a big convention in town and everything is sold out. You'll have to go out to the West Side to find a room—if there are any."

Walking over to her companions she said, "I think I screwed up again. They don't have any more rooms."

"We can get a cab and go to another hotel," Ryan offered.

"He says everything around here is booked. Big convention in town."

"Let me call my dad," Jordan offered. "He's got a lot of space. We'd have to rent a car, but we could probably do that here."

"It won't kill us to all sleep together," Ryan said. "I'm sure we'll have two queen beds. I just want a snack and sleep anyway."

"Mmm…I think it would be nice if we could have separate rooms," Mia said, shooting a look at Jordan, who looked very edgy.

Jordan gave her a grateful glance and took Jamie's proffered cell phone. She had to pull her organizer out of her bag to find her father's number, but she found what she was looking for and dialed while repeating the number quietly.

Picking up after a few rings, Jorgen Ericsson answered, "Hello?"

"Hi, Dad, it's Jordan."

"Well, hello, Jordan, how are things?"

"Good. Look, Dad, we're in town for the game, and we need a place to crash. Could you put us up?"

"Game?" he asked. "The UCLA/USC games aren't this weekend, are they?"

"Yeah, Dad. We beat UCLA tonight."

"Damn, I wanted to come to that game. Why didn't you remind me? I specifically told you…"

She cleared her throat and said, "I did. I left a message with your secretary a month ago, and I called to remind her last week. She said she'd put it on your calendar."

It was obvious that he was checking his calendar at that moment as she heard pages flipping and his muted mumbling. "I swear that she didn't…oh…well, I guess I blew this one, didn't I?"

"It's okay." Her voice was soft and clearly reflected hurt feelings.

"No, I feel terrible, Jordan. I swore I'd get to one of your games, and I didn't get it done."

"You could come to the 'SC game tomorrow," she suggested with a timidly hopeful expression. Ryan's heart nearly broke when she saw the look on her friend's face, then heard her say, "No, don't worry about it. It's not a problem. You saw me play a few times in high school. It's the same game." Ryan couldn't bear to hear any more, so she went over to some chairs in the lobby and pulled Jamie with her.

"Well, Jordan," her father said, "I'm happy to have you come by tomorrow. Candy and I are leaving for Europe in the morning, so you can have the place to yourselves. How's that?"

Her heart fell, but she bit her lip and accepted. "That's great, Dad. Can you leave a key under the mat?"

"Oh, no need. I have a new security system. Just key in Candy's birthday."

"I don't know Candy's birthday, Dad."

"It's 11-15-78. Make sure you mark that down, honey."

"I will. Thanks for the use of your house."

"Anytime. That's what fathers are for."

Jordan hung up and gave Mia a sad smile. "That was the easy one. Now I'll try my mother."

"No, you really don't have to. We can just stay here."

"No, it's okay. It can't hurt to ask. She's got a five-bedroom house."

Now Mia couldn't bear to watch. Jordan had just revealed more about her family than Mia could stand to think about, and she didn't have the heart to listen to this conversation. She gave her a gentle hug and walked over to join her friends on the chairs. "God. Remind me to call my parents when I get home and thank them for caring about me."

Ryan shook her head and asked, "Who's she calling now?"

"Her mom. Her dad said we could come tomorrow, but not

tonight."

They all watched her out of the corners of their eyes. Jordan looked very pained, but she didn't say much, merely nodding and occasionally sighing audibly. Letting out an exasperated groan, she finally came over to the group and flopped down in a chair, still listening. Occasionally she would say "uh-huh," but that was all until she said, "I know how hard it is to live on so little, Mom. Yes, I understand that he lives a very nice life, but..."

She closed her eyes and nodded for another few minutes, and when she could get another word in she said, "I've got to go. I'm on a cell phone and minutes are expensive." She nodded again and said, "It's okay. It's really not important that you come to the game tomorrow. I'll see you the next time I'm down here. No, really, I wouldn't want you to miss your aromatherapy appointment. I'm sure they're very hard to get." After another long silence she said, "I've really got to go." Then, "Uhm, I'm not sure. I think I have to stay in Berkeley for Thanksgiving. We have a game the next day." Another pause, then, "Yeah, probably Christmas, too. Yeah, this is my last year. Yeah. Time does go fast." She pursed her lips tightly together and blinked slowly as she said, "I love you too, Mom. Bye."

Clicking the off button she handed the phone back to Jamie with a terse, "No go."

Mia stood and twitched her head towards an empty area of the lobby. "Can I talk to you?" she asked.

Jordan got to her feet and followed Mia to a pair of chairs. Sitting down, Mia looked over at her friend and felt her heart ache when she saw the sadness that had settled in her blue eyes. She looked at her with compassion and asked, "What would you like to do? I would never have come if I knew that we'd be forced into sharing a room. I know you're not ready to sleep together yet, and if you're uncomfortable we'll get on the phone and find a room, even if we have to go to Orange County."

"I'm exhausted," she said. "I'm not up to the stress of running all over town trying to find a place. We'd have to rent a car, and Coach would probably not be real happy about us getting stuck somewhere. If you don't mind sleeping with me, I'd rather just stay here."

"I'd love to sleep with you. I bet you're really cuddly," she teased, giving her a tender smile.

Jordan looked at her for a moment and shook her head as she gave her a grateful grin and agreed. "Let's stay here."

When the pair informed Jamie and Ryan of their decision, they accepted it placidly. Jamie knew that she could get on the phone and find a hotel somewhere that would take them, but she didn't want to make a big deal out of the issue since Jordan obviously felt bad enough already. "I'm happy to stay anywhere as long as I get to sleep with my tiger."

That did more to perk Jordan up than all the reassurances they could jointly muster. "Tiger?" she asked with a luminous grin.

"Don't start," Ryan moaned. "Don't even start."

The room service menu was sadly lacking, but Ryan eventually settled for cereal and toast. The others decided to order a pizza, and as they waited for delivery Jordan said, "I really need a shower. Okay if I go?"

"Sure. I'll wait until you're finished," Ryan said.

"If you're a good girl, I'll wash behind your ears," Jamie teased.

"I'm a very good girl," Ryan smiled, "and you're a very good girl for coming all this way just to be with us."

Jamie had lived with Ryan long enough to know that one little two-ounce box of cereal would not hold her, so she had also ordered a fruit salad. Ryan polished off everything but wasn't tempted by the pizza that looked like little more than cardboard with ketchup and processed cheese-food slathered onto it.

Jamie was not really used to the vagaries of economy-class travel, and she had to admit that the pizza was one of the worst things she had ever had in her mouth—topping by a hair that goat's head stew she had been served in Sierra Leone.

When Jordan exited the bathroom, Ryan went in to run the water for a bath. She was staring at the complimentary lilac-scented bubble bath when Jamie came in.

"No, no, no," Jamie said, taking the bottle from her hand "I've got something that you'll like much better." She returned a minute later with a new bottle of shower gel called Spring Rain. "This has almost no scent. It's hypo-allergenic, too."

Ryan shrugged and squirted a dollop into the running water, pleased that it created only a gentle lather. "Nice," she smiled at Jamie as the faint scent wafted up.

"I thought we'd find a place with a nice, big tub…maybe a Jacuzzi," Jamie said, wistfully. "This wasn't what I had in mind." She snuggled up against Ryan who gave her a gentle hug.

Ryan ran her fingers through soft blonde locks. "It's a hell of a lot better than I was expecting. I thought I'd have old Jordan crawling in with me, hogging the bed. You are a decided improvement."

Jamie hadn't expected to need any pajamas, so she was wearing just her panties and one of Ryan's big T-shirts. "I just couldn't stand the thought of you down here all weekend when I knew I could be with you. Are you glad we came?"

"Couldn't you see my smile when I looked up and saw you? The highlight of every day is when I get to lie in bed with your warm body next to mine. It doesn't matter how big the bed is or who's in the room with us. It only matters that we're together." She dipped her head and placed a few lazy kisses around Jamie's tender lips, then slowly made contact with her target. As usual, Jamie was more than responsive, and the meandering kisses slowly became more focused and intense. "Maybe we'd better cool it. I don't think this is the ideal place to make love."

Jamie sighed and started unzipping Ryan's warm-up jacket. She undressed her quickly, not taking her time as she usually did. Ryan climbed into the warm tub and let out a soft groan. "Ooh, this feels nice. I don't know why I avoided tubs for all of these years. I'm a convert."

"Have we ever bathed together?" Jamie asked, cocking her head as she tried to remember.

"Just showers. I don't think we've been in the tub together. Are we going to correct that omission tonight?" Jamie was stripping out of her T-shirt, giving a fairly clear answer.

"Why the heck not? We won't get to do anything else fun tonight."

She surveyed the standard-sized tub, which was already full of her long, lean lover. "I think I'll get in behind you. I don't want the faucet in my back."

"Why not sit on my lap?"

Surveying the geometry, Jamie shook her head. "No, that won't work. If I'm in back, you can keep your knees bent. You're too long for me to sit on your legs if they're extended. I think this is the only way."

"Let's give it a try," Ryan agreed, scooting forward to allow her partner as much room as possible. Jamie climbed in and slowly lowered herself. The only way Ryan could lean back was if Jamie's legs were wrapped around her, draping over her flexed legs. It was an intricate puzzle, but it proved to be comfortable. Ryan leaned back and let out another sigh when Jamie started to cup her hands full of the warm water and splash it over Ryan's chest. "Once again, your ideas are top-notch, Jamers. I'm gonna lie here and soak every bit of stress out of my poor tired body."

Jordan and Mia were sitting on the small upholstered chairs that flanked the round table near the television. The chairs were not particularly comfortable, but Mia was afraid to make the move to the bed.

"Are you really okay with me being here? I swear I wouldn't have come if I'd known we'd have to share a bed. I know that's more than you're ready for."

"I'm glad you're here. I hated to leave after last night. I hated the thought of not being able to talk to you for three days." She batted her cool blue eyes at Mia and said, "I'm really sorry for running out on you. That was so lame."

"Hey," Mia soothed, "don't worry about it. It didn't bother me."

"Come on, how could it not?"

Mia smiled and leaned forward to reach out to grasp Jordan's hand. "Let's just call it payback for one of the times I left a guy in a car with blue balls. God, I would get guys so turned on and then decide that I didn't want to go any farther. They must have been cursing my name."

Jordan looked at her seriously, a question in her eyes then forming on her lips. "Is that what happened to you last night? Were you really turned on?"

Mia tapped at Jordan's forehead with her fingertip. "Hello? Earth to Jordan. Of course I was turned on. Weren't you?"

"Well, yeah, I just thought it wouldn't be as big a deal for you. You've done so much more."

Mia tossed her feet up onto the bed and gazed at Jordan for a full minute. Finally, she asked the question that had been bugging her. "Can I ask you a really, really personal question?"

"Uhm, sure…I think."

"Have you been sexually molested?" Her voice was full of empathy, but she didn't want to make it sound like Jordan being abused was the most horrible thing in the world, so she tried to sound more casual than she felt.

Jordan got up from her chair and crossed over to Mia's, folding her long legs to sit on the floor. She looked up and said, "No. No, I haven't." Her head dropped and she stared at the floor for a few seconds before she asked, "I act like I have been, don't I?"

Mia began to stroke the silky blonde hair. "Yeah, you do. You act really frightened. What's frightened you so much?"

The tall woman rubbed at her eyes with both fists, looking very frustrated. "It's…it's not really fear." She shook her head a bit as she corrected herself, "Well, that's not true. In a way, it is fear, but not fear of sex."

"Go on," Mia urged, not having gained any insight thus far.

"I've had a decent number of guys touch me, and it's never been a big deal."

"Did you go out with guys in high school?"

Jordan's head nodded quickly. "Yeah. Sure. I went out with guys. I went to prom. All of that stuff."

"And you've been kinda serious with a couple of guys at Cal?"

"Yeah. One guy last year and another when I was a sophomore. I've never had actual sex…like intercourse…with a guy, but I've done everything else."

"Did you like it?" Mia asked, a little surprised that Jordan had gone as far as she claimed, given her response to having her breast touched.

"Yeah," she shrugged. "It was good. Fine. But it wasn't the earth-changing think I thought it should be. I kept trying to fool around with different guys, thinking maybe they were the problem."

"But they weren't, huh?" Mia asked quietly.

"No. It wasn't them. It felt okay, but not great, you know? Nothing like it felt when those women kissed me. That was...that was great."

"So, you do have sexual desire? Do you uhm..." she looked down pointedly, letting her gaze linger on the area between Jordan's legs.

Jordan flushed as she nodded. "Yeah, I know myself pretty well. I've known myself an awful lot...lately." She shrugged, adding, "It's those dreams I keep having."

"Tell me about your dreams," Mia urged, still running her fingers through Jordan's hair.

"Sometimes they're not actual dreams. Sometimes they're daydreams. I lie in bed and think about how it feels when you kiss me, and before I know it, I'm...knowing myself," she said, an adorably embarrassed expression on her face.

"Tell me how it feels when I kiss you," Mia asked, leaning over to place a gentle kiss on Jordan's exposed neck.

Turning around and entwining her fingers through Mia's hair, Jordan pulled her down and placed a tender kiss on her lips. Her mouth was curled into a sly grin as she released Mia and whispered, "It's better than my dreams. It's magic." She locked eyes with Mia and said, "It's not the sex that frightens me. It's how I feel inside. It feels so powerful, like I can't control it." She made eye contact and added, "Control means a lot to me."

Continuing to stroke Jordan's hair, Mia murmured, "I understand. I really do. Sometimes the drive feels like it's more than you can handle." Smiling down at the lovely woman who was now leaning against her leg, Mia promised, "The good news is that now you have me to talk to when it feels like too much."

"Thanks," Jordan whispered, slowly rubbing her head against Mia's warmth. "That helps. A lot."

The bath buddies could hear the muted ringing of a phone, but neither paid much attention until Mia knocked and said, "Ryan, Bryant's calling on your cell."

"Do you mind bringing it in?" Ryan asked. "It'll take us an hour to get out of here."

Mia's curly head popped in, and she giggled as she took in the scene. "Nice position," she said to Jamie, then handed Ryan the phone.

"It's the only way it works, with her long legs," Jamie whispered, surprisingly calm about Mia seeing them in such an intimate clutch.

Ryan was chatting with Bryant, obviously making arrangements for their meeting. "Hey, Jamie?" she said as she hit the mute button. "Would you like to have Bryant meet you at the game tomorrow?"

"Sure. That'd be fun. I'll save him a seat."

Ryan finished her conversation, then handed the phone back to Mia. "Thanks," she said.

"No problem. I hope to be able to use your solution to the 'bathing with a long-legged lover' dilemma one day."

"Hey, would you mind letting some water out and adding a little more hot?" Ryan asked. "If I lean forward that much it will upset our balance."

Mia did so, looking up when Jordan popped her head in. "Come on in," Ryan said, deciding it was too late to be modest now. "Wanna join us?"

"Now that would be interesting," Jordan smirked. "You two don't have room for a bar of soap in there, much less me."

"You doing all right?" Ryan asked Jordan.

"Yeah. Fine. What's the agenda for the rest of the weekend?"

"Have a seat," Jamie offered magnanimously.

Ryan turned as much as she could and shared a smile with her partner, pleased that she seemed so much more comfortable with her body than she used to be.

Jordan sat on the floor, scooting up against the wall. Mia sat in front of her until Jordan tapped her on the shoulder and indicated that she could lean back. Mia did, sighing with pleasure as she felt the long arms and legs wrap around her body. "Ooh, Jamie, you got the raw end of the deal," she groaned. "These big girls are very nice pillows."

"Maybe," Jamie agreed, "but I've got a great view." She held her wet hand up and dripped a few drops onto Ryan's breasts, immediately causing the nipples to firm up.

"Hey," Ryan said, covering her breasts with her hands. "We don't have to show everybody my rapid response time, do we?"

"Oh, my little prude," Jamie teased, kissing Ryan's ear.

"Yeah, you're hiding back there, tough girl. I'm the only one on display here," Ryan reminded her.

"Right," Jamie scoffed. "If you had a nickel for every woman who saw you naked, you'd have more money than I do."

Ryan started to tell her she was wrong, but did a quick check of the math first, just to be accurate.

"So, what's up for tomorrow?" Jordan asked. "We've got our pre-game meal at two, a walk-through at three, and then we have to be there at 5:30 for the game, so our afternoon is shot. What do you two want to do?"

Jamie said, "We'll go find a rental car, maybe go to one of the museums down here. Don't worry about us. We'll be there to pick you up after the game, and we can go to your dad's house then, okay?"

"Sounds good," Jordan agreed. "He lives about halfway up Malibu. It's about an hour's drive from here."

"You sure that's what you want?" Mia asked.

"Yeah. It's a nice place and we can relax there. Seems like a shame to waste a day at the beach, doesn't it?"

"I'm up for it," Ryan agreed. "Will you call and see if we can change our tickets, Jordan?"

"Okay. Last flight back okay with everyone?"

Jamie shook her head and said, "Don't include me. I've got to fly to Portland Sunday evening. I've already made my arrangements."

"Two-sport family," Jordan said, shaking her head. "Bummer."

After another refill of the hot water, Jordan and Mia left the bathroom, with Jamie calling after them, "Hey, why don't you guys turn on the radio or the TV...loud."

"Gee, why would we want to do that?" Mia asked, intentionally obtuse.

Jordan yanked her out of the room, and seconds later the sounds of MTV reached the bathroom. "Good girl," Jamie called out, pleased to have her commands obeyed.

"Got something in mind?" Ryan asked, her deep voice echoing off the walls.

"You're starting to prune," Jamie said, holding up one of Ryan's hands for inspection, ignoring her partner's question.

"It's not permanent. I'm not in a rush to get out."

"This is nice, isn't it?" Jamie dipped her head to capture a damp earlobe. "I like being able to cuddle you like this."

"I like being cuddled this way. It's nice. Makes me feel small. I don't feel that way often."

"Why don't you sit up just a bit, and let me wash your back."

"Okay," Ryan sighed, not in the mood to argue about anything at the moment.

As she leaned forward, Jamie spent a moment just running the tips of her index fingers over the firm muscles in front of her. She didn't see Ryan from this position very often, and she found that she was crazy for the view. Ryan's upper body was draped over her bent legs, her broad back sweeping up in a neat V from her trim waist. Her skin was perfectly smooth, not one visible imperfection marring the view.

"God, I love your back," Jamie sighed, cupping her hands and dipping them into the water. She let the water trail down the sculpted surface, watching as it made dozens of independent tributaries, skimming off in many directions at once.

"Thank you," Ryan murmured. "We aim to please."

"Oh, you please, all right. If I was any more pleased, I'd burst."

Ryan chuckled mildly, her back muscles moving from the effort.

"Lean back now," Jamie said as Ryan detected the nice, light scent of the gel.

She leaned back and smiled as she felt a pair of soapy breasts start to glide against her back. "Like the soap delivery system?" Jamie asked, her taut nipples skimming across the slick surface.

"Mmm-hmm. Feels great."

Jamie lathered up her hands and started to work on Ryan's

breasts.

"You know," Ryan murmured, "I'm very grateful for the new appreciation you've given me for my breasts."

"Pardon?" Jamie's hands stilled even though she kept them right where they were, gently cupping the firm flesh.

Ryan laughed and repeated herself. "I didn't get that much pleasure from them before. I liked 'em, and I liked having them touched, but they weren't a prime pleasure zone for me. You've changed that."

"I have?"

"You get such pleasure out of touching me," Ryan said, reaching up to place her hands over Jamie's and squeeze gently. "Your pleasure's contagious."

"Really?"

"Really. I see how your eyes sparkle when you touch me, and it makes me throb." Ryan started to stroke her partner from her elbows to her hands, musing, "Sometimes I'll be lying there, and you'll have one of my breasts in your mouth and your hand on the other one, and you look so indescribably content that I can feel my pulse pick up. Every once in a while you'll look up at me, and you honestly look like a kid caught with her hands in the cookie jar." She chuckled softly and said, "It's so adorable. It makes me see the little kid that hides just under your typically mature self. I love that little kid."

Jamie laughed, the sound floating past Ryan's ear and sending tingles down her body. "Sometimes I feel like I've been caught doing something naughty. Not so much if I'm just concentrating— only if you look at me while I'm doing it. I get so much pleasure out of touching you. I guess it feels like it must be kinda wrong."

"Does that hurt your enjoyment?"

"No, actually it enhances it a little. You've taught me how to enjoy guilty pleasures. That's been your gift to me."

"Those are pretty good gifts," Ryan decided, giving Jamie's hands another squeeze. "The gifts that keep on giving."

"Uh-huh, and I'm gonna give generously tonight. Fasten your seat belt." Her breath was hot where it caressed Ryan's skin, and the taller woman could feel her partner's heartbeat begin to thrum a little more rapidly against her back.

Jamie's hands began to knead Ryan's breasts, letting the firm tissue slide through her hands as the gel created millions of tiny bubbles. Ryan could feel her partner's hips begin to twitch, her body expressing its needs. Soon the sensations overtook Ryan, and she began to moan softly, in time to the stroking. "Ooh, this feels too good," she gasped. The delicious sensation of her partner's breasts rubbing against her back as her own were played with was making her feel out of control, and she tried to scale back so their friends didn't hear them.

"Let it feel good, baby. Don't fight it." Jamie had scooted down as low as she could in order to be able to nibble on Ryan's neck, and she could feel her partner's hips start to sway under the warm water.

"We can't, honey," she moaned, frustrated. "This'll never work."

"Sure it will," Jamie soothed, assuming that she was referring to being overheard. "Just relax and enjoy my touch."

Ryan's head started to shake but Jamie's hand slid under the water, distracting her thoroughly as it parted her flesh and began to tease her most sensitive place. "Unh," Ryan grunted as the gentle fingers began to stroke her. "No, really," she moaned, pulling Jamie's hand away. "It doesn't feel good under water."

"What? Why?"

"Washes away the lubrication," Ryan insisted. "Water just doesn't work. Trust me. I've tried many times."

Jamie's mind raced, unwilling to halt the intimate contact. "Maybe you just haven't been using the right lubrication."

"I'm game for whatever you've got cookin'. You've rarely had a bad idea."

"I'm not going to let a little water stop me from loving you. It'll take a bigger obstacle than that."

Jamie took the shower gel and squirted it from Ryan's neck down to mid-thigh—as far as she could reach. Wetting her hands, she started to massage every part of Ryan's body, her hands gliding over soft flesh made softer still by the slick gel.

"Ooh, your muscles feel all tense," Jamie murmured. "You worked hard tonight, didn't you?"

"Yeah, I guess I did. This feels so good. I feel pampered and cared for."

"You are cared for," Jamie assured her. "I care for every cell in your luscious body. You're my life."

"God, it's such a short time to feel so completely and thoroughly known. I feel like you know me nearly as well as I know myself."

Jamie gently corrected her. "No, that's not true. I've got a long way to go before I know you as well as I want to. Luckily, we've got years to explore each other."

"Our whole lives," Ryan said, smiling as she watched Jamie's hands probe each of her stiff muscles. "Ooh, that's a sore one," she said when the searching hands began to work on a muscle high up on her inner thigh. "Wow…feels great." Ryan moaned as Jamie's fingers probed a little higher, trying to keep her sounds of pleasure to a minimum.

"Relax, they can't hear us. Don't give them another thought. They're probably wrestling around on the bed already."

"Good point," Ryan gasped, surprised by a very impudent touch. She finally tossed one long leg over the side of the tub to allow for better access.

Jamie's fingers slid between her legs and started a very erotic massage of her most hidden flesh. A lavish application of the shower gel had Ryan moaning in tandem with the pressure, and she let her head drop back against her partner's shoulder. There was something extremely sensual about being enveloped in Jamie's warm, wet embrace while determined fingers stroked her body into a frenzy. The slick touch was deliciously maddening, and she knew she needed some release as soon as possible. "Come inside," she whispered. "Let me feel you come inside me. Ooh," she moaned as her partner's other hand slipped under a muscular thigh to satisfy her request. Her hips began to pump, sloshing some of the water up the sides of the tub. "Ahh…ahh…ahh. Yes!" she cried as Jamie gently pushed her over the edge. Jamie delighting as goose bumps broke out from the tip of Ryan's toes to the top of her head. She shivered violently, but Jamie was sure it wasn't from the cold.

"Relax, relax, just lie back against me. I've got you," Jamie murmured, rocking Ryan in her arms until the last bits of stress left her muscles.

"Ooh," Ryan groaned. "That was such a good idea." She was still shaking, but she managed to sit up and turn the hot water on full-force. Settling back against Jamie's chest again, she asked, "How do you always know what I need, even when I don't?"

"I love you, silly. I know you intimately."

"That's true. Guess what I want now?" she asked lazily.

"I know the answer to that too, but you're not going to sleep in here."

The pair emerged from the bath nearly a half-hour later, to the amused gazes of their roommates. "Night," Ryan mumbled, falling into bed with a thud.

"G'night," Jordan said, and Mia echoed her.

"Good night, you two," Jamie said, unable to suppress a big yawn. "Stay up as long as you like. It won't bother us."

Mia had an impish look on her face, and as Jamie got under the covers she said, "I would remind you to say your prayers, but you apparently did that already."

"Huh?" Jamie mumbled sleepily, snuggling up against her lover.

"Why else have you been crying, 'Oh, God, Oh, God, Oh, sweet Jesus'?" Mia asked innocently.

The extra pillow from their bed was hurled so quickly that Mia didn't get a chance to duck. Luckily, Jordan's quick reflexes saved the day, preventing full-scale warfare from erupting between the feisty roommates.

Both Jordan and Mia were weary of sitting on the uncomfortable chairs, but there was only one other option. Mia finally brought up the topic. "I'm gonna go put on something to sleep in, okay?"

"Sure. Good idea," Jordan said, looking fairly composed.

Mia decided to put on a pair of sweat pants, but since it was warm she decided on just a T-shirt as a top. Jordan shot a quick look at her outfit, then went into the bath and emerged in a matching ensemble. Mia climbed in first, trying to stay fairly close to the edge to give Jordan some physical and emotional space. They lay facing each other, speaking very softly so as not to wake Ryan; Mia had explained to Jordan that it would take more than soft speech to wake Jamie.

"Are you sure that you can put up with me while I get comfortable with this? I know this must seem like kindergarten to you."

"Hey, don't put yourself down like that," Mia chided. "Yes, we're going slower than I'm used to, but that's not a bad thing. Having to wait for something you want can be rewarding. So I've heard." Brushing her fingers along Jordan's cheek she said, "I think it's gonna be worth the wait. You had me throbbing *so* hard last night. You're quite the little kisser, you know," she said, placing several soft ones on Jordan's lips, just to remind her of her talents. "And your breasts are really a turn-on for me. Every time we're together, I want to get my hands on them and give them a good squeeze."

Jordan batted her big blue eyes at Mia and whispered, "Wanna squeeze 'em now? If I faint, I'm already lying down."

Mia considered the offer, letting her gaze slowly wander down the long body. When her eyes lifted, Jordan was staring at her intently, giving her a look full of hope and desire. "I don't want our roomies to hear us," she whispered, "but that's not the kind of offer I'm willing to pass up." She smiled broadly, noticing Jordan's body start to grow tense as she waited for the touch.

"Have you dreamed about me touching you this way?" she asked as her hand reached out to cup the weight of Jordan's breast.

"Uh-huh." Jordan's voice was strained with tension, but her breathing was normal and her heart wasn't beating wildly like it had been the night before. "Even before you touched them. I just knew how your hands would feel," she murmured, with her eyes closed to allow her body to feel the touch without visual interference. "I was right."

Mia wasn't trying to excite the other woman so much as get her used to the sensation. She kept her touch light and delicate, just holding the flesh in her hand and hefting it a little to give her some gentle stimulation. Biting back a smile she remembered the first boy who had ever touched her breasts—feeling at the time like he was trying to knead suppleness into a stiff piece of clay. She was determined that Jordan would never feel like a collection of body parts when she touched her, and she gentled her touch even more, just running the tips of her fingers across the flesh through the T-shirt.

The experiment was proving to be a success, with Jordan actually relaxing into her caress. She rolled onto her back and sighed as Mia's hand moved from one breast to the other, maintaining her relaxed pace and tender touch.

"Good God, this feels nice," Jordan moaned as Mia's blunt nails scraped across a puckered nipple. She reached up and pressed the hand flat against her, increasing the pressure substantially as her breath caught in her throat. Mia could feel Jordan's heart begin to beat wildly, and she regretfully pulled her hand away from Jordan's firm grasp.

"We'd better stop," she whispered, finding that her own voice was a little breathy. "I don't want to lose control tonight."

"It just sounded like a good idea at the time," Jordan giggled.

Her smile slowly faded as Mia looked longingly at the swells of flesh. "Can I have a rain check? They really look scrumptious, and there are all sorts of things I'd like to do to them."

"Yeah, yeah. I'd really like to touch yours one of these days, too." She paused a beat and added shyly, "I've dreamt about them, too."

Mia clasped her hands behind Jordan's neck and snuggled close, letting their breasts rub against each other through the soft, thin fabric of their T-shirts. "Anytime your little heart desires, Jordan. They're looking forward to it."

Jordan gave her such an adorably shy smile that Mia had to stop the urge to pinch her cheeks, realizing that might offend her. Their faces were just inches apart, and as much as Mia was enjoying the view, she could see the fatigue on her friend's face. "You really look beat. Wanna break tradition and actually go to sleep?"

"Yeah," Jordan smiled, fighting a yawn. "Travel wears me out. I really should get some rest." She lifted her hand and delicately traced Mia's features, as if trying to memorize them. "I don't know if I can sleep with you so close to me," she whispered. "I've never slept with anyone before."

"No one?" Mia asked softly, rubbing her back.

"Just Ryan," Jordan chuckled to Mia's wide-eyed look. "I had a horrible nightmare when we were at volleyball camp, and she held me to put me to sleep. It didn't feel like this, though." Jordan nuzzled her face into Mia's neck and said, "I've never slept with anyone that I wanted to have sex with. I never trusted anyone enough." Her head lifted as her clear blue eyes locked on Mia's. "I trust you."

"I'm glad," Mia sighed. "I promise that I'll never try to push you too far. I'll be gentle with you." She brought her hand to Jordan's face and stroked it tenderly. "You're very precious, you know."

Jordan's head shook slightly when she said, "I've never felt precious before. The people I've been close to have made me feel like they wanted me for my body or for their own pleasure. It didn't feel like I mattered—you know?"

"You do matter," Mia whispered. "Very much."

"I dated a guy last year that I almost slept with. I liked him, and he seemed to like me." She chuckled a little as she recalled, "He was taller than I am, and blonde. He used to say that we had to procreate to keep tall, blue-eyed blondes on the planet."

Mia laughed as well and commented, "There aren't a lot of your species around. He might have been on to something."

"There are plenty of blondes in Sweden," she scoffed. "That didn't seem like the best reason in the world to be in a relationship with someone."

"So, what happened between you two? Why'd you break up?"

"It was a fight we had over sleeping together. Not having sex—sleeping together." She sighed and said, "Three separate times I told him he could stay over, and each time I got up and slept on the couch. I just couldn't relax when he was in my bed." Shaking her head, she rolled her eyes and said, "I think he was a little insulted. He'd get up in the morning and find my legs hanging over the end of the couch, my head jammed against the wooden arm. Telling him that I was more comfortable in that ridiculous position really pissed him off."

"Ouch," Mia grimaced. "That would sting."

"Yeah. I don't blame him at all. I just couldn't do it."

"Well, I hope you can relax tonight, but if not, please wake me up and tell me. I'll really be upset if I find you on the floor in the morning."

"Deal," Jordan agreed. "We can flip a coin for the bed if I can't sleep."

"No need. I'll fit in the bathtub just fine." Mia smiled. "One advantage of being short." She tightened her hold on the long body and placed a few soft, tender kisses on Jordan's lips. "Ready for sleep now?"

"Uhm…yeah. How should we do this?"

"Well, how do you normally sleep? Back, side, stomach?"

Jordan thought for a moment. "I usually start off on my right side. All bets are off after that, though. I thrash around a lot—fair warning."

"I sleep on my side, too, and I don't thrash around. This should work fine. Turn around now, and lie like you usually do."

Jordan started to, but turned back and gave Mia a few very gentle, emotional kisses. "You've been great. I really appreciate how patient you've been."

Jordan turned over and tried to get comfortable, digging her shoulder into the overly-firm mattress. Mia waited until she was settled, then snuggled up close behind her, placing her hand lightly upon Jordan's waist. "How's that?" she asked.

"Divine," the warm voice replied. "Just divine." She twitched her hips, pushing against Mia's lap. "You feel so good pressed against me like this."

"I love to sleep with a partner. Aside from sex, being in bed with someone is a wonderful sensation."

"If it's someone you really like," Jordan corrected her.

"Yeah," Mia said fondly, pushing the hair from Jordan's neck and giving her a kiss there. "It's much nicer with someone you really like."

She slipped her arm around the trim waist, snuggling tighter against Jordan's body. In a matter of seconds the tension began to leave the tall woman's muscles, and a moment later she collapsed against Mia, sound asleep. "Sleep tight, sweetheart," Mia whispered, knowing that her words would not be heard.

Chapter Six

For some reason, Jamie woke early and found that she couldn't get back to sleep. She was tired of lying in bed, so despite Ryan's incoherent protest, she got up and tugged on her sweats.

A soft voice whispered, "You getting up?"

Jamie snuck over to the other bed and leaned close to Jordan. "Yeah. I can't sleep." Mia was tucked up close to the taller woman's back, and Jordan gently disentangled herself from the warm embrace and stood, stretching a little.

"Wanna go scrounge up some breakfast?"

"Good idea. I'm absolutely famished."

Jordan smiled and said, "Maybe that's why you can't sleep. Whoever is responsible for that pizza should be arrested."

Jamie shuddered as she recalled the dreadful concoction. "You're probably right. My stomach's been rumbling for hours."

"Hey, maybe that's what woke me up."

"Watch it," Jamie whispered. "Big girls don't scare me."

"Point taken," she smiled, zipping up her warm-ups. "Let's go, before I pass out from hunger."

Once in the hall they surveyed their options. There was the hotel dining room, but the menu didn't look appealing to either of them. Striding outside, they looked up and down the busy street but saw nothing in the immediate vicinity. "We came from that direction last night," Jamie said, pointing north. "We passed a lot of fast food. Maybe there's a grocery store."

"Grocery store?"

"Yeah. I know it's bugging Ryan to pay room-service prices for cereal."

"Cool." They started to walk, and after a few moments Jordan said, "I think I know why I can't sleep."

"Why's that?" She slipped her hand around Jordan's arm, smiling when Jordan reached over to clasp the hand against her arm.

"I'm pretty freaked out with what's happening between Mia and me." She shot a sidelong glance at Jamie. "Is it okay to talk about this?"

"Of course. I've been through the same thing. I have a lot of empathy for what you're going through."

"What do you know about my story?"

"Mmm…not a lot. Ryan tells nothing." She laughed wryly. "Mia's actually been pretty close-mouthed too. I know that she likes you, and that you're having some trouble adjusting to this. Have you been with women before?"

"No, well, not anything more than kissing. Surprised?"

"Yeah, a little. I got big-time lesbian vibes from you when I first met you."

"One of my personas. I have more than I'd like."

"We all have different personas. Don't be so hard on yourself."

"I'm just being honest," she insisted. "I'd like to know who I am, so I don't have to act like the person I think people want me to be."

"Been there, done that. It's a hard thing to change, but it's sure worth it."

"Are you happy?" Jordan's question was very simple on its face, but Jamie knew that she meant it on a variety of levels.

"Yes. I'm happy that I went through the process, even though it was painful. I'm happy that I stopped trying to be who I wasn't. I'm happy to get to know myself for the first time. And most of all, I'm happy that I got Ryan in the bargain. She's the grand prize."

Jordan nodded, giving Jamie's hand a squeeze. "I had a feeling that you felt like that." They walked a little farther and she said, "It's a little different for me. This is a bad time for me, what with invitations going out for the Olympic team in another two months. This is not a good time for me to be exploring my sexuality."

Jamie shrugged and gave Jordan an encouraging smile. "Maybe your sexuality has a mind of its own. God knows that mine wouldn't listen to me."

❧

After a long morning spent watching cartoons while they ate an entire box of Frosted Flakes and sliced bananas, the athletes took off for practice while Jamie got on the phone and tried to find a rental car. Most of the large companies had a policy against renting to people under twenty-five, but she finally found one that was more lenient. It was a long cab ride to Santa Monica, but she finally procured a sexy, dull gray 1996 Ford Escort with 135,000 miles on the sporadically functioning odometer.

Determined to get a decent meal, the roommates settled upon one of the better spots along the water, just a few buildings down from the rental apartment Mia had used during the summer.

After a delightful lunch of fresh oysters, salmon carpaccio, and seared ahi, they hopped back in the car and returned to the hotel to check out and then dash over to USC. Luckily they were there forty-five minutes early, for, to their surprise, they found that North Gym seated only a couple of hundred people. It was an old facility right in the heart of the campus that had formerly been the gymnasium for the whole school. Now the basketball programs used the Sports Arena, a large, privately owned 11,000-seat facility, but volleyball was still relegated to the far-too-small campus gym.

Jamie caught Ryan's eye and the tall woman loped over to her, informing her, "I left Bryant's name at the door, and the guard assured me he'd let him in if they're sold out. Tiny place, huh?"

"My high school gym was twice this large."

"Welcome to NCAA Division One college athletics," Ryan grinned, running back to warm up.

The pair managed to secure seats at the end of one of the sections so that Bryant wouldn't have to climb over too many people to join them. The place was packed, made even more so by a substantial percentage of the USC band that was wedged into a tiny spot, the musicians so close together that they had a hard time turning their sheet music.

From their vantage point about halfway up in the stands, Mia was intently watching the cheerleaders warm up before they took the floor. Jamie finally elbowed her and said, "Hey, someone you want to sleep with is on the court, too. Stop drooling over the cheerleaders."

Mia shook her head briskly and said, "First of all—they're not cheerleaders. Well, the men are, but the women are song leaders."

Jamie peeked over and observed the gorgeous, well-built blonde women, clad in short, tight white turtleneck sweaters with microscopic white pleated skirts. "Oh yeah, they look like their purpose is to lead songs. They all have very nice…lungs," she observed popping her eyebrows a few times.

The women took the court just as the players went back into the locker room. Jamie and Mia watched them carefully, but not a song was sung. Instead, the women danced to a choreographed number designed to show off their beautiful bodies to good effect, and they did not disappoint. "Well, they sure can sing," Jamie decided. "Where do they get these girls, anyway? Central casting? They look like Hollywood's vision of the perfect woman."

"Are you gonna argue?" Mia chuckled. "They look pretty perfect to me."

The song leaders ran back to take their places along the front of the stands, ready to lead a song at a moment's notice. They were replaced by a group of women in sparkly black spandex tops and tights, and as they struck a pose and waited for the music to start Jamie leaned over and asked, "What's this group called?"

"I don't know," Mia mused. The music began and after just a few bars of the piece Mia turned to Jamie with wide eyes and said, "The women didn't dance this provocatively at that strip club you guys took me to on my birthday."

Jamie just nodded, amazed that a college needed two sets of dancers in the first place, but even more so that one set was clearly meant to inflame the loins of the young men and an interested minority of the young women in attendance. "I can't get over this," Jamie mused. "The dancers at Cal look like escapees from a convent compared to these women."

"I came down for the USC/UCLA basketball game last year when I was dating Jason," Mia recalled. "The game was at UCLA, and the whole band was there and they were really rowdy. While these poor girls were dancing the band kept doing this cheer asking how much for a lap dance. I felt sorry for them."

"Ew." Jamie pulled a face and said, "That's just gross."

"Melissa Johnston really wanted to come to 'SC and be a song leader," Mia said wistfully.

"Your Melissa?"

"Yeah. Remember Ryan said she was a cheerleader at USF? Well, that was her second choice—by far. She really wanted to come here, but she didn't make the cut. They asked her to try out for this group, but she says it's viewed by the students as the song leader rejects. She just wasn't up for it."

"Wow. That would've been cool to know one of the cheerleaders."

"Oh yeah," Mia grimaced. "Just what I need right now is to see Melissa again. Jordan's got me screwed up enough without asking for trouble."

Just before the game was scheduled to begin, six muscular young men ran onto the court to whip the crowd into a frenzy. They were clad in white oxford cloth button-down shirts, white v-necked sweaters with a large "SC" on the front, pleated white shorts, white crew socks, and white deck shoes. Jamie raised an eyebrow at the military-style haircuts the pristine men wore. The cheerleaders at Cal were a motley crew of two or three people in blue and gold rugby shirts who ran around during time-outs trying to drum up support to actually lead a cheer. Now having seen the regimented end of the spectrum, she decided she was much more comfortable with Cal's laid-back, informal style, although she wouldn't mind having a few of those song leaders to leer at during game breaks.

The game was almost ready to start when a tall, handsome man caught Ryan's eye, and she waved enthusiastically. Turning to find Jamie in the crowd, Ryan pointed at the man and sent him on his way. Jamie's eyes met his across the crowd and she immediately saw something familiar in him, even though Ryan had never described him. There was a warmth in his eyes and his wide smile that made him look like the kind of guy that Ryan would be fond of.

"Bryant?" she asked needlessly when he reached them. "Jamie Evans. This is my friend, Mia Christopher."

"Good to meet you both," he said, his friendly smile infectious. "You know, I haven't seen Ryan in a little over a year." He looked at the woman down on the court again, checking her out thoroughly. "Has she eaten during that time?" He gave Jamie a slow grin and she smiled back.

"She eats, Bryant. Lord knows she eats. She just uses as much energy as she takes in. She got sick a few weeks ago and lost over fifteen pounds. I don't know how she'll ever put it back on."

"Well, she looks healthy enough now," he smiled, watching Ryan enthusiastically go after a ball as the game began.

"Yeah, she's fine now. Still a little tired at the end of the day, but who wouldn't be?"

They settled down to watch the game, with Jamie filling Mia in to the full extent of her volleyball knowledge. Bryant didn't know much about the game either, but it was clear that Jordan and Ryan were the keys to the Cal attack. Their names were called repeatedly by the announcer, and some of the surrounding fans began to grumble whenever one of them recorded a kill. The match was much more lopsided than Ryan had predicted, and Cal won, three games to one.

Ryan hugged Bryant enthusiastically when they all met up after the game. He stayed for just a few minutes, since the women had to leave for Malibu, but they made plans to see him the next morning at Mass.

As they walked to the car Jamie looked up at her partner and said, "Why didn't you ever mentioned that Bryant was black?"

"Didn't I?"

"Nope. I didn't have any mental image of him, so I'm pretty sure that you never described him. It's funny, he looked so familiar," she said thoughtfully. "Something about his eyes and his smile makes it seem like you know him."

"Yeah, he's a great guy." She smiled at Jamie and said, "Our baby would be lucky to have him for a father."

"Well," Jamie said, wrapping an arm around Ryan's waist. "I think I'd like to spend more than two hours with him before we decide, but from the little I know of him, he seems nice."

"We have a few years to make up our minds. A lot can change between now and then. I just think it's a good idea to talk about it and make sure we agree. It's a very, very big decision."

"Of course it is. And luckily, we can put it off for a long time."

As Jamie led the foursome to the car, Jordan asked, "Is this the least fashionable car you've ever been in?"

"I'll have you know that my fiancé had an old Accord."

"Well, that explains why you dumped him," Jordan laughed.

"Hey, if money meant anything to Jamie I'm the last person she would have picked," Ryan said. "I didn't even have a car when she met me."

"Good point, tiger," Jordan agreed. "I still don't understand your allure. It must be very well hidden."

"It wasn't very well hidden last night," Mia jibed. "It was downright obvious."

"Hey, you were the voyeurs. I wasn't in the bathroom watching either of you."

"Also a good point," Jordan said. "I suppose you have endured enough torment for one day." As they rolled along on the interstate Jordan asked, "Do you know how to get to Malibu?"

"I just stay on the 10, right?" Ryan asked.

"Yep. When we get close there's a supermarket that's open all night. Let's stop there and get some supplies."

"How rustic is this place?" Mia asked, visions of log cabins dancing in her head.

"Oh, it's not rustic. But his girlfriend neither cooks nor eats, so all they ever have in the house is salad dressing and wine."

After buying enough food for snacks and breakfast, they ascended a narrow, winding road off Malibu Canyon until they reached a sprawling, glass-walled ultramodern home. From the entryway, all that they could see was the deep black of the ocean, and they could just detect the thrum of the waves. "Wow, some view, I bet," Ryan mused.

"Yeah. It's nice." Jordan searched in her wallet to find the code for the door. "Key in 11-15-78," she instructed Ryan.

"Cool," Ryan said as the door opened. "Jamie's parents use her birthday too."

"That's the girlfriend's birthday. I'm six months older," she added dryly. Ryan shut her mouth immediately and decided that she would not make another personal comment about any of the occupants of the house.

The place was beautiful in a spare, industrial sort of way. There were no mementos or family pictures around, but Ryan did see a couple of shots of a ruggedly handsome blonde man with a much younger, silicone-enhanced, model type. Jordan went out to the balcony that ran the width of the house on the ocean side and sat on the railing to breathe in the salt-laden air. It was obvious that she needed a few minutes alone, so everyone else went into the gorgeous but nearly empty kitchen. They finally found a knife and some forks and spoons, and they took the large fruit salad they had prepared out to the living room.

Jordan had come back in and put a calming CD on the player, and for several frenzied minutes she and Ryan ate in silence. When a sizable dent had been put in the platter, Ryan relaxed in the modern leather chair that wrapped around her, and a few moments later she was joined by her always cuddly partner. Seconds later, Jordan and Mia were wrestling on the couch in a passionate tangle. Ryan patted Jamie on the butt, and they quietly got up to find a guest room. They were halfway down the hall when Jordan gasped out, "Third door on the left."

Ryan was too tired even to notice if, or how, the room was decorated. All she saw was a big empty bed, and after she peeled her clothes off and went to the bathroom, she made a dive for it. She let out a pleasure-filled hiss as her bare skin hit the cool cotton sheets, and she lazily mused, "Sometimes when I'm really tired, it boggles my mind how good it feels to lie down. This is definitely one of those times."

Jamie snuggled up next to her and molded her body to fit tight. "It feels so good to lie next to you, I hardly notice how the bed feels. But I will agree that being horizontal right now is a very good thing. I love you, baby. Sleep tight."

"Mmm-hmm," Ryan murmured and was asleep within seconds.

When Mia blinked her eyes open to the bright sunlight of a warm Malibu morning, she turned her head to see Jordan, wide awake, her head resting on a braced hand. "You're so pretty when you sleep." Jordan tenderly traced a fingertip along Mia's jaw line.

Mia rolled onto her side and smiled up at her. "Thank you. You've never told me that you think I'm pretty."

Jordan visibly blanched. "I…I haven't?"

"No, but it's okay. You show me that you find me attractive."

"Well, I do. Think you're pretty, that is. Very much."

"I think you are, too, but I bet you hear that constantly, don't you?"

"No, not really. When I work, I'm much more likely to hear a bunch of people standing around criticizing different parts of me—like I'm a group of body parts unconnected to a person."

Mia chuckled. "What could someone possibly criticize you for? You're perfect."

"Ha." Jordan rolled onto her back and started the list. "Hair is too pale to work against light colors; eyes can look too cold; dark lipstick makes me too pale unless I have a tan; a tan makes me look too dark to sell the 'ice princess' look; shoulders are too 'mannish'; arms are too long to wear anything tailored; thighs are too muscular to look feminine…"

"My God. They say things like that to your face?"

"Mmm…sometimes, but even if they don't want you to hear, you do. The people from the ad agency are there, people from the product are usually there, and then the creative people. They argue while you're standing there trying not to feel like a piece of meat. It's no fun."

"Why do you do it?"

"Two reasons. It's great money for a pretty short amount of time. I just do local stuff, so I never have to travel. Plus, it's good for my image. I think USA Volleyball might like the idea of having one of the members of the Olympic team also be a model. They love to be able to categorize you like that."

"Volleyball means a lot to you, doesn't it?"

She nodded somberly. "I need to talk to you about this, Mia."

"Okay. "

Jordan sighed, and linked her hands behind her head as she gazed up at the ceiling. "Volleyball is more than something I like. It's what I've structured my life around. Since I was…oh…eleven, I'd guess, I've had this goal. That's ten years…ten years out of twenty-one that I've been working for this. I've been to every major national tournament, played on the best club teams in Southern California, gone to clinics all over the world. I've missed Thanksgiving and Christmas with my family for most of those years, since there are always holiday tournaments somewhere. I've sacrificed so much— and now it's close. It's really close, and I can't screw it up now."

"Why are you worried about screwing it up now?"

Jordan turned to her and said, "Because of you."

"Me? Why me?"

"Not you, per se," Jordan admitted. "But I'm worried about going further with this. I guess I want to make sure that we're on the same page before we get any deeper here."

"Okay. Tell me where you are."

"I'm focused on my sport and on my goal of making the Olympic team. If I can make it this year, that's great. But if I have to play in Europe for another three years, to get a chance at 2004, that's what I'll do. It's my priority. It's a much bigger priority than my sexuality, or my infatuation with you. I'm sorry if that sounds cold, but I have to be honest."

Mia rubbed her hand up and down Jordan's arm a few times in a reassuring fashion. "I think I knew that. I don't want to distract you from your sport."

Jordan chuckled. "You're distracting me from school. I'm actually playing better than I have since I hurt my shoulder four years ago. Why, I don't know, but even Coach Placer has noticed it. I guess I'm happier. You make me feel like I can jump higher and spike harder."

"Well, that's a good thing then, huh?"

"Yeah, it is for me. But is it what you want? I don't want this to just be about me getting my needs met. What do you want?"

"I'm not sure what I want, other than to be able to make sure we stay friends. I like you a lot, as I'm sure you can tell, but even though I'd like to have sex with you, I want to make sure we keep our friendship."

"I want that too," Jordan insisted. "That's vital for me."

"Sounds like we have the same goals," Mia ventured.

"But what about the big picture? I don't think I'm in any position to be in a relationship. I don't want to come out to my family or my friends. I don't want the people at USA Volleyball to know about me." She looked up at Mia rather helplessly and said, "I'm not like Ryan. It's going to take me a long time to feel comfortable being out."

"Jordan," she soothed. "I'm not a lesbian, and I'm not at all sure that I want to be in a lesbian relationship. I like you—a lot. I'd like to sleep with you, yes, but I'm not planning on making this a lifetime commitment. I don't think that's who I am."

"I think that's who I am," Jordan mused. "And I think it more and more when we're together. I can't see myself dating men after being held and touched by you. I really think I'm a lesbian, Mia."

Mia stroked her face, smiling over at her. "That's good to hear. I think you'll be happier once you make some decisions for yourself. I just want you to know that I'm not going to be jumping into lesbian land with you. That's not me."

"That's cool. I just want to make sure that you're not going to expect me to come out and tell everyone about us."

"No thanks," Mia said, her eyes wide. "This is private. I'm not ashamed of being attracted to you, but I have no interest in my family finding out. I don't want to take you home for Christmas."

"I'm sure I'll be at a tournament, anyway." Jordan laughed gently. "So let's summarize, shall we? I'm probably gay, you're probably not."

"I'm definitely not," Mia insisted, while laughing.

"Okay, you're definitely not. Neither of us wants this to be public, so we'll keep it low key."

"Yeah. No kissing on the steps of the library like Jamie did not two days after pledging that she and Ryan were just friends," Mia scoffed, still a little hurt by Jamie's deceit.

"Got it. No kissing in public. Also, no family introductions."

"Correct. No coming out to friends, either."

"Check. No friends—except Ryan and Jamie. I think they've already gotten the hint."

"Yeah, they're both pretty quick," Mia smiled, and added to the list. "No long-term commitments."

"Correct. Day-by-day commitment is enough for me."

"Fair enough. I'll give you twenty-four hours notice if I don't want to see you any more." Mia was clearly teasing.

"Good deal. One last big one," Jordan said, smiling broadly. "No falling hopelessly in love with me, then giving up school, family, and friends to chase me all over the world while I pursue my dream."

Mia acted as though she was considering all of the elements of the statement. "Hmm…that's gonna be tough. Can I fall hopelessly in love with you if I don't give up everything to chase you around the world?"

"Nope. I'd rather you didn't."

Mia sighed and rolled her eyes a little. "That's a tall order, but it's a deal." She shuffled closer and rested her head against her friend's chest. "I can't guarantee that I won't fall hopelessly in like with you, though. I'm only human."

❧

When Jamie and Ryan emerged from their room a little after nine, Jordan and Mia were sitting in the living room staring at them with concern. "I thought you guys had died in there," Mia said. "I assumed you were having sex, but when I listened at your door I didn't hear a sound."

"Do you always listen at our door?" Ryan asked with a smirk.

"Don't be silly. I've never been up before you, so I haven't had the opportunity."

"I will have to admit that this is a new able-bodied record for me," Ryan said. "I guess I didn't realize how tired I was."

Jamie sat on the couch and pulled her lover with her. "I'm beginning to get worried about you, honey. You've been much more tired than usual."

Ryan yawned deeply, still fighting the lethargy that seemed to have settled into her bones. "I guess you're right. I haven't had my same spark since I had the flu. Maybe I should go to the doctor."

"When do you have time?" Jamie asked, a little frustrated. "You're busy every minute of the day."

"I'll go during break if I don't feel better," Ryan promised. "Even though I'm tired, my appetite is perfectly normal. Let's eat."

"What about Mass?" Jamie asked.

"Shit." Ryan ran for the shower as she exclaimed her dismay. "We've got to leave in ten minutes. If you're not ready, I'm going without you."

Just because she loved Ryan more than she cared about making a good impression, Jamie spent her ten minutes making a snack that they could eat in the car. She looked decent enough, having put on a clean pair of chinos and a polo shirt, but her appearance did not live up to her usual crisp standards.

When Ryan emerged from the bedroom, she showed enough concern for how she looked for both of them. She was wearing a pair of black slacks that Jamie had never seen before, a crisp, white, banded collar blouse, and a black cotton sweater vest, every tiny button neatly fastened. "My, but you look nice," Jamie said. "Where'd you get those slacks?"

"Oh, they're really old—from high school. My proportions have changed since then, but these are long enough now that I'm thinner. My hips were a lot narrower then, so my waist wasn't much smaller than my hips." She pulled up her sweater, and Jamie could see that they rode rather low on her waist. "They should be up here," she indicated, pulling them up to the proper spot, "but then they're too short."

Jamie noticed that Ryan's sleeves were rolled up, as usual, and she asked, "Is that why you always roll your shirt up?"

"Yep. Haven't been able to find a shirt with sleeves long enough since…oh, I'd say sophomore year in high school."

Jordan and Mia had been watching this interplay and Jordan piped up, "I never wear shirts with long sleeves. I stick with sweaters."

"That's just not right," Jamie said. "Lots of women are as tall as you two."

"No, they aren't," Ryan laughed. "You're just hanging around the tallest of the tall. Manufacturers would go broke trying to make clothes to fit Jordan and me."

"Well, it's still not right," Jamie grumbled. "Big girls need to have their wrists and ankles covered, too."

"My champion," Ryan smiled after her partner as she grabbed the keys and made for the car.

The Sunday morning traffic was light, allowing them to make the journey to south central L.A. in a relatively short time. Jamie found one of the last parking spaces in the lot and trotted along behind Ryan, who was striding along the blacktop at full speed. They entered the church just as the previous service had concluded, and they found Bryant in the midst of setting up for the 10:30 Mass.

"Right on time, Ryan, Jamie," he said, a bright smile lighting up his face. Jamie hugged him and Ryan gave him a kiss and pitched in to help, expertly setting up the keyboard that Bryant had been working on. Since Jamie had no skills in this area, she secured seats for them in the front row right next to the choir, as Ryan suggested.

Various members of the choir entered, wearing long black robes with bright white trim. There was an enthusiasm and energy to the group that Jamie found infectious, and she sat watching patiently as Ryan finished with the organ and played a few bars to test the sound.

"Do you want me to accompany you, or do you want to play?" Bryant asked as he came up behind her.

"Either way," Ryan said, but then she reconsidered. "Actually, I think I'd rather accompany myself. Gives me something to do with my hands."

"Okay by me," Bryant said. "Are you nervous?"

"No, not really. I don't get nervous when I sing. Never have." She laughed wryly and added, "My only problem is that I get too into the music sometimes, and I tend to cry during emotional songs. I hate that."

"Michael would have liked that," Bryant reminded her fondly, giving her a hug.

"Yeah, he sure would have. He thought crying was as important as laughing."

"He'd have been proud of you, and very happy that you've found a partner."

"I know that he would have been happy that I've found love," Ryan agreed. "Come to think of it, he and I would be stepbrother and sister when Maeve and my father get married. Wouldn't he have gotten a kick out of that?"

"He would indeed. Any idea of when the wedding will be? I'd love to come."

"Probably January. As soon as we know the date, I'll let you know."

"Good deal. You all set here?"

"Yep. I'll see you after communion," she said, kissing him on the cheek.

When Ryan settled into the pew, Jamie said, "What do you two have planned? This looks like more than a casual Sunday Mass."

"A little surprise," Ryan said with a smile. "Don't worry, you'll like it."

"You seem to know your way around that keyboard pretty well, Ms. O'Flaherty. Have you been holding out on me?"

"Nope. I play a little when I get the chance. I just don't own a keyboard, and I hate to borrow Rory's."

"Ooh, Christmas is coming," Jamie teased.

"And I don't want any presents," Ryan teased right back, tapping the tip of her partner's nose.

"Okay," Jamie agreed. *But your birthday comes before Christmas, and all bets are off then.*

The church was full to bursting by 10:30, and the choir had quickly filled the available seats, spilling into the row with Jamie and Ryan. Bryant stood and welcomed the crowd, then began to play a soft tune on the keyboard as he urged everyone to join hands and prepare to hear the word of God.

The crowd fell into the obviously familiar routine, and as the music increased in volume the entire congregation began to sway to the slow beat as Bryant called on each part of the choir to join in, one at a time. The sopranos led off, followed by the altos, tenors, baritones and basses. The melody was simple, the words simpler still; each group adding to the previous, the sound building as more and more voices joined together. By the time the entire group was singing as one, Jamie felt a chill chase down her spine at the power and the enthusiasm that she felt rising up from the crowd. Everyone was singing—everyone was swaying to the gentle beat. As many times as she had attended services, she had never felt such an outpouring of feeling, and certainly not five minutes into the endeavor.

Now the voices continued to sing, but in a much quieter tone as Bryant called upon the Holy Spirit to enter their souls and make them receptive to the word of the Lord. He spoke simply, but so eloquently that Jamie found herself hanging on every word, closing her eyes as the sound of his warm, powerful voice merged perfectly with the choir. *Ooh, he is special. I can see why Ryan loves him.*

When the crowd was fully receptive, the priest entered, coming up the main aisle, shaking hands and hugging as many people as he could get his arms around. When he reached the sanctuary, he gave a few welcoming remarks, then launched into the Mass, following the traditional lines that Jamie had grown used to at St. Phil's, Ryan's home church. Everything seemed as usual until the Offertory. At St. Phil's, they sang a quiet, traditional song as the congregation presented their financial gifts to the church. It was very orderly and very proper, and lasted just a few moments as well-practiced ushers passed baskets around the church in a precise pattern.

Here at St. Agatha's, however, a very different practice was followed. Bryant stood and invited everyone to share their bounty with the Lord, and as people stood, he launched the choir into a very spirited rendition of "Jesus on the Main Line."

Everyone joined in to sing, most people clapping and swaying to the rhythm.

It was certainly different from anything in Jamie's experience. The songs that were sung at her grandfather's church were considered modern if they were from the 19th century; and the music at St.

Phil's, while more contemporary, never conveyed this much joy. At least half of the crowd left their seats, getting up to welcome friends and neighbors, greeting most with hugs and warm handshakes. Jamie and Ryan kept their seats, but Ryan was beaming greetings at everyone who ventured anywhere near her, her face so happy that Jamie felt her heart clench with emotion when she had a moment to spare a glance at her. She leaned over and said, "Thanks for bringing me here, honey. This was worth the entire trip."

"We'd be members if we lived anywhere near L.A."

"No arguments," Jamie smiled. "This place rocks."

There was another prolonged mass greeting during the kiss of peace, most of the congregants again leaving their chairs to tour around the church. It seemed like most of the people knew one another, but the greetings were just as enthusiastic for strangers. Jamie felt like she had been wrapped in a warm cocoon of acceptance and community, and even though the service had been going on for over an hour, she had no desire to see it end.

The Communion service was just winding down when Ryan leaned over and whispered, "Wish me luck."

Jamie squeezed her hand, which she realized she had been holding for the entire service, and sent her on her way. The tall woman slipped around the back of the choir and took her seat in front of the organ, looking up at Bryant as he introduced her.

"This week marks the anniversary of the death of someone who meant the world to me," he began. "AIDS has affected many of us here in this congregation, and it continues to be a scourge upon our cities. My friend, my lover, Michael, had a favorite song that he took courage from. When people questioned his belief in his creator, he just smiled and sometimes he'd quote a phrase or two from this song. In honor of his memory, I've asked his cousin Ryan to sing that song for us today." He nodded to Ryan and she began to play, her long, elegant fingers moving about the keyboard as though she was born to the instrument.

She closed her eyes, tossed her hair back from her face, and started to sing the song that had meant so much to her cousin.

The words spoke of prejudice and categorization. Things Michael detested. Ryan's plaintive voice wondered why God had been silent through so many centuries. Ryan tossed her head back and took in a breath, her deep, smooth voice rising up strongly—the emotion of her statement evident on her face and in her words.

With a smile that made everyone around her join in, she proclaimed her belief that God was right there, even though he'd had to travel very, very far. His spirit was with them then, and forever.

As she reached the chorus, the choir joined in, along with the rest of the musicians, the warm, melodic voices joining with Ryan's to form a perfect harmony. One of the women took over the lead, her powerful voice calling out to proclaim God's spirit.

The large group continued to sing, the words lost to Jamie as she focused intently on her partner, seeing the deeply felt emotions flitting across her beautiful face. Her voice never wavered, and not a tear escaped from her blue eyes—instead, she harnessed her feelings into her voice, the tones stronger and more powerful than Jamie had ever heard come from her lips. Chills chased down her spine as Ryan expressed her belief in her God as well as her dismay over the current state of the world, coming back time and again to her belief in the power of His spirit.

The woman who had shared the lead with Ryan closed the song, her voice building to such powerful levels that Jamie feared for the stained glass. She enunciated the final line clearly, making each word stand out. "*We can feel his spirit*," she cried to the heavens, and Jamie shared a meaningful look with her partner, both of them acknowledging that Michael's spirit was fully present along with the Lord's at that moment.

Bryant wrapped Ryan in a massive hug as the congregation gave her and the choir a heartfelt round of applause. Jamie had to restrain herself from running up there, but forced herself to wait for her lover to return, grabbing and holding her tenderly for a long while. "That was the most beautiful thing I've ever heard," she whispered. "He heard you. I know he did."

They sat down, holding hands through the end of the service, then Ryan stood by Bryant, accepting hugs and kisses from so many people that her head spun. As the last of the people left the church, Bryant gazed at Ryan and said, "My God, when did you develop that voice? You should be singing professionally."

"No, that's not gonna happen. I'd join this choir if I lived down here, but I only get pleasure out of singing songs that really mean something to me. I love singing too much to do it to please other people. I know that sounds odd…"

"No, no it doesn't. Michael was the same way. He played so beautifully, but he did it mainly for himself, or me. He said it was too personal to share with strangers."

"Yep. That's it," she agreed. "I don't mind doing it once in a while, like for Rory, but I know my limits."

"Thanks so much for singing today. I can't think of a better way to mark the anniversary of Michael's passing."

"It was my pleasure. Now I need the pleasure of lunch. Where should we go?"

"Do you like chicken?" he asked.

"Sure do."

"How do you feel about waffles?"

"Great. Love 'em."

"Excellent. Chicken 'n Waffles, here we come."

Neither Ryan nor Jamie had ever considered the merits of adding a waffle to a fried chicken dinner, but both were raving about the combination as soon as they were served. "I'll never be able to eat fried chicken without maple syrup again," Ryan declared, trying to decide if she should order another breakfast or just eat Jamie's leftovers.

Since it looked like Bryant was slowing down too, Ryan decided to scavenge rather than order more, and she was just one bite short of bursting when she had finished off both of her companions' meals. "I see what you mean about her eating," the amused man said to Jamie. "Where do you put it?" He leaned over and pinched Ryan's trim waist, not finding enough loose flesh to get a good handle on.

Ryan shrugged and said, "Maintenance. I've got a big plant to fuel."

"I guess I shouldn't be surprised. You ate like a hungry wolf when you were a kid. I don't know how your father kept you all fed."

"Thankfully I could sponge off Aunt Maeve and my friends. He would have gone bankrupt if he'd had to pay for every bite of food I ate."

"I wonder if it's genetic," he mused, looking at Jamie with a grin. "Maybe you should be the one to have the children." Turning to Ryan he said, "I assume you still want to have your own baseball team."

"Nah. We've scaled back. I might be satisfied with a basketball team." Cocking her head slightly she asked, "If we decide to go with a known donor, would you have any interest in contributing a little genetic material? Jamie's very talented, but she can't seem to manage a Y chromosome."

His eyes grew wide as he looked from one young woman to the other, seeing that they were serious about the question. "Gosh, that's a very nice compliment." He looked a little uncomfortable as he said, "Are you at that point now?"

"No, far from it. We're just pre-planning. We haven't made any decisions at all. It'll probably be five or six years before we're at a point to do that." She looked at him carefully and said, "You don't look like you think it's a good idea."

He sighed and leaned his head back, unkinking his neck for a minute. "No, that's not it. I think you'd be a fabulous mother. That's not an issue." He sat up fully and faced her. "I just don't know how I feel about creating a new life when there are already so many unwanted babies." He looked at Jamie and said, "I teach in the inner city, and I see so many kids languishing in the foster care system. I'm currently on the waiting list to become a foster father—I feel like I have to do something to help the problem."

Ryan reached across the table and squeezed his arm. "I think that's wonderful, Bryant. To be honest, even though I want to have one baby myself, we've talked about adopting the others."

"I'm not ruling it out, so don't take this as a firm no. But I wouldn't want to do it if I wasn't involved in raising the child."

"If we use a known donor, we'd want that too," Ryan assured him. "If we just want genetic material we'll go to a sperm bank."

He laughed for a minute and said, "Michael used to say that his dream job was being a teller at a sperm bank."

Jamie rolled her eyes and said, "If they had the equivalent for women, Ryan would be first in line. It must run in the family."

"It's a good family," he said warmly. "Let's see where we all are with the topic in a few years, okay? I'm actively pursuing being a foster father, but if that doesn't work out I'd consider moving back up to the city to do this, if we all agree. I really want to help raise a child."

"Whoever that child is will be very blessed," Ryan assured him, giving his hand a fond squeeze.

As they left the restaurant to get into the rental Jamie said, "He's a doll. So warm and open. I can see why he's on your list."

"He always has been. As soon as I decided I was a lesbian I started planning how I'd have children. There was a part of me that always saw Bryant being the father of my kids."

"I'm gonna have to adjust my mental picture, but I might just start a little fantasy of a Ryan/Bryant combo myself."

"Adjust your mental picture?" Ryan tilted her head in question.

"Yeah. I always imagine that the baby you give birth to will look like you. I think my imagination believes in cloning," she chuckled. "I picture the face from that photo of you from when you were about two. But if Bryant is the father, your baby probably won't share your features."

Ryan cocked her head even further and asked, "That doesn't bother you, does it?"

"No, not a bit," Jamie assured her. "I just need to adjust my mental image. I do think we'd need to have a serious discussion about having an interracial child, of course, but I'm certainly not opposed."

"Yeah, there are issues to consider if we use a donor of a different race, but as a biologist, I'm all in favor of mixing up the gene pool. Racial purity is the road to extinction."

"Conceptually, I'm sure you're right, but we're not having a science experiment—we're having a baby. There are more issues here than improving the gene pool."

"One more good reason to wait a few years," Ryan agreed. "We'll have time to argue and plan and discuss and argue some more." She smiled brightly and decided, "It'll be fun."

Jamie just rolled her eyes, believing that her partner could make nearly any discussion fun.

When the pair arrived back in Malibu, Jordan and Mia were in their beach attire. "Let's go," Mia demanded. "The beach is calling."

"Can we at least put on our suits?" Ryan asked.

She considered the request. "You've got five minutes…then we're taking the car."

The day was very warm for early October and for a change there was no foggy marine layer, which usually made it chilly by the ocean. Jamie had remembered to bring Ryan's suit, and Jordan had borrowed one from Candy, so they were all set. Since it was too far to walk and they had to drive anyway, they headed quite a few miles further up Pacific Coast Highway to Zuma beach. The big surfing beach was not as crowded as they had feared, and they were able to park in the lot.

By the time they got all of their gear down to an acceptable spot, Ryan was ready for a nap. She smoothed the sand carefully, then created a small depression for her butt and built up a sand pillow for her head. Her deep concentration was interrupted by Mia's chuckle. "What?" Ryan asked as she looked up to see three pairs of eyes staring at her. "I like to be comfortable."

"It's not brain surgery," Jamie reminded her. "Just toss your towel down and scoot around."

"Nope. Too much invasive sand. I've studied this, you know."

"I just bet you have," Jamie said fondly as she patted her cheek.

Ryan was just about to lower herself into her custom made depression when Jordan said, "You aren't really just going to sit in the sun are you?"

"Ahh, yeah, that's exactly what I was planning on doing."

"But you can do that anywhere. You don't need the ocean to get a tan. That's a waste of a precious resource."

A deep sigh preceded the question, "What do you have in mind?"

"Wind-surfing," Jordan said with a glimmer in her light blue eyes.

"I don't know how."

"Even better."

Jamie and Mia decided that watching wind-surfing sounded a lot more interesting than actually wind-surfing, but Ryan reluctantly agreed after Jordan reminded her that they didn't have a game until Friday and that Jamie would be gone for two nights, so she could catch up on her sleep. They were able to rent the equipment right on the beach, but they'd have to go without wetsuits, which Ryan was not at all happy about.

"Come on, don't be such a wimp. It's 69 degrees, for God's sake."

"Hey everybody has quirks. One of mine is that I don't like cold water."

"I guarantee you won't notice it once you start working. This is tough to do right, and you work up a sweat pretty fast. Trust me."

Ryan rolled her eyes and let Jordan have her way. They decided to rent just one board at first so that Jordan could train her properly. Jamie and Mia came down by the edge of the water and watched the lesson, but neither woman would go for a turn on her own.

As expected, Ryan was a very quick study. Her balance, strength and fearlessness allowed her to grasp the mechanics quickly, and within fifteen minutes she was skimming along atop the gentle waves. Jordan ran back to rent another board, and Mia and Jamie sat on the wet sand by the water's edge to watch them play.

"She's pretty hot, isn't she?" Mia asked as she tilted her head to get a better look.

"They both are," Jamie agreed, feeling a twinge of desire. Watching the women sail along side by side, it was easy to compare their radically dissimilar bodies and styles. Ryan looked powerful and strong as she clung to the sail. A wild look on her face evidenced her desire to tame the ocean to suit her purposes. Jordan looked light and graceful, almost like she was resting on the board. She looked absolutely serene as she skimmed along and, rather than fighting with the sea, she appeared to be a part of it.

Their personality styles carried through to their body styles also. Even though Ryan outweighed Jordan by only twenty pounds now, that entire twenty pounds was muscle, most of it in her rock-hard thighs, round butt, and cut arms. Jordan's body was muscular, but in a softer, smoother form. There were small dips and indentations here and there, but mostly her muscle was invisible, even though it was obviously present. She looked like a more compact woman who had been stretched to her full 6'3" with all of her muscles elongated at the same time. Ryan, however, looked like every robust muscle belonged right where it lay. Actually, when viewed from a distance or in a photograph, one might have guessed that she was 5'8" or so, she was so perfectly proportioned.

Jamie decided that no matter what look a person preferred, it was undeniable that these two women were strikingly beautiful. In Jamie's assessment, Ryan was like a wild mountain stream, while Jordan reminded her of a deep blue pool nestled in a fjord. Both beautiful, both alluring, but only one called to her.

"Yo, Jamie, where'd you go?" Mia asked as she nudged her side with an elbow.

"Oh, sorry, I was just looking at their bodies and my mind wandered."

"Yeah, mine's about to wander down there too."

Jamie aimed a half-hearted slap of rebuke at Mia's midriff, but the topic had been broached. "So…how is it sleeping with her? Did she get any more adventurous?"

"Well—yes and no. She let me touch her breasts a little bit, but we really didn't get that involved. I was worried about making noise with you guys there, and I knew it'd freak her out if you heard us messing around." She smiled serenely as she said, "I didn't mind a bit, though. It was so nice to cuddle up behind her and hold her all night." Giving Jamie a proud grin, she related, "She slept like a baby, and so did I."

"I'm married to the world's biggest cuddle-bunny. She's quickly made me an addict. It's very different from sleeping with a guy."

"Oh, yeah. Good different."

"So you think Jordan's making progress?"

Mia thought for a few moments. "I think so. But she woke up really early both days. I think this is really weighing on her mind."

"She does seem pretty confused," Jamie agreed, unwilling to tell Mia about the conversation she'd had with Jordan the previous day.

"It's clear that she's gay, but she's having a really tough time facing it. I believe her when she says it's not sex that frightens her. I think it's the label, and having other people know. Even on the night we met she was very evasive about being gay."

"Well, what about you? Where do you fall in the equation?"

"Me? I'm just an open-minded straight girl," she said, innocently batting her eyes.

"I don't know. I think there might be some cutoff point at which you're at least bisexual."

"Like what?" she asked, her curls tossing in the breeze.

"I don't know. Maybe there should be some objective standard. Like if you've touched a dozen breasts…"

"Pairs or individual breasts?"

"Pairs," Jamie allowed.

"I'm still straight," she decreed.

"Well, I've only touched one pair, and it's enough to convince me that I'm gay."

"Not me. I can actually feel the withdrawal pangs when I think of never touching a penis again."

Jamie patted her cheek and said, "I guess maybe you are just an open-minded straight girl."

"Well, whatever you call me, I've got to admit that Jordan makes me throb." Mia sighed deeply. "She's so soft and smooth; her skin just feels like satin. I loved lying in bed and talking last night. Her breasts felt so soft when they were rubbing against mine. Whew! I had to force myself not to pop one of those beauties into my mouth."

"Departing straight girl land," Jamie announced dramatically. "You are now entering bisexuality country."

"Get off the label fixation, James. If you must have a title for me, you may say that I'm Mia-sexual. That's the only one that fits."

They were allowed to drop the rental off at LAX, which made matters much easier, at least from a logistics standpoint. Emotionally, it was still very difficult for Jamie to leave. As much pleasure as she got from being on the golf team, she dreaded the time away from home. It wasn't so bad once she was actually playing in the tournament; then, she could give her complete concentration to the match. But leaving Ryan was horrible for her—and even though Ryan tried to put on a good face, Jamie knew it was nearly as hard for her.

Tonight was tougher than usual. They had shared so much emotion during the day that they both felt particularly close, and the thought of parting felt like a physical blow. Ryan had insisted on taking Jamie to her gate, even though it was quite a long jog back to her own flight. To avoid making a scene, they found an empty gate and spent a few long, tender minutes. Their good-bye kisses were always sweet and filled with emotion, and Ryan felt her composure start to slip as Jamie held her face and reverently kissed every inch.

"That makes me feel so treasured," Ryan murmured as she leaned in to the touch.

"You are treasured," Jamie sighed. "The more I know you, the more I love you. Thanks for sharing your heart with me today. I'll always remember your face when you sang that song."

"I'll always remember yours when we locked eyes after I was finished. The love you were sending my way felt like the warmest embrace I've ever experienced."

"This weekend was special. I'm glad we got to share it."

"Thanks for going out of your way to come. I'm really glad that you got to meet Bryant."

"So am I. I'll be home as soon as I can."

"It won't be soon enough. I'll count the minutes."

One final kiss and Jamie was off, striding confidently across the waiting area and into the line to board. As usual, she didn't turn around, and Ryan thought it best that she protected her composure that way. Sighing heavily, she made her way back to their friends, already feeling Jamie's absence pervade her senses.

When Ryan got into her own bed that night she studied the room, feeling like something was missing. It took her a long while, but she finally realized what it was. The stuffed tiger she'd given Jamie was not on her usual space on the loveseat. She looked all around the room, finally deciding that Jamie must have taken it with her. *That's my girl.* Only Jamie would have the nerve to sleep with a stuffed tiger that says "I love Jamie" on its shirt. *Her roommate's gonna think she's a whacko.*

Chapter Seven

Ryan was nearly asleep when the phone rang. "H'llo?" she said, trying to clear her throat at the same time.

"Do you have school tomorrow?" Conor asked without preamble.

"No, I don't. Don't have practice either. Why?"

"There's snow at Heavenly," he said, naming one of their favorite ski haunts.

"And?"

"Come on, Sis. We always go as soon as there's any snow. Don't be so whipped."

"I'm not whipped," she said archly. At his silence she said, "Okay, I am whipped, but in this instance, Jamie's not even home. She's in Oregon until Wednesday night."

"When should I pick you up?"

She sighed, knowing she couldn't resist the lure of fresh snow. "I should stay home and rest, but I'll go if you drive."

"Done. I'll be there to pick you up at four."

"Great," she muttered. "Bring my board, and my boots, and my overalls, and my ski jacket, and my gloves, okay?"

"Anything else? Jeez, I'll be packing all night."

"It wouldn't be that much fun to sit in the truck in my jammies, Conor. The equipment is kinda required."

"Okay, okay. You buy breakfast for my trouble, though."

"Deal. See you in…" she checked her watch, "six hours." *I should have my head examined*, she thought to herself as she tried to go to sleep quickly.

Conor was polite enough to call his sister when he pulled up, not wanting to wake Mia by ringing the bell. "Let's go," he demanded when she picked up.

"Be right there."

She ran down the stairs, making sure the note she left for Mia was easy to find. She planned on calling Jamie later, when she knew she'd be up, but she wanted Mia to know where she was in case Jamie called first.

Opening the rear door of the truck, Ryan checked to make sure all of her gear was packed away, then she pulled her clothing from the oversized nylon bag and made a reasonable pillow with it. She curled up as best she could, got the door closed and ordered, "Go."

"Aw, come on," her brother complained. "That's all I'm gonna get? How am I gonna stay awake if you don't talk to me?"

"Stop somewhere for a cup of coffee," she mumbled, but her wily brother knew one topic that would perk her up.

"Da was up when I left," he said.

"Mmm?"

"He's taking someone special to the airport today…"

"Shit! I forgot Aunt Maeve was leaving for home today." She grabbed her cell phone from her waistband and dialed home. "Da, it's me."

"Hello, sweetheart. You be careful up on that mountain today."

"I will. When are you leaving?"

"In about an hour. The flight is at seven, but we should be there an hour early just in case."

"I'm gonna call her, okay? I just didn't want to wake her up."

"I think it's safe to assume she's been up for a few minutes. I'd be surprised if she slept a wink last night."

"Okay. Give Aunt Maeve a kiss for me, will you, Da?"

"I think I can manage a spare," he chuckled. "Call me when you get home, darlin'. I want to make sure you're lucid."

"Will do."

After a quick call to her aunt, wishing her a good trip, Ryan hung up and glared at her brother. "You did that just to wake me up.

They're not leaving for an hour."

"Who, me? I was just making casual conversation. Just trying to keep you informed."

"Well, it didn't work, big guy. I'm going to sleep. Wake me when it's time to strap my board on. And not a minute sooner."

Since it was Columbus Day and the first holiday of the season, the slopes were more crowded than usual. Conor and Ryan were engaged in a spirited argument as the first light broke over the mountain, neither sibling willing to give in.

"I'm not going to do it, Conor. I don't do stuff like that anymore." She was shaking her head firmly, arms crossed against her chest.

"It doesn't hurt anything. We've always done this."

"I wasn't in a relationship then. Things have changed."

"You don't have to do anything. Don't tell me that you can't even flirt when you're in a relationship."

She rapped her fingers against his head, expecting to hear a hollow echo. "Yes, Conor, you most certainly are prohibited from flirting if you want your partner to trust you. Are you that clueless?"

"Aw, Jamie wouldn't mind. She's not a tightass. This is important."

"I'm not going to do it. You take a whack at her if it means so much."

He shook his head and started to walk towards the chair lift operator. "I'm telling you that she's gay," he insisted. "She'll be completely immune to my charms."

"Oh, yeah, like that would be the only possible reason for that," she called out.

He was only there for a few minutes, with Ryan watching his apparent lack of progress. When he returned he started to pout, making Ryan wish that she could have driven so that he had taken a nap. "You owe me," she grumbled, striding over to the woman.

"Hi," Ryan said when she approached, her normal friendliness shining through. "Do you have any siblings?"

"Pardon me?"

"Do you have any siblings?" Ryan asked again.

"Yeah. I have two older brothers. Why?"

"Well, my brother was just over here flirting with you…"

"Oh, yeah. You do look alike. Funny," she said, eyeing Ryan up and down, "he's not my type. He should have sent his sister."

"Yeah, well," Ryan said, trying to get out of this one with a minimum of damage. "We have a uhm…thing we do when we go boarding. We uhm…try to make friends with the chair-lift operator so we don't have to wait in the long lines." She looked adorably embarrassed, making her even more attractive.

"Is that what you're doing? Trying to make friends? I could always use another friend…"

"Ryan."

"I could always use another friend. Especially one that looks like you.

"Well, to tell you the truth…"

"Sandy."

"To tell you the truth, Sandy, I'm in a relationship and I can't really have any more friends at this point in my life. I was actually going to try to appeal to your sense of sibling rivalry, or if that didn't work, I was prepared to offer you a shameless bribe." She was bestowing one of her most charming grins on the woman, and she knew she was flirting…but just a little…almost too little to count.

"Make you a deal. Meet me for lunch—your treat, of course— and you have a deal."

"Happy to buy you lunch, Sandy, but that's all that I can offer. I'm quite attached."

"So am I," she said rather airily, "but I'm not too firmly attached."

"No problem," Ryan beamed at her. "I'm attached enough for both of us."

On the way home, Ryan offered to drive the truck since Conor had been up since three that morning. She had the stereo on low, singing to herself to stay awake when she heard a low voice from the back seat say, "You didn't really hit on the lift operator, did you."

"Of course not." Ryan laughed. "I told her the whole deal, and she played along for a free lunch. She was a pretty nice woman."

"You would have done her in the locker room a year ago," he chuckled.

"A year ago?" she said reflectively. "Yeah, I guess I probably would have. It feels better to just offer a bribe."

"No shit?"

Ryan didn't have to hesitate to consider her reply. "No shit at all."

Jamie's tee time was scheduled for ten o'clock, and as she was introduced, she turned at the exuberant applause to see her father, who had obviously just arrived, clapping for all he was worth. She gave him a wink, waited for her playing partner to tee off, then strode to the tee box to begin the tournament. She was pleased with her drive, and after she hit she walked back to the gallery to give him a kiss. "Glad you made it."

"It was nip and tuck," he admitted. "Great drive, by the way. Those muscles have really paid off."

"Gotta go," she said, as she saw her foursome getting ahead of her.

"Go get 'em," he said, giving her a smile filled with pride.

He was waiting outside the clubhouse when she emerged a little after two, having won her match, three and two. "Congratulations, honey! You really toughed it out over the last two holes. Great sand recovery on fifteen."

"Thanks. I was pretty happy with the way I played after the turn. It took me a while to get my rhythm."

"You did great. Cal's lucky to have you."

She giggled at that, and said, "I'm about to faint from hunger. Want to have some lunch?"

"It's five o'clock my time. I had breakfast at four a.m. Pacific time. I think I could stand to have a bite or two."

They decided to eat at the restaurant in the clubhouse, ordering identical meals, as frequently happened. As they waited for their food, Jim got on his cell phone and spent a few minutes talking softly with his secretary while Jamie observed him. *There's something both odd and reassuring about having someone in your life that you so resemble. I know I share a lot of traits with Mother, but sometimes Daddy and I act like the same person. It's odd…I wonder if I have the same inner desire that he has to win at all costs. God, I hope that stays buried if I do.*

Since her father was fully occupied, Jamie got on her own cell phone and called home. She didn't really expect Ryan to be there, but she wanted to leave her a message about her victory. Just a moment after she hung up, Jim finished his business and focused his attention on her.

"How are you managing golf along with school? Has it been very difficult for you?"

"No, not really. I'd say that Ryan's volleyball schedule has been tougher on us than my schedule. She has one or two games a week, and that really makes it hard."

"How is it going? With Ryan, I mean?"

She wasn't at all sure what he meant, and she looked confused for a second.

He smiled and said, "I was a newlywed once, too. It was a very tough transition for both of us. I guess I just want to make sure that you're handling the stress."

"It's not like that for us. Being with Ryan reduces my stress, to tell you the truth. I eat regular meals because I like to cook for her; we go to bed really early because she has to get up so early; she calms me down. She centers me."

He smiled at her and reached over to grasp her hand. "I'm really glad to hear that. That's what a relationship should be."

She grew pensive and spent a moment wondering if she should ask the question that played at the back of her mind. Deciding to risk it, she asked, "You didn't ever have that, did you?"

He shook his head, his face betraying his sadness. "No. We really didn't. We had the best of intentions, but we were far too young to get married." He looked at her for a second and added, "You and Ryan seem much more mature than we were. We were like two kids trying to act like adults."

Their food was delivered, and they spent a few minutes digging in. They said little until Jamie put her sandwich down and said, "Mom told me why you got married, Dad. I know it was a lot sooner than you wanted."

He looked ill as he nodded slowly. "It was too soon for us to marry, but I never regretted it. Not then, and not now. I was too young and immature to be a proper husband, but I think I did a pretty good job of being a father." He sighed heavily as he admitted, "I was better then than I am now. Odd, huh?"

"It doesn't do much good to talk about what happened, Dad. Let's try to build on what we have now. I think we'll both be better off that way."

He gave her a gentle smile. "I'm willing to try, honey. We have nowhere to go but up."

Jordan was waiting for Ryan after practice on Tuesday, practically wagging her tail as she waited to be invited over for dinner. "I've got my bike today," Ryan said, not even specifying why that was important.

"I can handle you. Don't worry your pretty little head about that."

"I'll go easy on you. We're ordering carry-out, by the way. I don't get pleasure out of cooking like Jamie does."

"Like I'm gonna complain?" Jordan chuckled. "I owe you twenty dinners already."

"Only eleven," the ever-accurate Ryan said, "but who's counting?"

Ryan rode her bike at a snail's pace so that Jordan only needed to walk at a brisk clip to keep up with her. "I think it really went well with Mia this weekend," Jordan said.

"Yeah? It looked like you were getting along well. How was it sleeping together? Kinda weird?"

"Mmm, no, to be honest. It was really nice. I was less anxious than I have been around her."

"Really? I'd think that being that close would have made you uncomfortable."

Jordan shot her a look and said, "It's not about sex. I'm not afraid to touch her or to be touched. The only thing that bothers me is how it makes me feel. Do you get the difference?"

"Not sure," Ryan said. "Seems like the same thing to me."

"No, not at all. I've had guys touch me…all over," she added. "No big deal. Actually, that's why I never had sex with any of them. It was no big deal. I didn't want to risk getting an STD or getting pregnant if it wasn't something that reached me, ya know?"

"Well, yeah, that makes sense, I guess. I forget that birth control thing." She shivered as she said, "Thank God for lesbianism."

"Yeah, that is a nice part of it. The difference is that when a woman touches me or kisses me, it's a very big deal. I feel my heart beating so hard that it feels like it's going to pop out of my chest."

"Hearts almost never do that," Ryan said seriously. "I wouldn't have made it past my first time if they did." She smiled and added, "The first time I kissed Jamie, I honestly felt faint. I don't think I've ever felt that lightheaded over something that I'd done thousands of times before. It was just so…intense," she said, shaking her head at the memory.

"Yes. That's it. It feels so intense that I'm trying to slow it down and stop when it feels too overpowering."

"That's not a bad idea. We did that, too. The difference was that Jamie was freaked out about the sex part, not so much the lesbian part."

"Well, the sex freaks me out, too, but in a good way," Jordan smirked. "I'm afraid I might wear Mia out when I finally let myself go."

"Oh, I think she can handle you," Ryan said, thinking that the randy young woman could handle Jordan and then some.

Ryan came trotting down the stairs on Wednesday morning, pleased to see the living room empty for a change. When she entered the kitchen, Mia was sitting on a chair, drinking a glass of juice. "Congratulate me," she said, a smile on her face.

"Congratulations," Ryan said dutifully. She took the container of orange juice from the refrigerator and gulped a half-dozen swallows from it, wiping her mouth with the back of her hand. "Don't tell Jamie," she warned, pointing a finger at Mia as she replaced the bottle. "Now, what am I congratulating you for?"

Mia wiggled her fingers, grinning evilly as she said, "Under the T-shirt. Both hands."

"Wow. Bare breast?"

Mia rolled her eyes and said, "Hey, it's only been a month. Don't expect miracles."

As usual, Ryan couldn't wait to welcome her partner home that evening, so she picked her up at the airport, stopping for a bite of dessert on the way home, since neither had eaten much for dinner. They entered the house via the back door, again surprising the trysting women occupying the living room. Neither woman had heard them, and once again they were forced to walk right by them to go up to their room. This time Jordan was lying on the loveseat, her long legs draped over the arm of the piece. Mia was lying atop her, twitching her hips as Jordan's hand disappeared up the leg of her shorts.

"Oh, shit." Jordan moaned, her face coloring as she spotted their friends trying to sneak up the stairs. "I'm sorry, guys. What in the hell time is it, anyway?"

"Nine-thirty," Ryan replied.

"I've got to study for a big test tomorrow," she groaned. "How did it get to be so late?"

"I don't know," Mia said, smiling coyly while Jordan extracted her hand. "I went to kiss you good-bye at eight o'clock. How could an hour and a half pass that quickly?"

"I've really got to go," Jordan said regretfully, waiting while Mia slithered off her body. She leaned in for one last kiss, grabbed her gym bag, and ran out the door, saying, "Bye," as she jogged down the porch steps.

Mia ran her hands through her hair and started to climb the stairs to her room, saying in a singsong fashion, "I got my butt squeezed, I got my butt squeezed."

"Bare skin?" Ryan called up the stairs.

"Must you diminish every one of my accomplishments?" She closed her door with a thud.

🐎

They were both tired, neither having slept well during their two nights alone. Jamie was curled up in bed, looking up at Ryan sleepily as the taller woman studied her computer screen, memorizing the number she was going to dial.

"Are you sure it's not too early to call?" Jamie asked, a huge yawn accompanying her question.

"Nah. It's fine. It's seven a.m. in Ireland. Moira has to get the younger kids off to school, and I'm sure Maeve isn't just lying about with all of that activity going on around her." She dialed the long string of numbers, and Jamie watched as a delighted smile came over her lover's face. "Brenna!" she exclaimed. "It's Ryan." She listened to her cousin's reply and said, "I'm just calling to check up on Aunt Maeve. Has Granny driven her to take up residence in the pub yet?" She nodded and smiled and said, "Sure, put her on."

"Ryan?" Maeve's clear soprano rang out.

"Just calling to see how you're faring."

"That's so thoughtful of you, dear," she said with her usual level of enthusiasm. Ryan could hear the lightness leave her aunt's voice as she related the truth of the situation. "I suppose things are going about like I expected."

"That bad, huh?"

"I shouldn't be surprised," she said, a hitch in her voice. "I knew this would be hard for Mam to take. I suppose I was fooling myself to think she'd gotten over…"

"How she feels about Da," Ryan supplied helpfully.

"Yes, that's mostly it, of course. But she's also upset that she won't be able to attend the wedding. She didn't see either your mother's or my first wedding, and it hurts her to miss this one as well. I think it brings back the pain of losing us both in the first place."

"There's no way she'd come here, is there?"

"I assume you're teasing. She still talks about the time she had to go all the way to Dublin to see your grandfather off to the war. She acts as though it was yesterday."

"Do you regret going, Aunt Maeve?"

"No, not at all. Regrettably, Moira can't make it either, so this is my only opportunity to spend time with her and the kids."

"That's a shame," Ryan said. "I know you were looking forward to her coming for the ceremony."

"Yes, it seems silly at this point in my life, but I will regret that no one in my family came to either of my weddings." Her voice broke as she said this.

"What would you ask for if you could have any wish granted?"

She thought about that for a few moments and finally said, "I wish we could have all come here for the wedding. I just don't know why I'm so emotional about this. I feel your mother's spirit so close to me when I'm here. And a very big part of me would like her to be near when I marry your father."

Ryan sniffed her own tears away as she said, "Aunt Maeve, I can't make your entire wish come true, but I can give you the biggest part."

"Pardon?"

"Jamie's mom gave us the other two round-trip tickets to anywhere in the world. I'm going to arrange for Da to come over there and marry you in Killala."

"Oh, but Ryan," she said wistfully, "then we wouldn't have the children with us."

"What's to stop you from having two weddings? This is the last time you'll marry, Aunt Maeve. I say you do it up right."

"Oh," she said breathlessly, her enthusiasm pouring out. "Do you think Martin would do that for me?"

Ryan barked out a laugh as she assured her, "He'd swim over there if it was important to you. The poor man's quite over the moon, you know," she added in her Irish lilt.

"I can't...I can't tell you how much that would mean to me, sweetheart."

"I know, Aunt Maeve, I know. I want you to go over to church and speak with the priest this morning. Find out what you have to do to get a license. Then get on the phone and call every cousin you can get hold of and tell them you're getting married on Saturday."

"Is there any way you and Jamie could come?"

She sighed and said, "I wish there was, but I've got two volleyball matches this weekend. There's no way I can get away." She thought of an even bigger reason to refuse and told her aunt, "Even if we could come, it would be unfair to the other kids if just I got to go. I'll play nice and wait until January. You will still have a service in January, won't you?"

"Oh, of course. It wouldn't feel right to not have a celebration with all of the children there with us." She paused for a moment and said, "You are the most generous woman. You make me so proud," she said as her voice quavered again.

Ryan smiled broadly at the compliment. "Much of what I am is directly because of you. You've been the best mother-of-choice anyone could wish for."

"I think that's the nicest compliment I've ever gotten," she sniffed. "My Lord, Moira must think I'm having a mental breakdown. She keeps poking her head in to see why I'm crying."

"Well, you've got a busy day ahead of you. Call me before you go to bed tonight and let me know what you've found out, okay?"

"I will," she promised. "Should I call your father or should you?"

"Why don't you call him right now and propose?" she suggested. "Tell him to call me in the morning and tell me when he wants to travel. I'll take care of getting the voucher traded in for a ticket."

"Bless you, Ryan. I love you."

"I love you too, Aunt Maeve. Call me later."

She replaced the phone and lay back fully on the bed, resting her head on her linked hands. "Not a bad night's work, huh?"

"You rule," Jamie said as she crawled over and wrapped her arms around her. "Now wrap those arms around me and cuddle me, baby. I've missed your touch more than I can say."

They were almost asleep, Jamie's embrace too comforting to allow for any other options, when the ringing phone caused Ryan to jerk upright, her eyes wide with alarm. "Damn. I hate to be wakened by the phone."

"Siobhán." Martin's voice rang through the line, "There are plans to be made, child, get out of bed."

"I'm awake, Da," she laughed. "I take it you spoke with your betrothed."

"Yes, and I've decided to let you run my life from now on. You're obviously more adept at it than I am. Why I didn't think to do this originally is beyond me."

"So you're not mad that I got involved?"

"Of course not, sweetheart. I'm entirely serious—you're in charge of all my important decisions from now on."

"What did he say?" Jamie asked excitedly when Ryan hung up.

"He is so excited. I've never heard him sound so happy."

"So when will he leave?"

"He wants to go tomorrow, but only because it's too late to get a flight out tonight. I'm going to take the morning off and take him to the airport. Boy, I can't remember the last time he took an unscheduled day off," she mused. "He called some of his friends and got people to cover for him, so he and my aunt will come home together on Sunday as originally planned."

"What about a honeymoon?" Jamie asked with waggling eyebrows.

"When I asked him that, he told me to get my mind out of the gutter."

"He is so funny about that topic."

"Well, he'd better get used to it, 'cause they'll be the butt of a lot of teasing for a very long while. Harassment about sex is a long O'Flaherty tradition."

"Don't I know it." Jamie wryly agreed, having been on the pointed end of those barbs more often than she cared to count.

Ryan lay awake in bed for a long while, her mind too filled with details of the events to allow her to relax. She was up at four, having decided to get dressed and get across the bridge before traffic became unbearable. After her shower she called Ireland again and spoke to her Aunt Moira, who was now alone in the house, Maeve having gone into town to speak to the parish priest. "Aunt Moira, I had an idea and I wanted to conscript you into helping me pull it off. Interested?"

"Of course. Your ideas always spice up my day. How can I help?"

Blowing a kiss to her still-sleeping lover, she took off while it was still fully dark, whistling a happy tune to herself as she got into her car.

Martin was packed and ready, looking quite dapper in a navy blue blazer, light blue golf shirt, and neatly pressed khaki slacks. "You look great," Ryan said, taking in her father's tidy appearance and giving him a hug.

"One of the most beautiful women in the whole of Ireland is going to be waiting for me," he said with a wide smile creasing his face. "I have to look my best."

"I hope Aunt Maeve knows how special she is to you," Ryan chuckled. "Switching days off…flying halfway around the globe at a moment's notice…borrowing Conor's jacket," she added, brushing a fleck of lint off his collar.

"That's enough out of you," Martin said, giving her a firm chuck on the arm. "I've seen the way young Jamie twists you around her tiny little finger, so if you plan on starting a bout of slagging with your father, be prepared to have the spotlight turned right back on you. You're as far gone as I am."

"Guilty as charged," Ryan laughed. "But I wouldn't change a thing."

"Nor would I."

As soon as she had her father deposited on the plane, Ryan called Jamie on her cell, smiling to herself when she heard the phone ring and ring. Finally, her lover answered, sounding winded. "Hi, sweetheart, what's up?"

"How'd you know it was me?"

"You have a distinctive ring. I can pick it out from among

thousands. Now, what's up? I had to sneak out of class to answer the phone."

"Sorry to bother you, but I'm about to spend a lot of money and I wanted to check with you before I did it."

"Ryan," Jamie said in a warning tone, "you know how I feel about this. We have about $25,000 in our checking account. As long as you leave a couple thousand dollars to cover outstanding checks, you can spend every dime. You not only don't need my permission, you don't need to inform me."

There was a long silence as Ryan tried to digest this information. "That's probably never gonna happen, but I appreciate that you trust me that much."

"I trust you with my life. Now let me get back to class. Have fun." She hung up before Ryan could utter another word, the tall woman staring at the phone in her hand for a long while.

🐎

When Ryan came home from practice that night, Jamie was in the kitchen, busily making dinner. "Hi," she said when Ryan entered. "How was your day?"

"Good." Ryan gave her a kiss. "Yours?"

Jamie proceeded to tell her about a funny thing that happened at golf practice, all of the details of her day's classes, and every other bit of minutia that she felt compelled to share with her partner. By the time she was finished, dinner was ready and Ryan spent a moment setting the table. As usual, two additional hungry mouths miraculously appeared, Jordan and Mia sitting down before Jamie could get the food on the table.

"Long time no see," Ryan drawled, having left Jordan's side not twenty minutes before.

"We'll clean up?" Jordan offered, giving Ryan a winning smile.

"It's a deal. Mia can give you the specifications."

"It's like cleaning the operating room in a hospital," Mia said. "It's an ordeal, but Jamie's cooking makes it worth it."

🐎

Leaving Jordan and Mia to their tasks, the pair went up to bed at 8:30 Ryan not even feigning an attempt at studying. She was stripping out of her clothes on the way up the stairs and had her T-shirt and bra off by the time she crossed the threshold.

Jamie was chuckling at her exaggerated attempts to get into bed quickly, and as Ryan went to brush her teeth she asked, "You seemed quiet at dinner, honey. Everything okay?"

"Yeth," Ryan replied, her mouth full of toothpaste. She finished up quickly and came back into the room, shucking her pants as she walked. When she climbed into bed, she rolled onto her side and rested her head upon her arm. "I had a revelation today," she said, her eyes unfocused as she stared at a spot on the wall.

"Tell me," Jamie urged, stroking her bare side.

"It's about the money. I got a taste of what having access to this kind of money is going to mean. It's weird. I'm still numb."

"You don't need to tell me how you spend our money, but I'm very interested in how you feel about this. Come on, tell me. What happened today?"

Ryan rolled onto her back and rested her head in her joined hands, letting out a long sigh as she related, "I was at the airport, thinking about my family. It dawned on me that none of this would have been possible without your...our money," she corrected herself. "I thought about the little town my family lives in, and it dawned on me that I could help Da and Aunt Maeve have a nice party."

She looked at Jamie and said, "I've never really talked about their situation, but my grandparents barely get by. I'm sure my Granny hasn't bought a new dress in ten years."

"I had no idea..."

"It makes me sad to think about it. I hate to see them struggle so much when they have so few years left."

"Oh, Ryan," she said, stroking her gently.

"Da's tried to give them money over the years, but Granny won't take it. I get the impression that she takes a little from Aunt Maeve and Moira, but that's about it." She laughed wryly and added, "My Uncle Eamon teaches at the national school, and I bet he doesn't make the equivalent of $20,000 American. They're the last people who should be trying to support my grandparents."

"Do they have pensions or something like Social Security?"

"My grandfather was a self-employed fisherman. He never made much, but they did all right. Their needs are very simple, so it wasn't too bad when he was working. Ireland has an Old Age Pension, but when my grandfather was working he wasn't covered by social insurance, so he didn't qualify. The government added a special provision for people in his situation, and he gets a pension now, but I think it's only about eighty Irish pounds a week."

"How much is that?"

"With the current exchange rate that would be about ninety dollars," Ryan mused. "In essence, they live on less than $5,000 a year." She shook her head and said, "It dawned on me today that I could help make the wedding nice and help my grandparents in the bargain." She looked up at Jamie and said, "It's a weird feeling. Really weird."

Jamie's mind was still reeling over the fact that Ryan's grandparents lived on such a meager sum, and she patted her lover absently, trying to imagine how it would feel not to be able to afford the simplest luxuries. "What did you decide to do? We can take my distribution and send them as much money as you want."

Ryan smiled and gently stroked her partner's arm. "I don't think that would go over well. My granny is more hard-headed about accepting money than I am. If you can imagine that," she said, while chuckling. "I decided to do an end-around, so I called my Aunt Moira and we decided that she'd take the money I sent and offer to pay for a reception in the local pub. She said she'd order some nice flowers for the church, and take my grandparents out and buy them each something nice to wear." Ryan smiled fondly as she said, "My grandfather's only suit is so shiny that it looks like it's made out of spandex."

Scooting across the bed, Jamie cuddled up next to her partner and said, "How do you feel about doing that?"

Ryan let out a long breath and said, "It feels really good. Scary good, to be honest. Making the day nicer for my...parents," she said, experimenting with the word for the first time, "feels awfully good."

"Wow," Jamie said, looking up into Ryan's deep blue eyes, "It sounds funny to hear you refer to them like that."

"Yeah, I've been trying to determine what feels right...you know?

I mean, after Saturday, she's not really just my aunt. I refuse to refer to them as 'my father and my aunt,'" she declared, a look of distaste on her face, "but I'm not sure what does feel right."

"It'll come to you. Don't rush it. It does make sense to refer to them as your parents, though, at least when you're speaking to people who don't know them well. Maeve has been a mother to you, and it's nice to acknowledge that."

"I know. I just can't call her 'Mom'. It doesn't feel right, and I don't think she'd even like it."

"Don't push it. You'll know what feels comfortable, and that's what you'll do." She had been softly stroking Ryan's back and felt her start to drift off. She tilted her head up and placed a gentle kiss on the rose-colored lips, surprised when Ryan's eyes opened fully and the kiss was returned.

"Thank you for letting me send that money. It means a lot to me," she murmured as she wrapped her arms tightly around Jamie and fell into a contented sleep almost immediately.

Friday was Jamie's easy day at school, and after golf practice she decided to balance their checkbook, a task that she was becoming more and more comfortable with. She opened the check register and saw the precise handwriting from Ryan's entry of the day before. $5,000, she mused. *My baby acted as though she'd written a check as big as the national debt. We've got to find a way to provide for her grandparents on a routine basis. I'll not have my sweetheart's aged grandparents living on next to nothing.*

Jamie was working away at her desk when Maeve called with a progress report, "My goodness, I've made more decisions and called more people today than I can ever remember."

"How's everything going?" she asked, Maeve's excitement bubbling over to infect her, too.

"Just lovely. I was so excited about seeing Martin that I nearly burst."

"Can I speak with him?" Jamie asked.

"He's not here, dear. The curate wanted to talk to him about the wedding, so I came back home to make more phone calls."

"How's he doing? Ryan says he was acting more like Caitlin than himself. She said she didn't think he even needed the airplane to get him across the Atlantic."

"He certainly does seem excited. This is all turning out so well. Our curate pulled some strings and helped get everything organized. I think Mam helped convince him of a few things." She laughed. "She's quite good at that. Then Moira and I took Mam and Da shopping today, and she bought them both the most lovely things. I don't know how she afforded it, but she insisted." She took a breath, her words spilling out so fast that she was hard to understand. "Did I tell you she's arranged for a luncheon for everyone at the pub after the ceremony? My goodness, I don't know when I've been so excited. This is the wedding I dreamt of as a girl."

"Don't forget to take pictures for us, Maeve. We want to see every little detail."

"I brought my camera, honey. I'll assign Cormac to that job. We'll do our best."

"Well, you'd better wander over to church to pick up your fiancé, Maeve. You don't want to keep him waiting."

"I wouldn't dream of letting that adorable man wait for me. Thanks so much for everything. If it wasn't for you and your mother, none of this would have happened."

"Don't mention it," Jamie insisted. "If it wasn't for Martin and your influence I wouldn't have the wonderful partner that I have. I just hope you're as happy as we are. You truly deserve it."

"Thank you," she sniffed. "I'd better go now. I've got to go fetch my Marty."

"We love you, Maeve. We wish you all the happiness in the world."

"Bye," the older woman said, her voice choked with tears.

After the volleyball team played a very successful match against Arizona on Saturday night, Jamie and Mia stood near the locker room, waiting for their dates. The team usually had a quick meeting after home games—just a chance for Coach Placer to compliment them on their play and make a few tactful suggestions where needed. No one showered after the match, which Jamie found very strange. Most of the women didn't even venture into the locker room; they just exchanged their sweaty uniforms for T-shirts and their warm-ups, which most of them left in the meeting room during the game.

As the pair waited, a legion of young fans tried to get as close to the athletes as possible, pushing and elbowing each other to be near the spot where the women exited.

Ryan and Jordan were among the first to leave, each toting her enormous gym bag on her shoulder. Ryan immediately handed her bag to Jamie, who gave her a kiss on the cheek as a reward for her excellent play. Jordan gave Mia a shy smile and Jamie held her hand out and accepted her bag also. Both players then went into the large, unstructured half of the gym and began signing autographs. Tonight the team had distributed posters with very flattering photos of Jordan and Ryan prominently featured, both because of their play and because they were the only seniors on the team.

The girls who sought them out were anywhere from eight to sixteen years old, and many of them wore T-shirts and sweats that identified them as members of a school or club volleyball team. In fact, many of them came to the game as part of a team, with their coaches hovering around them trying to keep track of the kids in the crowd.

Jamie couldn't help eavesdropping on one pair of girls, who were nearly giddy when they walked away with autographs from their heroes. "Ryan's so tall," one of them said, in the cross between a scream and a whisper that only pre-teens could manage.

"Jordan's so pretty!" the other exclaimed.

"They're both really nice," Jamie said, catching the girls' attention.

"Do you know 'em?" the bolder of the pair asked, her eyes wide.

Jamie held up the gym bag, with "O'Flaherty" embroidered on the side. "Quite well," she said, smiling impishly.

Mia hefted her bag, too, displaying the "Ericsson" on her burden.

The girls looked at each other, their eyes wide, then emitted twin screams and ran out the door, laughing the whole way.

"My God, were we that weird only ten years ago?" Jamie laughed.

"I'm that weird now," Mia said rather dreamily. "I'm kinda stoked just to be holding her gym bag."

Jamie gave her a look and said, "I've never seen you like this about anybody. You're positively smitten."

"Oh, I am. Maybe it's because I have to work so hard. But whatever it is, I'm absolutely goofy for her."

"I was surprised to see that she went home last night. What's up with that?"

Letting out a wry laugh, Mia said, "We've been staying up most of the night for a month, James. She's on her last legs. Besides, I know everything about her by now. I could write her biography at this point. We don't need any more all-night talks. Now, we just need to get busy and make love."

"Any progress?"

"No, as a matter of fact. We actually seem to be doing less, rather than more. I'm gonna take her home and push the envelope tonight. I don't want to lose patience with her, but I also don't want to hang on forever if she doesn't want to keep moving forward."

Slipping an arm around her shoulder, Jamie said, "I hope you hang in there. She's really pretty special."

They both gazed at the lanky woman, who was now lying on her stomach on the gym floor signing autographs for the line of kids who waited patiently, posters and pens in hand. Ryan was lying right next to her, adding her signature as soon as Jordan finished. Jordan spotted Heather standing around, looking lost, and she called her over and ordered her to hit the floor and start signing. The shy freshman did as she was asked, the kids now making over her as well.

Watching the scene unfold, Mia sighed and said, "She really is special, and one of her best traits is that she doesn't know how special she is."

As soon as they arrived home, Ryan grabbed a big bottle of sports drink and she and Jamie went to bed. They had only been gone a few minutes when Mia leaned against Jordan and wrapped her in a hug. "You played so well tonight. It was honestly fascinating to watch you."

"Thanks. I felt good about tonight, to tell you the truth. I worked my ass off."

As Mia released her hold Jordan got a whiff of herself and said, "Wow, I smell like I worked my ass off. I should go home, take a hot shower, and get to bed."

"You know," Mia said, trying to sound casual, "I have a really nice shower here. My bed's not bad either. Wanna see?"

"Uhh." Jordan looked like she didn't know whether to run for the shower or the hills, but Mia didn't try to influence her. She wanted her to make up her own mind, and after a minute she did. "I'd like the shower. We'll see about the bed later."

"Good deal," Mia smiled, taking her hand to lead her upstairs. While Jordan was in the shower, Mia paced around the room trying to decide if she should try to set a mood or just act like this was an everyday occurrence. She finally decided to go for it, then turned off the overhead lights and lit a profusion of candles, their flames flickering against the darkened ceiling.

A muffled voice came from the bathroom, "I forgot my gym bag, will you get it for me? I need some clean clothes."

"Uhm…sure," Mia said, instead handing her friend a blue silk robe. Jordan's hand reached out, and she accepted the offering without comment, then emerged a minute later, looking magnificent to Mia's appreciative eyes. She had washed her hair and it was wrapped in a white towel, showing off her exquisite bone structure even more distinctly than usual. The short robe highlighted her pale blue eyes, and her cheeks glowed from the warm water. She smelled fantastic, having used some of Mia's favorite freesia shower gel.

"Blow dryer?" she asked, her voice tight with tension, her blue eyes darting nervously about the room.

Mia indicated her desk chair and said, "Sit. I'll do it for you."

Jordan raised an eyebrow but complied, sitting stiffly on the edge of the chair while Mia grabbed a wide-toothed comb that Jordan extended towards her. She worked the comb gently through the thick strands, being careful not to pull too hard. She had never combed another woman's hair before, and she found herself fascinated with the thick, straight tresses. Actually, Mia didn't technically comb her own hair. Her curls did not respond well to any attempts at order, so she usually just fluffed her fingers through them to provide some loose organization.

When the tangles were combed through, Mia took the blow dryer and worked the warm air through the hair, running her fingers along Jordan's scalp and then letting them slide through the silky tresses.

It was clear that Jordan was nervous, but she seemed willing to go where Mia was leading her, giving hope that they would finally make some progress. As Mia continued to touch her gently, Jordan's body grew more and more relaxed, eventually feeling pliable and receptive as Mia started to massage her shoulders.

"It's getting dry out now that it's fall. Can I put some lotion on you?" she asked softly, breaking the silence. Jordan's head rested comfortably against her hip.

She could actually see Jordan swallow, but to her satisfaction, she shrugged the robe from her shoulders. Jordan clasped some of the fabric to her breasts, but exposed her back and shoulders to Mia's touch. A massive sigh escaped Jordan's lips as Mia's hands began to work the freesia-scented body lotion into her skin, her fingers gliding over the dips and swells of muscle. "My God, but you have a beautiful back," Mia whispered as Jordan closed her eyes and leaned hard into the touch. "Such soft skin. It's like silk."

"Y…your hands…feel good." Jordan grimaced as she heard the nearly inarticulate sentence escape her mouth. She had so much to say—to share with Mia, but she knew that it would remain locked inside. So much emotion was threatening to burst forth that she was terrified of allowing the floodgates to open even a tiny bit.

Mia continued the gentle massage, focusing on letting Jordan become used to her touch and the sensation of exposing a part of her body. "You feel very tight. You didn't have the trainer work on your back after the game, did you?"

"No, I was in a hurry," she said, her voice so soft that Mia had to lean around her to catch the last words. "I couldn't wait to see you."

With a fond smile, Mia turned the desk chair just enough to be able to reach Jordan's shyly grinning mouth. "You are so sweet," she sighed, capturing the soft, full lips for several loving kisses.

When Jordan's eyes opened, Mia had not moved a muscle and she met and held her gaze. "Why don't you let me give you a real massage? I'm good at it."

"I just bet you are," Jordan smirked, a trace of her usual sense of humor making an appearance.

"Come on," Mia urged, reaching out to grasp the large, fine-boned hand that trembled slightly when she touched it.

Jordan stood, looking awkward and shy as she clutched the bright blue fabric against her chest. "Where do you want me?"

Mia looked at her quizzically and said, "I thought the bed would be the best choice. Is that okay?"

Lips pursed tightly, Jordan nodded and walked over to the queen-sized bed, which seemed to grow before her eyes. By the time she reached it, it appeared to fill the room, blocking her exit with its bulk. She gulped audibly as she stood in front of it, looking at the orchid and white checked flannel sheets that were in the same state of disarray that they had been in when Mia had crawled out of them that morning.

The curly-haired woman came up behind her and placed a hand on her exposed shoulder. Deciding to adopt a casual attitude she said, "Come on, let's get those muscles loose. You don't want to stiffen up."

Jordan did better dealing with a direct order, and she slipped the robe back into place and tied it, then set about making the bed, twitching the sheets into place and fluffing the pillows before settling them just so. Mia didn't comment on her actions. She went into the bath and found some vanilla-scented massage lotion and was warming a healthy dollop of it between her hands when Jordan got into position.

"Why don't I cover you with the blanket? That robe is just going to get in the way." Again, her casual, businesslike tone carried the day, and Jordan pulled the fleece blanket up to her waist, then slipped out of the robe entirely.

"Excellent," Mia said approvingly. She climbed onto the bed, straddled Jordan's hips, and started to work on the stiff muscles, almost immediately drawing a heavy sigh from Jordan.

"Ooh, that's perfect," her soft soprano voice purred.

"Glad you like it. I love to give massages. It's actually a nice way to get to know someone. You learn about how they like to be touched, how much pressure they like, if they're ticklish. All sorts of things, if you pay attention."

As the massage continued, Mia learned that Jordan could take every bit of pressure she could bring to bear, but that she also liked a delicate, whisper-soft touch. She didn't seem to be ticklish, and as time passed, she stopped shaking and seemed to appreciate the loving contact.

Mia kept the massage completely chaste, not even venturing past horizontal on the surface of her back. She stayed well above the blanket also, since Jordan was the one who had placed it just above her waistline.

"That feels great," Jordan finally said. "You do a better job than the trainer does."

"I care more," she said honestly, as her hands stilled, remaining splayed across the pale skin.

"I uhm…was thinking about what you said before," Jordan ventured, her voice once again high, and thin. "Would you like a massage? I'd…like to get to know you a little better, too."

"Sure," she said immediately, before Jordan could change her mind. Sliding off the bed, she started to undress, removing her sweater while Jordan performed a stunning series of moves to get the robe back on while still covered by the blanket. Mia rolled her eyes at her friend's extreme modesty, but she knew that the only way to get her past it was to be patient with her.

Jordan stood by the bed, managing to look everywhere but at Mia. The brunette removed her bra, then considered, *Do I have on cute panties today?* She paused to think for just a moment, then remembered that she had on a deep purple thong that was just the perfect shade to compliment her olive-toned complexion. *Good job! It's unlikely that she'll look anywhere near your ass, but if she does she'll have a nice view.* She unzipped her slacks, rolling her eyes again as Jordan flinched noticeably. *Good thing she's in great shape, or I'd be afraid of her having a heart attack. I can see the headline in the* Daily Californian. *"Volleyball player succumbs to zipper fright. 'I didn't even get my pants off,' grieving near–lover laments."*

Smirking at her internal monologue, Mia climbed into bed, settling the blanket around her hips just as Jordan had. Jordan straddled her and began to give her a fantastic massage—managing to be gentle yet firm, alternating delicate caresses with deep, penetrating pressure. "Oh, my Lord. Where did you learn to do this?" Mia moaned from her trance-like state of bliss.

"I had a great trainer one summer at a clinic I participated in." Mia noted that her voice had its normal confident timbre.

"Tell me about him or her."

"It was a guy. Probably three years ago. He was just great at giving massages, but his best quality was his ability to explain what he was doing and why. He taught me a lot."

"Where can I send a thank-you card? You are well taught."

"Thanks. I haven't really had the opportunity to do this before. Except for Ryan, that is."

"Hey, no fair," Mia teased. "Ryan gets to sleep with you first, she gets a massage before I do…"

"There are still a few things that I haven't shared with her," Jordan teased back. But when she heard what she was implying, her mouth snapped shut and she reverted to concentrating on the massage.

Mia had a feeling that the mood was lost, and she quietly enjoyed the last few minutes of the fabulous massage. When Jordan's hands stilled, she decided to take a bold risk. Turning her head until she could make eye contact, Mia asked, as casually as she could manage, "Want me to turn over? I bet your touch would feel divine on both sides."

Stark, dead silence filled the room, and Mia realized she'd been too forward. Grasping the sheet to her chest, she turned over as much as she could and started to apologize, but the look on Jordan's face brought her up short.

Mia didn't think she had ever seen anyone who looked more like they were wrestling with a dilemma. She could almost see the internal dialogue in Jordan's mind, but she didn't say a word. It was important to her that Jordan only go as far as she was willing—and she decided that she didn't want to tip the scales in any way. However, she eventually couldn't stand it another minute and asked, "Tell me what you want. Not what you think you should do, or what you're afraid of. Tell me what you want."

The ice-blue eyes locked on her and she mumbled, "I want to run." The delicate lids snapped shut, and she began to tremble again, looking like she was about to cry.

Tucking the sheet under her armpits, Mia sat up and grasped her by the arms. "Jordan," she said firmly, "you don't have to run. We'll only go as far as you want. I promise that. If you want to stop, we'll stop. If you want to get dressed and stay and talk for a while, that's fine, too. I just want you to know that I will never push you. You don't have to run from me. It's safe here."

The blue eyes cracked open and immediately sought out the warmth of Mia's gaze. "Only part of me wants to run," she whispered. "Another part wants to touch you so badly that I feel like I'll go mad if I don't."

"It's safe," Mia whispered. She grasped a trembling hand and held it to her chest, chafing the soft skin with her hands. "I won't hurt you."

"I don't know how to touch you," Jordan said, her voice coiled with tension. "Will you show me?"

"Of course I will." Mia sighed, her heart breaking for the obvious distress that her friend was in. "How would you like me to show you?"

Jordan lay down on the bed and closed her eyes as she tugged open the tie to her robe. Spreading the fabric open, she revealed her body to Mia's stunned gaze. *Oh, my God. Thank you for having her close her eyes, 'cause it'd be embarrassing to let her see me drool.*

Jordan's shaking hand lifted, and Mia instinctively laced their fingers together. Jordan placed the smaller hand upon her breast and whispered, "Show me."

The blue fabric still covered the long body from waist to thigh, so Mia climbed astride her once more, the robe providing a thin, protective barrier for Jordan's modesty. Now it was Mia's hands that shook, nearly rivaling the trembling in the long body that she lovingly caressed. *She trusts me so much. What a gift that is.*

Mia massaged the stunningly smooth skin with reverence, keeping her touch light and delicate. She repeatedly replenished the lotion on her hands, wanting her touch to glide across Jordan's body, not even allowing the friction of her hands to mar the perfect flesh.

She continued the loving touch until Jordan had visibly relaxed and her breathing had calmed. The blue eyes had remained shuttered, but they slowly blinked open and gazed at Mia with a gentle question reflected in their clear blue depths. She obviously decided not to pose her query verbally, instead lifting her hand to trail the backs of her fingers up Mia's exposed side.

Mia twitched and involuntarily pulled away, stifling a giggle as she did so. "Yes, I'm ticklish. Ridiculously so. Like a three-year-old." She had a resigned smirk on her face, but Jordan's expression remained serious. Outlining Mia's lips with the tip of her index finger, Jordan promised, "I'll never take advantage of you because of your ticklishness."

Turning her head, Mia captured Jordan's fingers and kissed them gently. "I know that."

Jordan rose up on her elbows, holding Mia's gaze for a long time. Sitting up fully, she wrapped her arms around Mia's body and started to kiss, their breasts pressing lightly against each other. Unable to contain the moan that sprang up from her core, Mia held on tight and opened herself fully to Jordan's increasingly confident caresses.

Their bodies slowly grew hot to the touch, their skin tingling everywhere their flesh came into contact. Hands threaded through silky and curly tresses, mouths opened—sucking gently on tongues, moans mingling. Jordan's breath had grown so ragged that she was now softly panting, her eyes hooded with the desire that pulsed through her veins.

Finally, pulling away roughly, she grasped Mia firmly by the shoulders and said, "I can't fight this anymore." Her determined face and fiery eyes locked upon Mia's. "I don't care who knows…I don't care that I know. I can't deny myself any longer. No matter what the consequences—I've got to have you."

Mia grasped the long, lean woman by the shoulders and pulled her down, their breasts compressing against each other as Jordan settled onto her. "I've never wanted anyone like I want you," she murmured, her voice soft and gentle. Her hands roamed all over the smooth, strong, yet delicate body. "It makes me feel very special to share this with you."

"You are special. You're very special to me," her soft voice murmured, eyes full of confidence in her decision. Her smile broadened even as she began to shake again. With a look that merged equal parts stark fear and burning desire, she whispered, "Let's make love."

Mia let the wish hang in the air for a few minutes, stroking Jordan's cheek, letting her eyes convey her wholehearted acceptance of the offer. She wanted to give the shaking woman time to change her mind, while hoping fervently that she wouldn't. It soon became clear that Jordan wanted to continue, but equally clear that she didn't have any idea of how to begin.

Denying her almost painful desire, Mia concentrated on making Jordan feel loved and cared for. She knew the remarkably lovely woman didn't often feel lovely, and she silently pledged that she would do everything in her power to make her feel so.

Her hands glided with a whisper-soft touch, slowly pushing the silky fabric away. Eyes locked together, Mia smiled at the look of intense pleasure on Jordan's face as her hands caressed her. "I love touching you this way," she whispered. "You're such a beautiful woman."

Jordan blushed becomingly, averting her eyes as she struggled to accept the compliment. "You make me feel beautiful," she said, her voice soft and winsome.

"You're just as beautiful here," Mia insisted, placing a kiss on her temple, "as you are here." She placed delicate kisses down the long body, starting at the hollow between her collarbones, and continuing to her navel.

Unexpectedly, Jordan threw her arms around Mia's body and hugged her tight. She felt as if she would burst from the wellspring of feeling that pummeled her, but she didn't know how to express herself. Her instincts told her to grab on and hold Mia as closely as she could, but that's the only clear message she was able to decipher.

Mia was patient with her, letting her go at her own pace, even though she was about to combust. Her ribs were beginning to ache, and she freed an arm to stroke down the long, muscled back, soothing Jordan with her gentle caress. "I know," she murmured, "It's a lot to process, isn't it?"

"Yeah," Jordan's shaking voice agreed. "It's an awful lot."

"Just relax," Mia urged. "Lie back and let me touch you. Let me know what feels good," she soothed, "and what feels even better." Her voice had dropped into a low growl, and Jordan's toes curled at the frank sexuality of her tone.

She dropped to the bed inelegantly, her quivering muscles unable to support her any longer. Consciously opening her body to Mia's touch, Jordan held her breath as determined hands smoothly removed her robe, leaving her naked and more vulnerable than she had ever been. "Relax," Mia soothed as the long body continued to twitch with tension. "Just relax." The small, cool hands stroked across her skin, the gentle touch too appealing to resist. Jordan's body slowly calmed as the touch grew more focused, and her nerve endings began to tingle from the sensation.

"Ooh, yes," Jordan whispered. "That's fantastic."

Mia moved slightly, bringing her head up to rest on the same pillow with Jordan's. Their lips met and merged, the passionate kisses causing the blood to pound in Jordan's head as Mia's hands claimed her body. It was almost too much, but she forced herself to breathe deeply and focus on the touch rather than the emotion that was flooding her brain.

Body and brain warred for supremacy, the echoes of previous emotionless intimacies fighting to be resurrected. But she focused on Mia, chanting her name like a mantra to her mistrusting inner voices. Lifting her eyes repeatedly, she let the warm brown depths soothe her tumultuous thoughts, gaining strength from the sure, gentle regard she found there.

Eventually her mind calmed, and she opened her body and her heart to the gentle woman who held her in her arms, surprised by the strength and sureness of her embrace. All rational thought slowly ceased. Her body now in control, the deeply intimate caresses overpowered any shred of doubt about her sexuality that she harbored. This was right—so very right, and suddenly that was all that mattered.

Her breathing grew more erratic and her heart beat wildly, feeling like it would explode from her chest. The sensations grew to be so overpowering that all she could do was hold on and let them take her. Long, elegantly-shaped hands clutched at Mia, grasping at her hair, her skin—anything that she could reach to stay grounded. A fantastic burst of feeling washed over her as her body convulsed in sensation, the feeling at once brand new and deeply familiar.

Suddenly she was being cradled and soothed, warm gentle hands caressing her tenderly as her heart slowly calmed. She blinked up at Mia, desperately wanting to express the feelings that filled her heart, but she was completely unable to utter a single word. Tears formed in her blue eyes, spilling onto her cheeks, where Mia immediately kissed them away, lifting her head to lock her gaze onto Jordan's face, searching her expression for a gauge to her feelings. "Are you all right?"

"Perfect," Jordan whispered, a tired smile curling the corner of her mouth. "As long as you hold me, I'm just perfect."

Chapter Eight

R yan woke to a day that seemed wrapped in a gloomy gray fog. It was early in the year for rain, but as she looked out the window she saw the steady downpour pelting relentlessly against the house. *I thought I heard rain, but it's so damned windy I couldn't be sure.*

She was one of the many San Franciscans who actually enjoyed the worst that the climate could throw at her, and without regard for her comfort she decided to go for a nice long run. It had been over six months since any measurable rain had fallen, and she found that she missed it greatly. As a child spending her summers in Ireland, she had not been exposed to the months of bone-dry summer weather that most of California was subject to, and she didn't care for it. So when rain did come, she tried to enjoy it as much as possible.

Dressing as carefully as she could, she trotted down the stairs and slipped outside. *Good Lord! As my Granny would say, "Tis desperate."* It could not have been over 45 degrees, and the wind was blowing the rain almost horizontally, making it seem even colder. *Oh, this is gonna be fun*, she decided as she stretched. Fun, however, it was most definitely not. The rain stung her face and hands like millions of tiny needles, and before she had gone fifty feet she could hardly see because of the tears welling up in her eyes. *Oh, mama. This is torture.* But even though every sensible bone in her body urged her to return to her nice warm house, she kept on with a fiercely determined gait. It wasn't that she enjoyed torturing herself, it was that she couldn't bear to have the weather dictate her choice of activities. People all over the world carried on with their normal days even when it was bitterly cold, snowing, and sleeting—she wasn't about to let a little rain stop her.

As she ran along, she realized that she was feeling quite unsettled at the thought of her father marrying her aunt without her or any of her brothers in attendance. She knew that was small-minded, and that it wasn't for a lack of desire on her father and Maeve's part. Nonetheless, she hated to know that they were now married, and that only the European side of the family had been able to share in their joy.

She was so lost in her thoughts that it wasn't until after the first mile that she realized the stinging pain was lessening significantly, but then she realized that was only because her face and hands were now mostly numb. She compulsively shook her head to clear the icy water from her stinging eyes, but the motion did little good. She motored along more by instinct and feel than vision, but as she continued she felt herself slide deeper into an infrequently achieved trance. That wasn't the proper term, but she didn't have a better name for it. Strangely, she found it easiest to enter when the distractions around her grew too strong.

As her concentration deepened, she felt easy and light and completely disconnected from the mundane concerns of the world. She let herself become her stride and her breathing and the mass of dark hair that slapped against her back with each step. She just was…As simple as it sounded, that was the reality—she just was.

The rain no longer stung, the cold no longer bit her skin, the wind did not whip her hair into her eyes, every bit of the experience became her, so there were no more distractions. As she glided along, her mood lightened until she became absolutely euphoric. The miles flew by as she traversed streets she'd never consciously seen before. Everything looked new and fresh and unique. The earth actually seemed to shift under her feet, but she felt her body adjust seamlessly to the change. The muscles in her thighs seemed to grow as new demands were made on them, but her perfectly tuned body accepted the burden without complaint. Her lungs worked harder and harder to supply blood to her extremities, but again all systems cooperated to keep the machine functioning flawlessly. She turned a corner and gazed down at the cloud choked city and…*down?*

She jerked to an abrupt halt as the trance was shattered. *My God, where am I?* Her mind tried to accept the fact that she was high above the city, probably up in the Berkeley hills. But she had no idea exactly where she was, and even less of an idea how to get home. Glancing at her watch, she saw that it was nearly eight o'clock. *Shit. I've been out for two hours. Jamie's going to be frantic.*

Since it had taken two hours to get where she was, it was obviously going to take longer than that to get home, now that her broken trance allowed her body to recognize that it was thoroughly exhausted. Shoving her hands into the pockets of her thin nylon windbreaker, she extracted nothing but lint. *Shit. How can I go out running without I.D. or change? That's ridiculously irresponsible of me.*

She tried to stop her self-recriminations to logic out a solution to her problem. *First thing is to find someone who can tell me how to get out of this neighborhood.* She started to run again, wincing at the stiffness that was beginning to settle in her over-stressed thighs. *Oh boy, I've really done it this time. Jamie's gonna have my hide.*

She struggled along for about a quarter mile before she spotted a man doing some light stretching on his covered front porch. *Ahh, a fellow masochist.* She dashed up to him and asked, "Pardon me, but I've gotten a bit lost. Can you steer me out of the neighborhood?"

"Uhm, sure," he said, looking a little suspicious. "Where'd you come from?"

"I live a few blocks from Claremont and Ashby."

He blinked at her for a second, not quite able to believe her, but seeing no reason for her to lie. "You ran up here?"

"Yeah," she replied sheepishly as the water cascaded down her face. "I was in a zone."

"That was some zone," he laughed as he shook his head. "My wife gives me a hard time about running two miles in this weather. She should count her blessings."

"Yeah, I'm gonna get my butt kicked if I ever get home."

"Come on in and use the phone. Somebody's got to be worried about you," he said with an appreciative glance down her long, lean body.

She was about to say no, having caught the slight leer, but his curious wife came to the door and said, "Tim? Who are you talking to?" She leaned her head out and snagged a glance at Ryan, then another back at her husband.

"Oh, honey," he said. "This woman's lost. Can she come in and call her...husband?" This last remark was directed at Ryan, but she just smiled at him.

"Uhm, sure," the man's wife said hesitantly as she gazed at the water dripping off every inch of the leggy brunette.

"Actually," Ryan offered, "would you mind making a call for me? I don't want to drip all over your house."

"Sure, I'd be happy to." She dashed back in the house and grabbed a pad and pencil. "What's the number?"

Ryan gave her the particulars and waited as the woman darted back in. She cooled her already icy heels for a few minutes chatting with the man. By the time his wife returned he knew a substantial amount about Ryan, but she had learned nothing about him. *Must be a lawyer*, she mused. Rosemary, as Tim had identified her in her absence, returned with a smirk on her face and a much warmer attitude. "Jamie says to tell you not to move a muscle. You're in deep trouble."

"I thought maybe she'd go easier on me if I had you call." She laughed as Tim looked at her curiously.

"Well, she told me that if you tried to leave, I should hurl something at the back of your head to stop you," she explained with a smirk. "Does that sound like she's going to go easy on you?"

"At least I didn't ask you to call my father. He reacts much worse, since he long ago had his fill of bailing me out of trouble."

"I won't," the thoroughly contrite woman said from her spot on the kitchen chair as her lover towered over her.

"And you promise to never leave the house without money or a calling card on you?"

"I won't."

"But you know that I still have to punish you, right?"

"I guess I do. What are you going to do to me?"

"I'm going to take you shopping," she said, sliding onto Ryan's nice, dry, sweat pants-covered lap.

An hour later they emerged from the sporting goods store with a foul-weather running outfit. At Jamie's insistence, Ryan had purchased a lightweight shell that was completely waterproof and windproof and had the added benefit of being very quiet, since she maintained that she could not tolerate the "swoosh swoosh" sound that most nylon garments made. It was a bright gold color that they labeled "butternut," but Ryan failed to notice the similarity between the color and the squash.

She also carried a pair of wind-shield tights that were a cross between snug-fitting nylon tights and rain pants. They only came in black, but Jamie preferred that anyway since the dark color made her lover's legs look even more long and lean. When Ryan's attention was diverted, Jamie slipped a pair of wind-shield gloves in with the purchases to keep her partner's hands warm on the chilly mornings they were sure to have more of. As they neared the checkout counter, Jamie spied the last necessity—a bright gold waterproof nylon baseball cap. She tried it on her partner, pronounced it "cute" and added it to the pile, shaking it at Ryan as she ordered, "Wear this one with the bill in front for a change, Buffy. I want to keep the water from your pretty blue eyes."

"Did we really need this stuff?" Ryan complained. "I've been running in the rain for a very long time, and I've never suffered because of it."

"How did you feel when you first hit the street this morning?"

"Mmm, miserable?"

"Um-hmm," Jamie replied. "And what part of you thinks that is necessary?"

"The Spartan part?"

"That's right, precious, but running in this muck is plenty Spartan. You don't have to compound that by being drenched to the skin, goofball."

"Not many people could use 'precious' and 'goofball' in the same breath," Ryan mused. "You're very talented."

"Thank you. I get lots of practice with you since I so often feel like kissing you and kicking you in the butt simultaneously."

They stopped by the house to drop off their purchases before they left to pick up the newlyweds at the airport. "Hey, honey?" Jamie asked as she bent down to write a note to Mia. "Are these Jordan's keys?"

"Yep," Ryan said, taking a look at the set. She looked at Jamie as a smile broke out across her face. "Think our friends took the plunge last night?"

"Mia said she was going to try to push a bit. Maybe she finally fell."

Ryan shot a worried glance upstairs and said, "I hope it went well for them. I don't want Jordan to get hurt."

"Mia really likes her. This isn't just a conquest for her. I'm certain of that."

"I hope so," Ryan mused. "I really hope so."

"The plane won't land any sooner, no matter how many times you pace in front of that window."

Ryan looked at her partner with a sheepish grin, slightly embarrassed to be caught. "Okay, so I'm a little anxious." She turned her attention back to the dim, gray skies over San Francisco. "Oh, that might be them," she said excitedly as she pointed to a plane making a wide turn toward the gate.

Just as she spoke the flight was announced, and Jamie watched with amusement as her lover's anxiety turned to elation. She ran over to the gate and began to fidget as she craned her neck around, trying to observe every bit of activity occurring beyond the heavy double doors that opened and closed repeatedly with airport personnel. Finally the doors were fully opened and the first passengers began to file through. Jamie was a few feet away from Ryan, choosing not to be in the scrum of people waiting to fetch their loved ones, but it was patently obvious when Ryan spied her father coming down the passageway. Her face broke into a smile so luminous that tears immediately came to Jamie's eyes. Luckily,

Ryan's arms were quite long, and they allowed her to snake one arm around both Martin and Maeve. She wasn't very verbal, but neither of the newlyweds could have any doubt that they had been missed. She kissed both of them again and again, and Jamie finally decided that she needed to butt in or she would never get to greet them.

"Welcome home," she said as she lifted Ryan's arm from Maeve's back and slid into the group hug.

"It's good to be home," Martin responded heartily as he stood at his full height and stretched a bit. "It's no wonder Ireland seems so different. It's damned far. I thought we'd never get off that plane."

"Well, you're home now," Ryan assured him "I'll go pull the car up to the arrival area. I'll be waiting when you've collected your bags."

Fifteen minutes later they were headed home. "I'll bet you're starved," Ryan said, "but Conor's in charge of Sunday dinner. Would you rather stop at McDonald's?"

"Well, our bodies believe it's two a.m.," Martin reminded them. "The boy could make a bowl of porridge and a piece of toast and I'd be happy."

"That sounds good to me too," Maeve agreed.

"So…uhm…where will you…should I drop your bags at our house, or…" Ryan knew she was fumbling, but she had no idea of where the happy couple was going to live until their house was ready.

"Kevin can come get me after we have a bite," Maeve said.

Jamie bluntly asked, "Aren't you going to sleep together? You're newlyweds, for goodness sake."

Martin laughed at her impudence and revealed, "There's a little more to it than that, girls. We didn't talk about this on the phone, but we aren't actually, technically married."

"What?" Ryan barked out as she her head swiveled around so quickly that the car nearly swerved out of the lane.

"The problem was," Maeve explained, "that we didn't have the required three weeks to post the banns of marriage. Father tried his best, but the bishop would not allow an exemption from the rule, especially since we had both been married before."

"What's a ban of marriage?" Jamie asked, now thoroughly confused.

"It's one of the church's requirements to guard against bigamy and the like," Maeve explained. "They post the upcoming marriage for three weeks to allow anyone who has knowledge about a prior marriage to come forward. It's one area where the church encourages gossip."

"So, what kind of married are you?" Ryan asked, thoroughly confused.

"Father married us in the church building, but he could only certify a civil marriage, so we're still not married in the eyes of the Church. But only Moira knew that. I wanted Mam and Daddy to think they'd finally witnessed the real thing."

"And knowing you two, you don't consider yourselves married at all," Ryan guessed.

"You're right on that one," Maeve answered. "So the good news is that our January service is not just for show. It's the real deal."

"But the bad news is…" Ryan smirked, turning and shooting a glance at her father.

"Your mind is focused on the desires of the flesh as usual," he chided her as he gave her a playful tap on the back of her head.

"Gee, Da, I didn't expect you to emulate the way Jamie and I structured our relationship. We waited for almost three months before we had sex. You want to go for the record?"

"That's enough out of you, Siobhán," he warned.

"My mother always said that nothing created good character like a little self-control," Maeve joked.

"Yeah, she's all about self-control," Ryan said as a grim look passed over her face.

Jamie turned slightly and caught an astonishingly similar look on Martin's face, but Maeve didn't seem to notice.

"When I was in high school, Mam gave me the lecture about self-control," the older woman related with a chuckle. "I was so terribly naïve that I truly did not know what she was talking about. All she managed to do was frighten me terribly and make me fear the boys at school. Poor Charlie really had his work cut out with the likes of me," she laughed, referring to her first husband.

"Yes, it was quite the shock when we boys got to San Francisco in the 60's," Martin related. "Ireland was still very backwater then, very provincial and proper. To be thrown over here during the beginnings of the hippie movement was quite the experience."

"So did you avail yourself of all of the free love, Da?" Ryan asked with an impish look.

"I most certainly did not," he huffed. "Unlike some people I know, I was brought up with a good, healthy fear of any such behavior. The fires of hell seemed like a terrible price to pay for a fleeting pleasure." He playfully reached into the front seat and slapped his grinning daughter on the shoulder.

Ryan's face grew serious as she turned slightly and said, "Thank you for not putting that fear in us. You never made us afraid of suffering eternal damnation for expressing our sexuality."

"Well," he said thoughtfully, with a smile struggling to get out, "I certainly hope I wasn't wrong on that point. Because if I was, you'll be stuck down in the lowest rungs of hell, Siobhán."

"Yeah, but at least I'll have Conor to keep me company. And the girls down there will be hot…in every way."

🐎

Jamie called the house from her cell and asked Conor to cook up some oatmeal for the jet-lagged travelers. By the time they reached the house, Brendan and Kevin had joined the group to welcome the new couple home. Both Martin and Maeve were very appreciative of the welcome, their happiness supplanting their exhaustion.

Despite their fatigue, the pair managed to relate most of the details of their trip. The boys were also shocked to hear that they were not married according to church law, but after enduring some good-natured teasing, the nearly-newlyweds continued with their stories. "And which one of you sprites was responsible for bringing a photographer all the way up from Galway?" Martin asked as he cast a stern gaze on the two women.

"Not me," Ryan said honestly. "I have no knowledge."

"I couldn't let you get married without pictures," Jamie explained. "Did he do a good job?"

"He seemed confused," Martin admitted with a chuckle. "I don't think he'd ever been that far out of the city. But once he got used to the scale of things, he did a fine job."

"How did you arrange for that?" Ryan asked, slightly amazed.

"You can find anything on the Internet if you look hard enough."

"We truly appreciated it," Maeve said sincerely. "Everyone was so generous. Moira acted like she'd won the Sweepstakes this year. She even bought my dress."

"So, how many people attended?" Ryan asked, trying to steer the conversation away from money.

"Oh, my, the church was nigh onto bursting. I'm not sure how many came, but we have the guest books here. We can count them up later."

"Did any of your family come up, Da?" Brendan asked.

"I was quite surprised that several carloads came up from Kerry."

"Do you have many relatives still in Ireland, Martin?" Jamie asked.

"Oh, yes. One of the blessings of coming from a large family. My father was one of seven, and my mother was the eldest of nine," he related. "Naturally, I've still got a few uncles and aunts there, and my first and second cousins are legion."

"Now, what's the name of your town?" Jamie asked Maeve.

"If people know Ireland, we say we're from near Ballina—that's the big town. Our village is Killala, and you have to be familiar with County Mayo to have even heard of it."

"How many people live there?"

"Oh, not more than seven hundred. It's just large enough for one pub, one shop for necessities, and of course a church."

"A town that small can support a church?" Jamie gaped.

"Oh, certainly. There are smaller villages nearby and forks in the road with a few more people to add to the roster. Since nearly everyone is some degree of Catholic, it's actually necessary to have a church. It's a very small affair, though," she said. "The big church is in Ballina, and that's where the parish priest, Father McConnell, is. Father Kearney is the curate for our church. He's the sweetest young man, didn't you think, Martin?"

"He was very nice. Even though he looked like he hadn't started to shave yet."

"Mam says he was just ordained last June. He said we were just his fifth wedding."

"I'm really happy it went so well," Ryan said. "But you'd better get to bed soon. Da, you have to work tomorrow, don't you?"

"Ahh, don't remind me," he scowled. "I want to stay home and just moon over my beloved half-bride."

"That's a rather odd term, but I suppose it fits," Maeve agreed. "I'll make you a deal, Martin. Be a good man and go to work, and I'll bring you a nice lunch. We can walk over to Mission Dolores and have a picnic."

"You're really not going to stay overnight?" Conor asked.

"Of course not," Martin said indignantly. "Weren't you paying attention, boy? We said we're not married yet."

"You're civilly married. That counts."

"Not all of us take the laws of the faith so lightly, Conor."

"Boy, I'm glad I don't have any morals," Conor mused. "That's brutal."

❧

They returned home at nine, and Ryan was puzzled to see that nothing in the house had been disturbed: the keys were right where they had been that morning, the note hadn't been moved, there were eight messages on the machine, and Mia's pager was dancing across the table. Jamie hit the message button on the answering machine and heard six messages from Mia's mom, as well as two from her brother Peter, each one more perturbed. Jamie checked the pager and saw Mia's parents' number keyed in. "Honey, do you think they're even up there?" she asked, casting a glance at the stairs.

"How could they not be? Jordan can't get into her apartment without her keys, and Mia never leaves without her pager. They've got to be here."

Jamie poked her head into the kitchen and saw that there was not a single thing out of place—no glasses in the sink, no dirty plates piled up on the counter. She took a look in the refrigerator and saw that all of the leftovers from the night before were still in their containers. "Honey," Jamie said, now worried, "they didn't eat or drink anything all day. We have to check on them."

"Okay," Ryan said, giving her partner a raised-eyebrow smile. "Check on them."

"I thought maybe you could check on them."

"Nope. I've stayed in bed for twenty-four hours plenty of times. It's no big deal."

Jamie scowled at her and said, "I don't know what her mom wanted, but she sounded pissed, didn't she?"

"Yeah, a little, I guess," Ryan admitted.

The phone rang again, and Jamie answered, "Oh, hi, Mrs. Christopher. Yeah, it's Jamie. I'm good." She was rolling her eyes at Ryan the entire time, finally saying, "I just got home, and I'm not sure if she's here. I'll go check and have her call you, okay?" Her face dropped as she said, "No, it's okay, you can hold on. Be right back."

She scowled at Ryan again and ran up the stairs, pressing her ear against the door to determine if there was any sound coming from the space. When she failed to detect any movement she knocked lightly, but didn't hear any response. A louder knock still produced nothing, so she shrugged her shoulders and ran back down. "No, she's not here, Mrs. Christopher. She forgot her pager. It's lying here on the table, so that's why she hasn't called you back. Yes, she could drive a saint to drink sometimes," she chuckled. "Okay, I'll tell her, bye."

"Weird," Jamie said as she gazed at her partner. "Where in the hell do you think they are?"

Ryan gave her a frown and marched upstairs. Not bothering to knock, she opened the door to find Jordan, stark naked, her body nestled between Mia's legs, head resting upon her thigh. Her long legs were hanging off the end of the bed, the top sheet and comforter thrown to the floor, along with all of the pillows. An empty quart of orange juice lay on top of the discarded bedding, obviously the only nourishment the pair had enjoyed. She walked over and lightly touched Jordan's back, shaking her head when she felt how chilled her skin was.

Ryan grasped Jordan's shoulder and gave it a shake, repeating the movement with more force when she didn't respond immediately.

Jordan finally let out an unhappy whimper, but Ryan persisted and finally got one blue eye to open. "Time to shift up on the bed," Ryan whispered.

The full lips quirked into a lazy grin, and she started to shimmy up the bed. She dropped her head onto the pillow that Ryan had put into place, but now Mia's head was several inches below hers. Ryan started to move over to the other side of the bed to put a pillow under her head, but Jordan handled the situation by snaking her long arms around her and tugging her into place—curled up against her side, with Jordan's shoulder as a perfectly acceptable pillow substitute.

Ryan unfurled the sheet over their bodies and quickly tucked it in, then added the light blanket, smiling to herself when Jordan made a vague kissing sound in her direction. "I love you too," she whispered before tiptoeing out of the room.

As she closed the door, she nearly ran into Jamie, who was lurking just outside.

"Are they okay?"

"They appear to be just fine…exhausted, but fine."

"Are they awake?"

"Nope. Well, Jordan was semi-conscious, but Mia's dead to the world. Even without verbal confirmation, though, I do believe that our little Jordan lost her virtue last night…and this morning…and this afternoon…and this evening…"

The excitement of the weekend caught up to both of the women, and Ryan overslept for the first time in ages. She didn't even have time for breakfast before class, running down the stairs at full tilt… then screeching to a halt at the passionate good-bye being said in the entryway.

Mia was wearing a blue silk robe, and Jordan had on her warm-ups, the only clothes she had brought with her on Saturday. Their arms were locked tightly around each other, their mouths so firmly glued to each other that they were practically fused. Ryan tiptoed around them, grabbing her book bag from the spot she had dropped it on Friday, nary a book having left the cozy nylon confines the entire weekend.

She secured the bag onto her back and tried to pass by the new lovers, stopping abruptly when Jordan's hand reached out and grabbed her jacket as she passed. "Wait for me," the tall blonde murmured, her lips just far enough away from Mia's to be able to speak.

Ryan rolled her eyes and walked across the porch slowly, waiting for Jordan with as much patience as she could muster. Jordan started to pull away, Mia still hanging on tenaciously as Jordan backed up. By the time they reached the stone steps, Mia was bending over, trying to hold on for yet another tender buss. Jordan reached out to gently break the suction. "Gotta go," she whispered. "See you… tonight?"

"Oh yeah," Mia drawled sensuously, crossing her arms across her chest to hold her robe closed. "I've got plans for you."

Blowing the curly-haired brunette a kiss, Jordan practically skipped down the sidewalk, catching up with Ryan as they reached the street. "Have a nice weekend?" Ryan asked, smirking.

Jordan shot her a goofy-looking grin, then launched into a set of three cartwheels, finishing up with a neatly tucked somersault, landing gently on her feet, a laugh bubbling up from her chest. "Why wasn't I informed of how absolutely fabulous it feels to make love?" She threw her arms out and turned in a tight circle, intentionally trying to make herself dizzy.

"I don't remember you asking my opinion." Ryan smiled, slinging an arm around the happy woman's shoulders. "I would have given you my enthusiastic endorsement."

"It's not just the physical sensations," Jordan said earnestly. "It's… God, I don't even know what it is. It's looking into her eyes when you're touching her, and knowing that you're the one who put that adorable smile on her face."

Ryan just smiled at her friend, knowing exactly what she was talking about, but not feeling the need to give her any feedback. Jordan had grown so animated that she was running backwards while she spoke, trying to make sure that Ryan understood the importance of her point. "Jesus, I had no idea it'd feel like this. I thought it would be about what you did and how you did it, but it's not. It's about how you feel, and how you make the other person feel," she decided, sure that she had an insight into this mystery that few others understood.

"It is," Ryan agreed, unable to keep the wide grin from her face. "It's all about feeling if you do it with the right person." She cocked her head a bit and asked, "So, did you do okay…technically? You said you were worried about having to learn on the job."

Jordan looked at her with an amazed expression, obviously trying to come to terms with her feelings. "I was horrible! I didn't have any idea of what to do, or how to do it, but Mia was so wonderful. She was right there for me, helping me to get over my nervousness… just making me feel wonderful. I got better as the weekend went along," Jordan said, smiled, "but I finally realized that it doesn't matter. You just have to show her how you feel, and everything works out okay. Isn't that weird?" she asked, still dumbfounded.

"Weird, but true," Ryan nodded. "All true."

"I kinda thought that I'd have to act like a guy—you know?" Ryan's eyes widened, and the surprise on her face made Jordan blush fiercely. "I know I'm a total dunce, but you always hear guys talking about how big they are and how long they can last. I guess I thought that was the important thing—like there was some technique to pleasing a woman that I wouldn't be able to master."

"No way. Guys would do a hell of a lot better if they could understand that. Penis size doesn't matter…heck, I don't have a penis at all, and I've never had any complaints. It's not about equipment—it's about connecting emotionally."

"Yes. Yes. That's it." Jordan launched into another cartwheel. "It's about connecting emotionally. Too true."

Ryan smiled at her friend's antics, having never seen Jordan act so free or jubilant. A thought flittered through her mind, and she spent a moment examining it. *It took me until I fell in love with Jamie to understand what Jordan's talking about. Is she just gifted, or is this fling a lot more than a fling?*

"Hey, James? Is that you?" Mia called out when she heard someone walking down the hall.

"Yeah." She entered Mia's room and immediately walked to the window, throwing it open to get a little air circulating. "I don't even want to tell you what this place smells like."

"I bet it smells like twenty-four hours of some of the best sex I've ever had," Mia mused lazily. She was stretched out in bed, obviously naked under the sheet, her arms tossed casually over her head.

"Really?" Jamie asked, dying to learn some details. "I thought it would be kinda rough, what with her not having any experience."

"Well, technically, on a scale of one to ten, I'd honestly have to give her a negative six." Mia laughed. "She was so nervous on Saturday night that she must have lost five pounds just from shivering. She acted like she was lying on a bed of snow. Seriously."

"Okay, so where did the great sex come in?"

Mia looked up at her friend with a slightly puzzled gaze. "It's hard to say, to be honest. It felt so wonderful to be with her that way. She was so nervous, and so hesitant, but the trust in her eyes just took my breath away." She shook her head as she said, "She was so tender and gentle with me, like nothing I've ever experienced before. She didn't just focus on making me come either, although she took instruction well," she added with a smirk. "I feel like I saw what's in her heart, James. I don't know how else to say it. I felt like I saw her heart."

Smiling at her friend, Jamie admitted, "I know how that feels. It's really something, isn't it?"

"It's the best, James. She holds me like I'm some fragile object that she treasures. I've never felt like that before."

Jamie approached the bed and gave her friend a hug, adding a kiss as she pulled away. "Everyone should feel like that. That's why they call it making love."

"I don't like this," Jamie murmured into the navy blue nylon jacket that covered her partner's chest.

"I don't like it either, but it's fine. I'd prefer that you didn't come to the game tonight."

"But I've never missed one of your games if I could get to it," she protested.

"I know, but you said yourself that you can't afford the time. Even though San Jose isn't far, it'd take at least five hours out of your evening, and with your accounting mid-term tomorrow, you really can't spend that much time."

"Will your family be there?"

"No. Da has to work, Rory's got a gig, and I told Conor not to come. He gets up so early that it's not fair to expect him to come down for every game. Besides, the whole clan is going to make an effort to come on Friday to watch Stanford kick our asses, so I'll see everyone then."

"Hey, you beat them last time," Jamie pointed out.

"Uh-huh, I know that, punkin, but they haven't lost at home in over four years. No good reason to think we'll stop that string. I think we just caught them on an off night in Berkeley. We are their only loss, you know."

"Well, I know you can do it. I have nothing but confidence in you."

San Jose State gave them no trouble at all and the mood was very upbeat when they straggled out of the locker room. Ryan took the time to take a shower since she didn't want to stiffen up on the long ride home, so she was the last to leave. As she poked her head out of the locker room she was amazed to find Catherine waiting patiently for her. "Catherine." she exclaimed with delight. "I had no idea you'd be here. I didn't even look up in the stands because I didn't expect anyone."

Catherine gave her a hug. "Do you really think I would miss a game that was only an hour from my house? What kind of mother-in-law do you think I am?"

Ryan slid her arm around her shoulders. "The best kind I could ever hope for."

The equipment manager was just coming out of the locker room and she advised, "Let's go, you're the last one."

"Oh, I've got to go, Catherine. I wish I could stay for a while, but they'll leave without me."

"Will you stop for a snack on the way home?"

"No, not tonight. It's mid-term week so everyone wants to get home. I'll just get something there."

"Nonsense. Go tell them you've got a ride. We'll stop and get a snack, and then I'll take you home."

"But…" Ryan started to protest.

Catherine narrowed her eyes and said, "We're family, remember?"

Ryan pursed her lips and gave her a quick nod as she ran to tell the Coach that she would get home on her own.

⁂

"Hi," Ryan said from Catherine's cell phone when Jamie answered.

"Hi, baby. How did it go?"

"I had a great night. We won three-zip, and I got picked up by the most gorgeous blonde. We're in her car now, and I wanted to let you know so you didn't worry when I was late."

"Let me talk to that blonde right now," Jamie demanded, suppressing a giggle.

Ryan handed her the phone and Catherine said, "Hello, dear. I'm taking the star of the game for a snack. I'll return her as soon as I top off her tank."

"Thanks for going, Mom. I couldn't bear the thought of her not having anyone watch her play."

"I was planning on it anyway, dear, but thank you for reminding me."

⁂

After studying the extensive menu at the closest diner, Ryan settled on a club sandwich and a chocolate malt. As usual, Catherine stuck with a cup of coffee.

They chatted about the game for a few minutes, but when the food was delivered Catherine said, "I wanted to make a proposal to you, but I want to make sure that you understand that you do not have to agree."

"Okay," Ryan said as she put her sandwich down and looked Catherine in the eye.

"I want to call Jim and invite him to come home for the weekend. I know it would mean a lot to him to see Jamie play Stanford, and it might give you a chance to be around him so that he could get to know you better. I know that Jamie wants to facilitate a relationship between you and her father, and this seems like a perfect time to start." She blew out a breath after she got the thought out, and Ryan patted her hand to reassure her.

"Does it make you nervous to ask me that?"

"Yes, it really does. If I were in your place, I'd have no interest in being in the same room with him. I feel uncomfortable even asking you this, but I think it's something that would make Jamie happy."

"Catherine, I'd move to Washington and share an apartment with him if it would make Jamie happy. I'd think it's an excellent idea, and I'm sure Jamie will appreciate it."

"I haven't mentioned this to Jim or Jamie. I just wanted to see if you were willing before I did."

"I won't say a word," Ryan said with a smile. "Why don't you see if Jim is interested, and then you can tell Jamie."

She shook her head slightly and stirred her coffee absently, saying, "Your capacity for forgiveness just amazes me. I don't know how you do it."

"It's not really that hard. And it's not all that selfless. There's an old Irish expression that sums up my philosophy on the subject. 'Animosity is like drinking poison and hoping that your enemy dies.' I really do believe that, Catherine. I can't spend my life being wrapped up in this little drama. I've forgiven him, and I'm perfectly willing to move on."

Catherine tilted her head just a bit as she asked, "What does that mean when you say you forgive him?"

"Well, I'll tell you what it doesn't mean. It doesn't mean that I've forgotten what he's done—to any of us. He tried to hurt you, and me, and I'll never forget any of that. When I say I forgive him, it just means that I'm no longer invested in continuing the fight. I won't ever try to exact revenge."

"So you just mean that you don't need to get even or force him to make amends?"

"Yeah. That's about it. He can't really make amends because what he did will always be between us. I have a very, very long memory, and I'm certain that I'll never trust him. What he did was calculating and callous and terribly cruel. He fully intended to hurt you and me in any way he could just to have his own way. That wasn't just the heat of passion talking. He meant everything that he did, and I have no doubt that he would've hurt me physically if he'd thought it would help. It takes a certain kind of self-centeredness to act like he did, and that's not something that'll ever go away. I'll always keep an eye on him."

"But you still forgive him?"

"Sure. To keep the wound open will only hurt me, and I refuse to participate in that. I can be perfectly civil to him, and I'm sure I'll eventually even enjoy spending time with him. But I will never trust him, and I will never, ever give him the opportunity to hurt me again."

"I just find it remarkable that you are willing to do this for Jamie."

Ryan looked at her with her piercing blue eyes and leveled her gaze. "I'd die for her, Catherine. Having a topically friendly relationship with her father is nothing compared to what I would do for her."

Catherine grasped her hand and squeezed it gently. "I am so glad that she found you. You've brought out the best in her."

"I'm the lucky one. And to get you as a mother-in-law is a great bonus."

As they left the restaurant Catherine dangled the keys in front of Ryan. "Care to drive?"

With reflexes as quick as a jungle cat's, Ryan snatched the keys away, just in case Catherine decided to withdraw her offer. "Can I drop the top?"

"For that smile you can drop the top and choose what we listen to on the stereo," Catherine said, linking hands with her daughter-in-law as they walked down the street to the Mercedes.

Ryan got the seat and mirrors adjusted to her satisfaction, then hit the button and listened to the cloth top secure itself into the trunk. "I love this car."

"It suits you," Catherine decided, thinking that the bright red convertible matched Ryan's personality quite well.

"Thanks. Now I'll just find some tunes I like, and we're off." She started to run through the CD's that Catherine had in the changer, giving her mother-in-law a slight frown as she did. "All classical all the time, huh?"

"Yes, I'm afraid so. My knowledge of what songs were current came to a grinding halt around 1978, I'm afraid."

"One of my favorite years," Ryan smiled. "I actually have a few selections from your era in my bag. Would you pull my CD case out?"

Catherine did so, and she spent a minute flipping through the choices. "I don't recognize most of them, but I owned a few of these when I was in college. Why the interest in ancient history?"

"It's not so ancient. I like some of it because it's the music my mother liked," she said. "Some of it appeals to me because my cousin Michael got me hooked. It's hard to say why some music touches your heart, to be honest. I've never gotten into rap or hip-hop, and I hate the current group of pop artists, so I tend to go retro." She smiled as she. added, "No offense, full-courtof course."

"None taken. So what's your choice?" she asked, shaking the CD case.

"Pick something that you know. We can sing together to stay awake."

Catherine chose a disc that she hadn't heard in many years. Popping it into the cartridge Ryan smiled and said, "I pulled this one out of my stash to work on a song I sang in honor of my cousin. The anniversary of his death was a couple of weeks ago."

Catherine gave her a sympathetic smile and nodded. "Jamie told me about that. She was very moved by your performance."

"Eh..." Ryan shrugged. "The choir was great, I just helped out."

The CD whirled in the player, song after song forcing Catherine to think back to her youth until she finally took the lyrics out of the jewel case to recall the words of the once very familiar tunes.

The pair sang along companionably, the brisk wind blowing their hair in the breeze. The night was clear and the stars were dotting the sky, the lights of the city obscuring all but the brightest of them. When Ryan didn't hear Catherine's voice for a few minutes she shot a look at her, dismayed to see tears streaking down her cheeks. "Hey, what's wrong?" she asked, turning down the volume of the player.

Catherine sighed, embarrassed to be caught in such a vulnerable moment. She shook her head briskly, trying to dry her eyes with a tissue and ignore the question. But Ryan was too determined for that, and she pressed the point. "Catherine? You can talk about how you're feeling if it'll help."

Something about Ryan's soothing, gentle tone make her open up a little, sharing her feelings in a way she was only just now getting used to with Jamie. "I remember playing this album when Jim and I were dating. I identified very strongly with a few songs on here, especially the one about being too shy to say you're in love. It made me think of how it felt to be falling for Jim and not having the nerve to let him know how I felt."

Ryan moved her right hand from the wheel and gave Catherine's thigh a squeeze. "I like that song too," she said. "I felt a little like that with Jamie."

Catherine smiled and placed her hand atop Ryan's, feeling the smooth skin that covered her powerful but gentle hands. "It's hard to think that the song playing now had no meaning for me then," she said. "Now it's the only one that makes sense."

As the song played, Ryan thought of how it must feel to have this sad song be the only one that stood out. Loss, regret, distrust and pain filled the verses.

Ryan shot Catherine a sympathetic gaze and patted her leg once again. "I can't tell you how sorry I am. I know you loved him...I think you still do."

"Yes, yes, I do," she whispered through her tears. "Through everything that he's done...all of the ways he's hurt me and my child, there's something that isn't dead yet. I don't know if that means I'm too hard-headed to let go, or if my love for him is still alive, but it eats at me. It honestly breaks my heart."

"It's not over yet. You never know what'll happen."

"That's true," Catherine sighed. "I suppose I need to see how this story ends." Looking up at Ryan, she pasted on a brave smile and said, "Maybe there's still a happy ending in store for us."

They were now in front of the house and Ryan asked, "Do you want to come in and say hi to Jamie?"

"Oh, honey, I'd rather not. I don't like her to see me when I've been crying."

"She can handle it, Catherine. She's a pretty strong woman."

"You're right. Perhaps it's just my own insecurities." She looked at Ryan and said, "I'd still rather not."

"Okay," Ryan agreed quietly. She put the car into park and got out, going over to the passenger side. When Catherine exited and looked up at her, Ryan encircled her with her long arms, holding her close until Catherine began to lean more heavily against her, finally allowing the warm hug to break through her carefully erected defenses. She sagged against Ryan, feeling younger and more vulnerable than she had felt in years.

"Let it out, Catherine," Ryan whispered. "It's okay. Just let it out."

The distraught woman cried for several minutes, her tears flowing unabated. Ryan hated to see her so upset, but she knew that her mother-in-law couldn't get through the coming months without a lot of tears falling from her warm brown eyes, and she was glad that she was here with her now, providing what comfort she could.

Catherine's blonde head finally lifted, and she reached into the car for another tissue, blotting her eyes repeatedly. "You've certainly seen me at my worst," she said, a mild chuckle rising up from her chest.

"I've seen you at your best, too. Any way you are is just fine with me. We're family, remember?"

"Yes, I remember. It's one of the things that's kept me going over the last months. I hope you know that."

"You mean a lot to me, Catherine. Are you sure you can drive home? We have an extra bed, you know."

"No, no, I'm fine. Please don't worry about me."

Ryan stroked her still-wet cheek and said, "I do worry about you. One of the pleasant duties of family. Call when you get home, okay?"

"I will. Thank you," she added, standing on her tiptoes to place a kiss on her daughter-in-law's cheek.

Catherine walked into her kitchen a little before midnight. She slipped off her butterscotch suede jacket, exposing the off-white cashmere turtleneck, and twitched the sweater smooth over her dark brown wool slacks more from habit than need, since no one was up to see her.

She had called Jim from the car just a few minutes after leaving Ryan, but he had not answered the phone at his apartment. She left a message telling him that she'd be home around midnight if he wanted to call back. To her surprise, the phone rang at twelve on the dot, and she answered immediately.

"Hello?"

"Catherine, it's Jim," he said, sounding concerned. "Is everything all right?"

"Yes, everything is fine. I was calling to see if you were interested in coming home this weekend."

"Home?" he said slowly, not at all sure of her meaning.

"Yes. Both Jamie and Ryan are playing in tournaments at Stanford this weekend."

"And…?" he asked, thinking that she was inviting him, but having his doubts.

"The girls are staying here for the weekend, and Ryan's entire family will be here for a party on Friday night. If you would like to come, it might be a good opportunity for you to meet her family and get to know her better, too. I think Jamie would like it," she added needlessly.

"I'd be happy to come. I appreciate that you're inviting me." He paused for just a second and asked, "How do you feel about me coming? Are you all right with it?"

"Of course," she said quickly. There was a tense silence as she added, "I'd like you to come, too."

She could hear his smile even though she couldn't see it. "That's great. I'll have my secretary make the arrangements. I suppose I should stay in San Mateo so I don't have to drive all the way into the city…"

"Stay here," she said before she had time to stop herself. "Surely we can manage to share a house for one weekend." Her tone was light, and it was clear that she was trying to inject some humor into a relatively tense situation.

"I'd like that," he said quietly. "I've missed you."

"It's hard to have your routine destroyed," she ventured, trying to take the emotional note out of the conversation. "I'm sure Jamie will like having you here." She added, deciding that she'd better be clear, "Will you have a problem with her and Ryan sleeping together?"

He whistled through his teeth, letting out a low chuckle as he said, "You certainly know how to destroy a perfectly good mood."

"I just don't want there to be any nasty surprises this weekend. The girls are lovers, and they act very familiar with each other. I doubt they'll censor themselves because you're here, and I'd rather that you didn't come if you don't think you can tolerate it."

He tried to brush off her concern, saying, "No 'don't ask, don't tell' policy at the house, eh?"

"This is serious," she warned.

He sighed and said, "I know it is, and I wish I could lie and say that it doesn't bother me, but it does. I think the sexual element is a big part of my discomfort with Ryan. I just don't want her in my daughter's bed," he said, his voice tight with tension.

"You can either get over that on your own, or you can try to work through it with Jamie. Those are your only options if you want to be close with her."

"I know it's not politically correct, but it's how I feel. I hate to have to compromise my beliefs to be close to my own child."

"No one is asking you to compromise your beliefs." After a pause she asked, "What are they anyway?"

There was a long silence as Jim tried to control his temper. "I don't believe that straight people should always have to tread lightly to avoid offending gay people. I don't want my child to be gay, and I'd prefer that I didn't have to witness her behavior, but I realize that isn't my choice any longer."

"Jim, I don't mean to belittle you, but those are not beliefs. Those are prejudices."

"How do *you* do it, Catherine? How do you handle seeing her with that woman? Doesn't it bother you in the least to know what they do together?"

She sighed heavily and took a moment to think about her answer, assuming that his question was sincere. "I don't know why, but it bothered me more to think of Jamie with Jack."

"What?"

"You heard me. I knew what she and Jack did together—I knew they did the same kinds of things that I did and it was hard for me to face. But I don't know what it's like to love a woman, so I don't really have many mental images to deal with. Ignorance can be bliss."

He shook his head, mentally chiding himself for all of the XXX movies with a lesbian theme that he'd watched from his hotel rooms over the years. "It's different for you," he insisted. "She's not rejecting your entire sex."

"She's not rejecting yours either. I certainly didn't feel that she was rejecting women when she was with Jack. Where do you even come up with arguments like this?"

"I don't know," he said glumly, sounding like a little boy who had been scolded. "I just don't want to have to think of them like that."

"Look, Jim," she said firmly, "I try to treat Jamie like what she is—an adult. I don't get involved in my friends' sex lives, and I don't think I should intrude on Jamie's either. It's still odd for me when I see them kiss, but I'm happy that they act naturally around me. I guarantee that she won't spend any time alone with you until you make her believe that you accept both her relationship and her lover."

"Do you have to call her that?" he winced.

"What would you prefer?"

"Anything that sounded less sexual."

"All right, let's call Ryan her partner. You can delude yourself into believing it's a business relationship."

"This isn't funny, Catherine."

"I agree this is far from humorous. You seem nearly phobic about the sexual aspect of their relationship. I think you have to put that out of your mind and focus on their emotional bond."

"Fine. I'll focus on the bond Jamie has with her and ignore the fact that she used to have that with me."

Catherine actually felt some empathy for him at that moment. She knew that her husband needed to control every aspect of his life, and she could well imagine that no longer being able to control Jamie was wreaking havoc on his psyche. "She never had that with you, Jim. The love you have for a parent is nothing like the bond you feel for your lov...partner," she said quickly as she corrected herself. "She has the capacity to love you both, if you will only let her."

He sighed, a thoroughly defeated man as he whispered, "Is this the only way?"

"Yes," she said firmly. "It's the only way."

On Wednesday morning Jim put in a call to Jamie's cell phone as soon as he thought she might be up. Ryan had already left, and she was just about to head to class when the call came in.

"Hi, Daddy," she said, finding that she no longer experienced a sense of dread when she heard his voice. "What's up?"

"Your mother called last night, honey, and she has generously asked me to come down this weekend for the Stanford matches. I'd love to come, but I wanted to make sure you'd like me to."

"Oh, well, yes, that would be great." She paused for a minute and asked, "Do you think you're ready for that, Dad? Ryan's whole family will be there."

"I want to get to know her better. I can't think of a better way to know someone than to see them with their family."

"Okay, Dad, if you feel like making an effort, I'd be glad to have you come."

"Great, honey, that's just great. I think I'll come this afternoon and spend some time at the office. I'm still trying to wind up some work that I couldn't get finished before I left for Washington."

"Great."

"Any chance we could have dinner together?"

She considered the offer for just a moment. "Sure. But I have a lot of studying to do since it's mid-term week, so it'll have to be a quick one."

"Great," he said, sounding very happy. "I'll come by and pick you up. I think I'll be there around 5:30. Is that all right?"

"Yes, that's fine. That'll just give me enough time to stop and buy something simple for Ryan to have for dinner."

He smirked to himself, thinking it rather ironic that his daughter had fallen into a homemaker role, given her upbringing. "All right, honey. I'll pick you up this evening."

Chapter Nine

Ryan dragged her tired body into the house on Wednesday night, Jordan trailing right behind her.

Mia poked her head out of the kitchen, giving Jordan a wave and blowing a kiss. "I'm in charge of feeding you two. Are you ready to eat?"

"I'm too tired to eat," Ryan moaned as she tossed her legs over the arm of the loveseat and reclined fully.

"No way. Jamie will have my head if I don't pour some calories into you."

"Where is Jamie, anyway?" Ryan asked. "Did she leave a note?"

"She's out with her dad. He came into town early, so she decided to have dinner with him."

"That's nice."

"Look on the table for your messages," Mia instructed. "Some girl's been calling here every fifteen minutes looking for you. Jennie something or other."

Her fatigue forgotten, Ryan leapt to her feet so quickly she got a head rush. "Damn, damn, damn," she said as she dashed to the table by the stairs and looked at the message that merely stated Jennie's name. "How do I get in touch with her?"

"She said she has to call you 'cause she's not at home. She sounded really upset. What's going on?"

"I mentor her. She's really a handful," she said, sitting down on the wooden chair they kept by the table.

As if on cue, the phone rang. Ryan picked up and heard the tremulous voice say, "Ryan?"

"What's wrong, Jen?"

"I got thrown out again."

"Oh, sweetheart," she said sympathetically, "Where are you? I'll come get you and see if we can't work this out."

"I'm sick of this," she wailed. "I want to go home."

"We can talk about it when I get there, Jen, now tell me where you are."

"I'm over by the office."

"Jennie," Ryan said, "the office is closed now. What are you doing there?"

"I'm just hanging out. It's no big deal."

"It is a big deal, and you know it," she chided her gently. "You're just going to get into more trouble. I'll be over to get you within fifteen minutes. Are you at the pay phone on the corner?"

"Yeah, but I have to keep moving. Just ask some of the kids. They all know me."

I bet they do, Ryan thought to herself. "Okay, don't leave and don't talk to anyone in a car. Do you hear me?"

"Yes, I hear you. See you soon."

Ryan hung up and blew out an aggrieved breath. "Maybe we shouldn't have kids," she mumbled to herself.

"Ryan, what's going on?" Mia demanded.

"I've got to go," she said absently as she started for the door, but Mia's surprisingly strong grasp pulled her up short.

"No way. You're going to eat something before you walk out that door. That's final."

"Jesus! She really did put the fear of the Lord into you didn't she?"

"I'm not afraid of Jamie, but I care about you. I want to make sure you stay healthy."

Ryan's face broke into a shy grin as she agreed. "Okay, but I've gotta eat quickly. God knows how much trouble she can get into in an amazingly brief period of time."

"Well she's been calling here since five, so another fifteen minutes won't kill her. Now tell us what's going on?" Mia led both athletes into the kitchen.

Ryan took a deep breath and gathered her thoughts, knowing that Jennie wouldn't mind some disclosure of her situation. "As

I said, I work with Jennie, and have for almost eighteen months. She's a very sweet kid, but she and her mother are like oil and water, and regrettably her father's not in the picture, so it's just the two of them. Her mom discovered she was gay and threw her out of the house—absolutely refused to allow her to return."

Mia and Jordan were staring at her, their eyes wide with shock. Ryan nodded in agreement, "Amazing, isn't it? Well, the Department of Children and Family Services got involved, thanks to one of Jennie's friend's mothers. They finally agreed that Jennie could not go home, given how tense things were, so after a couple of unsuccessful attempts at placing her in foster care, she eventually wound up in this group home for 'throwaway' kids as they're called. That's how I got involved."

"Her mom would rather have her in a home? Just because she's gay?" Mia asked.

"Well, that's open to interpretation. In Jennie's case, being gay doesn't help, but she probably would have been thrown out even if she was straight. She and her mom are both really volatile, and they're on each other constantly. Her mom is very authoritarian, and Jennie just has to push her to the edge on every issue."

"How long has she been at the home?"

"She was there almost a year. She finally went home to her mother a few months ago. Jennie's social worker has been doing everything she can to keep them together—which is what they both say they want, by the way—but it sounds like Mrs. Willis snapped again."

"So where is she now?" Mia asked as she spooned a generous portion of vegetable soufflé onto all three plates.

"The Gay Teens in Crisis office is where the kids hang out during the day. They can use the phone there and get referrals to various programs. They also have counselors and substance abuse meetings. But at night it becomes a big pick-up place for the scum that prey on young, troubled kids. One of the few times I wished I had a firearm was when I went to get her one night and saw a forty-year-old man trying to talk a little boy into his car. I pulled up alongside and made a show of writing his license plate number down. He took off, but I assume he came back as soon as I left."

"That's beyond disgusting," Jordan muttered as she shivered involuntarily.

"Anyway, that's why I don't want to waste time. Jennie's prone to act out when she and her mom fight. I don't think she's ever tricked, but I honestly wouldn't put anything past her."

"Should we go with you?" Jordan asked. "Sounds like a rough neighborhood."

"Nah. It's not dangerous for adults. It's just vulnerable kids who are at risk in this place."

"You sure?" Jordan asked.

"Positive. I've done this several times."

"Will you be home late?"

"Probably not, but I'll have to bring her back here first. I want to talk to her mom on the phone, and if she agrees then I'll take her home. Damn," she muttered, "Jennie was just starting to feel comfortable in her new school. She just started high school, by the way. I hope to God that she doesn't have to go back to the home—she'll have to switch high schools if that happens." Ryan had gulped down all of the food that Mia had doled out, and she bent to kiss her friends, then made for the door. "Tell Jamie where I am if she gets here before I do."

"Oh. She took your car. She said yours is always low on gas so she took it to fill it up for you."

Ryan shook her head as she headed for the door. "I am so spoiled," she said as she shot her friends a guilty look.

"You spoil each other," Mia corrected her, "and that's the way it should be."

Jamie had the top down on the car and rather than waste time, Ryan left it as it was. The night was cool and foggy, but she thought the cool air might revive her a bit. *Thank God I took a shower tonight. My clothes were so wet they would have frozen right on me.*

She arrived at the run-down industrial neighborhood about ten minutes later. The young kids hung out in about a three-block area, most of them standing in groups of two or three. The older kids and young men liked to work a corner alone, so the area they worked could be six or seven blocks long, depending on how many of them there were on a given night. There were always a few transsexuals on one particular corner, and tonight was no exception. Because of the near-constant harassment and the possibility of gay bashing, during business hours they stayed close to the office in case they had to make a run for it. At night, however, there was no safe haven in this very rough neighborhood, despite the fact that the Oakland police had been trying to crack down on prostitution. It seemed to Ryan that too often the victims became the targets of such initiatives, starting with the transsexuals.

About three blocks from the office, Ryan spotted the first group of young men. Three boys about fifteen years old were having a discussion and when Ryan slowed down, one of them immediately came to the car and leaned over, holding on to the top of the windshield as he did so. "Oh no, honey," he said dramatically. "You're in the wrong place."

"I'm looking for a friend."

"Aren't we all?" he coyly replied as he batted his big brown eyes.

"I'm looking for a girl named Jennie. Do you guys know her? Shaved head, baggy bell-bottoms? Usually has on a big white T-shirt?"

"Oh, she's here," the young man assured her. "She was by a little while ago. But she doesn't trick, girlfriend," he said in a dismissive tone.

"I'm glad to hear that. She really is my friend."

After her fifth stop, the occupants of an unmarked police car looked to each other and nodded with a knowing smirk. They radioed ahead to the detectives waiting behind the office of the teen center. "Yellow Porsche Boxster. Driver has long brown hair. Obviously looking for something special. License number JDSE 211. Vehicle registered to James Evans, Hillsborough. Looks like Mr. Evans is keeping company outside of his neighborhood tonight. Pull him over if he snags anyone."

"Roger," crackled the radio.

Moments later Ryan finally spotted Jennie. She was standing with two other girls, both of whom looked like they were hooking. *Damn, damn, damn. If she lives to see fifteen, I'll be surprised.*

Jennie ran to the car and leaned into the passenger compartment. "Do you have any money?" she asked anxiously. "My friends haven't eaten since yesterday, and business is so slow they're not gonna eat tonight either."

Ryan rolled her eyes and reached for her wallet but stopped short when she realized it was still in her gym bag. Luckily she remembered that Jamie always kept money in the ashtray for emergencies. She reached inside and pulled out two twenties and stuck her hand out to offer the money to Jennie just as both of her friends began to run for their lives. The spotlight of the unmarked car hit her at precisely the same time that Jennie accepted the money and started to get into the car. "Don't anybody move," the disembodied voice from the loudspeaker ordered.

Jennie looked panicked, and before Ryan could say a word, she took off in the same direction as her friends. "Fuck!" Ryan cried as she watched her run down the dark street, holding up her outrageously huge pants.

"Put your hands on the steering wheel," the voice boomed, and Ryan immediately complied.

The two officers approached her car with their weapons drawn. They had parked about ten yards behind her, and one officer came from each side. The one on the right stayed behind the car with his weapon aimed at her head while the other approached the driver door. "Keep your hands on the wheel. Do not make any sudden moves," he commanded.

Ryan knew enough about law enforcement to know it was futile to argue at this point, so she immediately complied with each of their instructions, while remaining silent.

The officer yanked open her door and ordered, "Put your hands above your head and exit the vehicle." She had removed her seat belt when she reached out with the money, so she was able to get out without impediment. "Walk around to the hood of the car," he directed. When she got there he said, "Step back two paces and lean forward with your hands on the hood." As soon as she complied, he whipped a pair of handcuffs onto her right wrist and yanked her arm behind her back as he pulled her left arm back and snapped that cuff on.

"License and registration," the officer demanded.

"Registration in the glove box. I don't have my license with me."

The second officer went to the radio to communicate with the lead officer. "We have the perp in the Porsche cuffed. Forty dollars confiscated. All three juveniles escaped. No identification. Registration looks clean. Check for vehicle reported stolen."

The radio crackled back, "That car belongs to our new senator. If it's Evans, you'd better let him off with a warning."

"Not him," the officer replied. "It's a woman."

There was a pause, then the voice asked, "It's not his wife, is it?"

"No way," the officer confidently said. "I'll identify her."

He walked back to Ryan and asked, "What's your name?"

"Siobhán O'Flaherty."

Walking back to the car the officer reported, "She's not an Evans. Some kinda Irish sounding name."

"There's been no report of theft, but I think the Senator's in Washington already. She might have stolen the car. Run her in. Impound the vehicle. We'll wait for the tow."

The officer went back to Ryan, grasping her firmly by the bicep as he led her to the squad car. He placed his hand on her head to make sure she didn't hit it on the frame of the car and pushed her into the back seat. "Does it matter what my explanation is?" she asked, her anger boiling at both Jennie and the officers.

"Nope. Tell it to the judge," he instructed as he punched the accelerator, causing her head to snap back sharply.

It took almost forty-five minutes to get her processed enough to allow her a phone call. She briefly thought of calling Brendan, but knew that Jamie would be upset if she wasn't called first. One handcuff was removed to allow her to use the pay phone by the door to the lockup, but the other was firmly attached to one of the arresting officers, who listened to every word she uttered.

"Hi," she said in as normal a tone of voice as she could muster. "You'll never guess where I am."

"Well, you should be in bed. It's after nine. Where are you, anyway?"

"I'm in a holding cell at the North Oakland police station. Any chance you can come bail me out?"

The silence that greeted her indicated that Jamie was less than pleased with the news. "I'm sure you have a very good explanation for why you've been arrested," she said calmly. "I really can't wait to hear it."

"I didn't do anything wrong."

"Why are you in jail?" Jamie cried, tired of waiting for an explanation.

"Uhm…solicitation of prostitution?"

There was a terribly long pause until Jamie let out a sigh and said, "This I gotta hear."

"My three minutes are up. If you don't want me going steady with the really scary-looking woman in the lockup, you'll hurry over here."

"What's the address?" she sighed, continually amazed at the trouble that one woman could get into.

Ryan gave her all of the particulars and reminded her, "You have to bring cash or go to a bail bondsman. Can you get $1000?"

"Yes, I can get $1000. I'll be there as soon as I can. And, honey?"

"Yes?"

"If you drop the soap, just leave it on the floor."

"Very funny. It's nice that you can keep your sense of humor while I sit in a cell with Big Bertha."

Forty-five minutes later Ryan was brought from the holding cell back out to the desk sergeant. Jamie was accompanied by her father, and Ryan could only think, *This doesn't seem like the best way to make Jim start to trust me.*

Jamie tossed her arms around Ryan and gave her a fierce hug. "I think Daddy has convinced them to let you go. Trouble just follows you, doesn't it?"

"It didn't used to."

"What happened?"

"I went to pick Jennie up. She and her mom had a big fight, and she got thrown out again. She was with two of her friends and they hadn't had anything to eat, so I was giving them the money from your ashtray when the spotlight hit me. Of course they all ran, so I was left in your car with no ID and three teenaged prostitutes running down the street."

"Jennie's not a prostitute. You'd know if she was."

"I'm not so sure," Ryan admitted. "There's not much I'd put past her at this point."

Jim walked over and said, "They've agreed to release you. All they really had to go on was the fact that you were in a car that wasn't registered to you and you didn't have ID Since they didn't catch the girls, they'd have a hard time making the solicitation charge stick."

"Thank you so much for your help," she said gratefully.

"Well, I have a lot of questions I'd like to have answered. This whole incident is very suspicious."

"I understand that," she conceded.

"She doesn't have to defend herself, Daddy," Jamie began, automatically springing to Ryan's defense.

Ryan stopped her as she said, "Why don't you come by the house for some coffee, Jim? I'll explain everything."

Fifteen minutes later they were sitting in the kitchen listening to Ryan's tale. Luckily Mia came downstairs for a drink, and so provided corroborating testimony. Jim seemed placated after she backed Ryan up, and he stood to leave when his coffee was finished. As they walked to the door Ryan said, "I hope I don't get arrested again, but I have to go find Jennie. Otherwise, God knows where she'll end up tonight."

"I understand, honey," Jamie agreed. "We can go in your car."

"Absolutely not," Jim said, then immediately backed off when he saw his daughter's expression. "Why don't you let me go with Ryan? You said you needed to study."

She hesitated and Ryan stepped in and said, "It's really fine if you stay home. We shouldn't be gone long."

"Are you sure?"

"Positive," Ryan said, kissing her on the cheek. "Get some work done while we're gone, okay?"

Jamie walked them to the drive, where Jim said, "We'll take my car," he walked to a full-sized sedan that he had obviously rented, since it wasn't sexy or fast.

"Hurry back," Jamie said as the pair got into the car and took off.

While they drove along, Jim turned to Ryan and asked, "Tell me more about this girl."

Ryan launched into the same spiel she had given Mia, adding some of the more explicit details just to show Jim how lucky he was to have a child like Jamie.

"How does she do in school?"

"Well, that's a tough subject," she said. "She's very malleable, and the other kids can talk her into anything. She's been suspended three times in the year and a half I've known her. I'm about out of ideas for how to reach her. When we're together, you couldn't ask for a sweeter kid. If she was given any love at home, she'd be fine. But she gets so angry at her mom that she does incredibly stupid things to get back at her, but of course it only hurts Jennie."

"Why is her mother so antagonistic?"

"Partly because Jennie's gay. A couple of years ago her mom got religion, and since that time she's tried to force Jennie to follow her beliefs. That's hard to do with any twelve-year-old, but nearly impossible with one as headstrong as Jennie. She gets into a lot of situations that she wouldn't ordinarily be tempted by, but she willingly dives in just to prove that her mother doesn't control her. It's really dangerous, and it worries me sick."

"She's lucky to have you," he said, staring straight ahead.

"Thanks," she replied, "but I feel lucky to know her. She's such a bright, sweet kid, and I know she'll be fine...if she survives these tumultuous times."

They reached the neighborhood just as things were starting to heat up. Every corner was filled with kids from ages twelve and up. Some were selling drugs; most were selling their young bodies. Jim looked physically ill as he stared at the young kids struggling to survive with the only tools they knew how to use. "I...I had no idea," he murmured as they passed each group. Ryan directed him to the side street from which she had seen the police car emerge. About a block down the street, the same car that had picked her up was waiting to be called again.

The passenger window rolled down as Jim pulled up. "Evening, officers," he said calmly. "We're just trying to find a young woman and take her to a group home. I trust we won't be disturbed?"

The officer merely nodded and rolled his window back up. "Chatty fellow," Jim laughed as they pulled away.

Ryan recognized one of the young women who had been hanging out with Jennie earlier in the evening. "Hey," she said, rolling the window down, "did Jennie come back?"

"Yeah, she's down the street about a block. Are you gonna kick her ass?"

Ryan laughed as she said, "No. I don't kick many asses. Did you get enough money for some food?"

"No. And I've only blown one guy all night," she said disgustedly.

"Here's forty," Ryan said, handing her the money that she had reclaimed from the police. "Why don't you call it a night?"

"Hey, thanks," the girl said. "What you want for this? I'll go down on you." Looking past Ryan to the driver, she twitched her head at Jim and added, "Or him."

"No, thanks," Ryan choked out, a deep flush traveling up her cheeks. "Just get some food."

Jim gave her a wide-eyed look as they drove away, and Ryan just shrugged her shoulders. "Most people want something from them. They're suspicious of people who don't want sex. It makes them think that you'll want something worse down the line."

"What could be worse?" Jim mumbled, his hands tight on the steering wheel.

They pulled up alongside the small group that Jennie stood with, Ryan opening the car door just as her young friend caught sight of her. She turned and took off again, running as fast as she could, but Ryan was in no mood for her nonsense tonight. She took off after her like a defensive end chasing down a streaking wide receiver and grabbed onto her XX-large T-shirt with enough force to slow her down, then snaked a long arm around Jennie's slim waist and lifted her off her feet, using her momentum to toss the young girl over her shoulder. "One word and I'll spank you in front of all your friends," she threatened as she marched back to the car. She opened the back door and checked the side of the door, flicking the switch she found there before tossing Jennie into the car and dashing around to the other side to get in next to her. "I activated the baby lock on that side, Jim," she informed him. "I don't want this little hellion to sneak out at a stoplight."

Jim turned around to get a look at his passenger, and Ryan could tell that he was astounded by what he saw. Jennie was a very young-looking fourteen-year-old. She had an angelic round face, with pink cheeks and dancing blue eyes. With her nearly bald head, when she smiled she looked like one of the adorable babies from a baby food ad. The eyebrow and ear piercings ruined the innocent look, however, appearing so incongruous on the sweet face that it did take some time to get used to her appearance. "Jim Evans, this is Jennie Willis," Ryan said.

"Good to meet you, Jennie," he said. "Where to, Ryan?"

"Our house," she said decisively.

Jennie looked up at her warily. "Why your house? Are you gonna beat me?"

"Jennie," she said as she placed her hand on her leg, "I've known you for eighteen months. Have I ever given you reason to think I would hit you?"

"No," she said slowly, "but I never got you arrested before."

"Good point. But I'm not the type of person who hits. I just want to talk to you and then call your mom."

They proceeded to the house, and Ryan showed her in as Jamie ran to the door to see what had happened. "God, I was afraid you got arrested again. What took so long?"

"My friend didn't want to be found. And when I did see her, she ran away. So it took me a few minutes to run her down and carry her back."

Jamie looked over at the youngster who looked like she wanted to slink away when no one was looking. Jamie slipped an arm around her shoulders to escort her inside. Leaning over, she whispered, "Don't worry about it, Jen, sometimes she picks me up and carries me, too."

That got a small laugh out of Jennie and served to relieve some of the tension in the room. Jamie took her into the kitchen to get her a snack, while Ryan got on the phone and woke Jennie's none-too-happy mother.

"Hi, Mrs. Willis, it's Ryan O'Flaherty."

"Oh great," she groused. "I assume Jennie has convinced you to come to her rescue again?"

"Well, I wouldn't characterize it like that, but she is at my house."

"Aren't you the lucky one. If you have any sense, you'll give her a good beating and throw her out. That child needs to learn that her actions have consequences. She wanted to stay out all night Tuesday night. Let her see what it's like on the streets. She'll change her tune."

"So you'd rather I let her sleep on the street?"

"She'll be fine," she said curtly. "She's just got to learn."

"I can't do that, Mrs. Willis," Ryan explained. "I'll bring her home, take her to the Youth Authority or keep her here."

"She's not welcome here. I will not let her return here until she shows that she's matured."

"Let her stay here overnight at least, Mrs. Willis. I can't bear to take her to the Youth Authority. God knows where they'll put her at this time of night."

"You can't coddle her," she insisted. "She'll run roughshod over you."

"Mrs. Willis, if I take her to the Youth Authority, I'll have to tell them that you threw her out," Ryan said, playing her trump card. "Do you want to have your parental rights revoked? I don't have to remind you that her social worker wouldn't hesitate to petition the court to do that."

There was a pause as the older woman considered whether or not Ryan was bluffing. Deciding not to take the risk, she snapped, "Fine. Keep her as long as you like. But don't say I didn't warn you."

Jamie had hustled Jennie back out of the room as soon as it was evident that her mom was giving Ryan a hard time, but Jim stayed in the living room with his mouth gaping open. "How could anyone care so little for their child?"

"She told me to toss her out on the street so she learns her lesson."

"That's unconscionable."

"I agree, and I wish she didn't have to go back, but tossing a rebellious, gay kid into the foster care system is no picnic either. She does pretty well in the group home," Ryan said. "It's a good atmosphere for her. Lots of structure—she has jobs to do around the house, really firm curfew. The problem is that the court doesn't often approve permanent placements with a home like that."

"Why not?"

"Well, for one thing, it's much more expensive than keeping a kid in a foster home. For another, it's hard to supervise one troubled kid, much less eight or ten. The older kids can sometimes prey on the younger ones; they really need to be watched constantly."

"How old is she?" Jim asked.

"She just turned fourteen," Ryan said, "but she's seen more in those years than I have in twenty-four."

"Has she a father?"

"Yeah, and Jennie's crazy about him." Ryan rolled her eyes to show that she didn't agree with the child's opinion. "He's career Navy, remarried with a new baby. He pays child support—the Navy sees to that—but all he's good for is a few broken promised per year. Besides, he's on a ship for months at a time, and the stepmother has no interest in having a fourteen-year-old to take care of. I doubt she'd be better off with him—even if he'd have her."

"No grandparents? Aunts? Uncles?" Jim asked, grasping at straws.

"No one who wants to be involved. She's really on her own," she said, the pain she often felt when she thought of Jennie's situation grabbing her heart yet again.

Jamie and Jennie came back into the living room, and Jennie gave Ryan a very cautious look. "Can I stay?"

"Yeah, you can stay. I'll take you upstairs and get you settled." She placed an arm around her shoulders and guided her upstairs, asking, "Did you get a snack?"

"Yeah, Jamie fixed me up."

Jim sat in a depressed silence as the pair went upstairs. "I have such a hard time believing that sweet little girl is so horrible to live with."

"I don't think she is. Her mother's trying to force her to be straight in every sense of the word. She won't let her hang out with other gay kids, she makes her dress very conservatively, she forces her to go to some conservative church where they try to pray her sexuality out of her. It's just a mess. It'd be one thing to try to guide Jennie, but her mom just lays down these inflexible rules and then punishes her too harshly when she breaks one. And she invariably breaks one," she said with a smirk. "Usually a big one." As Ryan descended the stairs, Jamie asked, "What happened this time?"

"She stayed out all night with one of her friends. Hard to imagine she thought she was going to get away with that one," she chuckled.

"Nonetheless," Jim argued, "you don't throw your child out of the house because you don't approve of her behavior."

"Obviously we agree with that opinion, Daddy," Jamie said, as the upstairs door opened and Jennie came out into the hall and looked over the railing. She was dressed in a pair of Jamie's flannel pajamas, the roomy red and black plaid outfit making her look even younger than her fourteen years. "I'm going to bed," she announced. "I just wanted to say good night."

"Good night, Jennie," Jamie said as she ran up the stairs and kissed her cheek and gave her a hug. "Do you have everything that you need?"

"Yeah, this is an awesome house, Jamie."

"You're welcome any time," Jamie told her, giving her another squeeze. "But next time don't make Ryan spend the evening in jail first, okay?"

"Okay, I won't," she said, looking down, obviously embarrassed. "Good night, Mr. Evans," she said politely. "It was good to meet you. And thanks for coming to get me. I would have been outside all night if you hadn't."

"My pleasure," he said briskly, but Ryan caught just a glimmer of a catch in his voice. *This has really affected him*, she marveled.

After Jennie went back upstairs, Jim got ready to leave. "You were a lifesaver tonight," Ryan acknowledged. "If I'd gone back alone, they probably would have arrested me again."

"They didn't look very fond of you," Jim admitted with a chuckle.

Jamie slid her arm around her partner's waist and said, "But to know her is to love her."

Jim wasn't ready to make that concession, but he shook Ryan's hand in a friendly manner and said, "I admire how much you've tried to help that child. You can tell it means a lot to her."

"Thank you," Ryan said. "She means a lot to me too."

"See you Friday," he said as he kissed Jamie goodbye.

Ryan walked over to the loveseat and flopped down with a groan as she said, "I thought I was tired at seven."

"Let's get to bed, jailbait," Jamie said, tugging her to her feet.

"Jailbait is what they call a minor who sleeps with an adult," she said, chuckling at Jamie's faux pas.

"Nope. If you were in jail, I'd commit a crime just to get in there with you. You would definitely be jail bait."

As they snuggled in bed, Jamie said, "I guess we should be good chaperones and just go to sleep, huh?"

"Yeah, we should. Besides, I've had enough exploration of my more intimate parts for one day."

"What?" Jamie exclaimed indignantly, abruptly sitting up.

"They booked me. Before they put you in a cell, they do a very thorough pat down."

"Somebody had their hands on you?"

"Yep. It was not an experience I'd like to revisit."

"You poor thing. They manhandled you."

"It was a hell of a night," Ryan agreed, trying to stifle a yawn. "I guess monogamy isn't as restrictive as I thought, though," she chuckled. "I thought you'd be the last woman to touch me quite that intimately."

"Well, you'd better not have gotten aroused by her," Jamie whispered as she climbed on top of Ryan and touched noses.

"Honey, this woman was absolutely scary and she acted like I was toxic. If being touched like that aroused me, I'd seek professional help."

"Boy it makes my blood boil to think of those people roughing you up. It frightens me how easy it is to abuse power."

"Well, in their defense, it did look pretty incriminating. And since I'm so much in favor of cracking down on pedophiles, I guess I can't really complain."

"I can complain plenty," Jamie said. "And if I ever see the woman who put her hands on you, I'll give her a pop."

"Mike Tyson would run from this woman. She looks like she eats nails for breakfast. She'd crush you like a grape."

"I'd go up against a hydra to defend you, sweetness. She doesn't scare me."

"She'd scare you plenty if you saw her snapping a rubber glove onto those big mitts. I'm used to a more delicate touch," she teased, lifting Jamie's small hand and kissing each finger. "And just for the record, I'd be very happy if no other hands ever touched me again."

As a concession to Jamie, Ryan managed to remain in bed until eight o'clock, when she padded downstairs to rustle up breakfast. She was on her second helping of oatmeal when Jennies' sleepy face peeked into the kitchen. "Hi," she yawned as she shuffled in and sat down. "Got any more breakfast? I'm starved."

"Sure. You name it and I can make it for you," Ryan offered. "Breakfast is my specialty."

"Can you really cook?" Jennie asked in surprise.

"Yeah, I cook pretty well. Why, does that surprise you?"

"I don't know. You just seem like the type who would have people cooking for you."

Ryan smirked at her assessment, thinking it too accurate for her comfort. "Well, Jamie does most of the cooking, but I can handle myself just fine, thank you. Now what will it be?"

"Can you make pancakes?" Jennie asked hopefully, not often meriting a hot breakfast at home.

"Absolutely. What do you want in them?"

"Uhm…syrup?" she asked, unsure of her choices.

"Don't you want to spice them up? I like mine with bananas and blueberries or pecans or chocolate chips."

"Really? You can do that?"

"Yes, Jennie, I can do that. Now, make a decision," she ordered as she started to mix the ingredients together.

"I'll have them the way you make them for yourself."

"Okay. Bananas and blueberries coming right up." She mixed the ingredients together and put a little butter on the griddle. Waiting until the butter was hot, she took a paper towel and wiped the pan until the butter was invisible. "Trick of the trade," she said with a wiggling eyebrow. "Too much butter makes the first pancake turn out flat."

"This is fun. I wish I could live with you," she added wistfully.

Ryan gave her a crooked grin as she said, "I'd like that too."

Two minutes later the first pancake was ready, and Jennie dove into it like she hadn't eaten in days. "This is so totally fine," she said happily. "You really can cook."

"I don't lie to you, Jennie," Ryan responded seriously. "And I hope you don't lie to me." She removed the pan from the heat and sat down next to the young woman. "Tell me what happened on Tuesday night."

"Uhm, I went out with my friend Axel."

"Why did you stay out all night? You had to know you'd get in trouble."

"His parents were gone, and we were just hangin' out. I didn't think it was late until it was too late."

"What were you doing?" Ryan persisted.

"Nothing much." She took another bite, her attention focused on her food.

"Jennie, tell me what you did that night. There's no reason for you to stay out all night if you weren't fucked up somehow."

She stared at her plate for a long moment. "We had some wine," she finally admitted.

"What else?" Ryan persisted.

"A little ganja."

"Anything else?"

"Huh-uh, that's it."

"How many times have we had the conversation about drinking and doing drugs?" she asked, her eyes darkening.

"Uhm…a bunch?"

"A bunch sounds about right. Has nothing I've said reached you, Jen? Do you understand why it's dangerous to do these things at your age?"

Her nearly bald head nodded, and she mumbled, "'Cause my brain's not cooked yet."

"That's right," Ryan insisted, grasping her chin to force eye contact. "Your brain isn't fully mature, and exposing it to drugs and alcohol can permanently impair its ability to form itself properly. I'm being totally honest with you here. I'm not just saying this because I disapprove of drugs and alcohol."

"Okay," she said, nodding.

"It's truly dangerous at your age, and it can have lasting consequences." The child nodded again, her sweet, innocent-looking face making Ryan's heart clench with emotion. "What did you do all night? It doesn't take all evening to drink a little and smoke a little." Ryan's tone indicated that she thought "a little" might have been an inaccurate description of the girl's consumption.

"We were just playing around, you know."

"No, I don't know. I want you to tell me." There was something very evasive about the child's demeanor; she seemed almost embarrassed. Acting on a hunch, Ryan asked, "Did you have sex with your friend, Jennie?"

She laughed nervously, her eyes never leaving her empty plate. "He's gay."

"Did you have sex with him?" Ryan asked again in a quiet but determined voice.

Her full lips were pressed together so hard that they were nearly invisible. "Not really...I mean...well, maybe...but just a little bit," she stuttered.

Ryan placed her hands on the wooden back of the chair. She easily moved it so that Jennie was facing her fully, then lowered her head just enough to be able to stare into the girl's eyes. "Tell me exactly what happened. I want every detail."

A heavy sigh came from the small body, but she blinked slowly and began her tale. "We were a little high. Not that bad, but just enough. I've never really seen a guy, and he's never really seen a girl, and after a while we started undressing each other. It was kinda fun 'cause it was really different, you know?"

"I know," Ryan said, blinking slowly as she fought the nausea that was starting to build. "Go on."

"Well, when we were naked, I asked if I could touch him and he said okay. It was really weird but kinda cool, so I played with it for a while. He got hard and said he wanted to do it, but I was afraid. You know?" she asked with a childlike expression on her sweet face.

"I know," Ryan assured her as she placed her hand on the thin shoulder. "Go on, Jen, tell me the rest."

"We started kissing and stuff, and he kept putting my hand on it. But it kept getting soft—I guess 'cause I'm a girl. So after a while he had me get on my hands and knees so he could act like I was... you know."

"So he could imagine you were a boy," Ryan supplied.

"Yeah. I guess so. I told him we couldn't really do it 'cause I didn't want it to hurt, so he just kinda rubbed against me. It felt pretty good, and he liked it too, I think."

"Jennie, this is really important. Think carefully about everything you remember. Did he put his penis in your vagina?"

"I don't think so," she said slowly. "Would I know for sure?" She looked up at Ryan with such trust that the woman felt like going to Mrs. Willis' house and knocking her silly for letting her child face such adult experiences alone.

"Was he wearing a condom?"

"No, he said he was just gonna rub against me," she explained.

"I understand that, honey, but this is important. Did he come inside of you?"

"I'm not sure how you know that. I'm not really sure," she reiterated, looking as confused as she was embarrassed.

"Oh, Jennie," Ryan said, dropping her head onto the small shoulder. "You're so young to be playing games like this. I just hate to see you put yourself in so much danger."

As Ryan straightened up, Jennie looked up at her with big blue eyes and asked, "Will it be okay?"

"I'm not sure. I'm not sure." She shook her head slowly, gazing at her young friend and watching her composure shatter. Within seconds she was crying fiercely, her small shoulders shaking as she sobbed deeply.

"I'm scared. I...I...didn't want to do it, but he really wanted to and...and I didn't want to be a big baby."

Ryan grasped her shoulders and pulled her onto her lap where she rocked her and hummed a soft tune for a long while. "I'll do my best to make sure you're okay," she promised, "but we have to go see the doctor today."

Jennie tensed up noticeably but Ryan reassured her. "I'll be with you. I promise I'll take care of you."

Ryan knew that she should just call Jennie's social worker and tell her everything that had happened, but she couldn't bear to think of the child spending the day at some impersonal clinic. She decided to take Jennie to the doctor first, then call the social worker.

When she was composed, Ryan got up and made another emergency call to Alison Aiken, recalling that it had been nearly a year since she had taken Jamie down to see her. Ryan hated to go so far, but she didn't know any other gynecologist and from her experience with Jamie, she knew Alison would be gentle with the child. She spoke with the very competent receptionist and told her that she had a young friend who might have had sex with a boy and that there was a chance the boy was HIV positive. The receptionist told her to bring the girl down, but she couldn't promise that they wouldn't have a long wait.

They had to wait nearly an hour and a half, but they were finally shown into Alison's private office a little before eleven. The doctor strode into the room and gave both women a friendly smile. "Hi," she said, looking from one to the other. "Who am I seeing today?"

"This is Jennie," Ryan explained, "and I'm Ryan. We met about a year ago when I came down with Jamie Evans."

Alison smiled and said, "Oh yes, how is Jamie?"

"She's great," Ryan said, her smile brightening at the mere mention of her partner. "Jennie isn't doing so well, though. She had a sexual experience on Tuesday night, and we want to make sure that she isn't pregnant. She didn't use protection, so we can't rule out STDs either," she said, giving a small nod at Alison's severely raised eyebrow. Jennie was staring down at the floor, and Alison used her best bedside manner to draw her out.

"Do you want to tell me what happened, Jennie?"

"I was fooling around with a guy and he was rubbing his thing against me. He came, but I don't know if he was in me or not when he did it," she said quickly, having learned the important points from Ryan's questioning.

"Okay," Alison said slowly. "Do you know that there's a significant amount of sperm that comes out of a man's penis even before he ejaculates?"

Jennie's eyes grew wide as she shook her head slowly. "I...I thought that if he didn't...you know..."

"No, it's very possible to get pregnant if his penis was inside of you at any time during the act. How old are you, Jennie?"

"Fourteen," she said.

"When did you first get your period?"

"Right before I turned thirteen," she stated, her voice shaking.

"Would you like me to prescribe birth control pills for you today?"

"No, I'm gay."

"It doesn't matter what you are if you have a penis in your vagina. You can still get pregnant."

"I know," she said. "I just made a mistake. I won't do it again," she sniffed, trying to hold back the tears.

"Have you ever had a gynecological exam, Jennie?"

"Uhm," she looked at Ryan for help as her eyes grew wide. "I don't know."

"Let's do one today," Alison suggested. She buzzed for the nurse and asked her to do the preliminaries. Ryan got up too, but Alison indicated that she should stay for a minute.

"I'll be in as soon as you're ready," Ryan assured the girl as she got up to follow the nurse. Jennie looked panic-stricken so Ryan reassured her, "She's just going to weigh you and get you to give a urine sample. No big deal."

Jennie nodded and followed the nurse. As they left, Alison blew out a breath and asked, "What's the story here?"

"I mentor her through a program for gay teens at risk. She has a very shaky home situation, and her mom threw her out on Wednesday. It turns out that she threw her out because she was out all night with this guy. Jennie definitely identifies as gay and so does the boy, but knowing the crowd she hangs out with, he might be a prostitute. So you should check her for every known STD, including HIV," she said, feeling the bile at the back of her throat from merely saying the word.

"Well, most of them won't show up this early. Is there any way you can find out if the boy is HIV positive?"

"I can try," she agreed, shrugging her shoulders. "But I wouldn't be reassured even if Jennie assured me that he was negative."

"No, of course not," Alison agreed. "We'll do an HIV test today, and then she can have another done in six months. Do you feel comfortable being in the room with her, or should I have my nurse be there?"

"I think she'll do better if I stay," Ryan said, "but I sure hope her mother never finds out about this. She's not very friendly towards gay people in general, but I'll be damned if I'm going to let her intimidate me from being there for this kid."

"Okay, let's go," Alison said forcefully as she escorted Ryan to the examining room.

Much to Ryan's relief, Alison found no signs of penetration, commenting casually that Jennie's hymen was intact. That threw Ryan for a loop, but she didn't want to make an issue out of it at this point, so she just exchanged glances with Alison and nodded. Nothing abnormal showed up during the exam, which made sense since the incident was only two days before. Alison told Ryan that she'd call her with the results of the blood tests since Jennie didn't want her mother to know about the incident. Just before she left, Alison bent over until she was eye to eye with Jennie. "I'm sorry you had to go through all of this, but I hope you understand how dangerous it is to play around without proper safer sex precautions. You're risking your future and your life."

Jennie just nodded and continued to stare at the floor. When Alison left, Ryan went over to the table and gave her a hug. "Are you okay?"

"Yeah, but I didn't like that exam."

"Nobody really likes them," Ryan said. "And if you keep your private parts private, you don't have to have another one for a few years."

"That's good enough for me." Jennie agreed immediately. "Off limits. Once was enough."

❧

Ryan paid for the office visit and the lab tests, silently thanking Jamie for the American Express card. Jennie had insurance, but Ryan knew the claim information would go to Mrs. Willis, and she definitely did not want that to happen.

On the way back to the city, Ryan tried to tactfully get some more information about the boy that Jennie had been with. "Tell me about this guy you were hanging out with."

"He's just a guy I know from the neighborhood."

"Which neighborhood?" Ryan asked.

"My uhm…my mom's neighborhood."

"How old is he?" Ryan asked.

Jennie stared out the window for a minute before replying, "I'm kinda embarrassed to tell."

Oh, God. This kid doesn't embarrass easily. "You can tell me, Jen."

"Okay," she grumbled. "He's thirteen. He's still in grade school."

"Really?" Ryan asked in surprise. "How do you know him?"

"He just hangs out with some other people I know. He's kind of a loser."

"So why were you with him?"

"I don't know. I kinda feel sorry for him. The guys pick on him a lot cause he's pretty obvious about being gay. That kinda bothers me, so I talk to him."

"Has he been with many other boys?"

"No," she said, laughing and shaking her head at the mere suggestion. "The guys would torture another guy that even talked to him. He told me he hasn't even kissed anybody," she said with an embarrassed giggle.

"So you're sure he hasn't had sex with a guy?"

"Yeah. I think he would've told me if he had. I mean, it's kinda pathetic to be gay and have the first person you kiss be a girl, isn't it?"

"I wouldn't say it's pathetic, but how does he know he's gay?"

"Everybody knows he's gay," she said dramatically. "He's *so* gay."

Ryan gave her a pointed look and asked, "If he hasn't had any sexual experiences, how did he know to get you into a position that he liked?"

"He watches tons of porn," Jennie said, rolling her eyes. "He said he comes home every day and gets on the Internet for hours. I think he was just doing what he sees in movies. I mean, I really don't think he was trying to come inside me. He just didn't know what to do."

Thank you, Jesus. Ryan prayed silently. "I believe you, Jen, but we should still go back to the doctor in six months and have you checked for STDs again. We can't be sure your friend is telling the truth."

"Will she have to put that thing in me?" she asked warily.

"I'm not sure. I know it's uncomfortable, but when you become sexually active you just have to do it."

"Okay, I'll go," she agreed glumly. As they rode along Jennie looked up at Ryan and said, "If I could choose a mom, I'd choose you."

Ryan lifted her hand and rubbed Jennie's stubbly head. "If I could choose a younger sister, I'd choose you," she said with a smile. "I wouldn't have been a very good mother if I'd had you at ten."

She grinned up at her and admitted, "It seems like you're a lot older than me. I forget it's just ten years."

"Sometimes ten years seems like a lot. Some of the women I used to date were ten years older than I was, and it seemed like forever."

Jennie looked at her with a quizzical expression and asked, "Have you ever been with a guy?"

Ryan shook her head briskly. "No, I was never interested in guys like that. And since I went to an all girls school, I didn't have many boy friends my age. My brothers' friends were always interested, but my brothers would have killed them if they had even asked me out."

"I don't blame them."

"Who, my brothers?"

"No, their friends. You're about the best-looking woman I've ever seen," Jennie said as she gazed at her friend appraisingly.

"Trust me on this, kiddo. The best-looking woman you'll ever see is the one you fall in love with."

When Ryan stumbled in the door from practice, Jamie was waiting for her with a warm embrace and a hot dinner. "I fed the children earlier so we could have some time alone," she smiled. "Now tell me all about your day."

"Whew. There's a lot to tell," Ryan said. "I learned a lot about my young friend today."

Jamie tilted her head in question as Ryan continued, "It seems that our little radical queer friend just had her first real sexual experience on Tuesday night."

"Are you kidding?" Jamie gasped. "I thought she had more experience than you do."

"Gee, thanks," Ryan smirked.

"You know what I mean. Tell me what happened."

"Well, the kicker is that her first time getting naked was with a boy."

"A boy? Jennie?"

"Yep. I was as surprised as you are, but it seems that her worldliness is a carefully cultivated image. She's had plenty of crushes on girls, and she was thrown out of the house the first time because her mom caught her kissing her best friend, but she's never actually had genital contact with another girl."

"That's amazing. But why didn't you know this before?"

"I bought her act completely. When we first met, I gave her a very frank lecture on safer sex…"

"Without the visual aids, I assume?" Jamie asked with a smirk.

"Yes, dear. No hands-on demonstrations. Anyway, she listened patiently and has continually assured me that she's never had unprotected sex. Little did I know that was because she wasn't having sex at all."

"Amazing," Jamie muttered. "So what happened on Tuesday?"

"It seems that she and a younger boy from her neighborhood got drunk and high and played 'you show me yours and I'll show you mine.' Neither of them really knew what to do, so this rocket scientist puts her on her hands and knees to simulate anal sex. He was just going to rub against her, but neither of them had a clue about what they were doing, and Jen didn't even know if he entered her."

Jamie blew out a breath. "Let's make sure we only have boys, okay? This is terrifying." After another moment she asked, "But how does she not know if he was inside her or not? I mean, I don't have a lot of experience, but believe me, I knew when Jack was inside."

"My guess is that he was just bumping around in the general

vicinity. He's only thirteen, probably not even fully developed. Given her position, I don't think he would've been big enough to reach her vagina. But if he was just pushing against her opening it could feel like he was inside, given her inexperience."

"But she can't afford to take that risk, can she?"

"No. Of course not. That's why I took her to the doctor. I took her to see Alison since I didn't know any other gynecologists. Oh…I charged the exam and the tests since I didn't want her mom to find out. Is that okay?"

"Of course. What did Alison say?"

"She was confident that she hadn't been penetrated, so I guess we can relax. Jennie and I had lunch together, and I gave her another long lecture about sex. She seemed pretty freaked out about the whole incident, so hopefully she'll stay away from loaded penises for a while."

"What happened after you went to the doctor?"

"I was able to get in touch with her social worker, and she met with Jennie and Mrs. Willis this afternoon. After a good deal of begging on my part the social worker agreed to let her stay in the group home for a few days while she investigates placement possibilities. I just hope to God they don't put her into another foster care situation," Ryan sighed.

"Why not, honey?"

"She was in two foster care homes after her mom threw her out the first time," Ryan said. "She ran away from both of them, and the second time she was on the street for more than a week. I spent every evening looking for her, and by the time I found her I nearly did beat her."

"Good Lord. What can we do to help her? I thought she was so jaded that she was past redemption. But it sounds like she's still pretty impressionable."

"I know. I'm really worried about her hanging out with the street kids. She doesn't have very much common sense, and I'm afraid her friends will lead her to do things she wouldn't do on her own."

"How does she do in school?" Jamie asked.

"When she's not making a point to her mother, she does really well. She's a very bright kid. She's very creative and quite talented. She hasn't had much instruction since the high schools don't offer art anymore, but her drawing skills show a lot of potential."

"How about sports?"

"She hasn't done much, but I think she'd get a lot out of athletics. Her school only offers the standard girls sports, and she's not interested in them. I think she'd do better with something like golf or tennis."

"I just wish we could do more," Jamie mused.

Ryan looked thoughtful for a moment, then said, "You know, I would even be willing to be her guardian, but Mrs. Willis would fight tooth and nail to stop that from happening."

"Well, we'd have to have a very, very long discussion before I'd give the okay to have her move in with us," Jamie said, smiling at her partner's generosity but not at the thought of being a parent to a fourteen-year-old. "But I understand how much she means to you."

"I guess we just have to wait and see what happens," Ryan said. "I hate to feel so powerless, but in this situation I guess I really am."

"Yeah, I guess that's so. But if you think you're powerless, think how Jennie feels."

Chapter Ten

On Friday morning, Jamie looked nearly as tired as she felt as she walked down the stairs to find her keys. She had an 8:30 tee time at Stanford, and briefly regretted not staying in Hillsborough to knock 45 minutes off the trip.

Much to her pleasure, Ryan was in the kitchen making her a big bowl of oatmeal—something to stick to her ribs and get her through the morning. "I don't know if I can eat at five a.m.," Jamie grumbled as she sat down at the kitchen table.

"Come on, love," Ryan urged. "You've got to eat, and this will give you energy."

"Okay, I'll eat it…but only because it's made with love," she said, smiling up at her partner.

The first pair to tee off strode up to the tee box at eight o'clock on the dot. Jamie was scheduled for the fifth group, and she was in the process of limbering up on the driving range when Jim quietly approached. "Hi, Cupcake," he said.

She turned and gave him a generous smile. "Hi. I'm glad to see you, Dad." Looking over his shoulder she asked, "Are you alone?"

"Yes. Your mother is going to come over separately. I think these early tee times aren't to her liking," he chuckled.

"No big deal," she said. "If you're not into it, I realize that watching golf is a little like watching grass grow. I'm thankful she makes the effort." She smiled at her father and added, "I'm really happy that you made the effort too, Daddy. It means a lot to me that you flew across the country just to see me play."

"I wouldn't have missed this for the world. I'm so proud of you, I could burst." He said this with more enthusiasm than she thought she'd ever heard from him. "I don't even mind that you're not playing for Stanford."

She knew that sentiment was a lightly veiled jab, since he was a Stanford man through and through. Actually, her decision to attend Cal was the first real disagreement they had ever had, and she knew that he had always considered it a particular slap that she'd chosen to attend Stanford's biggest rival. The thought flitted through her mind that her decision to attend Cal had allowed her to make more than one momentous change in her life, none of them particularly welcomed by her father.

⚓

Ryan's class was over at 9:30 and as soon as she could get away she went home, grabbed her car and swung by Jordan's. Next they headed over to Amy's, and then Michelle's. Most of the players were taking the bus to Palo Alto later that afternoon, but Ryan had talked a few of her friends into going down early to watch Jamie's match.

Traffic wasn't too bad on that Friday morning, and they were at the golf course by eleven. Jamie's foursome was on the 15th hole when they approached, and as she looked around, Ryan was delighted to see four more of her teammates already trailing the group. All four freshmen were raptly watching play when Ryan snuck up behind Heather and said, "Boo."

The poor young woman nearly jumped out of her skin, but luckily Jamie had just rolled in her putt so the startled scream that came from her throat didn't disturb anyone's play. Heather blushed furiously as Ryan put her arms around her for a hug. "This was so sweet of you guys to come." Ashley, Lauren and Cami all smiled shyly, and Ashley admitted, "You should thank Heather. She's the one who got us organized."

Ryan gave her young protégé another hug, and this one caused Heather to blush a deep pink. Catherine was also following her daughter's foursome by this time, and she walked over to the volleyball players to greet them all. Most of them recognized her, and after a moment of small talk she reminded them all of the party at her home after the game. Ryan stayed with her to talk privately while the Cal group followed Jamie to the next hole. "Do you really think this is a good idea?" Ryan asked, her anxiety beginning to get the better of her. "I can't imagine that Jim will like all of my friends hanging out at your house."

"Jim is the one with the problem. Coddling him hasn't made things any better, so I'm going to live my life as I see fit. He's the one who has to change this time."

❧

Ryan said hello to Jim as they caught up with the group, but she quickly grabbed her teammates and went to stand with the gallery along the fairway where the balls would land rather than standing close to the golfers. She didn't want to make Jamie nervous so she thought it best not to actually talk to her during the round, plus she wanted to give Jim as much space as she could.

She'd never told Jordan the extent of the animosity that Jim had for her, but Jordan knew about Jim's edict that Ryan move out— which had obviously not come to fruition. Jordan stole glances at Jim occasionally, finally commenting, "Jamie looks a lot like her dad, doesn't she?"

"Yeah, physically, she does; but in my opinion, she gets most of her wonderful qualities from her mother. *She's* really special."

❧

When she putted out on the 18th hole, Jamie finally looked up and made eye contact with her partner. Ryan gave her a brilliant smile and a wink, but waited patiently until Jamie shook hands with the woman she had beaten. Jim and Catherine were standing relatively close to the volleyball team, but when Jamie trotted off the green she immediately went to give Ryan a hug and a kiss. "That was so sweet of all of you to come watch me."

"It was fun." Ashley piped up. "I've never been on a golf course before."

"Well, I admit it doesn't have the drama that your games do, but the atmosphere is nicer." Turning to Ryan she lightly patted her stomach and asked, "Isn't it time for your midday feeding?"

To the chuckles of her teammates, she grinned indulgently and admitted, "I could use a snack. Can you go with us?"

"I have to stay until my team is finished. But you need to get a good meal in you now so you can digest it before your game. Why don't you guys go on and have lunch?"

"I hate to leave you," Ryan said.

"Go on now," Jamie smiled. "I should spend some time with my parents anyway. When the match is over, we'll have a late lunch together."

"Okay with you guys?" Ryan asked.

"Yeah, I'm starving," Jordan admitted. "And if I'm hungry, Boomer here is probably close to eating small animals."

"Let me suggest a few places," Jamie said, describing a few spots close to Stanford.

When the eatery was agreed upon, they began to say goodbye to Jamie. Giggles broke out among the group when Jamie asked, "Ryan, do you have enough money?"

"Yes, Mom."

"Now remember to eat enough to get you through until 9:30."

"I will," she said to the snickers of her friends.

"You play well tonight," she added, standing on her tiptoes for a kiss.

"I will," she said mechanically. That got her a hard pinch that she fended off by wrapping the pincher tightly in her arms. "I'm proud of you," she whispered while everyone looked away. "You played great."

"Thanks," Jamie replied. "It meant a lot to have you here."

As Ryan released her, she looked over to Jim to wave goodbye. The unguarded look on his face was far less than friendly, but as soon as he realized she was looking at him, he forced himself to smile. "See you later," he called out.

When they walked away, Amy said, "What's up with Jamie's dad? He looked like he was ready to kill somebody."

"I hope that's not the case," Ryan worried without verbal

elaboration. *'Cause I'd be the victim.*

❧

By the time they'd finished lunch, it was time to head over to the gym. Coach wanted them to spend an hour getting used to the court, so they practiced some low-intensity drills and worked on service technique for a while. At around three he released them until 5:30, but that wasn't really enough time to go anywhere, so most of the team dressed in their warm-ups and wandered around campus.

Ryan didn't want to spend another afternoon looking through a campus bookstore, so she opted to hang out at the gym. "I think I'm going to take a nap," she decided.

"Are you going over to Jamie's?" Jordan asked.

"No. Since we didn't arrange that, I don't think I'd better. I don't want to seem like I think it's my home, too."

"So where are you going to go?"

"I've had some of my best naps on the training table. Care to join me?"

"Sure. It's better than looking at Stanford T-shirts for two hours."

❧

When the student manager came in at a little after five, she had to laugh at the sight of the two six-foot tall women sound asleep on the five-and-a-half-foot-long training tables. They had fashioned pillows from towels, and even though the tables were too short, both women looked quite comfortable. At the first small noise the trainer made, Ryan's eyes popped open. "You two look happy," the woman said.

"Nothing better than a long nap before a big game."

Jordan woke a little more slowly than Ryan, but within a few minutes she was her normal perky self. "Now what do we do?" she asked. "We can't start warm ups until six."

"How about a game of horse?" Ryan asked seductively.

"You're on."

Jordan actually had a great touch for someone who hadn't played basketball in years. "Hey, you're damn good," Ryan said as her shot was matched again.

"Why's that?" she asked airily. "Just because I can keep up with you?"

"Well, uhm, yeah, I guess that's what I meant," she conceded.

"I played on my high school team. I was recruited by a lot of colleges, but I liked volleyball better."

"You should come try to walk on with me," Ryan said, missing from center court.

"I don't think I can risk it. I can't afford to blow out a knee."

"I see your point," Ryan said, her mouth dropping as Jordan swished it from center court, "but we'd kick ass if we played together."

"Well, I'd kick ass if I played alone," she said, patting Ryan on the cheek indulgently, "so I suppose it wouldn't hurt to have you tag along."

All three of the Evans family members rode down to Stanford in one car. On the way over to campus Jamie warned, "All of Ryan's family will be there tonight. Knowing Martin, he hasn't told the extended family about how you behaved this summer, Daddy, and I'm not even sure what the boys know, but don't expect a rousing welcome from him."

"I won't," he said with yet another fake smile, already feeling jealous of the man for whom Jamie obviously felt so fond.

Everyone was very warm and friendly to Jim even though there had been a buzz in the group when he appeared at the door with Jamie and Catherine. There had been some discussion among the family about why this was the first time the man had gone out of his way to attend any of the family functions, but they didn't show it. Tommy and Annie were in attendance together for the first time, and as soon as they were introduced to Jim they began to thank him enthusiastically for the use of his home for their vacation. It was obvious to Jamie that her father had no idea that these people had been in his house, but his years of training as an attorney prepared him to handle the situation smoothly. As the young couple went back to their seats, Jim leaned over towards his wife and whispered, "Why do all of these people act like they know you so well? And who was the couple that stayed at the house? You've never mentioned any of this."

She shrugged mildly and said, "They're a lovely group of people, and they've welcomed me into the family. If you play your cards right, they'll do the same for you."

Martin and Maeve had been in line for refreshments when the Evans family had entered, and as they came back to their seats Martin made eye contact with Jamie and escorted his beloved up to meet Jim for the first time.

Maeve had given Martin a rather stern talking to on the way down to Palo Alto, finally convincing him that he should not even allude to the trouble that the senator had caused for Jamie and Ryan. Martin wasn't happy with the order, preferring to take Jim aside and tell him how close he had come to paying him a surprise visit, but he knew that Jamie wanted the evening to go smoothly, so he agreed to keep his anger bottled up.

After the introductions, Jim tried to make small talk. "So, Jamie tells me that Ryan is quite the gifted athlete. Was she always involved in sports?"

Martin stretched his mouth until he could contort it into a reasonable facsimile of a smile. "Yes," he said without elaboration.

"Well, it must have been hard raising such a big family without your wife. You've obviously done a fine job," Jim commented, trying to butter up the stern-looking man.

"Thank you," Martin said, with his steely-eyed gaze never softening. The tense interlude was mercifully brought to a close as the game was set to begin. Martin pointedly picked out seats next to his brother Francis, four rows away. "Not a very friendly bunch, are they?" Jim asked his daughter.

"They usually are. They're just very protective of Ryan…and me." She patted her father's arm and said, "I have to go say hello to everyone. Be back in a few."

Caitlin hadn't been able to properly greet her friend Catherine, and just before the game started she made it clear that she wanted to go to her. The giggling baby was passed down the row, finally reaching her target. She threw her chubby arms around Catherine's neck, slobbering all over her extremely expensive sweater. "Since when are you a fan of babies?" Jim asked with a puzzled glance, wincing as he heard how harsh his words sounded.

"Since I realized what I lost by being so distant from my baby."

"It's drooling on your sweater," he helpfully pointed out.

"She may drool wherever she wishes. Dry cleaners can clean a sweater with ease."

He leaned back in his seat, staring at the interaction between his wife and the small child. "She looks like Jamie did at that age," he commented, sticking his finger out for the baby to play with.

Caitlin looked mildly interested in him, but she was fascinated by the heavy silver chain that Catherine wore around her neck, and she occupied herself by trying to make a dental imprint on the smoothly polished metal. "Yes, she does a bit," his wife agreed. "Less so now than when I met her. She looked more like Jamie when her features were still indistinct. I suppose it was the blonde hair and the green eyes."

"That's a nice combination for a girl," he said, once again trying to engage the baby. "I miss my little Jamie," he said softly as he trailed a finger down the baby's pudgy cheek.

"With any luck, we'll have a grandchild or two in a few years," she said lightly, now beginning to look forward to the possibility.

"Yeah," he said tersely. "There's always that to look forward to."

Catherine gave him a look and shook her head. "They are planning on having children. You have a few years to get used to the idea, but you're not going to dissuade them. I think they'll be fantastic mothers."

He nodded somberly, unwilling to even imagine his daughter being that adult. "I'm sure Jamie would be."

"Ryan is the one," Catherine disagreed. "She had the proper example at home. Jamie will learn how to mother from her."

Catherine looked up when the three O'Flaherty brothers entered the gym. All three lumbered up the stairs, greeting everyone as they passed. Since Jim and Catherine were in the top row of the group, the men squeezed into the row behind them for their introductions. Conor, of course, was friendly, asking Jim all about his adventures in Washington. Brendan was very reserved, being formally polite—nothing more. Rory was his usual shy self, but he acted as though he bore no animosity towards Jim. After just a few seconds, Brendan indicated that their cousin Frank had saved them seats, and he and Rory climbed through the crowded bleachers to reach their spots.

"I have the feeling that your brothers aren't in my fan club," Jim mused to Conor.

"I don't think Rory knows much about what happened," Conor said, "but Brendan knows enough. He's not the kind of guy that can tolerate having Ryan hurt."

Jim looked at his young friend and asked the obvious question. "What about you, Conor? Why do you still speak to me?"

Conor thought about the question for a minute and decided to be honest. "It helped when you called me to tell me what had happened," he said. "I don't approve of what you did, but I guess I tried to put myself in your shoes. If my kid was doing something that I really didn't approve of, I'm sure I'd be pretty heavy-handed, too."

Jim nodded and said, "It's been hard, Conor, but I really am sorry for hurting your sister."

"You didn't really hurt her. You upset her, and made her really anxious, but you haven't actually hurt her."

"Are you sure of that?" he asked, casting a glance down at the young woman playing her heart out down on the court.

"Oh yeah," Conor assured him. "If you had, you'd be dead." He gave him a friendly pat on the back, his face curling into a smile.

Jim couldn't help but notice, however, that the normally warm blue eyes now bored into him like a pair of surgical lasers.

There was a small break between the first and second games, and some of the other players' parents came over to say hello to Catherine and Jamie, and finally meet Jim. Jim nearly gagged when Amy's mother introduced Catherine to her husband as 'Ryan's mother-in-law', but he managed to smile and graciously accept a few compliments about his recent appointment.

As the couple left, Jim leaned over to his wife and whispered, "How many of these games have you been to?"

"All of them," she said lightly. "It's important to Jamie."

The match was the most emotionally draining one that Ryan had ever played in. Stanford had gotten so much better since they'd last played each other that they seemed like a different team. But against all odds, Cal was having an extraordinary night. The match was so close that every game extended beyond the normal fifteen points. Cal won the first 17-15 with Stanford taking the second 18-16. When Stanford also took the third 16-14, Jamie was afraid that the tide was turning. But Cal roared back and rescued the fourth game on a beautiful dig by Michelle that Ryan put away for a kill to take it 17-15.

Every point in game five was hard fought, with neither team ever being up by more than two points. When Stanford missed an easy block that would have given them the match at 15-13, Jim's voice echoed through the gym as he shouted out, "Hit the damned ball."

Twenty pairs of mostly blue eyes turned and stared at him in shock, but Jamie did her best to avert a mutiny when she said, "He's a Stanford alum. He gets carried away."

Most of the relatives smiled at his faux pas, but Brendan locked his gaze on Jim, looking like he wanted to take him outside and teach him a lesson. Martin put his arm around his eldest and whispered something to make him turn around and concentrate on the game again, but he couldn't keep himself from turning around another time or two, his eyes burning with unveiled animosity.

The match was knotted at eighteen when Jordan and Ryan rose as one to extend their arms up and over the net to block a ball powerfully off the Stanford setter. All of the O'Flahertys stood with the other Cal fans as Erika served for the match. She looked entirely focused as she tossed over a high percentage serve just to be safe. The rally went on so long that Jamie's stomach was in knots, but to everyone's amazement, the shortest person on the team, five-foot-four-inch Michelle Chang, leapt as high as she was able to record her first kill of the match. The Stanford team was so utterly devastated that they could hardly bring themselves to go to the net for the traditional handshake. Even the crowd lapsed into silence, except for the very vocal Cal rooting section.

Jamie noticed that Ryan was wiping her eyes as she hugged the seniors from Stanford, obviously feeling empathy for the team that had never lost at home. The Cardinal coach came up to the net and threw an arm around both Jordan and Ryan and spoke to them for a few moments, finally releasing them to continue their celebration.

Ryan could not contain her joy for another moment, and she raced over to the bleachers and gingerly climbed up to grab Jamie in a powerful hug. "Oh, baby, I'm so proud of you." Jamie cried, hugging the overheated and thoroughly drenched body.

Catherine started to put a hand on her back, but she pulled it away quickly when she felt the sweat, not sharing that particular affinity with her daughter. Jim shook Ryan's hand, sincerely praising her efforts.

She smiled at him as she turned to head back down, saying, "Next time you'd better sit with the Stanford rooting section, Jim. Your cheering could be dangerous to your health with my family around."

Jamie just smirked at her, amazed at Ryan's ability to focus so intently on her game and still hear nearly everything going on in the gym.

It was ten o'clock by the time the last of the guests arrived, and Catherine and Maeve spent a minute marveling at the energy that flowed from the young women as they cavorted in the pool. "Ahh, youth," Maeve said fondly.

"I never had that kind of energy," Catherine said. "I think athletes are just different kinds of animals."

"You could be right there," Maeve agreed as Ryan went barreling into the deep end, executing a perfect cannonball.

"Come sit and tell me how married life is treating you," Catherine urged, leading Maeve over to a table.

"Ahh. I just so happen to have some snapshots of the trip. Your daughter arranged to have a professional photographer come, I'll have you know," she said with a big smile, "but we don't have those pictures yet. I just had my nephew take a few rolls of film with my camera."

Catherine looked at one of the first pictures, taken the day Maeve arrived in Ireland. "Oh, these must be your parents," she exclaimed.

"Yes, that would be them. John Ryan and Brigid Casey—married fifty-nine years in July," she said proudly.

"My, oh my. Such a long time to be married."

"They're still daft about each other," Maeve chuckled, and Catherine had to admit that she could see the affection the two shared, even in a simple photograph. "I don't think Martin and I will have anything close to their longevity, but I certainly wish our time would come."

"I was surprised when Jamie said you weren't living together yet. Is that because you haven't had your church wedding?"

"Yes," Maeve sighed. "I didn't mind at first—I suppose I was still so excited about the trip and everything. But I'm fifty-seven years old, Catherine. I don't want to waste a quarter of a year waiting to live with my Martin. It's actually been wearing on my mind. I'm afraid I'll be so cranky by late January that he won't want to marry me any longer."

"I think it would take more than a bad mood to scare Martin off. He's clearly very much in love with you, Maeve. How's he faring?"

"Well, Martin is nothing if not disciplined," she commented.

"He believes that one just does what one has to do. We're actually spending less time together than we did before." She blushed mildly as she said, "I think it's too tempting for him to spend our evenings snogging."

"Snogging?" Catherine asked.

"Oh…you know…kissing," she said, embarrassed.

"Then why wait, Maeve? Surely you could come up with an alternate plan. Would it bother Kevin if you and Martin lived at your house for a few months while you waited for Niall's house to be completed?"

"We haven't even asked him," she said, looking puzzled. "I suppose we hatched this plan, and now we're stuck with it."

"Nonsense," Catherine said. "We can put a wedding together in a week or two. Talk to Martin and see if he feels like you do."

"All right," she said tentatively. "I suppose I could be ready sooner—although I had planned on buying a nice dress." She shook her head briskly and said, "Ahh…no need. I can wear the one my sister bought for me in Ireland."

Catherine was thumbing through the pictures, and she came upon the ones from the actual wedding. "Is this the dress you mean?" she asked curiously.

"Yes, that's it," Maeve said. "It's perfectly serviceable."

Catherine surveyed the plain ivory colored gown and thought privately that it did nothing for her friend. The color was too close to her skin tone, making her look exceedingly washed out, and the dress was of a style more suited to an older woman, not showing off Maeve's trim figure in the least.

"My darling younger sister took me shopping, since I'd not brought anything special enough to get married in. We could have done a better job if we'd had the time, but we were forced to go to a shop in Ballina. They only had three dresses in my size," she commented. "This was really the best of the lot."

"I would love to go shopping with you, Maeve. This dress is very nice, but it won't do to wear it twice. Isn't that some kind of bad luck?" she asked teasingly.

Unhappily, Maeve said, "I can't spend the money on something so frivolous. I have a nice navy blue dress that I can wear. I'm sure that will be fine."

Catherine cocked her head and asked, "Do they have the good luck aphorism in Ireland that you should wear something borrowed for your wedding?"

"No, but I know what you mean," Maeve said.

"Let's go up to my room for a few minutes. I'd like to test a theory."

Maeve was more than taken aback as Catherine led her to her walk-in closet. She looked around with a wide-eyed expression and finally was unable to stop herself from exclaiming, "My goodness, this looks like the finest clothing store in Dublin."

"It's rather ridiculous," Catherine said. "I had to attend so many social functions with Jim and for my own charity work. It's just not done to wear the same thing to multiple functions, so most of these things have only been worn once."

Maeve gazed around at the gorgeous clothing that was arranged according to color, shaking her head in amazement the entire time. Her hand lifted as she fingered some of the garments, stunned by the rich feel of the fabrics. "Remarkable," she murmured, unable to come up with anything more complex.

Catherine placed a hand on Maeve's shoulder and said, "My theory is that you and I are about the same size. Would you be interested in testing it out?"

Maeve blanched noticeably, as she said, "You want to lend me one of these gorgeous things?"

"No, I want to give you a dress to wear to your wedding," she said, her eyes locked upon her friend's. "I'd be honored if you would do me that favor."

The green eyes were dancing with delight, but Maeve felt duty-bound to try to refuse. "Oh, Catherine," she said, "that's really not necessary. I have a perfectly serviceable…"

"Maeve," Catherine interrupted, "no woman wants to get married in a serviceable dress. Some of these dresses would look positively wonderful on you. Will you at least try a few on?"

Giving Catherine a nearly giddy smile she said, "Well, it couldn't hurt to just try a few, now could it?"

"That's the spirit." Catherine enthused, running her eyes down the long racks, trying to pick the dress that would allow Maeve to stand out as the lovely woman that she was.

Jamie noticed her mother's absence, and after a half-hour she went to search for her. She was a bit surprised to find Maeve standing in the closet, wearing only a full slip, but when the task was explained she immediately pitched in to help.

Another half-hour later, both Jamie and Mia were sitting on the floor of the big closet, giving their expert opinions on the fashion show. They had been trying to focus on the colors that would go best with Maeve's hair, the auburn clashing badly with much of Catherine's wardrobe, which tended towards the colors that highlighted her light blonde hair.

Mia finally jumped up from the floor and went to an untapped source, pulling out a sterling silver silk shantung two-piece suit that immediately caused Maeve's eyes to light up. "Oh my goodness," she said as she lightly touched the fabric. "I don't think I've ever seen anything so gorgeous."

"Give it a whirl, Maeve," Mia insisted, having warmed up to the delightful woman immediately.

She did so, fastening the tiny covered buttons and twitching the jacket into place. The skirt was a little shorter than she was used to wearing, hitting her above her knees, but she had very shapely legs, and the look was extremely flattering. As she gazed at herself in the three-way mirror, she shook her head slowly as three other heads nodded in tandem. "I hardly look like myself," she mused, wondering who the sophisticated woman was who looked back at her.

"We have a winner," Mia declared, settling the issue to everyone's satisfaction.

At around eleven, Jim had had enough of making small talk with the O'Flahertys, so he excused himself to Jamie by saying, "I need to get up early and go in to the office for a few hours. You don't mind if I say good night, do you?"

"No, but are you sure we won't disturb you?"

"No, no, I'm sleeping in a guest room in the front of the house. I won't hear a thing."

"Okay, good night, Daddy. And thanks for trying so hard tonight. I really appreciate it."

"Anything for you, Cupcake," he said automatically, before he realized that he really meant it.

It was after midnight when they finally were able to pluck the tiring baby from her fifteen baby-sitters and get her back into her clothes. All of the O'Flahertys thanked Catherine profusely for her generosity as they slowly departed. The team finally got squared away with dry T-shirts and their warm-ups, and took off shortly thereafter. As Coach Placer got ready to leave he took Ryan aside and said, "The luckiest day of my year was when you walked into my office. It's been a pleasure to be your coach."

"Well, given that volleyball was my least favorite team sport, I have to thank you for elevating it significantly in my estimation," she teased.

"I don't know what your favorite is, but I'd switch to be able to coach you in something you really love," he said as he patted her back.

One of the things that the O'Flahertys had trouble with was refraining from cleaning up after a party at Catherine's. "We can't just leave this mess," Martin said as he surveyed the damage.

But even as he spoke, Marta, Helena, and Helena's son, Antonio, came out to attack the mess. Antonio did not work for Catherine regularly, but the nineteen-year-old college student helped out on an hourly basis when Marta thought they needed an extra pair of hands.

"It's okay, Da," Ryan assured him. "Jamie and I will help out. You guys head on home. It's late, and I know the boys have had a long day."

"All right, darlin'. But it just doesn't feel right to expect other people to clean up after us."

"I know, Da," she said indulgently. "But things are different down here."

"You can say that again," he muttered so that only she could hear. "The nerve of that sorry excuse of a man to root for Stanford. And then to leave in the middle of his own party. I'll tell you one thing, Siobhán, wealth doesn't assure good manners."

"That's for sure," she agreed, giving him a kiss on the cheek.

By the time the mess was cleared away it was nearly one a.m., and Catherine decreed that the dishes should be washed in the morning. The staff gratefully retired to their quarters, exhausted from the rare flurry of activity that the day had brought.

"It's awfully late, Mia," Catherine said. "Would you like to stay over so you don't disturb your parents?"

"Gee, I guess I could do that," she said, thinking, *My bag's already in Jordan's room.*

"I'll have Helena prepare an extra room for you, honey," Catherine said, starting off in the direction of the servants' wing.

"No, don't bother, Mom," Jamie said. "We'll set Mia up. Helena's already in bed."

"All right," Catherine agreed. "Just let me know if you need anything."

Mia smiled, thinking, *I've got everything I need, all wrapped up in one big, tall package.*

Catherine kissed the girls good night and headed straight for bed, one o'clock being close to her normal bedtime. Jamie looked at her partner with very alert eyes and said, "I'm still keyed up."

"Yeah, I am too. I should be exhausted, but I'm full of nervous energy bubbling out of me."

"Let's hop in the spa," Jamie suggested. "Maybe that will relax us." Turning to their friends she asked, "You guys wanna come?"

Mia batted her eyes at her friend and said, "I haven't been able to touch Jordan all night long. I think I need to make up for lost time."

"I'd hate to disappoint Mia," Jordan smiled as she took her friend's hand and led her into the house. "'Night, girls," she said over her shoulder. "Don't do anything we wouldn't do."

Ryan looked down at Jamie and said, "I'm not sure what that would preclude at this point. The house feels like it's gonna shake off its foundation some nights."

"Jordan's making up for lost time." She gave Ryan a smirk and said, "Mia just loves sex."

"I think she loves more than sex. I think she loves Jordan."

"You could be right, Buffy," Jamie agreed, grinning up at Ryan. "It's easy to fall in love with a big, sexy volleyball player. I know I have."

"Flattery will get you everywhere," Ryan joked, taking Jamie's hand to lead her to the spa. They spent a good fifteen minutes soaking in the warm water and were both beginning to relax as the water worked its magic.

As she always did when she was relaxed, Jamie started to get a little frisky and she asked, "Wanna burn off a few more calories? I'd really like to get you onto that chaise over there," she indicated the extra-wide piece, "and have my way with you."

"Ooh…I like your way," Ryan agreed, "but I think it would be nice if we went upstairs."

"You know," Jamie purred as she slid onto Ryan's lap and started to nibble on her neck, "I think you're right about my exhibitionistic tendencies. There's something so totally erotic about making love outside." She shivered as she tried to describe the sensations. "I love the cool air that flows over my hot skin, and the goose bumps you get when I touch you. I love the contrast between your hot skin and the cool breeze as it glides over my body." Her head dipped as she started to work on Ryan's sensitive ears with a focused intensity. "What do you say?" she asked seductively as she rubbed her breasts against Ryan's, intentionally trying to influence her vote.

"But people can see us," Ryan protested weakly, her resolve easily swayed when Jamie put her mind to it.

"No, they can't," Jamie insisted as she wrapped her arms around Ryan's neck and twitched her hips in a slow, sexy beat, making her partner's eyes roll back in her head. "The servants' quarters windows face the street, not the pool," she added, bending to kiss Ryan's full lips tenderly. "Daddy's in a front guest room, so the only person who could possibly see us is mother, and that's only if she went to the window and really tried to focus. There's a lot of foliage between the upstairs and the pool, so it'd be hard even if she tried."

"But you can see from the kitchen," Ryan protested, knowing full well that she could see the pool area while she was eating breakfast.

"Yeah, you can, but no one is in the kitchen. It's after one a.m."

"Jordan and Mia?"

"Yes, they have a good view of the pool. Now tell me, what are the odds of them going to the window to watch us?" She raised one eyebrow, reminding Ryan of where their friends' priorities lay.

"Uhh…" Ryan's head had dropped back against her shoulders as Jamie escalated her attack, working on her neck with a relentless enthusiasm. "I guess I'm out of excuses," she said, nearly forgetting what they were discussing.

Backing off for a moment, Jamie sat upright and grasped Ryan's face in her hands. "If you want to go inside, that's what we'll do," she said. "I never want to make you uncomfortable."

"Jamie, I've had sex in a phone booth. You know I'm a shameless hussy. I'm only concerned for you."

"I can take care of myself," she reminded her. "I wouldn't ask for things I didn't want."

The time out for discussion had allowed Ryan's mind to focus again, and she discovered that she was having as much fun playing the game as she expected to have when she gave in. "I like it when you try to seduce me," she whispered, drawing Jamie's ear close so that she could give it several long swipes with her warm tongue. "I really love it when you act like you're dying to have me."

"I like it too," Jamie agreed. "It's different for me—but really nice."

"You're not finished, are you?" Ryan asked, batting her big blue eyes at her partner. "I'm not thoroughly seduced yet."

"Oh, I'll seduce you, tough stuff. And if my charms don't work, I'll drag you out of here with brute strength and have you on the pool deck."

Ryan chuckled, the sound rumbling deep in her throat. "You'll have to call for reinforcements," she said, laying down the challenge. "If I don't want to get out—you can't make me."

"And I suppose that you could make me?" Jamie asked archly. "You think I can't defend myself?"

Ryan crossed her arms against her chest, narrowing her eyes as she surveyed her opponent. "That's exactly what I think. You can't touch this."

Unable to resist a challenge, Jamie spent a moment looking for a weakness, deciding to launch a full-scale attack in the hope of catching Ryan off guard with her ferocity. She hurled herself at the taller woman, tickling every spot she could sneak a hand. Ryan fended her off pretty well, finally dunking herself under the water to escape the questing fingers. When she emerged, Jamie was draped over her shoulder, slapping at Ryan's back, the blows sounding much worse than they were on her partner's wet skin.

"I want some privacy," Ryan declared. "We're going into the pool house."

"I don't want to!" Jamie cried, her laughter mingling with her outrage at being handled so effortlessly. She continued to slap at Ryan, demanding, "Put me down right here. I want to make love to you under the stars."

"Nope. You'll see stars all right," Ryan promised, "but they won't be in the sky. I'm gonna make you scream," she growled, "and no one will hear you. No one will rescue you tonight. You're mine—all mine."

"Put me down, you brute! I don't want to go in there." She was slapping furiously now, the sharp sounds echoing off the stucco walls that surrounded the yard.

"Quiet," Ryan cautioned, afraid that Catherine might get up and look out.

Jamie complied, knowing that she had been too loud. Instead of complaining verbally, she contented herself with trying to wriggle out of Ryan's grasp, finding her efforts largely futile. Ryan had a very firm hold on the backs of her thighs, using one of her tricks of letting Jamie dangle far down her back to render her largely helpless. All Jamie could do was slap at Ryan, or tickle her, and the infuriating woman had the capacity to convince herself that she wasn't ticklish when the situation warranted it. It seemed as though Jamie had to either go along or utter her safe word, and it would be a cold day in hell before she voluntarily said, "Ryan rules."

Chapter Eleven

A fter tossing and turning in the unfamiliar bed for over two hours, Jim finally decided that he needed a drink. Slipping into his slacks, he stumbled downstairs and found the Scotch, but he couldn't stomach hard liquor without ice so he poured two fingers worth and went into the kitchen to fetch a few cubes. *What in the hell?* he thought when he heard muffled voices and splashing.

He had to strain a bit to finally focus on the sound, but he could just make out his daughter's small body being hoisted from the spa by her much larger partner. *Oh, Jesus, just what I wanted to see. That should make me sleep better.*

He averted his eyes and went to the ice machine to fill his glass. He was just about to go back upstairs when he heard Jamie's voice rise...sounding like she was being hurt. *What in the hell is she doing to her?* He went back to the window to see Ryan carrying his daughter towards the pool house, Jamie's legs kicking in the air as she beat on Ryan's back. *She's forcing her! She doesn't want to go with her. I'll kill her,* he vowed as he gripped his glass so firmly that it shattered in his hand. He bit his lip to keep from screaming, not wanting all of the servants hovering about if they heard him. Sparing a glance at his hand, he watched as the blood gushed from the sizeable gash, the pain not really registering because of the adrenaline that flowed through his body. When he looked up again, Ryan had lowered Jamie a bit, rendering her even more helpless as she struggled valiantly.

He opened the back door, unable to hear every word, but he caught his daughter calling the large woman a brute and Ryan ordering her to be quiet. He padded across the pool deck while wrapping a kitchen towel around his hand, the blood coloring the white cloth immediately. His pace grew quicker until he was running across the slate surface, finally catching up with the pair. Before either woman knew what was happening, Jim grabbed Ryan by the back of her suit and yanked her to a halt. "Put her down…now!" he screamed, his face so red with anger that it looked like it would explode. "Put her down!"

Ryan blinked at him, unable to form a single word. She crouched down and gently set Jamie onto the ground, staring at the man as Jamie said, "Daddy, we were just playing. Really." She was blushing wildly, her face nearly as red as his.

Trying to make the reality fit his perceptions he said, "But you were fighting. I saw you struggling. You don't have to defend her."

His last sentence pissed Jamie off, and she heard herself say, "I was seducing her. We like to do that sometimes. She was not hurting me…we were on our way to the pool house to make love." She gave him a withering gaze as she stated unequivocally, "I wanted to make love. Neither Ryan nor anyone else has ever forced me to do that."

He felt sick to his stomach and faint, and he remembered about his hand. His eyes went to the bloody towel just as Jamie and Ryan's eyes tracked to the same spot. "What did you do?" Jamie cried, trying to grab his hand to assess the damage.

"Nothing," he growled, his embarrassment over spying on them merging with his reaction to Jamie's words to make him start to run in the direction of the house. He grabbed another towel and ran back upstairs, sticking his bare feet into his loafers before running back downstairs. He grabbed his keys and ran for the door, not bothering to turn off the alarm before he jumped in the car to drive himself to the emergency room.

Within seconds, the entire household was awake, most of them gathered near the kitchen. The servants reacted quickly, getting the alarm turned off while Catherine ran across the living room to find Jamie and Ryan in the kitchen, a vivid trail of blood smeared across the kitchen floor. "My God! What happened?" she gasped, grabbing Jamie by the shoulders as she anxiously surveyed her from head to toe, looking for the source of the blood.

"It's Daddy," Jamie said, feeling sick to her stomach as she focused on the blood. "He cut his hand somehow."

Jordan and Mia poked their heads in the kitchen, both looking wide-awake but very haphazardly put together. "Are you okay?" Mia asked, looking at the two women.

"Yeah. Fine," Ryan said. "Sorry guys, you can go back to bed."

Jordan gave Ryan a doubtful glance, but did as her friend asked, tugging Mia along with her.

Helena went to the supply cabinet and took out some cleaning cloths, then set to work on the sink and the floor, trying to get the blood out before it soaked into the stone.

Catherine exchanged meaningful glances with her daughter and twitched her head towards the stairs, leading the way to the second floor. Both women followed her into her room, where Jamie immediately began to explain. "We were in the spa," she said, already embarrassed, "and we started playing with each other."

Catherine furrowed her brow, but didn't comment.

"I don't know why, but all of a sudden we were playing that, 'you can't make me' game," she said weakly, looking ill.

Catherine smiled and nodded as she said, "I'm familiar with that one, girls. Everybody does that at some point."

Ryan interrupted, not seeing the need to go into details. "We were going into the pool house. I was carrying Jamie over my shoulder when Jim showed up."

Catherine's eyes bugged out as Ryan continued.

"He grabbed me by my suit and demanded that I put Jamie down. He apparently thought I was trying to force her to…"

"I get the picture," Catherine said, holding up a hand. "But where did the blood come from?"

"He cut himself in the kitchen," Jamie said. "There was broken glass all over the sink. I guess that's where he was when he heard us."

"Well," Catherine said, running her hands through her disordered hair, "I suppose the excitement is over now. I hope he wasn't hurt too badly," she said worriedly. "There was an awful lot of blood."

"It didn't look good," Ryan agreed. "What hospital would he have gone to?"

"Probably San Mateo," Catherine mused. "Should we call?"

"Yeah. If he's not there, I'll go look for him."

"Oh, honey, I don't want you to go out driving around here. You don't even know the neighborhood."

Ryan didn't want to worry her unnecessarily, but she was honestly quite worried about the cut. She thought it entirely possible that he could have lost enough blood to render himself unconscious.

Catherine got on the phone to the hospital, and after wasting ten minutes trying to get an answer, was finally satisfied that he had not gone there. In the interim, Jamie had pulled out the phone book and was dialing all of the urgent care facilities that were reasonably close by—with no luck.

Ryan knew that her partner was correct and that she shouldn't be driving around aimlessly. She didn't want Jamie to go with her, since she didn't know how long she would be gone and Jamie needed some rest to be able to play golf in a few hours.

Her musings were interrupted by the ringing doorbell, and all three women shared a puzzled look as Jamie ran to answer it. She opened the door to a Hillsborough police officer who asked, "Is everything all right here? We were notified that your alarm went off."

Jesus, you could have a four-alarm fire in my neighborhood with a slower response time. Ryan thought.

"Yes," Jamie said, but Catherine came up behind her and said, "Actually, officer, we have a problem."

She explained the entire situation to the man, and he asked for the information about the car. Jamie found the paperwork from the rental car company. The officer went to his car and got on the radio, notifying the station to be on the lookout for the car that Jim was driving, and promised to call the house with any news.

After the officer left, all they could do was sit and wait, and they decided to do so together.

After going upstairs to put on some sweats, they went into the living room, and within a few minutes Jamie was curled up on the couch, her head on Ryan's lap as the indulgent woman gently trailed her fingers through her hair. Seconds after the tender touch began, Jamie was sound asleep, much to Catherine's amusement. "She has the most uncanny ability to sleep anywhere, at any time. I envy her."

"Yeah, I do too," Ryan agreed. "I tend to lie awake and worry if I have something to worry about."

"I tend to sit in the living room and drink myself into a stupor," Catherine said wryly, getting up to fix the first of what she assumed would be many.

"Catherine?" Ryan asked, looking up at her intently.

"Yes, dear?"

"Why don't you try Jamie's tactic, instead?" She picked up her lover's head and laid it back down on a soft pillow, taking a moment to cover her with a throw. Moving to the other couch, Ryan sat on the end and patted her lap, smiling at her mother-in-law as she issued the invitation.

"This works very well, thank you," Catherine said, holding her glass up.

"Humor me," Ryan insisted. "Come on. You might need to have your wits about you later on." She didn't want to sound like such a pessimist, but she thought there was a chance that they would, at the least, have to go to the hospital, and she didn't want Catherine to be looped if they did.

"All right," she said, understanding Ryan's unspoken worry. She lay down and placed her head gingerly upon Ryan's lap, moving her head around to get comfortable. Ryan pulled the chenille throw from the back of the couch and covered Catherine with it as she began to run her fingers through her soft blonde hair.

"Your hair feels very much like Jamie's," Ryan said, as she continued to trail her hand through the tresses. "I'd love for one of our kids to have hair like this." She laughed and said, "I guess that precludes using one of my brothers as a sperm donor."

"Don't forget Caitlin," Catherine reminded her. "There must be some gene for blonde hair in your mix."

"No. Don't think so. Tommy's dad was very fair. I think that's a Driscoll thing. The O'Flahertys go from dark to darker." She sighed and said, "Eh…less chance of sunburn. No big deal."

"It must feel odd to know that you can't create a child together," Catherine said, her voice growing soft and a little sleepy.

"Mmm, probably odder for Jamie. I never had the fantasy of being able to do that. Don't get me wrong, I'd love to be able to merge with her and create new life from our love. I've just never assumed I would do it, so it doesn't seem odd now."

"That makes sense," Catherine agreed. "I suppose you have a different way of looking at the world than I do."

"I think everyone has their own view. It's only when we think our way is *the way* that we get into trouble." Her thoughts drifted to Jim as she considered that was his main problem.

"True," the older woman said, a yawn escaping. She cuddled up tighter and slowly fell asleep, her face losing the few lines of tension that it carried when she was awake.

Ryan leaned back and regarded the two women, so similar and yet so different. *Some day I'll sit back and watch Jamie and our daughter and think the same thing*, she mused, smiling to herself as she also drifted off.

🐎

The young clerk looked up as a man walked quickly down the hallway, heading for the exit doors. "Oh…Mr. Jones?" she asked, certain that she had identified the correct patient. The tall, sophisticated man stood out from the crowd, not just because he wore only a pair of slacks and shoes. There was something that was vaguely familiar about him, but she couldn't place him.

She turned to the woman at the next desk and asked, "That last patient left without his receipt. Did he remind you of anyone?"

The other woman looked at the receipt and said, "Yeah, he reminded me of the fifty other John Joneses we've had in here in the last year. Can't these guys think of something more original?"

🐎

As he pulled up to the house, Jim surveyed the place and pondered why the lights were on in the living room. *Well, time to face the music*, he decided. He had a notion to just head over to his apartment, but his briefcase was in the house and he couldn't leave without it, much as he wanted to.

He entered through the kitchen, noticing that the alarm had been turned off. "Could I have screwed up any worse tonight?" he grumbled as he walked towards the living room. Coming up to the room at an angle he saw bodies lying on both couches, with Ryan sitting up, sound asleep. *They probably stayed up so they could all watch when Jamie tells me to go to hell.* Walking a little closer he saw his daughter sleeping on Ryan's lap and begrudgingly thought, *Well, she does look very content lying there with her.* As he crept closer still, he gasped when he saw that it was not Jamie but Catherine who lay so contentedly in the dark woman's loose embrace.

Jesus Christ, he cried, feeling irrationally angry at witnessing the tableaux. *She's taken my daughter, now she's got my wife. Thank God we don't have a dog.* He shook his head slowly, carefully observing the woman as she slept. *I don't understand the attraction. Yes, she's pretty, but I don't think that's it. It's something more than that. She has potential, but no track record. Jack was a much surer bet. He's definitely going somewhere. Ryan might be content to just run around playing sports; she might turn into another freeloader like Catherine's cousins.* But even as he thought this, he knew it wasn't true. His investigation had showed a very determined, very focused young woman about whom very few people had a bad word.

Well, he thought as he slowly trudged upstairs, *I doubt that I'll have the chance to find out what her allure is. I'm sure that I've finally pushed Jamie over the edge this time.*

He gathered his things, packing quickly, then put on a fresh set of clothes, throwing his bloodstained shoes and slacks into the trash bin. When he was ready to leave, he removed a notepad from his briefcase and sat down to write.

You were all sleeping so soundly that I thought it best to leave you alone. I'm fine—nothing that a few dozen stitches couldn't mend. I'm going to work a bit at the office, and then go home as planned on Sunday evening.

I would apologize, but there comes a point at which even I have to acknowledge that my words mean little. I guess I'm just too set in my ways to even try to change. I truly wish that I wasn't so angry and suspicious of people—it just seems second nature to me now, and I don't have a clue how to stop.

I'm sorry for being such an abject failure as a father.

You deserve so much more—I hope that Martin can serve in that role for you.

I'm heartsick over how this weekend turned out, but I know it's too late to repair the damage I've done. For what it's worth, I am very sorry. I hope…well, I suppose my hopes and wishes won't come true—but it's no one's fault but my own.

He didn't sign the note, not having a clue how to refer to himself. He was addressing all three of the women who slept on the couches, but his role was so nebulous that he was utterly confused. No longer a husband, no longer a father…who was he? Placing the note on the writing table near the front door, he hefted his bag onto his shoulder, blew a kiss to the women who meant more to him than he could fathom, and left quietly, fully expecting this visit to be his last.

🐎

The phone rang at four, and Ryan jerked awake, slipping off the couch when Catherine sat up halfway, a dazed expression on her face. Jamie, of course, didn't flinch, sleeping away contentedly on the other couch. "Hello?" Ryan managed to say, fighting with the cobwebs that still choked her mind.

"Mrs. Evans?" a brusque voice asked.

"No, but I can take a message for her. Can I help you?" The phone was on the writing table, and as Ryan spoke she scanned the note that Jim had left.

"This is Sergeant Hallihan of the Hillsborough Police Department. I wanted to give her an update on our search for her husband."

"Oh," Ryan said, thinking quickly. "Actually, Mr. Evans just got in contact with us. He seems fine, officer, so you needn't continue the search."

"All right, Ma'am," he said warily. "I'd prefer to speak with the senator, just for our records. We like to have a statement from the missing person before we close our files."

"I don't think he's reachable right now," Ryan said. "Give me your name and number, and I'll have him call you when he's in contact again."

The officer did as requested and hung up after obtaining similar information from Ryan.

Catherine was running her hands through her hair, trying to organize her thoughts, when there was a sharp rap on the front door. "Now what?" Ryan moaned, going to the door to open the tiny window that allowed a view of guests. "Yes?" she asked the young man who stood on the steps.

"Steven Hawkins," he said. "San Francisco Chronicle. I'm here investigating the missing persons report filed on Senator Evans earlier this evening. Will you comment for the record?"

"Sure," Ryan said, hoping to nip this in the bud. She thought quickly, deciding to give the bare bones of the incident just to appear like they had nothing to hide. "The senator cut his hand on a glass earlier this evening. It was in the middle of the night, and he thoughtfully didn't want to wake his family up to drive him to the hospital. He obviously thought he'd return before anyone woke, but that wasn't the case. His wife was alerted to the blood in the kitchen, and she wisely thought to call the police in case he was disoriented from blood loss."

"Where is the senator now? What hospital did he go to?"

"He's resting now," Ryan said, assuming that he was resting somewhere…just not in his bed upstairs. "His choice of hospitals is a private matter for the moment, but I'm certain that he'll authorize the doctor who attended him to release a statement. Anything else?"

"Can you comment on the reports that there was a rather wild party at this address earlier in the evening?" he asked, obviously having been told this by a disgruntled neighbor—made more disgruntled by being awakened at four a.m. for a comment. "Was the senator's injury connected to the party?"

Ryan smiled through the tiny opening and said, "His daughter is a senior in college. The party was just a few of her friends gathered for dinner. It would hardly qualify as wild, I assure you. The guests had been gone for hours when the senator cut his hand. No connection whatsoever."

"All right," he said thoughtfully, glad that he could wrap this one up and get back to his desk. "Any further comment?"

"No. That's the whole story," she assured him. *Or the whole of the story that you're going to get.*

"Who are you, ma'am? You didn't identify yourself."

"You may attribute my comments to an unnamed family spokesperson," she smiled, having always wanted to attach that moniker to herself.

As Ryan returned to the living room, Catherine was beaming a grin at her. "You do that very well. Have you ever thought of a career as a public relations specialist?"

"I'm Irish," she smiled. "Telling tales is our birthright."

Saturday morning found Jamie wrapped around Ryan's body, snug in her childhood bed. She opened her eyes and tried to figure out how they had gotten there, finally deciding that it wasn't really important—they were there now, and that's all that mattered.

Ryan felt her move and lazily commented, "Maybe I do want you to take off a few pounds."

Jamie smiled as she understood the reference. "Had to carry me again, huh, tough stuff?"

"Either that or leave you on the couch, and that's just not acceptable."

Jamie sat up, brushing her hair out of her eyes. "What happened? Did Daddy come home?"

"Yeah. We were all asleep on the couch, and he came in and went out again. He left a note."

"Oh, please. He took off?"

"Yep. Hard to tell if he was mad at us or just himself. It sounded like he was pretty depressed."

"What am I going to do with that man?" Jamie moaned, falling back to the bed heavily.

"He is pretty high maintenance," Ryan agreed. "We need to get in touch with him at some point. A reporter came to the house and wanted details. I placated him, but your dad needs to issue a statement of some sort."

"Jesus. It's not like things weren't bad enough. Now we have reporters interested in our drama?"

"Yep. Never a dull moment with you people. I've got thirty people in my family, and we have less going on than your threesome does," she chuckled.

"Well, let's go see what awaits us today."

"Hopefully nothing," Ryan said, knowing that the odds of that were unlikely.

Their attempts to contact Jim were fruitless, but they did leave messages at his apartment in Washington and the one in San Francisco, where they assumed he'd spent the remainder of the night.

Jamie had to get to the golf course, so she and Ryan took off, Jordan and Mia still sound asleep—or not, depending on the moment.

Catherine stayed behind for a while, finally deciding to use all of her resources to track down her elusive husband. It took quite a few calls, but she finally found someone in his senate office who was working on Saturday. They provided her with several numbers, and she finally reached his secretary at home. The efficient woman was able to provide his new cell phone number.

Dialing the number, Catherine smiled to herself when Jim answered on the first ring. "You can run, but you can't hide," she said in a gently mocking tone.

"Oh, hello, Catherine," he said, sounding more wary than she could ever remember.

"What's going on? Why the need to play hide and seek?"

"I'm ah…I'm at work, Catherine. I have some things that I have to clean up here."

"Uh-huh," she said calmly, not buying his story for an instant. "We're concerned about you, Jim. Really."

"I've caused enough harm for one weekend, Cat. Let's just move on, shall we?"

"Jim, please don't be so melodramatic. This was a small incident… don't act like it's fatal."

"I don't think I can do it, Catherine. I just don't think I can change." He sounded totally defeated and very sorry for himself, neither trait particularly appealing.

"Maybe you'll feel better after you talk to Jamie. She wants to speak with you, you know."

"I'll call her when I get back to Washington," he said, obviously trying to evade the issue. "I've got a lot to take care of today, and I'm really struggling with these damn pain pills."

Ahh, that's probably why he seems so depressed. "Did you get proper medical care?"

"I'm not sure, to tell you the truth. I'm going to find a specialist in DC to have it checked out."

"You do that, dear," she said, surprised that she had used that term for him. "I assume you know that the newspapers picked up on the story."

"Yes. I was on the other line with my press secretary when you called. Public life sucks," he groused, using a term that she had never heard him utter before.

"You'll get through it. You always do."

He sighed, his voice slower and his mind less sharp than usual. "How do you get through it, Cat? Have you ever seen them… together?"

It took her a second, but she finally understood his question. "I've had a couple of close encounters. I've learned my lesson now. When we're in the house together it would take an act of God to get me to leave my room once I've announced I'm going to bed. A pair of earplugs is also not a bad idea," she laughed, hoping to lighten the tone of the conversation.

"I don't think I can ever get to where you are with this," he said, the sadness flowing through the phone lines. "I just don't think I can."

"Honey, you're tired, and you're not yourself when you're taking pain medication. Give it some time. I think you did very well this weekend, to tell you the truth. Don't give up."

"Thanks for saying so, Cat, but I think you're being too generous. I think I've blown it for good this time."

She found herself wanting to reassure him, but it was obvious that he wasn't in a receptive mood. "I don't think so, but we'll just have to wait and see, won't we?"

"Yes. That's what we'll have to do," he agreed, his voice sounding raspy and full of dread.

In retrospect, she wasn't sure why she said it, but Catherine heard herself say, "It's possible to severely disappoint people and still have them forgive you and want you in their lives. Don't give up hope… for either Jamie or me."

There was absolute silence coming from his end, lasting a good minute. "Do…do you mean that?" he whispered.

She sighed heavily and said, "I honestly don't know what I mean, but I certainly haven't done anything about moving forward with the divorce. There must be a reason that I haven't wanted to do so."

"Catherine…Cat…if there's anything that I can do…"

"No, really, there's nothing you can do right now. Let's just take it slow and see how things develop."

"Okay, okay," he said, an eager tone replacing the morose one of moments earlier. "I'll uhm…wait to hear from you, Catherine. I look forward to it."

"Goodbye, Jim. Take care of your hand. I'll call you in a few days to see how you're faring."

"Excellent. I'll be waiting for your call."

Well, wasn't that odd? Catherine thought as she hung up. *I swear I don't have a clue what will come out of my mouth next.*

When they all returned from the golf course on Saturday afternoon, Jordan and Mia were gone. They'd left a nice note, thanking Catherine for her hospitality and wishing Jamie good luck in the remaining match. "They seem like they've become good friends," Catherine commented.

"Oh, yes, they're close all right," Jamie agreed. "They don't have much in common, but they hit it off very quickly." She omitted just how quickly or how deeply their relationship had developed, knowing that Mia would not appreciate having her secret revealed.

"I'm really glad that you and Mia have stayed such close friends," Catherine said. "She seems very fond of Ryan, too."

"Well, that's an entrance requirement for any of my friends, but it's really nice how well we all get along. I think Mia genuinely likes Ryan."

"I always thought she had good taste," Catherine smiled. "Now I'm sure of it."

Waking early on Sunday morning, Jamie stretched and cuddled up to her partner, feeling immensely glad that her tee time wasn't until eleven.

"You awake, love?" she asked, not able to see Ryan's face.

"Uhm-hmm. Have been for a while. You just keep lulling me back to sleep," Ryan yawned.

"Wanna have a nice big breakfast with me? I don't have to be at the course until ten."

"Yep. Sounds great. Are you ready for another round today? Three days in a row would be a lot for me."

Rolling over to lie on her back, Jamie looked at her partner carefully and asked, "Do you get any pleasure out of playing golf?"

"Yeah, I do," Ryan said, sounding unconvincing. "I mean, I'd never play alone, but I like to play with you or with my brothers. It's kinda like bowling for me. It's not something I love, and it certainly doesn't seem like exercise. Although, I guess it's superior to bowling since it's a decent way to spend time outside."

"So, you don't think you'll ever get the golf bug, huh?" Jamie asked, wistfully.

"No. Don't think so, babe. It's a little slow-paced for me, and I kinda suck at it, which always hinders my enjoyment." She was chuckling gently, but Jamie knew that she was serious.

"I've been surprised that you haven't gotten better at it. I think your height is actually part of the problem."

"Yeah…that makes sense. I think I'd be okay if I'd started young, but I've got a lot of body flying around during that swing. Lots of things can go wrong. I actually remind myself of Michael Jordan when I play. He's obviously a talented athlete, but he'll never be great at golf. Too tall."

"Things do tend to go pretty wrong for you," Jamie laughed, a small part of her quite happy that she could so thoroughly kick

Ryan's butt at something.

"You know, I don't generally handle being humiliated very well. I think you should prop up my self-esteem before we leave." The blue eyes were twinkling, and Jamie had a very good idea where this train of thought was heading.

She rolled onto her side again and snuggled up tight to Ryan's long body. "How can I help improve your poor self-esteem?" she whispered.

"Mmm, let me think," Ryan murmured, grasping Jamie's hand and slowly trailing it down her body. "Maybe you should remind me that being tall and having long arms can come in handy sometimes. Like this," she said, wrapping her arms around Jamie from behind and slipping a hand into a warm, humid place. "I couldn't do that if I wasn't blessed with a large wing span."

As her right leg lifted to allow for better access, Jamie sighed, extremely pleased that her lover's reach equaled her grasp. "You have beautiful wings," she whispered thrusting her hips against the soft curves that she nestled against.

Turning to face Jamie fully, Ryan enveloped her in a warm embrace and promised, "Wait until my beak starts sipping your nectar. That's when my talents really shine."

The entire immediate O'Flaherty family, along with a smattering of cousins, showed up to watch the team championship on Sunday. Catherine and Maeve walked along at the back of the large group, chatting quietly, more about the plans for the wedding than the golf, but their main purpose—to show support for Jamie—was accomplished perfectly.

Cal did not prevail on this dry, warm day, but Jamie wasn't terribly disappointed. She didn't have the same drive to win that Ryan did, usually being happy as long as she put forth her best efforts. She had played well, shooting a seventy-one on the difficult course, and she was happy with the play of her teammates against a team that was superior in every way.

Even though Catherine offered to host another dinner, the family decided to head home after the match, not wanting to get stuck in the usual Sunday night crawl along the 101.

Jamie and Ryan decided to head home also, and after stopping in Hillsborough to pack up their things, they returned to the 101 and started for home. As they drew near the airport, Ryan turned and asked, "What time was your dad's flight out tonight?"

"Mmm…I think around five," Jamie mused. "He didn't want to get back to Washington too late. Why?"

"Wanna take a chance and see if we can find him? I bet you'd feel better if you could see him in person before he leaves." She paused a second and added, "I know he'd feel better." Jamie tilted her head and stared at her partner for a long while, with Ryan finally turning to give her a questioning look. "What?"

"This is one of those 'I'm falling in love with you again' moments," she sighed. "I can't think of another soul that would put up with his shit like you do, and I love you for it."

Ryan gave her a warm smile and said, "I feel bad about Friday night. Playing around like that outside was really rude. We should both know better. He was really making an effort to be nice to me, and I paid him back by going into my caveman routine." She shook her head and said, "I should have been more considerate."

Jamie patted her leg and said, "No, it's my fault, Ryan. I was pushing you. I know better."

"You gave me a perfectly acceptable cooling off period. There's an insolent part of me that got off on being sexual outside, knowing that we could have been discovered. I know that I'm a bit of an exhibitionist, but this was more than that."

Jamie sighed and said, "Let's try to find him. Mom will know how to get in touch with his secretary."

Several phone calls later, they were waiting at the gate for the flight, having nearly an hour before the scheduled departure. They didn't have long to wait before Jim showed up—with Jamie gasping aloud when she saw the massive bandage that covered him from forearm to fingertip, making his hand look more like a club.

She waited until he had checked in, then got up and approached him, Ryan staying in her seat to allow Jamie to have some time alone with him.

"Can I buy you a cup of coffee?" she asked, when he did a double take upon seeing her.

"Do…do you want to?" he asked tentatively.

"I don't normally hang out in the airport on Sunday afternoons looking for men to pick up, so I'd say that I do." She smiled, slipping her hand under his elbow to guide him to a coffee bar.

He looked over his shoulder at Ryan, but she just gave him a nod and a wave, and opened one of her textbooks. "Is Ryan…?"

"She's fine," Jamie assured him. "I want to talk to you alone." As they walked along the concourse she asked, "Your hand is pretty bad, isn't it?"

"Yeah," he admitted, casting a quick glance at it. "I think I might have some nerve damage. I'm going to see a hand specialist as soon as I can get an appointment."

"You broke the glass when you saw us, didn't you?" she asked, deciding there was no other logical explanation, given the chain of events.

He nodded, looking very embarrassed. "I got so angry," he whispered, his face full of pain. "Thank God I don't keep a gun in the house. I might have killed her."

She shivered at the mere thought, but managed to say, "I don't blame you for being angry, Dad, but wanting to kill her is just too extreme a reaction. I think you need to figure out some way to control your anger. It's going to get you into trouble some day that you can't get out of."

They approached the coffee bar, and he led her to a seat, grabbing a chair for himself which he pulled up close. "Do you mean that, honey?" he asked, looking more than a little pale.

"Yes, it's dangerous to let yourself get that out of control."

He shook his head briskly and said, "No, no, honey, I know that's true." He blinked at her slowly and asked, "Do you mean that you're not angry with me for what I did?"

"No, I'm not angry," she assured him, while placing her hand upon his uninjured one. "Are you angry with me?"

He blushed deeply as he said, "I know that you and Ryan are uhm…that you enjoy each other's company. I'm doing my best to get comfortable with it."

He looked helpless as she gave his hand a squeeze and said, "I know that. That's not what I meant. I'm wondering if you're angry with me for being inappropriate with her in your house. That was irresponsible of us, and I'm really sorry that you had to see it."

His body collapsed back against his chair, and he gave her a thoroughly dumbstruck look. "You're apologizing to me?"

"Yes, of course," she said earnestly. "I know this is hard for you, and I know you're doing your best to control yourself. Playing around like we did is really improper where there's even a chance that someone could see us. It's disrespectful—and I'm really sorry."

Running his good hand through his hair, he stared at her for a few long moments. Finally, he smiled and said, "I think we should have gone to a bar-bar rather than a coffee bar. I could use a drink."

She shrugged and indicated, "There's one right over there."

"No, I shouldn't drink with this pain medication. I've had enough publicity for one day—causing a scene on the plane isn't a good idea." He was smiling as he said this, and it looked like some of the tension was leaving his body.

"Let me get you something," Jamie said. "Coffee? Latté?"

"Do you know what I'd really like?" he asked, looking like his answer surprised himself. "I'd like a cup of hot cocoa."

"Cocoa it is," she said. As she rose from her seat, she leaned over and kissed the top of his head. "It's okay, Dad," she said. "We'll get through this."

He sat quietly and watched his daughter as she strode to the counter. *I don't deserve her*, he thought to himself. *I never have.*

When Jamie returned, they sat in silence for a few minutes until Jim said, "What do we do now?"

"We don't have to do anything. This isn't going to go quickly, and if that's your goal, you're going to be very disappointed."

He looked sheepish as he said, "I'm not a very patient man. This is going to take some getting used to."

"We've got time. As long as we each try hard, we'll get there."

"I do better with tasks that I can beat into submission," he chuckled. "That's not going to work this time, is it?"

"No. Neither Ryan nor I do well with a heavy-handed approach. You're going to have to finesse this one." She smiled at him and joked, "This will be good practice for your day job. I imagine that consensus building is a good thing for a senator, isn't it?"

"So they tell me," he chuckled. "So they tell me." Patting Jamie on the shoulder he said, "No time like the present. Let's go try to mend some fences."

When they arrived back at the gate, Ryan was nowhere to be seen. Jim looked around, assuming she had gone to the rest room or was in one of the shops, but Jamie said, "Look for a quiet corner."

True to form, the tall woman was curled up on the floor in the corner of the gate opposite Jim's. Her knees were drawn up nearly to her chin, her heels just inches from her butt. Long arms were wrapped around her knees, and her head was resting atop them. Jim and Jamie were just a few feet away, but Ryan didn't twitch. "She's asleep," Jim said.

"No, she's not. She's thinking." Looking up at her father, she wrinkled up her nose in a grin that reminded him of her youth and said, "She thinks a lot." Leaning over, Jamie gently touched Ryan's head, which turned and swiveled to allow her clear blue eyes to lock upon her partner's.

"Ready?" she asked, a placid expression on her face.

"In a few," Jamie said. "Daddy won't be able to board for fifteen minutes or so." She extended a hand and Ryan grasped it, allowing Jamie to help her up.

"So, what were you studying, Ryan?" Jim asked, puzzled by her study posture.

"Oh, I wasn't really studying. I was just thinking about something."

"What subject are you working on?" he asked, trying to make small talk.

"Oh…well…they all kinda merge at a certain level." She looked over at Jim and asked, "Do you know what I mean?"

"Ahh…no," he said, "I don't have a clue."

She searched for a way to explain herself, finally saying, "I'm working on a math problem, technically, but the way I'm thinking about it today seems a little more like quantum physics." She shrugged her shoulders and said, "If you open your mind, things tend to surprise you."

His mouth started to curl into a grin, growing wider and wider as the impact of her words hit him. "You know, Ryan, you are absolutely right. As a matter of fact, that's going to be my personal motto from now on." He stretched his arms out, the young women bracketing his body. Wrapping both of them in a hug he looked from one to the other, each returning his bright smile as he tried Ryan's statement out for himself: "When you open your mind, things tend to surprise you."

The End

By Susan X Meagher

Novels

Arbor Vitae
All That Matters
Cherry Grove
Girl Meets Girl
The Lies That Bind
The Legacy

Serial Novels

I Found My Heart In San Francisco
Awakenings
Beginnings
Coalescence
Disclosures
Entwined
Fidelity
Getaway
Honesty
Intentions

Anthologies

Undercover Tales
Outsiders

To purchase these books: *www.briskpress.com*
Author website: *www.susanxmeagher.com*
twitter.com/susanx
facebook.com/susanxmeagher